CW00394864

Red Tempest Academy
Omnibus

NATHALIA BOOKS

Published by Purpleheart Publishing

This is a work of fiction. Similarities to real people, places or events
are entirely coincidental.

Red Tempest Academy Omnibus

First edition, January 4, 2023
Copywrite © Nathalia Books
Written by Nathalia Books

Trigger Warnings

This story contains bulling, LGBTQ+ discrimination and sexual assult

Unexpected

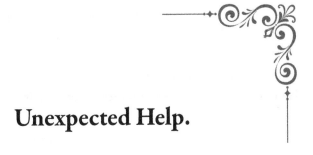

Unexpected Help.

The raindrops cut down on the family like small knives. Sediana Lumina looked down on her childeren as they pushed themselfs agains a wall in a dark alley, hidding from the people who were after them. The angry voices came closer and closer, Sediana motioned to her children to be quiet. Adelidis her daughter responded with a short nod, but her son Bertin looked anxiously at the mouth of the alley. The men who were hunting them came into view, some looked into the dark alley and one pointed at them.

"Shouldn't we look there? It's dark enough there to hide in it."

But the other men ignored his words. "Van Helsing, you are getting more disturbed every day!" one shouted. The man called Van Helsing sighed deeply before walking on.

SEDIANA BREATHED A sigh of relief for the first time that night, even though she knew the night was not over yet. "Mother, do we still have to go far?" asked Adelidis wearily, it had been a long night for them too.

Sediana sympathized. "Hold on, we are almost over the border. Your father is waiting for us there and then we will be safe in Narinor." Sediana said, at least that is what she hoped.

She listened carefully, but all she heard was the rain still falling on them and their own breathing. Carefully they crept out of the alley, silently cursing how poorly lit it was, Even though that had just

1

been their salvation. The three of them snuck along the streets of the sleeping city. With every sound they froze, ready to run.

The voices of the hunters came closer, Sediana grabbed the hands of her children. Pulling them closer, while she started to walk faster. They were walking along an alley when Bertin was caught out of nowhere. Sediana let out a little cry before putting her hand over her mouth to muffle the sound. From the alley came the man called Van Helsing, along with Bertin.

"Let him go, it's just a kid. He's not even drinking blood yet." Sediana said as softly as possible. Van Helsing looked at her in surprise and turned Bertin around, shaking his head with a sigh. "Have the vampire hunters really fallen that far? Do we really spend our nights chasing women and children, instead of looking for the leeches that can't control themselves?"

Van Helsing let go of Bertin. He watched Sediana take care of her son, taking is pale white face in her hands and with her thumbs she whipped away his tears. "Don't worry; other than my respectful collegues. My mother did her best to raise me." said Van Helsing as if their conversation was commonplace in the world. "Around the corner is a horse and carriage from the Ventilas. I always have one ready if necessary. The driver will take you and yours to Narinor."

Sediana looked at him in disbelief, this couldn't be a vampire hunter trying to get them to Narinor. "Why should I trust you?" she hissed under her breath, shielding her children with her body.

Van Helsing shrugged ", probably for the same reason why your son is still alive." he said as if this were the most natural thing in the world.

SHE WALKED AROUND THE corner with the children in hand, followed by Van Helsing. As he prommised, there was a black carriage with the crest of the Ventila family on the door. "Good evening Hendrik." Van Helsing said to the driver now that he was standing next to the carriage. Hendrik patted his top hat. "Good evening Abraham, it's not bad. Only the weahter."

Van Helsing opened the carriage door and nodded. "Yes, actually, I have a lady here with her two children." Sediana looked at the driver and nodded politely.

"So which family is this?" Sediana still kept her children out of the carriage.

"I can also ask you the same thing. Hendrik, was it?" Sediana was still wary.

Hendrik laughed and pointed at her. "You will stay alive with that attitude, I am a son of the Ventila family. Hendrik is just a cover name, Dadrick Ventila at your service, Mrs. Lumina." Dadrick said. Sediana let go of her son's hand and put one hand on her pendant, Dadrick nodded. "Don't worry, I think you are Markus Lumina's wife. He passed my father's land house yesterday." Sediana's disbelief slowly melting away.

"Have you seen father, sir?" Bertin asked. Dardrick opened his mouth to answer, but was interrupted by the clearing of Van Helsing's throat.

"Can we discuss this some other time, maybe in the Ventila mansion." Sediana nodded and motioned for Bertin to get in, the boy eagerly got into the carriage. Sediana had to help Adelidis because of her long skirts, Van Helsing in turn helped Sediana in the carriage. Before he even got in, which surprised Sediana. Van Helsing probably saw her in surprise, and he shrugged. "I wouldn't be able to sleep peacefully if I'm not sure if you're safe." he said. Sediana stared at him.

THE CARRIAGE LEFT TOWN, the children on either side of the carriage had already fallen asleep. Van Helsing pushed aside the blood-red curtain and looked out and Sediana did the same "Why did you and your husband travel separately?" Van Helsing asked, probably to break the silence.

Sediana put her hand on her pendant, which had once belonged to her husband. "We got separated." Sediana said quietly, she didn't want to wake her children. "After those two were born, we heared rumours about hunters attacking vampire villages. My husband and I feard the rumours, but that was all what they were, rumours. We lived in harmony with the humans who were our friends so what did we had to fear?" She took a deep breath.

"But just in case we got a plan. If our village was attacked we would go to Narinor. A few weeks ago hunters found our village, the sun was setting. I don't know why I was awake that early, but I'm glad I was." She took again a deep breath, it was painfull to think about the attack, not knowing if the rest of family escaped. "Our house was on the opposite of were the attack started, so we got time to change to wake up the children. Only just outside our village we were spotted, my husband pushed me and the children in a cave. Before he run away, he led the hunters away from us. After it was save for us to come out, I decided to stick to the plan, we traveled mostly during the day. I hunted small rodents to drink their blood and feed my children. But when we arrived in that cursed border town. Well you know we were hunted again, until you came along." Van Helsing waited a moment, she saw that is eyebrows frowned a little.

"I am sorry this happened to you and your family." He said eventually, She knew he meant it.

"WHY ARE YOU HELPING us, Mr. Van Helsing?"

He raised his shoulders. "I know what it's like to be hunted, but by members of your race. I've lost all my family to that hunt, so I don't wish that for another child."

Sediana's heart shrank, she'd heard about vampires killing humans before. The thoughts alone made her nauseous. "I'm sorry, those vampires disgust me." she said and meant it. Van Helsing looked at her and he nodded. "I believe you, but that's why I joined the vampire hunter. But I'm disgusted by the hunter who do exactly the same thing as those vampires. That's why I help you and yours, I don't want innocent lives on my conscience."

Sediana looked at her children. She herself had drunk human blood several times, but never more than was necessary and never had she had to hunt for food. "Thank you, Mr. Van Helsing." He let go of the curtain and nodded slightly. "Don't thank me until we get safely to the Ventila's mansion."

She nodded and turned her attention back to the road.

THE CARRIAGE CAME TO the iron gate, Sediana studied out at the large mansion from the window. In her life she had heard several stories about size of the manor of the Ventila, but the stories were nothing compared to reality. The gate opened with a loud squeak, the children woke up and looked around in alarm.

"Mother, where are we?" Bertin asked a little anxiously as he looked at the mansion that was getting closer and closer.

"This is the Ventila mansion, young Lord Lumina." answers Van Helsing in Sediana's place, Bertin's fear disappeared like snow in the sun and looked at the house in admiration. Adelidis also looked at the house in wonder.

The carriage stopped right in front of the door and it flew open. An elderly vampire woman ran outside, holding up her skirt with her two hands as she ran. "By my soul. Dadrick, Van Helsing you stayed away a little too long for my taste!" She cried.

"Don't worry mother, everyone in Traimora knows the Ventila crest and especially the hunters." Sediana looked at her children.

She actually wanted to speak to them about their behavior before the Countess, but Van Helsing already opened the carriage door. "Countess Ventila, don't worry I will always protect Dadrick. But you have guests." He got out and helped Adelidis out of the carriage, holding out his arms to Bertin who shook his head. Bravely he jumped out of the carriage. Van Helsing looked with a smile at the boy who bowed his head reverently to the countess. "By my soul, who have we here?" she asked.

"My name is Bertin Lumina, ma'am and this is my sister Adelidis." Bertin said, Sediana's chest grew with pride.

Van Helsing's hand came back into the carriage, Sediana took his hand and stepped out of the carriage. She bowed her head slightly. "Countess Ventila, it is an honor to meet you."

The countess walked up to her and grabbed Sediana by the arm. "Don't be formal, honey. You and your childeren will be exhausted and hungry." The Countess pulled Sediana in, Sediana looked over her shoulder and saw Bertin shake Van Helsing's hand before running after her. Van Helsing put on a hat and walked away from the house.

"BY MY SOUL DEAR; YOUR husband left less than an hour ago. My son is driving to him right now." They sat at the kitchen table in the mansion, Sediana tried her best to listen to the Countess, but there was so much to see. "Honey, let's get you out of those damp clothes and then those cute little ones can sleep. Tomorrow you can continue on to Narinor." said the Countess, got to her feet. "Follow me." Sediana's children also got up and followed the Countess.

SEDIANA SAT ON THE edge of the large bed where her two children slept under a warm sheet. There was a soft knock on the door. She got up quietly and she pushed the heavy handle down as gently as possible.

She had barely cracked it before it was pushed open. Her husband burst into the room.

"Markus!" she said a little too loudly, but she didn't care. She threw her arms around him. The children leaped out of bed. Tears of joy glisenend in Sediana's eyes. At last, they were safe and together again.

Unexpected Friend

Sediana took a deep breath, Markus and she stood in front of the large door that led to the throne room. Just before they left the Ventila's mansion they were told by Dadrick that the vampire king would like to meet them, this he did for all the new vampire inhabitants of Narinor. At least that was what Dadrick Ventila had told them. The Countess had given Sediana a new dress so that "she didn't look like a vagrant", the Countess had described it.

"Mother! Father!" her children's voices buzzed down the gray stone hallway, Sediana turned and caught her daughter, who was also wearing a new dress. The Countess followed the two. "Those children of yours are really lovely, just like my son Dadrick when he was that age." said the Countess, her eyes visibly dreaming away to past times. When the Countess realized that she was being looked at, she put a hand over her mouth ashamed. "I'm sorry, but I miss my grandson. He's staying with his other grandparents, I wonder where he is.?"

Sediana caught sight of her son who also looked dapper, probably he was wearing the Countess's grandson old clothes. "Mother, when can we go in?" asked Adelidis. Sediana glanced at the door, which was still closed. "Patience. You can enter soon, young lady."

Dadrick Ventila now also entered the hall with a boy in tow. The boy pointed to Bertin. "Father, why is that boy wearing my old

9

clothes?" Bertin looked at the clothes he was wearing. His cheeks slowly turned red with shame.

"Derick!" the Countess rebuked him. "Apologize!" Derick winced, but kept his lips tight. "Derick, these vampires have fled their home and these childerem had to leave their clothes behind. When they arrived at our mansion, their own clothes were soaked and torn. That's why Bertin Lumina wears your old clothes." Dadrick said to his son.

Derick reached out to Bertin. "I am very sorry, we will play in the garden after this meeting. Your sister can also come, of course." Derick looked quickly at Adelidis, then at his father. "If my father and your parents allow it, of course." Derick added.

Dadrick laughed and nodded. "We won't go back to our estate until tomorrow." Bertin and Adelidis looked at Sediana now and she nodded too. The children jumped up and down with excitement.

THE DOOR FLEW OPEN. "Lumina family, your majesties." said a voice from the throne room, Markus quickly reached for Sediana's hand and she took it. Together they walked into the front of the hall. At the end, a man and woman sat proudly on their gilded thrones. A golden crown rested on both their heads. Behind the woman was a young man leaning against the wall, his arms crossed. Just before the platform where the thrones stood, Markus and Sediana stopped. Sediana heard the footsteps of her children behind her. A man walked past them and turned a quarter turn so he could look at them as well as the king and queen.

"Your Majesties, may I introduce you to Markus Lumina and his wife Sediana Lumina." said the man. They bowed at the hearing of their names. "And their children, Bertin Lumina and Adelidis Lumina." he continued. The children now walked past them and bowed their heads. "Welcome to Narinor, Lumina family." said the king, Sediana glanced from the king to the man behind the queen. He tore himself away from the wall and came towards them. "It is good to be welcomed, your Highnesses. My wife and I could never have hoped that we would receive such a warm welcome from yourself and the Ventilas who opened their doors to us." Sediana hardly paid any attention to her husband's speech. She was watching the man fehind the throne, who was now almost in front of them, giving her a polite nod.

"This is our son, Mrs. Lumina. Armand Barnier." Sediana seemed to wake up and looked from the queen to Armand. "I'm sorry for staring. But after being on the run for a while you start to distrust everyone." she said, cheeks glowing red with shame. She looked quickly at Markus, who gave her a scornful look.

"It's all right, Mrs. Lumina as a father of three, I understand completely," said Armand, giving her another polite nod. "You're just on your guard when strangers get too close to your little once." He turned his attention now to Bertin and Adelidis. "I heard from my nephew that you are going to play in the gardens after the meeting was over." Sediana watched her children bow their heads reverently, then nodded with enthusiasm.

Armand turned his gaze to a woman Sediana had not seen before. "Helana, would you like to take these children to the gardens?" Armand asked her. The woman stepped forward and nodded. "With pleasure, my love." Bertin and Adelidis looked at her and she nodded. Sediana smiled as she watched her childeren run to Helana. It was such a pleasure to see them carefree after all this time.

"MRS. AND MR. LUMINA, we took the liberty of searching the city for a place for you to live. We found one on the edge of the Human Quarter." Armand told them after his parents left. He gave Markus a map of the city and took his place next to Markus. "Here is the vampire palace and there is the dwelling." He pointed to a square on the parchment. "I'll walk you to the house in a minute. I'll show the blood bank right away."

Sediana blinked at him in surprise. She had never heard of a blood bank before. "It's a place where blood is stored. People in this town give it up here voluntarily." explained Armand, seeing her surprise. "Shall we go then?" Armand pointed to the door and walked over without waiting for an answer. Sediana watched in amazement as Markus followed Armand.

Sediana looked at the door through which her children had just disappeared. "Mrs. Lumina?" Armand's questioning voice echoed across the room.

She looked at him. "It's not that I don't appreciate it, Your Highness. But I'd rather stay as close to my children as possible."

A smile appeared on Armand's face. "Don't you trust my wife, Mrs. Lumina?"

Sediana shook her head quickly. Her blonde hair flew in all directions. "It is definitely not that my prince, but this is a strange environment for them and..." Armand interrupted her with a loud laugh. "Don't worry, if you walk down that hallway you will end up in the gardens. I will take you and your children to the house, later. My wife would most likely appreciate the company." Sediana looked at her husband, who watched after her, shaking his head.

SEDIANA WALKED DOWN the gray stone corridor, the sound of her shoes echoing. Moonlight glistend at the end of the hall. When she was almost standing in its glow, the screams of children playing came to her.

She walked out of the hall and her eyes fell upon the garden with a large tree in the middle, millions of white flowers hanging from the tree in strings. The petals lit up when the moonlight touched them. She was awestruck.

"Yes, that tree still takes my breath away. Every time I walk into this courtyard." said Helana, Sediana cried out in shock, but quickly covered her mouth with a hand. "My apologies, princess." Sediana said as she lowered her hand again.

Helana's hand lifted until it touched a string of blossoms. "It's not a problem. You were enchanted by the Wisteria." When Helana lowered her hand, several petals fluttered down.

Adelidis ran over, Sediana knelt slightly and caught her daughter. "Mother, look at that tree!" Adelidis pointed to it, a few petals landing on her blond hair.

"I see it. Where is your brother?" Sediana said, but immediately her eyes fell on the group of boys emerging from behind the thick trunk of the tree. Bertin ran behind and gave his mother a wave when he saw her. Adelidis let go of her mother and ran back to the boys.

"The two in front are mine. Derick has already met you. Oh, and there is my daughter." Helana said, pointing to the girl who came running down the hall, panting to a stop. "Andrea, where were you?"

The girl looked at her mother a little ashamed. "In the kitchen, Mother." Andrea said in a very soft voice.

"And are you allowed to come there?" Helana asked.

The girl shook her head gently.

Helana looked at Sediana who smiled at the mischievous child. She estimated the girl to be about four years old. "Andrea, you see that girl over there. That's Adelidis and this lady is her mother, Sediana Lumina." said Helana, putting a hand on Sediana's shoulder.

Andrea wasn't looking at Sediana, but at Adelidis. The girl ran away without words.

Sediana chuckled softly, but Helana shook her head. "Armand spoiled them too much." she sighed, Sediana didn't know what to say and watched the children play in silence.

"YOU SHOULD HAVE WALKED with us right away, Sediana." Markus said angrily.

The happiness Sediana had felt the day before when she saw him had disappeared. "I didn't want to leave the children alone." she snapped at him. "You know, the two little vampires sleeping in the other room?" She pointed to the door that led to the bedroom where the children were sleeping. He hit the table with his fist. "They were perfectly safe in the vampire palace. Now Prince Armand had to walk twice."

"He didn't mind. He said, more than once, both to you and me." She reminded him. "And I know our children were safe there, but I just don't like it when I don't know exactly where they are. We fled for a reason. I just have to get used to the idea that we are really safe."

Markus marched over to her and grabbed her arms. "Are you accusing me now?" he hissed through his teeth.

She shook her head. Where did he get that from? But he did not let go of her. "I gave you what you wanted; a house, children, clothes on your body."

Sediana was fed up and pushed him away from her. He started to reach for her again, but she walked to the front door. "Where do you think you are going?" he almost shouted.

"Outside, then you have time to cool off." She walked out and slammed the door behind her and stormed down the street, not careful where she was walking.

Sediana bumped into someone with a bang. "I'm terribly sorry." She started and looked up at the person she was pitted against.

To her surprise, Van Helsing stood in front of her. "What are you doing outside? The sun is shining!" was his first reaction.

She looked up at the blue sky and let the sunlight caress her pale skin. "I had to get out of the house for a while. My husband was stepped om his ego." she said.

Van Helsing looked at her inquisitively. "May I ask why?"

She nodded and ran a hand through her blond hair. "I stayed in the palace with my children, while he walked with Prince Armand to our new home. I know my children are safe here in Narinor, but old habits are slowly wearing off. Is it really weird that I want to know where my children are? Who they are with? "

Van Helsing shook his head. "Not if you consider where you are from." he replied, and she gave him a warm smile.

"I'm sorry for this the question, but what are you doing here in the capital of evil?" she asked.

Now he gave her a smile, "I live here, if I don't hunt leeches in Triamora. Something the vampire hunters don't need to know, because they do call it the capital of evil." Music was rising in the distance. The surrounding street grew busier, Sediana tried to suppress a yawn but it was too late.

"I saw that," said Van Helsing. "I better take you home."

Sediana nodded that might be for the best. There had been time for Markus to cool down now, and so had she, but it was getting late; or early in a human's point of view. "Do you know where I live, Mr. Van Helsing?" she asked, and to her surprise he nodded.

"I make it my duty to know where all the vampires live." he said as if it were the most normal thing in the world. Maybe it was for him.

They didn't walk long before they got to the street where her new house stood. "Thank you, Mr. Van Helsing, I appreciate it." she began, as the door of her house opened and Markus stormed out.

"Sediana, where were you and who is this man?" The tone in Markus voice changed from worried to jealous.

"I was at the town square, Markus, and this man here is Van Helsing. He saved me and the children last night." Sediana said with a sigh. She never understood why Markus could react that way.

Markus nodded to Van Helsing and grabbed Sediana by the upper arm. "Then you have my thanks, Mr. Van Helsing. But it is late." he said as he gently pulled her along with him.

NIGHT FELL AGAIN. THE streets were lit with lanterns, and where the lantern light did not reach, the moon took over. Sediana walked the streets with Adelidis and Bertin to the blood bank, Markus said he had to work.

"Mother, where is father?" Bertin asked her, as if he could read her mind. "Your father had to work, dear."

Bertin tilted his head a little. "We haven't been in town for a night yet, where did father find work?"

Sediana shrugged. That was a good question. Only she didn't have the answer.

"Mother, it's Mr. Van Helsing!" Adelidis called out before running to the man. With a smile on her face, Sediana waved to him as he caught Adelidis. He picked her up with ease and carried her back to Sediana. "I believe this is yours, ma'am." he said when he put Adelidis down again. Sediana nodded. "I believe that too, Mr. Van Helsing."

He shrugged as if to say it was nothing. "Where is the journey going to?"

"To the blood bank, Mr. Van Helsing." answered Bertin in her place.

Van Helsing nodded. "May I accompany you then?" Van Helsing asked Bertin in return, who nodded enthusiastically.

"I want to apologize for my husband this morning." Sediana began.

Van Helsing shook his head. "There's no need for that, is he always like that?" She heard the doubt in his voice. It wasn't really appropriate to ask for him to ask, but Sediana didn't care. "Yes he is always tense. Just before we had to flee he almost climbed the walls."

"Did he ever hurt you?"

Another question that was not appropriate. She quickly looked at her children running ahead of them. "Once in a blue moon." Sediana replied, ashamed of it. But for some reason, she trusted Van Helsing.

"Did you choose him or your parents."

She stopped walking for a moment. Why did he want to know this? "Why are you asking me this, Mr. Van Helsing?" Her voice was to loud, and she knew it.

He raised his shoulders. "I have to admit that I have no answer for that myself."

She nodded, they were now in front of the blood bank. "My parents chose him for me. Apparently we played nicely together as childeren. But he wouldn't be the man I would have chosen myself. Still, I can't complain, I have two beautiful children and we're safe now."

Multiple vampires walked in and out of the blood bank. A few children standing in front of the blood bank came running to Adelidis and Bertin. "We're playing tag. Do you want to play? Is it okay with your parents?"

Van Helsing immediately opened his mouth, probably to say that he is not their father. "Do you know the way home?" Sediana asked Adelidis and Bertin, both nodded. "Then go home at the sunset." The two dashed off, and Sediana smiled after them.

Van Helsing chuckled, "It's been a long time since I could run so free." he laughed. Something gnawed at Sediana about what he had just said. "I really have to go in. Are you coming?" she asked.

He shook his head. "I'll wait here."

SEDIANA HEADED INTO the blood bank. The outside of the building was made of gray stone, like the rest of the vampire part of town. But the inside of the building was covered with strange white tile on the floor and walls. A male vampire stood in front of a wooden counter. He waved at her and weaved at her to join him.

Something about his manner was reassuring. She came to stand by hi without hesitation, and she noticed that there was a book in front of him. "Good evening ma'am,"he said. "I don't think I've seen your face before. So, you've moved from another place in town or you're new."

"The second." Sediana said.

The man immediately picked up a swan feather and a jar of ink. "May I have your last name and the number of your household? Young children included."

Sediana gave him a questioning look. "Why, if I may ask?"

The man sighed as if it were the dumbest question in the world, Sediana tried to see the symbol on his pendant, and caught a glimpse of a Phoenix. "This is so that if your husband or one of your children comes to get blood, we know how much they need." Sediana still wasn't happy about it, but she gave what the man asked for.

"Thank you for your cooperation, Mrs. Lumina. Two adults and two children. Well that means three blood bags." The man walked away from the counter.

A MOMENT LATER SEDIANA came out of the blood bank. Van Helsing was standing in the same place where she left him.

"How was Michal Stryder today?" he asked, she turned her head slightly to make sure no one else heard her answer.

"Is he always like that?"

Van Helsing nodded. Sediana saw a few women coming their way, but when they saw Van Helsing, they turned back quickly. "I have that effect on vampires, don't worry about it." he said soberly, Sediana nodded. Suddenly she knew what was bothering her. "Mr. Van Helsing, when we first met you said you were well-behaved. But later in the carriage you told me your entire family had been murdered by vampires."

He nodded. "That's right, my parents were indeed murdered by vampires. When the Ventilas heard what had happened they were ashamed of their own kind and took me in. So, I was raised by the Countess and am a respected member of the noble families, but feared by the rest. I need not tell you that the Countess was not happy with my career choice, but she could understand."

Sediana did indeed understand it. He bent down to her and took the bag from her hands. "Let me carry this to your house."

Sediana brushed a stray blonde tuft behind her ears. "Please call me Sediana." she said. He nodded. "All right Sediana, please call me Abe."

She too gave him a nod.

THEY WERE AT THE CORNER of her new street. "I don't know if your husband is home yet. Did you know Armand hired him as a member of his guard?"

Sediana shook her head. "No, he just said he had to work. He didn't say anything to the children either."

Van Helsing sighed and handed her back the blood bags. "Next week there will be a ball in the humans' palace. Since I unofficially belong to the Ventila family, I have to be there. But I can bring extras and the Countess insists that I take you and the children."

She saw that he was a bit nervous. She wanted to say she needed to ask Markus, but something, some internal voice, stopped her. "My children and I would be honored Abe." she said finally.

He nodded and a broad smile appeared on his face before he turned and walked away.

Also smiling, she returned to her house, where Markus was already waiting for her.

Unexpected Love

The moon was still low, but it was a busy event in the little house. The Countess had sent new clothes for the children and for her, which Markus did not appreciate. "Who does she think she is! I can get some new clothes myself for that stupid ball!" Sediana heard him say when the dressmaker came by to take their measurements.

She ran a brush through Aedelidis hair one more time, "Mother, why was father so angry when he left?"

Sediana finished running the nightingale feather brush through her daughter's blond locks. "Your father misses the old house, honey. He misses our old life and his parents. He doesn't know who is still alive after the hunters invaded our village."

Sediana could see from her daughter's posture that she did not have to go any further. "I don't miss our old village at all, I like it more here." Adelidis said, and Bertin came over to them and nodded violently.

Sediana looked at the necks of the two children, where each wore a pendant of red wood engraved with the symbol of a tiger. "I have something for you." Sediana said. She got up and went into the bedroom she shared with Markus. She took two boxes from a drawer.

When she turned around and saw two curious faces at the door, she beckoned to them to came in. "What is that, mother?" Bertin asked cautiously, looking at the box in his mother's hands and then quickly at the door.

Sediana cursed this. Markus did not want the children to come into their bedroom and he had made it clear to them several times. "This is for you, open it up in the living room."

The children grabbed the boxes from her hands and ran into the living room. Sediana sat on her bed for a moment, listening to her children's cries of joy.She caught a glimpse of her reflection in the mirror on top of the chest of drawers. Her blond hair hanging down her back. Her blue eyes sparkled with excitement and a gold pendant with a tiger on it sparkeld at her throat.

"Mother, can you help me with this?" Adelidis pleaded.

Sediana startled for a moment. Her daughter was standing next to her with her new gold pendant in her hands.

"Sure honey." Sediana took the juwelery, and Adelidis turned around and with a single stroke, she swept the hair from her neck. Sediana fastened the chain and immediately Bertin ran into the room too.

"Mother, I can't get it around my neck." he said in a whine, something Sediana hadn't heard from him since they fled the village.

"Give it here, and I'll help you."

THERE WAS A SOFT KNOCK on the front door. Adelidis ran straight out of the bedroom jerked it open. Van Helsing stood in the doorway. "Mother, it's Mr. Van Helsing." Sediana was already leaving the bedroom with Bertin following her.

"Good evening, young lady and young Mr. Lumina." said Van Helsing as he walked in. "Sediana, you look beautiful. Vanessa Lazar will be jealous." He took off his hat.

"Who is that, Mr. Van Helsing?" asked Adelidis.

Van Helsing was shocked by her question. "Don't you know who that is? You know that Narinor is ruled by vampires and humans."

The children, who both nodded. "Well Vanessa Lazar is the queen of the humans," Van Helsing continued.

Sediana saw their surprised faces. "Mr. Van Helsing, shall we go?"

He nodded "Good idea, your coach is ready." he said, bowing slightly.

The children rushed out with shouts of joy. Sediana followed. At the door stood the same black carriage that had taken them to the Ventila's mansion.

Sediana closed her eyes for a moment. "Was that really just a week ago?" she thought to herself. She opened her eyes and Van Helsing opened the door of the carriage. Bertin jumped in and turned to Adelidis. "Come on, it's easy."

Before Adelidis could jump, Van Helsing grabbed her and picked her up. Bored, Bertin folded his arms and sat down. "Girls always get special treatment." he grumbled.

Adelidis walked up to him and punched him before sitting across from him. "I can't jump that easily with this skirt on," she snapped. Sediana shook her head with a sigh and, with the help of Van Helsing, got into the carriage too. "Bertin, Adelidis. Stop that or I'll leave you at home." she said sternly, sitting down. The children looked at her in alarm.

Van Helsing climbed into the carriage and sat down. The carriage jerked into motion.

"Mr. Van Helsing, are there other children present?" Bertin asked. Sediana knew that since they were in Samaria, the capital of Narinor, he had made many friends.

"Derick is present and the young princes." Van Helsing answered him.

Bertin clapped his hands with pleasure, and Sediana chuckled for a moment.

THE CARRIAGE DROVE through the streets of white houses, which was a big difference from the gray houses in the vampire district. A large building rose from the human quarter. The building was made of the same white stones as the surrounding homes. "Is that the palace, Mr. Van Helsing?" asked Adelidis, glued to the glass.

"Yes, that's the humans' palace. If you're up there." answered Van Helsing as he leaned forward and pointed to a tower, "then you see that the two palaces line up directly opposite each other."

The children were beaming, and Sediana knew what those two were up to. If the could they would climb up to the tower to see for them self. "Adelidis, Bertin. You behave yourself; we are guests." she reminded them. The two looked at her disappointed, but nodded anyway.

The carriage stopped at the gate of the palace, the red wooden doors stood wide open, and a man hurried out of the palace and opened the carriage door. "Welcome."

Van Helsing got out of the carriage. "Good evening Harold, how is the little one?"

Harold sighed and a smile appeared. "I can't complain Abe, she finally sleeps through all the nights now."

Van Helsing helped Bertin and Adelidis out of the carriage. Harold Leant a hand to Sediana get out. "If she has trouble sleeping again, put some lavender or jasmine close to her crib. I got that tip when these two had trouble sleeping and it works." Sediana said to Harold, who nodded gratefully.

"I'll remember that, thank you." Harold looked at Van Helsing. "I'm actually surprised to see you here. Normally you look for an excuse not to be." Harold began to mention a number of reasons, which always came back to vampire hunting.

"Okay, okay. Harold, I get your point."

Sediana looked at the children laughing behind their hands. Van Helsing saw that too. "You see, those children are laughing at me now."

Harold shrugged. "That is nothing new." He slapped Van Helsing's shoulder.

Van Helsing and walked through the door of the palace with a defeated face. Harold looked at Sediana. "Abw and I grew up together on the Ventila estate. My parents were servants there." he said lightly.

Sediana nodded and followed Van Helsing with a smile on her face. The children in turn followed her.

THE WHITE STONE CONTINUED here, just as she had seen in the vampire palace. For a moment she wondered whether there was a Wisteria in the courtyard here too. But before she could ask Van Helsing, he stopped walking. They stood in front of a double door.

Two lackeys looked at them and shrugged. Without saying a word, they opened the doors synchronously, revealing a descending staircase. Music and several voices drifted their way.

Van Helsing stepped through the door. Sediana and her children followed him. The four of them carefully descended the stairs. A man was waiting for them at the bottom.

"Name?" said the man. Van Helsing leaned over and whispered something in the man's ear. The man gasped.

Sediana's eyes, meanwhile, danced across the room. The ball room was build up from white sparkled stone, with on them little decorations of gold. A giant cristal chandeler hung in the middle of the room. Under it couples in the where dancing on the music, the woman all in colorful dresses of expensive fabric. There jewels shimmered in the light of the many candles.

"SEDIANA LUMINA, BERTIN and Adelidis Lumina and Abraham Van Helsing!" the man shouted, his loud voice startling Sediana. Immediately some attendees looked their way, but then resumed the conversations they were engaged in.

Derick and the young vampire princes broke away from the crowd and ran to them. Derick looked questioningly at Sediana. "Can we play with Bertin and Adelidis?" Derick asked when he stood in front of her.

Sediana looked at Van Helsing. "Can I let them go or do we have to greet our hostess first?" Van Helsing hissed and looked pained. "It is expected of us."

Sediana looked at Derick, who had already understood. "As soon as we're done, they can come with you." Sediana said to Derick, to answer him anyway. The boy nodded and ran away with the princes.

VAN HELSING GUIDED them through the crowd until they arrived at a woman in the exact same dress as Sediana. She felt a little torn, the dress was a gift from the Countess. When they came closer she saw that the fabric was more expensive, the light pink satin of the womans dress was laid with small little diamonds. Something that Sediana's dress had not. Prince Armand was standing next to woman, unable to take his eyes off her. Markus was right behind Armand. Sediana struggled not to look at him. Only the children rushed to him.

"Wow!" Armand called in surprise.

"I'm terribly sorry, Your Highness." Markus said, pushing Adelidis away from him. "Markus, I didn't know your wife and children were coming." Armand said, amused.

Markus looked at Sediana, seeing the rage burning behind his gaze. "I knew they would come at the invitation of Countess Ventila, Your Highness." said Markus.

Sediana nodded her head towards the woman. "I'm sorry for my children, Your Highnesses. They were glad to see their father."

"Van Helsing what a surprise, never in my life did I expect to see you voluntarily at a ball. But here you are and you have this woman and her miracles of children with you." said Queen Vanessa, her voice so light she seemed to be singing. "I believe my announcer announced you as Sediana Lumina. What a beautiful dress."

Sediana raised her head, sillently hoping that the queen was not offended. "Thank you Your Highness, allow me to introduce you to my son Bertin and my daughter Adelidis." Hearing their names, the children turned to the woman and nodded politely.

Vanessa gave them a smile. "Welcome Adelidis and Bertin Lumina. It is an honor to meet children who love their parents so much."

Armand turned to Markus. "Lumina can you still find the playground?" Armand asked.

Van Helsing already took a step forward. "I can take the children there, Prince Armand. I know exactly where it is and I suspect Sediana would like to see the playground with her own eyes."

Sediana as he spoke glanced at Markus, who gave Van Helsing a hostile look. "It's not necessary, Mr. Van Helsing. I'll take *my* children to the playground." Markus said, already taking the children's hands and pulling them with him.

Van Helsing watched him go. Sediana put a hand on Van Helsing's arm. He looked at her and nodded. "I wish the Highnesses a pleasant evening," he said, taking her hand and pulling it with him.

VAN HELSING AND SEDIANA followed Markus through the corridors of the human palace. They had just taken the children to the playground, where the princes and Derick were already playing. Suddenly Markus stopped in the path, and Van Helsing almost bumped into him. "Mr. Van Helsing, may I speak to my wife privately?"

But Van Helsing made no move to walk away "I'm sorry, Mr. Lumina. But like you, I am a man who takes orders from another. My orders come straight from the Countess." Van Helsing said.

Markus spun around. "She's my wife!" cried Markus, no longer hiding his anger.

"I know that, Mr. Lumina. I know it all too well." said Van Helsing calmly.

Markus now turned his anger on Sediana. "Why are you with this man? You said you were invited by the Countess," he ranted.

Sediana folded her arms. "I *am* here at the invitation of the Countess. Abe picked us up." She had trouble to keep her voice down.

"Abe? Are you calling him by his nickname already?" Markus sneered at her, and at Van Helsing. "Enjoy your evening with her, it's your last. *Abe.*" He turned and stomped away.

Sediana sighed deeply and closed her eyes angrily. Van Helsing put a hand on her shoulder and she opened her eyes and looked at him. "Should I apologize for my husband's behavior?" she asked, and Van Helsing slowly shook his head.

THE TWO OF THEM ENTERED the ballroom again. The attendees were dancing to music played by an orchestra in the void of the alcove above the ballroom. The orchestra played the last note, just as they arrived. Those present applauded. The conductor bowed and started the new song. "Do you want to dance?" asked Van Helsing.

Sediana narrowed her eyes for a moment. If this was her last night in town with her only friend, she'd better make the most of it.

"Please, Abe," she said, taking his outstretched hand. He escorted her to the dance floor and she took the first steps of the dance.

SEDIANA LOVED EVERY step she took.

Suddenly the music was interrupted by a cry. A female servant came screaming into the ballroom. "The king! The king!"

Van Helsing tightened his grip on Sediana's hand. The vampire king stepped forward.

"What about King Matteo?" he asked quietly.

The servant looked at him in horror, an unknown shiver went to the ballroom "He was killed by your son!" she cried.

Sediana's eyes widened. Van Helsing cursed.

The ballroom was suddenly filled with human soldiers running towards the vampire king with their weapons drawn. Sediana pressed herself against Van Helsing. "Abe, the children." she whispered softly so that only Van Helsing could hear her.

He looked at her and nodded. "Take off your pendant and give it to me." She did as he said. They carefully walked into the hallway that led to the playground. Just before they left the room, Sediana saw Markus defending the vampire king against a human soldier.

PANTING THEY ARRIVED at the playground, where the soldiers had left the playing children alone. "Adelidis, Bertin, Derick!" cried Van Helsing.

The three children immediately came to them and the two vampire princes did too. "What's up Uncle Abe?" Derick asked.

Van Helsing looked at Sediana, who sat down on her knees with a sigh. "You two," she said to the princes, there was no time for formalities. "Is Andrea here too?"

The boys shook their heads. "She's in the vampire palace, with mother."

Sediana bit her lip for a moment and sighed. "I want you all to listen to me carefully, take off your pendants and give them to Mr. Van Helsing. Quickly."

The children immediately understood that something serious was going on and did as Sediana asked of them. Sediana got up and looked at Van Helsing. "Is there a way that we can leave unseen?" she asked him and he nodded.

"Follow me," he said as he put the hangers in a bag.

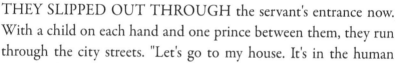

THEY SLIPPED OUT THROUGH the servant's entrance now. With a child on each hand and one prince between them, they run through the city streets. "Let's go to my house. It's in the human quarter, they won't be looking for the princes and Derick there so quickly," said Van Helsing.

Sediana nodded, it was a good plan. They made a few detours down some small alley. She couldn't tell if she imagining it, but the sound of heavy footsteps buzzed the streets wherever they went.

"We are here!" Van Helsing rattled his pocket and took out a key, opened the door and let the princes and Derick in. Sediana followed in with her children, followed by Van Helsing. He closed the door behind him and locked it. "Children go to the bedroom and stay there until we call you." He pointed to a door and the children ran to it.

"DO YOU REALLY THINK Armand really killed King Matteo?" Sediana asked.

Van Helsing shrugged. "Not without good reason. It's suspected that Prince Armand and Queen Vanessa are in a relationship. If

Matteo caught them in the act..." Van Helsing, looking intently at the door.

Sediana took his hand. "Thank you." she said and he nodded. Slowly he bent his face towards her and gently pressed his lips to hers.

Her heart was pounded in her chest. She closed her eyes and melted into the kiss. She didn't know how long they stood there, but they both jumped back when there was a knock on the door. "Who's there!" cried Van Helsing.

"Dadrick and Armand, are our boys here?" Dadrick's voice came through the door.

Van Helsing went to the door and unlocked it. Sediana reached for a knife on the table. Van Helsing opened the door, first ajar and then completely. "Yes the boys are here, we thought it would be better to get them to safety." said Van Helsing as Armand and Derick entered the house.

Armand looked at Sediana and bowed his head. "Mrs. Lumina, I was hoping to meet you here. Unfortunately, I have to report that your husband was killed in the fighting tonight."

Sediana gasped and Armand nodded. "It's all my fault. You should know, Mrs. Lumina that I have had a secret relationship with Vanessa for years. I am also the father of her two children. Matteo found out about this tonight and threatened to kill the children." Tears streaming down his face. He turned his attention to Van Helsing. "Thank you, for watching over my sons."

Van Helsing, who shrugged. "We thought it would be better to keep the vampire children from the playground. Before anyone got into their heads to use them as a bargaining chip."

Sediana went to the bedroom door and opened it. "Derick, princes. Your fathers are here," she called into the room.

Immediately the boys stormed out of the room straight into the arms of their fathers. "Thank you again. Both of you." Dadrick said, escorting Derick out, Armand also thanked them, before he too left the house.

"ARE YOU OKAY?" VAN Helsing asked Sediana, and to her surprise she nodded. He took her in his arms. "Sediana, I don't know what the future holds. All I ask is for you to stay with me. You and your children." He said.

She leaned her head against her chest and smiled. Then she nodded.

"What do you think of it?" he asked and Sediana pulled away from him and turned to her children.

They nodded slowly, their faces white with fear.

Out of the corner of her eye she saw Van Helsing gesture to them and the children darted over. The children hugged Van Helsing and their mother like they never wanted to let go.

Sediana only now felt tears streaming down her cheeks. Tears of happiness, tears of fear. Because Van Helsing was right, they didn't know what the future would bring them, but if they stayed with Van Helsing they were hopefully safe. She looked out the window as the soldiers marched through the streets. Danger was in the air. But no one could take this moment from them; really, no one.

Twin Souled

1

A new school year begins and Siobhan couldn't wait, or could she. This was the first time she entered the school gates as a she and not a he. She looked at the solid iron gate and then looked on her watch. The digital figures told her only that she was probably late, but she couldn't fight the nerves.

"Siobhan O'hEaliadthgthe is that you? " Shaken Siobhan looked at the door of the old mansion that was the Red Tempest Academy, the oldest boarding school for vampires. In the big wooden door stood a very familiar face, Ceira Vigil one of the teachers. The woman walked towards her, but stopped at the iron gate. "It is you, and look at you." Ceira spread her arms and Siobhan sighed, she rather not. Not sure what she would see, a boy in a girls clothing or a girl looking like a boy. She hoped that after the operation... Ceira smilled. "Give it time, but for now come in. You are the last student to come in." Siobhan wanted to curse, but instead of doing that she walked reluctantly through the gate.

Together with Ceira she walked over the gray stones towards the door. The graystoned hallway with its view on the massive library greeted her. The torches were not light yet, which was a pity. She loved the spooky shadows between the lights, that were places she used to hide in.

"Professor Vigil, what nice to see you. How was your summer?" The so famialer voice, was like a slap in her face, alright maybe not a slap but something not very pleasent. Siobhan had hoped she could slip into school without facing...

"It was wonderfull, thank you for asking Nathalia." Nathalia Tomes, a girl from her clas and one of the nicest people in this building. Nathalia moved her gaze from professor Vigil towards Siobhan and all what she wanted to do was turn around and run.

"Siobhan, you got your last operation." Nathalia's voice was a bit louder, but she tried her best not to scream. "Why didn't you tell us?" Siobhan looked to the ground, that was a good qeustion. Nathalia and Nick, her cousin, were her friends. Nathalia grabbed Siobhan's arm. "You know what, never mind. I am so glad for you. Let us go to the dorms and then you can unpack." Nathalia gently pulled her with her.

NICK LUMINA STOOD AT the door of the boy's dormitory waiting for his friends, Gala was probably already inside. Taking care of his pet. But what about Brian, he looked up and saw his cousin walking with another girl he didn't recognize. Typical, Nathalia was always nice to new students, something she never took credit for. At least not openly. Nick looked towards the two girls, who were quickly joined by a thirth girl. The thirth girl was unmistakably Katrina , her cat like ears made her so reckonable. He saw her jump up and down, did Katrina know the unknown girl. Nick stared walking towards the group, when he got closer a shimmer of recognition stuck him. The unknown girl, she looked a lot like Brian. Or Siobhan as he or she wanted to be called, Nick kept it up she. The group of girls watched him as he came closer.

"Hello Nick." That voice, that was Siobhan. He wanted to ask her so many questions, but when he opened his mouth not one of them came out, except.

"How was your summer?" He could hit himself, he could see how her summer was. Very painful, and when he looked into her eyes, he could see that the pain was still there.

"It is crazy, right, I know we talked about it before the summer, but now Brian finally did it." Katrina slapped a hand before her mouth, all looked shocked at her. From the corner of his eye, he saw Siobhans reaction. Katrina lowered her hand. "I am truly sorry, Siobhan. I was not thinking."

"Clearly." He said, a little angry. Katrina looked at him, clearly not happy with his rejection.

"Well I am sorry, but one of my best friends didn't tell me that he, sorry slipped up again, you know what never mind. Forget I said anything."

"Gladly."

"Nick, Katrina . Please." Nick felt his anger fade, when he heard Siobhans voice. "Katrina is right, I didn't tell you about the operation, and it must come as a shock to you to see me like this."

"We she you as you, Siobhan." Nick loved his cousins safe.

"Thank you, Nathalia. Now I need to see that as well. Well, I need to unpack, see you later." and she walked away. Nick looked at Katherina.

"Nicely done, Dazzlonkat."

"My name is Katrina, Nick."

SIOBHAN HEARD THEM argue when she left them, she didn't want them to see her crying. Katrina's words cut deep. The dorm was not far, and it felt a bit strange to walk into the left building instead of the right one. Before the summer she was transfer from the boy dorm to that from the girls, when she entered no one really paid much attention towards her. So she went straight to her room on the ground floor. Professor Vigil had explained to her that her room, was a room designed for those who transition. The rooms were transformed, so that they got their own bathroom. Siobhan entered her bedroom, everything was exactly the same as she left it. An overflowing book cabinet, boxes with the books that didn't fit were everywhere, which made it difficult to walk around the room. On the nightstand laid a small paperback, *Twinsouled* was standing on the cover. It was the book written by professor Vigil, she was reading it before the summer, and she forgot to bring it with her for the summer. With a sigh, Siobhan maneuvered herself between the boxes and put her new pink bag pack on the bed. She looked around, maybe she needed to find room for the other books, or donate them to the library. No, that last thought was ridicules, the library was well stocked Cleon Crypto made sure of that. A knock on her door a woke her from her thoughts, maybe it was Nathalia or Katrina. Again she needed to maneuver between the boxes to get to the door. But as soon as she opened it she wanted to slam it in the persons face, on the other side of the door was Ayslin her younger sister.

"What do you want, Ayslin?" Ayslin shrugged, but said nothing. "Ayslin, I really don't have the time for this nonsense!" Siobhan didn't mean to shout, but her sister was driving her crazy.

"Sorry, were you talking to me, silly me. I heard we had a new girl in the dorm and I came to welcome her. Have you seen her." Siobhan felt her heart sink, she had to put up with her sister's harsh comments all summer. But that was at home, this was school. This was the only place she thought was safe.

"Ayslin, do I need to remind you that there are rules." A voice came from what seemed out of nowhere. Siobhan stepped outside the door and saw Nadia Dracul standing. Or rater laining against the wall, both the O'hEaliadthgthe sisters looked at the daughter of the Headmaster. The girl was a senior just like Siobhan and vice president of the student counsel. Ayslin recovered somewhat quickly.

"It is none of your business, how I treat my brother."

"Your sister, Ayslin. She is your sister now. And when you bully one of my fathers students, then it is my bloody business." Ayslin looked at Nadia, her hands balled into fists.

"I will never, do you hear me, never. Call him my sister, I have two brothers and Brian..." She pointed at Siobhan. "Is one of them, and there is nothing in the world that can change that!" The last bit she shouted so that everybody who was interested, or not, could hear her. Nadia didn't flinch, but Siobhan saw the anger grew in her light purple eyes.

"Ayslin O'hEaliadthgthe, I am warning you. Keep this up, and you will be in front of the student council in no time." Siobhan knew that was not an empty promise.

"It is fine, Nadia. If I am not used to it be now, I never will." Nadia looked at her, but she shook her head.

"It is not the matter of getting used to it, there are rules, and they need to be followed." She turned her attention to Ayslin again. "So am I clear?" Ayslin said nothing but nodded, then turned away. Siobhan took a deep breath.

"Thank you, I think." Nadia shrugged but did not look at her, she kept her eyes on Ayslins back.

"Your little sister is an annoying brat, a brave one. I might add, but still annoying." She turned her gaze towards Siobhan. "I there is no need to thank me, Ceira is my aunt after all and if somebody like your sister..." She didn't finish the sentence, and she didn't have to. "Well I better get going, my bags don't unpack themselves." She wanted to walk away. "By my soul, I almost forgot." She turned around. "The reason I came here is because I went shopping before I came here. So I have a closet full of clothing I don't want and need. Do you want them?" Siobhan was flabbergasted by the offer, she knew that Nadia had a passion for fashion. So the clothes that she offered were not cheap. Siobhan closed her eyes for a moment, the only question was, will they fit her? There was only one way to find out.

"Sure, I am in the need for some new clothing. My mother refused to go shopping with me, or ratter she refused to go alone with me. And I didn't want Ayslin to tag alone, you can guess why." Nadia nodded slowly.

"Alright then, I will drop them off later." Siobhan gave her a well-meant smile.

2

Siobhans stomach growled, she looked at her alarm clock that was standing on her messy desk. It was almost three o'clock in the morning, so it was almost time for diner. She left the clothing that she got from Nadia on her bed and made her way to the door, right before she wanted to open it, there was a knock. Her heart dropped, and her stomach turned slightly, was that Ayslin again? She hastened for a short moment, should she open the door.

"Siobhan, it is me." The voice of Nathalia came through, and Siobhan could breath again.

"I am so sorry." She said, while opening the door. Nathalia gave her a friendly smile.

"It those not matter, I was wondering if you wanted to join us." Siobhan saw the picknick basket in Nathalia's hand, and she nodded. Together they walked through the hallways.

"Did you also invite Nick and the others?" Stupid question of course she had invited them, after what happened to her parents and grandparents, Siobhan couldn't blame her. But it gave them something to talk about, something other than what was currently on her mind.

"Yes, I have invited them. Gala too and yes I already told him about your operation. So he would not act to surprised." Siobhan laughed, for the first time since the operation. She knew she could trust Nathalia to prevent some uncomfortable invents, like the one earlier in the day. "But tell me, what is really on your mind?" Siobhan cursed, and Nathalia kept on walking.

"It is my sister, she was standing at my door earlier. Doing what Ayslin does best, stirring in already over boiling pot. Luckily for me, Nadia was there to save the night." Nathalia growled softly, something that was unlike her. But that meant she was furious.

"Your sister is one of the reasons, that I am, consider myself lucky that I am an only child." Siobhan knew that was not true. After the death of Nathalia's parents, she ended up with her grandparents. But they also passed away soon after that, luckily Nick's parents stepped up and took her in. So they were more like brother and sister, then cousins. They arrived at the weeping willow, the standard spot of Nathalia's picknicks. Her uncle had told her that her parents met each other under this tree, the others were nowhere in sight. "They are late, again." Said Nathalia with a sigh. "As usual, it seems. I hoped the summer had changed that." Nathalia was talking more to herself, so Siobhan said nothing back. Instead, she helped with the blanket.

"SORRY THAT I AM LATE!" A young boy came running, and waved at them. "Was busy with the final touches to my friend's room." He smiled a bit secretly.

"Hello, Gala, how is that slimy friend of yours?' Gala sat down, add the blanket. Nathalia gave him a plate, while he started laughing.

"He is alright, didn't like the travel. But now he is back in his cozy and warm home." Siobhan rolled with her eyes, she didn't like snakes that much. Nathalia handed her a plate as well. "Where are Nick and Katrina, I am starving."

"I really do not know, Gala." But as soon as Nathalia said it there came Nick and Katrina, running towards them.

"Sorry." The both said, but she waved there apologizes away.

"You are here now, so let's eat. Madam Valè gave us the very best of the BBQ." She pulled three plates of, what Siobhan assumed, cooked meat out of her basket, and got off the tin foil of. Showing the thick sausages, spareribs and chicken wings, the ribs and wing were covered in a very special sauce of Bloodberries. All of them made her stomach growl even more, of all the thing she missed about school, the cooking of Madam Valè was number one on the list. As if a start shot was fired, everybody grabbed a piece of meat and started eating. Siobhan just wanted to grab her second rid when she noticed Gala staring at her. A wave of self concusses rushed in, quickly she looked away.

"Gala, stop staring." Katrina had seen it to, and now everybody looked at him.

"I am sorry, but Siobhan, you look different. Nice different, if you were interested, I would have asked you on a date." Siobhan almost chocked on her bloodberry juice. "And thank you for that response, I know, were to look for a confidence boost." Siobhan whipped her mouth of with a paper towel.

"No, it is not that Gala. It is just I didn't expect to hear that." He started to grin, and she knew he had her. "You monster." He shrugged playfully and all the others, including her, started laughing. She was so worried that her friends didn't accept her, Luckily now she saw that she was afraid for nothing, for the first time since the operation she felt at ease.

"What is so funny." The laughter died down, Selara Crypto appeared what seems out of nowhere. Her Raven black hair played with the late summer breath. "O, please tell, Fathalia and Dazzolinkat." Nick almost jumped up, but Nathalia held him done.

"It was just a jest between friends, and the last time I checked you are not one of them." Nick did his best to hold back his anger, not that it matters, Selara didn't paid much attention to what he was saying.

"Brian, o wait no, it is Siobhan now. You look so divergent, I almost didn't recognize you. But maybe that is a good thing, however I need to run Student Counsel meeting. Nice seeing you." And she ran away. Nick cursed, and Katrina joined him.

"It still amazes me that she is part of the student counsel." Said Siobhan and everybody nodded in agreement. Siobhan looked at Nathalia. "You are more suited for that." Nathalia shrugged.

"They didn't ask me."

"Yet. The school year is just started." Everybody looked at Nathalia who shrugged again.

"We will see." That was all she was saying, and maybe hoping that this topic was at an end. The rest of the picnic they eat in silents, nothing more had to be said. The care free moment was gone, and they had Selara to thank for it.

KATRINA WALKED TOWARDS her room, her cellphone in her coat pocket buzzed. She picked it out and looked at the screen. It was a text from her father.

'Good luck, Katrina. Stay out of trouble.'

She smiled, this was a standard text for her father. Zeldar Link was not a man known for his many words, and she loved him for it. Also, she was grateful. He picked her of the streets, when her own parents abandoned her.

"Katrina." Katrina looked up from her phone and looked straight into Ayslin's dark blue eyes. Katrina sighed.

"What do you want, Ayslin?" She was not in the mood to talk with Siobhan's little sister.

"Your help, really. With my sister." Katrina frowned a bit. "I was horrible towards her and I want to make amends." Katrina didn't trust her, but decided not to say anything about it.

"Why not go to her and just say you're sorry. My father was always against a middle man and so am I" Ayslin shrugged.

"Siobhan does not want to talk, and the dragon Nadia won't let me near her room." This came as no surprise, but again she said nothing about it.

"Never show them your cards, although you are not playing." Those were her father's words, and they are wise words. Ayslin looked at her questionably.

"So, are you going to help me?" Katrina shrugged.

"All I can do is talk to her, but I can't promise anything." Ayslin nodded and Katrina wished that she had let her through.

"Ayslin, may I." Ayslin nodded and stepped a side. Katrina resumed her way towards her room. Finally, she could close the door behind her. Her room was as always clean, the citrus smell of the all cleaner was still hanging around, all was it what faintly. "Home sweet home. Time to get some work done." She said, walking towards her computer. "So, Ayslin, let me see how truly sorry you actually are."

3

Siobhan closed her eyes and groaned.

"Wait, her sister said what?" exclaimed Nick. Katrina motioned with her hand, asking him to lower his voice. The group was sitting in the cafeteria and the first lessons of the year would start over an hour. Nick shrunk down a bit and looked quickly around. "Sorry."

"I said, that Siobhan's sister says that she is sorry. And when I was doing my thing in the shadows of the web, well, I found nothing to prove that she was not sincere."

"Except for what I told you yesterday, she basically told Nadia and me that she would never accept my transformation." Siobhan could detect anger and a hint of desperation in her own voice. How could Katrina betray her like that. Nathalia and Nick also looked surprised towards Katrina.

"All that I promised her is that I would talk to you. Nothing more, nothing less." Siobhan looked towards her empty tray, she really wanted to jump up and storm away. Nathalia stood up instead.

"I am going towards the classroom, Siobhan, do you want to join me." Siobhan was silently praising Nathalia for her ability to pick up her mood. She nodded and got up from the table.

"THANK YOU FOR THAT." Siobhan said when they left the cafeteria, Nathalia nodded slightly.

"Not a problem, I was done eating and wanted to leave anyway. And it would look bad on my file if it said I was late on my first day." Siobhan couldn't help it and started laughing, Nathalia looked at her in surprise, but started laughing to. "I am glad that I know you so well. Otherwise, I might think that you are laughing at me." Siobhan shook her head and pinked away some tears of joy.

"Never. I will never laugh at you, always with you." Nathalia smiled when they came close to the science lab. The door was still closed, but they were just early. "I am wondering what things we get to cook this year." Nathalia tilted her head slightly.

"We will see, it still amazes me that they still haven't changed the name." Both nodded, the door opened and professor Blackwood appeared.

"Good evening ladies, you are early." The woman looked at them. "But that does not surprise me, you are always early, miss Tomes." She stepped aside so that the two girls could enter the classroom.

"I am going to sit at my usual place." Already walking towards a desk in the back, Nathalia sat down at a desk in the front. Slowly, the other students of their class were pouring in. Katrina looked at the desk next of Siobhan, but Nick shoot right past her and sat down.

"So this is a nice spot, no wonder you always sit here. You can do almost anything." Siobhan knew that was not the reason why he was not sitting next to Nathalia, as always. She wanted to thank him, but Katrina sat down on the desk in front of her. She turned around.

"I am sorry, but all I could see was that Ayslin spoke the truth. Not knowing what she said offline, of course." Siobhan nodded, but she really didn't want to talk about it. She wanted to focus on the lesson that was about to start.

IT WAS STRANGE TO SIT in a classroom again and listen intensely to somebody talk. But it kept Siobhan's mind of what happened earlier. She cursed when the bell for lunch rang, and they had time for themselves again.

"Hey, are you alright?" Nick asked, as they walk through the hallways. She shook her head, no, she was not. She didn't know what her sister was planning and if she was honest with herself she did not want it to find either. Maybe if she ignored Ayslin, maybe just maybe she gives up. Again Siobhan shacks her head, no she knew her sister better than that. Ayslin would never give up. They entered the cafeteria and immediately all the eyes were focused on her. Gala came running toward them.

"Siobhan, you better turn around and wait for me in the library." He looked at Nick. "Trust me, this is not something she can use right now." Nick's gaze went over all the students in the cafeteria and nodded.

"Nathalia, do as Gala suggested." Siobhan felt Nathalia's arm around hers, and it pulled her away. "No worries, we will be right there." Siobhan nibbled on her lip, but turned around.

"What do you think, that was all about?" Katrina asked. The two other girls shrugged as they entered the library.

"Siobhan!" Nadia came out of the glass cubical, a closed area where the student council held their meetings. Siobhan noticed something in her eyes, she didn't like. "By my soul did she saw it?" Siobhan frowned, what were they hiding from her? "By my soul." Nadia was noticeably relieved.

"Is there somebody going to tell me what the heck is going on here?" She almost screamed, but she was in desperate need for an answer. The two girls looked at her, clearly not knowing what to say.

"Well, if you are not going to tell her, then I will." Alex-Lucas stepped out of the glass cubical. Nadia wanted to protest, but he shook his head. "I know you want to protect her, Nadia. But there are things..." He didn't get the chance to finish is sentenced, some kind of paper floated down. Everybody looked up towards the vide.

There was no one there, more pieces of the paper were floating like snowflakes through the air. Siobhan couldn't see what was on them.

"By my soul?" Said Siobhan in surprise, she grabbed one of the pages out of the air. Slowly she turned it around.

"Don't!" Yelled Nadia, but it was too late. But she immediately wished she had not....

"I am so sorry, the rest of the student council is looking for the culprit." Siobhan's blood almost reached its boiling point.

"Don't bother, I know actually who had done this, and I think it's a lost battle to find anything that will point to her."

"Do you mean..." Started Nathalia, but Siobhan left with great steps the library.

4

Siobhan slammed the door behind her shut, she couldn't believe this. It was the first day of school, and already she faced humiliation. Would Katrina believe her know, or those she only believed what the computer is telling her. She let herself fall on the bed, face down in her soft pillow. Tears were already dripping on the soft pink fabric. Why could somebody be so cruel? A soft knock landed on her door, but before she could tell the person behind the door to go away. The door already opened, and Nathalia and Katrina came in.

"Go away." She said, her voice was almost lost through her tears and the pillow. She turned her face to the pink fabric and hoped that they would leave her alone.

"Never in our right minds." Said Nathalia, Siobhan felt a small shock on her mattress inclining that somebody sat down. A soft pet on her head, confirmed this. "I am so sorry." Why was Nathalia sorry, she was not the one who had done this. Siobhan wanted to tell her this.

"Nathalia, it is not your fault." That was Nick's voice, so he too had entered her room. "We hoped by sending her away and cleaning up the mess in the cafeteria would protect her from this. Not knowing that the perpetrator had followed you." Siobhan heard a loud bang, probably Nick hit the wall out of frustration. "When I find out who did this."

"Almost all the students, find this a sick joke. And will not say anything about it, respecting the protocol." Said Katrina. Siobhan raised herself up from the pillow.

"I had hoped that the protocol would protect me against this." She held up the piece of paper. Nathalia seized it right out of her hand, surprised about the sudden movement, she watched as her friend tore it to scraps. "Why did you do that?" Asked Siobhan while Nathalia walked over to the bin.

"What do you think, the same thing I will do if I find another piece of that crap." Siobhan gave her a smile, she was truly blessed with good friends.

KATRINA WALKED WITH great strides towards her room, cursing herself. If Siobhan was right, and Ayslin was behind it. Katrina shook her head, she needed facts before her emotions get in the way. That is what her father taught her to do. She entered her room, and went directly towards her computer. When her trustful companion jumped on the starting screen, she looked at a picture of her with her father. They were standing before the Linked Coin, the bank that her father owned. His hand was on her shoulder, a proud smile was on his face. The photo was taken right before she went to the Red Tempest Academy, four years ago. Katrina closed her eyes for a short moment, her memories brought her back, not to the day of the picture. But to the day that her father found her.

A LOUD NOISE CAME FROM outside, Katrina lifted her head slightly. It was not strange that she heard loud noises on the junkyard where she lived. There were people earning an honest living here. But often they go around the dusty old trailer, that she called home. She got up and walked towards the make shift door, she moved it slightly, so she could look outside. But before her eyes were adjusted to the sunlight, she needed to jump outside. The arm of the excavator came already through the rooftop.

"By my soul! Stop, stop immediately!" The voice of a man just came above the noise. "Richard, why in the Vamporeta, did you not tell me that the trailer was inhabited!" There was no answer, but Katrina felt that she was picked up. She opened her eyes, not remembering that she closed them. She looked at the man, his blue gray eyes looked concerned. "Are you alright?" He asked, she shook her head. No she was not alright, her home was destroyed. She looked at the trailer that she had called her home for almost five years. "Where are your parents?" She again looked at the man.

"You tell me, I have not seen them in five years." The man nodded.

"How old are you?" She did not know why the man asked her that many questions.

"Ten and can you put me down, I have legs you know." The man grinned and put her down. "Before you ask, my name is Katrina. Don't know what my last name is." The man nodded and looked to another man.

"Do you have anymore to add?" The man that Katrina knew him as the owner of the Junkyard shook his head. But she never knew how he was called.

"I have not seen her in a couple of days, I thought that she had left."

"Well, apparently not, and we almost killed her." The man that had held her, was angry. He turned his gaze back to her, his eyes softened. "Well, Katrina, it seems that we need to find you a new home. Because we destroyed yours." She nodded and folded her arms. A smile appeared on his face. "Here is a thought, why are you not coming with me. Then you can get cleaned up, while we are looking for a new forever home." It sounded tempting. But she did not know who the nice man was, could she trust him.

"I... I..." She looked at her trailer. He laid a hand on her shoulder.

"I understand why you hasted, you don't know who I am. Well, let's clear that up, shall we. My name is Zeldar Link." She gave him a what awkward smile, not knowing what to say. "Come Katrina. Let's leave this junkyard." He reached out his hand, she grabbed it and he took her away.

THEY WERE SITTING IN the largest car that Katrina has ever seen. The car drove through the part of the city that she knew, the three level high building made from boring red bricks. She expected that the car would stop in front of one of those. But it kept on driving, into the part of the city she did not know. The houses here looked a lot older, and were bigger, only not in height. Finally, the car stopped in front of a house, made from dark gray stones. That was surrounded by a large iron fence.

"Home sweet home." Said Zeldar Link. He stepped out of the car and again reached his hand out to her. Was the man kidding? She took his hand, and together they walked towards the gate. Which swung open, a yellow brick road laid towards the massive wooden double door. They also swung open, when they stood in front of it.

"Welcome home master. You are a bit earlier than expected. The maidens are still busy cleaning the house." Said a creaking old voice, behind the door stood an old woman.

"Thank you, Miranda. This here is Katrina, she was living on that junkyard." The woman looked with her dark green eyes toward Katrina. "She is going to live here."

"Here? But master, I hope that this is your taste of a bad joke?"

"It is not, Miranda. This girl lived on the junkyard, and I bought that yard to build my new bank. What means, I made this girl homeless." The woman narrowed her eyes.

"What will people say, master?"

"That I have adopted a homeless girl, Miranda. Which is the truth, I will ask Charlie to set the adoption in order. Good thinking, Miranda, where will I be without you." Katrina frowned, what those this all mean. "Miranda, is my housekeeper. Katrina." Katrina nodded to the old woman.

"Hello." Miranda said nothing back.

"Miranda, will you be so kind, to give her a room. I need to call Charlie." Zeldar left her with Miranda.

"THE MASTER LOST HIS mind." Muttered the woman, when they walked through the hallways of the mansion. The floors and the walls were pristine white, beautiful golden chandeliers were hanging from the ceiling.

"Well, lost kitten. Here is your room, no doubt the master will decorate it in a little girl's room. There is a bathroom in the door on your left." The door from the room opened and Katrina entered. The room was big, again with white walls and floor. A massive four-poster bed dominated the room. "If I were you, I would jump under the shower. You have dirt everywhere, and it smells like you don't have seen one in ages." The voice of Miranda sounded like a whip. After the shower, Katrina entered the big room. Dressed in a bathrobe made from a soft cloth. Zeldar was sitting on her bed.

"Look at that, you are cleaned up."

5

The days flew by, and nobody mentioned the picture. It was as Katrina predicted, they respected the protocol. The days of summer changed into the early evenings of autumn, and the cold night of winter were not far away. It rained almost non-stop, not that Siobhan minded, she spent almost all of her time in the library. Studying, at least that is what she is telling Katrina. Who still believed that Ayslin was an innocent bystander. Siobhan tried to push those thoughts away, she needed to focus on the text in the book. Nathalia sat next to her, busy with writing some notes in an old notebook. Siobhan looked up, and saw that Gala came running towards them.

"Siobhan, Nathalia!" He apparently had forgotten that they were in a library. Cleon Crypto came out of his office.

"Mister Kor'thrall, can you watch your volume please?" Gala faltered in his step and almost tumbled.

"Yes, Cleon Crypto. I am sorry." Gala waved at him, and he waved back, before he disappeared into his office again. Gala looked again towards them, and resumed his step.

"Hey Gala, good evening." Said Siobhan, calmly. He groaned, clearly popping with news he wanted to share.

"Good evening, can I now tell you what I have learned?" Both of them nodded. Gala sat down at the chair next to Nathalia. "There is a new boy coming to this school tomorrow." Nathalia shrugged slightly, what was there so strange? "Well it is in the middle of a school week, why those he come tomorrow, instead of the weekend?"

"Maybe his parents needed to work, or they just moved." Said Nathalia.

"Or there was something with the transfer. Happens all the time." Added Siobhan, and Nathalia nodded. The shimmer of excitement on Gala's face washed away.

"Fine, be boring. I will go then and find Nick. Maybe he will understand." he runned away before they could ask what he meant. The two looked at each other and shrugged.

"I WONDER IF THE NEW boy will get my old room." Said Siobhan after a short while. "He will, that one is the only room left. In that dorm, except for the special bedrooms for trans. And if he is a trans male, he will get one off those." Siobhan grinned softly.

"Are there things you do not know?" She was only joking, but Nathalia nodded.

"There are things that I do not know, and I like to keep it that way. But there is one thing I like to know, and that is the reason why." Siobhan sighed, she wanted to give her the same answer she had given Nick and professor Vigil.

"I do not trust Katrina, not anymore." But it was so much more than that, was it? She didn't know.

"I don't know, Nathalia. Every time that I see her... That I see her with Asylin." Nathalia reached out to take her hand.

"Maybe it is hurting you so much, because you have feelings for Katrina." Siobhan wanted to pull her hand away, but Nathalia didn't let her go that easily. Feelings for Dazzlinkat? No there were non, or were they and she kept those under lock and key.

"Nathalia, I do not know. Please let go of my hand?" She did that and Siobhan gathered her stuff. "I am going to my room."

"Siobhan, I am sorry. I went too far..." Siobhan didn't listen to the rest and stormed out of the library.

IT STILL RAINED BATS and dogs, when Siobhan stepped outside. Protecting her homework with her body, she run towards the girl's dorm. With the appearance of a drowned kitten she entered the building.

"He, this is a girl's only building." Asylin's voice echoed through the entrance hall. Siobhan shrunk a little. "O never mind, it is you. Did not recognize you." Siobhan straighten her back, and whipped the wet hair out of her face.

"Yes, it is me. So what?" She had it with all this bullying. Ayslin shrugged.

"Nothing, really. According to school regulation, I can't thatch you." Siobhan nodded and wanted to walk towards her room. Only Ayslin was blocking the doorway. "But that those not mean that I can't hurt you. Your friend is pleasant company, by the way. I will say hi on you're behave." Ayslin stepped aside so that Siobhan could walk on. Siobhan almost longed for the pouring rain outside. Everything was better than her little sister.

"Siobhan, can you help me with me math homework?" Nadia appeared in the hallway. Giving her an excuse to walk on.

"Sure, Nadia, I quickly grab a shower and I will be right up." Nadia nodded.

"Thanks."

1

The car stopped before the massive iron gate, thick rain drops are falling down on the roof. It was the last day of the autumn session, and it seems that the clouds wrung out their last drops of rain. Through the misty windows Realm Stryder saw a first glimpse of his new school, The Red Tempest Academy. He had begged his mother to let him come here, she was of course not happy about it. But this was maybe good for him to start somewhere fresh, at least that was what he told her. The old mansion looked grim and uninviting.

"Young master Stryder, I know that it is hard to start somewhere new. But your lessons are starting soon and your mother needs the car." Realm looked at the gray driver, who looked at him through the rear view miror.

"I know Henry, I only need a moment. This is the school were my parents went." Henry Graystone nodded.

"I know young master. I went there too, you know, the best four years of my life." Realm saw the sadness in Henry's eyes, he knew that he need to say something. But instead of doing that he quickly opened the door and climbed out of the car.

"Like you said Henry, my lessons are starting soon. Give my mother, my love." Before Henry could reject Realm slammed the door of car shoot. He run through the iron gate, the squeak of the gate created goose dumps on his skin. He ran over the crushed shell path to the old mansion, with force he opened the double red wooden door. The gray stone hallway greeted Realm with burning torches which were casting shadows on the floor and hallways.

"There is my new student." Realm looked at the man how walked towards him, with his arms spread. Realm nodded slowly, why was he so nervous.

"That, that is right sir." The man came to a stop and smiled softly.

"Well, welcome at Red Tempest Academy. I am the Headmaster Vance Dracul." Realm swallowed, this man was from a noble family. Realm took a good look at the Headmaster, was he one of those nobles?

"So, your lessons are going to start over a half hour. With that said I'm going to give you you're school uniform and the books you're going to need for school." Realm nodded, the Headmaster waved at him. "Well follow me, Realm." Realm did just that, the Headmaster walked trough an archway. Realm's mouth fell open, when he saw the space. The library was massive, the bookcases where up to the ceiling. The shelfs are stucked with leather-bound books. Their was a mental spiral staircase that laids towards a mezzanine where more bookcase where. In the back of the library their was some kind of office made of glass.

"Yes she is a beauty, I can't take al the pride, but still I'm the one who keeps her clean and stocked." Realm looked side wards, in the doorway of an office Realm didn't see.

"Well you must be the new arrival. Cleon Crypto. Don't be alarmed, I'm not one of those Crypto's, I'm better known as the white spider of the family." Realm smiled at the remark, he had heard about the white spider. All good ones, at least in his opinion.

"Noted." Mister Crypto smiled for a moment.

"Well, your uniform is in my office. You can change in there, in the mean while I'm going to get your books."

———— ⬥ ————

REALM WALKED INTO THE office, while closing the door behind him. He looked around, there was a desk with above it a painting from a man in very old fashioned clothing. On the golden tag stood *Count Dadrick Ventila*, Realm pressed his lip so hard that they became colorless. So this was a school run by the nobles and the most of the students will be nobles as well, that was something new. He found the uniform on the desk, a white shirt with blue pants, white socks, black shoes and a royal blue jacket with blood red extents. Realm undressed himself until he stood in his shorts. Quickly as he could he put on the pants, the socks and the shoes. Only when he put on the white shirt, it itched so much that he took it off and put on his own. Before he could put on his the jacket there was a knock on the door.

"Realm are you ready?" Mister Crypto's voice came through the door.

"Yes, mister Crypto." The door opened and Mister Crypto came in, also the Headmaster entered. Both looked at him and nodded approvingly.

"Well you are in uniform, Mister Crypto here has your books. So now you are ready to get to class. If you walk out of this library and follow the signs on which stand science lab, that is where you find you're class and classmates."

Realm nodded again.

"Yes sir."

REALM WALKED TROUGH the hallway, the sound of loud talking already came to him before he exactly saw his new classmates. Some of the girls where standing in the doorway and they didn't look up. He sighed.

"May I?" One of the girls with long raven black hair and light gray eyes hiding behind a golden framed glasses, looked at him and started to laugh.

"What happened to you?" He frowned a little bit, the girl laughed again.

"It's your hair." Another girl with long golden hair came to the doorway, the girl with the black hair rolled with her eyes. Realm's hand went through his hair, it was lying on his head like a dead animal.

"Yes, I forgot my gel and comb." The girls all are starting to laugh, excepted for the girl with golden hair.

"Well let him through, the lesson will begin at any moment." The girl with raven black hair rolled with her eyes.

"Lets go girls, lady Fathalia command's it." The rest of the girls laughed, but walked away from the doorway. Again except for the one girl, the others called Fathalia, and Realm was sure that was not her real name. He entered the classroom in and stopped before the girl.

"Thank you, I'm Realm Stryder." The girl gave him a little smile.

"You're welcome, my name is Nathalia Tomes."

"Please can all of you take their seats." A woman came into the classroom, her red stiletto heels are ticking on the floor. Realm sat on an empty seat. He looked at the woman with silver blond hair and light gray eyes, looked back at him.

"It seem like I have a new mind to, disappoint." Realm frowned for a minute, but the Professor looked away from him and started her lesson.

"Can somebody here tell me about the Bloodberry?" Nathalia raised her hand and the Professor nodded.

"The Bloodberrie has the same properties as blood, that is why we are drink its juice to stay alive. Professor Blackwood." Professor Blackwood nodded.

"Very good, Nathalia Tomes. Very good." Professor Blackwood, bowed and picked up something behind her desk. When she straightening her back she had a bucket in her hand. Realm saw that the bucket was filled with bloodberries.

"Well your assignment for today is making a nice bloodberry jam. You will do this in pairs." She has to say nothing more, and the rest of his classmates, they stood up and walked to the area where he suspected was made for experiments. The area was totally covered in white tiles, also the working benches. Nathalia stood also up and walked towards him.

"He, Realm. Should we pair up?" Realm nodded, why would he not be her partner for this strange assignment?

"Sure, why not." He stood up and walked with her to the white tiled area.

"Nathalia?" She looked up from her pan with water and gelatin.

"Whats down, Realm?" Realm shrugged his shoulders.

"I thought we where in science, but this looks a lot like cooking to me." Nathalia gave him a smile.

"You are correct, Realm. Only professor Blackwood doesn't like science that much." Realm looked surprised.

"But why is she then teaching science."

"Because Realm Stryder," He turned around behind him stood professor Blackwood. In her eyes where burning flames. "I love teaching and this was the only open curriculum available! Cooking is coming very close to those disgusting experiments!" Her words hit him like a wipe, he shrunk a little.

"I am sorry, professor." She nodded, but the fire in her eyes were still there.

"Forgive his ignorance, professor. He is new and of course we could suspected that he would have a lot of those uncalled for questions." A boy with ice blue ice and short brown hair, stood at the bench next of Realms. Professor Blackwood nodded, towards the boy.

"Well Barnier, I will count on you to teach him some manners." After those words she walked away, Realm looked a little shocked.

"Do not worry about it." said Nathalia, Realm looked at her and sighed.

"Thank you for the warning ahead." Nathalia started to laugh.

"You're welcome."

THE SCHOOLBELL TOLLED, Nathalia just turned the lid on the jar with their jam.

"So that was that." she sighed. The only thing Realm could do was agree with her. She put the jar on the corner of the bench, and walked away from it. "Come up Realm, history will start soon and I don't want to be late." While she was talking she walked to her backpack. He also walked to the table he was sitting on earlier, his worn out briefcase stood ready to pick up. As quickly as Realm could he followed the rest of his classmate.

"Stryder!" He looked behind him to the one who called him. The Barnier boy came from behind him

"That is my name." Barnier raised his left eyebrow.

"If I were you, I wouldn't sounds so cocky. Currently not after the stunt you just pulled." Realm opened his mouth, ready to defend himself.

"Lucas, don't you dare to go hard on him. Like you said against professor Blackwood, he is new. How does he suppose to know?" A girl with long red hair and light purple eyes jumped up from behind Lucas.

"Nadia, can't you see that I am busy?" Lucas looked at her while she nodded.

"Yes I can, but as your vice chairman I need to rein you in from time to time." Nadia winked to Realm.

"What he was trying to say Realm, Welcome to our school." Realm nodded.

"Thank you, both of you. I am happy to finally be here." Nadia gave him a smile, and took him by the arm.

"Let us lead you towards history class."

2

Realm looked around the history classroom, something he didn't do with the science classroom. The walls of the room were completely covered with posters about the first war, and some other events in vampire but also human history. A woman with silver blond hair, with a red glow on it, was sitting behind a red wooden desk. She looked at him with her brown eyes, did she smile at him? His heart stopped for a second, she was there that night. He wanted to turn around and run away. He saw vaguely that the woman stood up and walked towards him.

"So you are my new student, mister Stryder." He closed his eyes and nodded.

"Yes, yes I am Professor." She smiled at him.

"Well go sit down and then I can start my lesson." He nodded, he bit on his lip and walked to the empty table next to Nathalia's.

"Are you okay?" He didn't even heard her question. Her hand landed on his shoulder. "Realm?" He shock up.

"Yes!" He crawled together.

"Sorry mister Stryder did you say something?" The Professor looked at him, questioning him with her eyes.

"No professor, I'm sorry." Realm looked at Nathalia, who also looked at him. He lowered his head, he could have known that someday he would have to face the vampires who were there that night.

"Okay, what is wrong with you?" Nathalia asked, Realm sighed.

"I really don't want to talk about it." One of Nathalia's eyebrows shoot up, but she kept her comments to herself.

"Professor Redfang, is a nice teacher." He wanted to react but no sound came out of his mouth.

"Alright class, we go further were we left yesterday." Around him his classmate went to work, before he could wonder what they where doing. Professor Redfang stood before him. "Well mister Stryder, now I can explain the assignment to you." He nodded, she laid down a notebook on his table. "The assignment is to write about your own history." Realm froze up, she saw that and smiled at him. "May not seems like it, but everyone in this classroom has his or her own secrets."

REALM SIGHED ON THE canteen bench, Nathalia sat down next to him.

"Are you alright?" Realm shook his head, no that would be impossible. He had always liked history, but now he wasn't so sure. "Don't worry, as Professor Redfang said everyone here has his or her secrets." Realm wanted to say that was not the problem. But he knew it would be a lie.

"Shouldn't you eat?" A somewhat dark voice startled them. A boy was standing at their table, holding a tray of food in his hands. The smell of fried chips plagued Realm's nose.

"Hey Nick." Nathalia said to the boy. "I was just about to go get some, this is Realm Stryder by the way, he's new here."

"I know who he is Fathalia, I have eyes and I have seen him in class." Nick said as he sat down at the table. He reached his hand out to Realm. "Hey Nick Lumina is the name." Realm took the hand, Nick shook for a moment, then quickly it let go. Before turning to Nathalia. "If I were your it would be fast, Madam Valé those not wait for anybody." Nathalia stuck out her tongue and got up.

"Alright, I'm going, Realm come on. You have to eat too." Realm did as he was told, still a little confused about what had just happened. They walked towards the kitchen, where the most deliouse smells came from. Realm's stomach began to growl violently, which was strange he had eaten. Nathalia picked up a tray and moved between the counters. Realm looked at the menu and calmly read what it said.

"Hey new blood." Realm turned and looked at the girl standing behind him, her arms folded and looking straight into his eyes. Her silver eyes glittered dangerously. She had said only three words to him, but he felt he should be careful now. She nodded to Nathalia, who took something from a heated bowl. "I'll be kind enough to warn you. If you want to make a good impression, stay away from little miss Fathalia Tomes." Realm looked at Nathalia whose shoulders slumped slightly, she had heard the words of the silver-eyed girl clearly. Realm didn't know why, but he didn't like the way this girl spoke.

"And why should I?" Realm asked. The girl sighed and rolled her eyes.

"Didn't you hear, she's dangerous." Realm felt anger burn in his veins, he'd dealt with this kind of vampire before. "Both her parents died in a car accident and when her grandparents took her in. Well there is a reason she was dumped at her uncle and aunt. I am really surprised they haven't dug their graves yet." Realm had heard enough.

"Thanks for the warning, but I'm afraid it was lost to me." He wanted to walk away from her, but she grabbed his arm. Filled with anger, he looked at her neck on the gold pendant engraved with a spider. The sign of the Crypto family, a noble family. But he didn't care, he pulled his arm free and looked straight at her.

"I will only say this once, I am not a fly to catch in your web. I can make my own choices and with this one I did." The Crypto girl glared at him, like a cat looked at a mouse.

"Selara, what are you think you are doing?" Lucas came over to them and the girl raised her hand as if innocent.

"I am warning new blood here of the danger that Nathalia Tomes carries." Realm saw Lucas' eyes narrow.

"Selara, you are a member of the student council. So behave like a member of the student council." Lucas folded his arms and then looked at Realm.

"Go get something to eat quickly, otherwise Madam Valé will close her kitchen in front of your noses." Realm nodded and walked away from the two arguing vampires.

REALM WALKED BACK TO the table where Nick and Nathalia were sitting, with a sigh he sat down. He quickly put the still too hot Cheese Crub in his mouth, it felt as if his mouth was on fire.

"I heard Selara Crypto had been kind enough to warn you about Fathalia." Realm sipped his Bloodberry juice. As soon as he put the plastic cup back down, he nodded, hearing the difference Nick called Nathalia's somewhat odd pet name. "Well Realm, my cousin here is one of the few students who is genuinely nice and only I can call her Fathalia. Keep that in mind."

"Nick, why would I want to call her that?" Nick shrugged, then looked at Nathalia, who continued to eat.

"I do have a few ideas." Realm sighed.

"Nick, I know you don't know me and I know you don't trust me, but I can tell you right now I wouldn't treat anyone like that." Nick nodded and picked up a chip from his plate.

"Good to know." Nick took a bite.

3

After dinner, Nathalia disappeared, lips pressed together, Realm walked out of the old building. It was still raining

"Stryder, follow me." Lucas appeared out of nowhere next to him, Realm nodded and followed the stocked up noble. To one of the three outbuildings. As soon as the door closed behind Realm, Lucas turned. "Stryder, this is the boys dorm here. Mister Crypto already gave you your room key?" Realm nodded and took the brass key from his pocket. "Good, I think your room is on the third floor." With these words Lucas turned, Realm watched him go as Lucas walked away.

"He is a ray of sunshine in this dorm." Realm was almost frightened, a boy with black hair and pierced eyebrows had appeared next to him. "Wow, don't be scared, it's just me." Realm's heart was still beating faster than it should. "Okay, let's see. I haven't seen you here before, which probably means you're new. Which means that empty room next to mine isn't empty anymore. Come on I'll give you a tour around the dorm." Realm looked at the strange boy who beckoned him along. For no apparent reason as to why, Realm walked with him.

REALM LOOKED AT THE boy who pointed to a closed oak door at the end of the hall.

"That's the shared bathroom over there. Oh, shoot forgot to show you the laundry room. Oh well, we don't use it often. My room is here and yours is there." The boy pointed first at the door across from the bathroom door, then at the door next to it. "See you later, newbie." And the boy disappeared into his own room. Realm, still not sure what to make of it, looked at the closed door. Realm went to his own room, put the key in the lock, and turned it with some effort. The door clung slightly and the hinges squeaked violently. Realm walked into his room and immediately turned to walk out of the room. The white walls were slowly moving towards him and the cardboard boxes were in the center of the room. The bare bed and empty bookcase stared at him. "By my soul what a sad event." Realm did also jump up this time. The boy from earlier was standing next to him again.

"By my soul, you can stop that!" The boy smiled at him and nodded at the boxes. "Fine, even if I will miss that jump. My name is Galakrond from the Kor'thrall family, but anyone with a bit of sense calls me Gala. I heard the chairman called you Stryder, but I don't think that's you. real name." Realm now shook his head, laughing.

"No, I'm from the Stryder family. My name is Realm." Gala nodded, then folded his arms.

"Looks like you could use some help, Realm. Those boxes are almost running towards me." Realm rubbed his hair and sighed.

"Well I would never ask, but now that you offer it." Gala walked to the first box and opened it.

"Looks like your parents packed your things." Realm rushed to the open box, afraid of what was in the box. He looked over the edge and the box was filled with his beloved hair products. Gala had seen him look relieved.

"So you packed this yourself?" Realm shook his head and his hand entered the box.

"No, my mother packed the boxes. But I am glad there were no baby pictures in the box, wait while I think about it, it is still a possibility." Gala groped and reached with his hands between the hair products.

"By my soul, are you really using all of this?" Realm looked at the desk, which was now filled with gel, shampoo, hairspray and different sized combs.

"Not all at the same time, but yes." He opened another box that contained his casual clothes.

LUCKILY, IT DIDN'T take long for everything to be unpacked, only once all his things had been taken out of the boxes and scattered around the room, everything still needed a place. Gala had bailed at this point.

"I'm not even cleaning up my own room. So I'm not going to start on yours either." What Realm couldn't blame him for, with a sigh he picked up his clothes from the bed and put them in the wardrobe, disheveled. With a bang he slammed the wardrobe door and started with the rest of the stuff, he put the books in a pile on the desk and he put his hair products neatly on brand and at size in the bookcase. He stretched and crashed to the bed. The matras protested violently and a large cloud of dust flew up, then fluttered down like snowflakes. Realm had to shield his face from all that dust, he stood up coughing and toasting. He glanced briefly in the mirror that immediately wished he hadn't. His black hair, with crimson hairlights, was covered with dustflacks. He tossed through it with his hand, but it didn't help - it just made it worse. With a sigh, he went to the bookcase and grabbed his shampoo and conditioner. Maybe it was time to investigate that shared bathroom. He left his room with a towel thrown over his shoulder.

"By my soul what happened to you?" Realm nearly bumped into Nick, who stepped back and pointed at Realm's hair.

"My bed turned out to be a dust collectior. Please stop staring." Nick just didn't look away, there was a big grin on his mouth.

"Well, I see that you were planning to take a shower, which is actually something that is not recommended." Nick put a hand on Realm's shoulder and then walked past him.

REALM FELT RELIEVED when he was back in his bedroom, unable to say he had not been warned. Realm opened the window above his bed and this time sat quietly on the bed. He rubbed his hair dry with the towel. There was a knock on his door and before he could answer Nick entered his room.

"So you decided to ignore my warning." Realm nodded and sighed.

"Something I will not do again." Nick walked over to the bookcase and examined Realms' products, Realm watched him closely. "I thought, I had left primary school behind me." Nick turned to Realm.

"Well think agian, because some guys do not know that fact." Nick pointed his thumb at the bookcase. "You know that is for your books, right?" Realm nodded, and he was already expecting a strange comment about the amount of hair products he had. "Nathalia just came by at the training and she asked me if I wanted to ask you. This is so strange being her errand boy, but she asked if you would like to have breakfast with us tomorrow." Realm frowned for a moment and Nick shrugged. "Her words, not mine."

"Why not." Nick nodded and started to walk away. "Nick why do you call her Fathalia?" Nick froze for a moment and Realm shifted.

"Why do you want to know that?" Nick closed Realm's room door, Realm had heard the anger in Nick's voice.

"Calm down man, I was just curious. You called her that when we were having dinner, but the way you said it was so different from how that Crypto girl said it." Realm noticed that Nick's shoulders relaxed slightly.

"Nobody, really nobody can call my cousin by her nickname. Except me, because I don't mean anything by it. Nathalia lost her parents in one fell swoop, my uncle and aunt were rightfully snatched from her life. After the car accident, our grandparents took her in, but they also died in an car accident. From that moment on my cousin was seen as a curse, her father's family did not want her. My father could not stand it and so my parents took her in. She is not so much my cousin, but she's more of a sister to me. That's why I tease her where I can." Realm nodded slowly, he could understand that.

"Thank you." Realm said, Nick turned slightly.

"Why are you thanking me." Realm shrugged lightly.

"It's not an easy topic and yet you share this with me. I thank you for that." Nick nodded, pulled the door open with a loud creak, and left the room.

4

"So Realm?" Nathalia was standing just outside the locker room wall, Nick had changed from his basketball uniform to his school uniform. Several of Nick's basketball team who left the locker room starred at Nathalia strangely, Something that was not new but always bothered him.

"What's wrong with him?" Nick came out of the locker room, basketball in hand. Nathalia grabbed the ball from his hands and ran into the gym. "Come on, I just took a shower." Nathalia started to dribble the ball.

"Yes a deodrant shower, come on you are the basketball player in the family, come on try to snatch that ball from me." Nick laughed and ran after her. She aimed at the ring and threw the ball towards it, the ball went through without effort. A smile appeared on her face, and Nick had to admit he loved to see her like this.

"Nice shot Fathalia." The smile on her face disappeared, and he hated himself for it.

"Please, can you stop calling me that, it is now used as a name for bulling instead of just a fun joke." Nick picked up the bouncing ball from the air.

"I can't promise anything, Nathalia. But I'll try, but you started this conversation with Realm Stryder. What about him?" Nathalia walked over to him and she nodded.

"Well what do you think of him?" Nick sighed and sagged to sit on the floor, she followed suit.

"I don't know what to think of him, to be honest. But who well do we know him, he's not been here for a day and Gala just told me, that he helped him unpack his boxes. There was a box filled with her products." Nathalia started to chuckle.

"As long as your hair is looking good, right?" Nick started to laugh with her. "And we both know that Gala can exaggerate." Nick stopped laughing and looked straight at her.

"What are you hinting at, cousin of my heart?" Nathalia sighed.

"Nick we have no secrets from each other, even if we think we have them. I know you don't like girls."

"I've never said anything like that, and I've had girlfriends!" She motioned for him to lower his voice. He shook his head and Nathalia knew his business.

"You don't have to say that to me, Nick and I would never betray your trust by running my mouth, but I've seen you look at different guys. The same way the other guys are looking at girls." Nick narrowed his eyes. "Nick you don't have to be ashamed of anything, especially with me. You know that!" Nick nodded slowly and lay down on the dirty gym floor.

"I know, really. Do you think others are aware of this?" Nathalia got up and brushed off her skirt.

"Nick, if I'm not worried about what people think of me, why should you?" She reached out to him and helped him to get up. They walked out of the gym together and he sighed.

"I think I repeat myself, but I know that. You are my cousin, but also my best friend." Nathalia took hold of a golden string of hair with her hand and threw it back, almost slapping Nick in the face.

"I know that, so what do you think of Realm, because he also plays for the other team." Nick paused at the door and his jaw dropped.

———— ⌘ ————

NATHALIA WAS SITTING at the cafeteria table with a cup of Bloodberry coffee in her hands. Her eyes darted back and forth across the faces of the students who slowly trickled in.

"So is Fathalia waiting for her cousin." She winced, it couldn't be anyone else then Selara. Selara, with her straight black hair, sat down next to her. "It's still a mystery to me to this day, why Nick's parents took you in. Have you promised them not to kill them like you did with your parents and grandparents?" Nathalia silently cursed, couldn't vampires let her parents and grandparents rest?

"Is there something wrong?" Realm's voice echoed through the cafeteria, everyone else had fallen silent. Nathalia looked up for a moment and saw that Nick was standing behind Realm. Selara got up and shook her head.

"No, nothing for you to worry about." Realm took a step forward.

"Well then you better go, black widow. And leave Nathalia alone, she has been through enough." Nathalia couldn't see Selara's expression, but she could guess.

"It's a shame you didn't heed my warning, Stryder. But then again, Fathalia has an innocent and pretty face." Realm shrugged.

"She's a good friend, nothing more or less." Realm said quietly, Selara rolled her eyes.

"Do I have to believe that, you guys are all the same. You all fall for the most dangerous girl in the room, without even trying to resist her."

"Then it is strange that we do not like you, but maybe we *guys* do not like your sharp tongue." Nathalia had never heard Realm speak so sharply before, but how well did she know him. Like Nick said the day before, he was here only a day. Selara gasped, Realm saw this and straightened his back. Nick passed Realm and Selara, and sat across from her in the meantime.

"Are you okay?" He whispered softly and she nodded. Together they watched how Realm folded his arms. Selara had her arms at her sides, her fist clenched.

"How dare you, I am ..."

"A spoiled noble vampire, whose family was smart enough to make a deal with the Barniers when the kingdom of Narinor was formed. The only difference between your and my family is that my family was not big, important, or wealthy. So what did you want to say?" With a cry of frustration, Selara turned and stomped away. Realm looked around the cafeteria and shrugged before sitting down too. "Hopefully this was the last time, she bothers you." Nick chuckled.

"Don't hold your breath, Selara is stuborn."

NICK GOT UP TO GET everyone a cup of Bloodberry coffee.

"Did you hear, some idiot put Selara Crypto in her place." Gala came with a tray filled with cheese and liverwurst sandwiches. Without waiting for an answer, he took a bite of a sandwich.

"Did you hear who?" Nathalia asked and Gala shook his head.

"No, but you don't have to be in your right mind, to choose her as an enemy. She's a member of the student council in soul's name. Where she doesn't belong in my opinion, but in my opinion is not asked and why are you so quiet?" Realm chuckled and she joined him.

"Gala, it was Realm." Gala looked at Realm in amazement, then back to Nathalia.

"I don't get it. What was Realm?" But as soon as he asked the question, his eyes widened. "Realm, I'm sorry. I called you an idiot and said you're out of your mind." Realm laughed, Nick sat down next to Gala. He passed the cups of coffee to the others and chuckled.

"Well Gala, you are not far off. But he defended Nathalia, so I can't directly condem him for that." Nathalia took a sip of her second cup of coffee and chuckled with him, Realm shrugged.

"Selara is no different from the bullies I faced at my old school." Gala looked at him.

"You were bullied, but you are a cool dude. If you don't count all those hair products then." Realm nodded.

"Yes Gala, I was bullied. But not for my many hair products, nobody knew about that. Except my mother and Henry the family butler. No, I came out openly two years ago and not everyone appreciated that." There was a moment of silence at their table and also at the tables around them. Gala leaned over to Realm and started to speak, but Nick pulled him back.

"Realm, how brave that you dare to say it so openly and although it is not allowed to bully anyone with his or her sexuality. That does not mean that this is stopping Selara."

"That's something I know all too well Nick and to be honest it doesn't matter to me. I'm proud of who I've become." Nathalia glanced at Nick, but Nick shook his head. Realm took a sip of his coffee and quickly gaped a sandwich from Gala's tray. Nathalia looked at the three men talking to each other and strangely enough it didn't feel strange. As if the four of them had been friends for a long time.

5

Nick walked to the gym, he had basketball practice today and couldn't say he was really looking forward to it. As soon as he entered the dressing room, he knew why.

"Did you hear, that the new blood is *gay*." One of his teammates spoke to him and Nick nodded.

"Sure he heard it, he was sitting at the same table as Realm, when Realm mentioned it. But then again, we have several of the LGBTQ+ community members here at school." Said yet another team member and a heated discussion took place. Nick put on his sports clothes with a sigh and left the locker room without saying a word. After the training it was not much better, because the discussion just continued.

"Well, I now understand why we are losing every game." Everyone on the team was startled as Nathalia came into the locker room. Nick sighed, but is silence he thanked her for the distraction. But ofcourse he couldn't say that to her.

"You can't just come in here." He said instead, and Nathalia shrugged.

"Why not? If these guys have sex with a girl, they probably do it in her; so I will not the first girl in here, and probaly wouldn't be the last, either." Nick covered his eyes and sighed again. He could really leave this to her, he lowered his hand agian. His eyes quickly went over the red faces of his teammates. "In addition, I wanted to let you know that I have a picnic planned for the two of us, we desperately need to talk." Nick lowered his head, he already knew what she wanted to talk about.

"Is that really necessary, we talk every day." Nathalia nodded and he could see in her eyes that there was no room for discussion, his mother had the same look.

"Alright then." Nick heard a few members of his team chuckle. Nathalia nodded contentedly and walked out of the dressing room satisfied.

"Hey Nick, do you know what that is called?" Said a team member who put his hand on Nick's shoulder, Nick nodded slowly.

"I'm on a leash. Just like you my friend, because I think I see your girlfriend standing just outside the locker room." The boy cursed and immediately shot into the showers.

NICK RELUCTANTLY WALKED over to the thick weeping willow tree, rumored to have been there since the first war. Nathalia was already under the tree waiting for him, next to her she had her mother's wicker basket, one of the few things she still had from her parents. He sat down with a deep sigh and put his basketball next to the basket.

"Here I am." Nathalia nodded and reached into the basket, fetching a plate with sandwiches wrapped in plastic.

"Here you are. Have something to eat, before we start our heart-to-heart conversation. One that will most likely lead to a well-intentioned fight." Nick dropped into the grass with a groan, he knew it.

"Nathalia please let it rest." But Nathalia shook her head and carefully removed the plastic from the plate. She offered him a sandwich and he scrambled to get one.

"I can not let it rest Nick, and you know why that is." Nick took a bite of the Red Tempest salmon sandwich, knowing why Nathalia was so worried about him. She had no other choice, she was not even eight years old when she first lost her parents and then their grandparents. His parents took her in and then dump her at this school a few years later, with him. He was the only thing, she has concetned in her live, he came all the way up now and took her hand.

"Don't worry about me, I'm not going anywhere." Nathalia looked at him with her light blue eyes for a moment, then pulled her hand free. Nick smiled at her, then moved closer to her. "I know what you are thinking."

"That's great, I often don't even know what's going on in my head myself, so what am I thinking?" Nick had to do his best not to laugh. He could leave that to her too.

"You wish I came out, just as Realm. I only don't know if I have the courage to do that. You heard the guys in the locker room, although the Red Tempest Academy is known for its tolerance towards the LGTBQ community. Those not say everyone here agrees, with that concept." Nathalia now also took a bite of her sandwich, he could not see what she had on it. But he suspected it was Bloodberry jam, her favorite topping. She washed it down with some bloodberry juice poured into a bottle by Madam Valé, the chef of the cafeteria.

"I know that, all too well. But Nick what about your happines, I'm the only one you really hang out with and that's because I can help you with your homework." That was true, but that was not the only reason, and she knew that.

"And you are my cousin, Nathalia. Yes, we can fight like brother and sister sometimes." Nick put an arm around her. "And in addition to that, you are still haunted by the deaths of your parents and our grandparents. Not because you can't let it go, but because some noble bitch has decided to keep reminding you about it." Nathalia leaned against him and sighed.

"I'm not as hopeless as I look, Nick." He smiled, he knows that better then anybody else. If her words could leave marks, his skin would have being covered by scars.

"I know that all to well, and as for my happiness, give it some more time."

NICK DIDN'T KNOW HOW long they sat there, but suddenly Nathalia got up. She had mumbled something about homework and left it with the wicker basket. Nick looked up at the sky for a moment, dark thick clouds gathered. It wouldn't stay dry for long, stiff off the hard ground he got up and picked up his ball. He walked with long strides in the direction of the old manor. The corridors of gray stones, lit with candlelight. Brought the students of the modern era, still back to the time before electricity. Nick did not know why but he enjoyed this, he could actually say that his ancestors had slept under this roof before the first war. His grandparents had told him the story of Sediana Lumina and the vampire hunter van Helsing whenever he wanted. Nick walked into the cafeteria which, in contrast to the hallways, looked modern with the metal tables and chairs and the counters where food was kept warm or cold. Madam Valè came out of the kitchen.

"Good night, Nick Lumina. Did you enjoy it?" Nick nodded and grabbed a bottle with bloodberrie juice out of the fridge, which always were stocked. The mealtimes were very stricked, but the students could always grab something to drink.

"It was wonderful, as always. Madam Valè, you have my cousins thanks too." Nick wanted to turn and walk away.

"Nick, your cousin is a very special girl and she cares about you a lot." Madam Valè said, she gave him a thin smile and he nodded.

"I know, Madam and I care about her a lot. We might fight a lot, but that doesn't mean I don't care about her. She's not so much my cousin, she's more of a sister to me." Madam Valè's thin smile disappeared and a broad smile took its place.

"That's good to hear, Lumina. Anyway don't you have homework." Nick sighed.

"Madam, you just sound like my cousin."

NICK OPENED THE DOOR to the stairwell on the third floor, walking down the hall with the basketball under his arm. As he passed Gala's bedroom, the door flew opened and Realm walked out. Realm had a funny look on his face, Nick's look entered Gala's room and saw Gala holding his snake. Nick knew Gala was keeping a snake in his room against the rules. But Nick had always urged him not to advertise it.

"Hey Nick." Gala walked away from the doorway, Nick walked past Realm into Gala's room. Nick had been to Gala's room before and wasn't surprised to see it was a mess. Gala put his banded water snake in the wardrobe that was converted into a terrarium.

"Gala, what did the new blood think of your cold-blooded roommate." Realm appeared in the doorway.

"Oh, I have no problem with that cold-blooded roommate." Gala nodded and closed the glass of the terrarium. Nick glanced at Realm and he nodded at the plastic box. Nick had to hold back his laugh, the box had contained mice. He then looked back at Realm who looked a little uncomfortable. "Yes, yes I know that the snake has to eat too." Realm took a few steps back and walked away, Nick glanced at Gala who was too busy staring at his snake. Before following Realm to his room.

"Realm can I talk to you for a moment?" He asked before Realm had a chance to shut the door in Nick's face. Realm looked at him in surprise and nodded.

"As long as you don't pay attention to the mess." Nick chuckled a little and he walked into Realm's room, Nick glanced around the room and then wondered where to see the mess.

"Where's the mess?" He finally asked and Realm visibly relaxed.

"Well what do you want to talk about?"

6

Realm was on a sheet, Nathalia had convinced him and Nick, that it was a good idea to have breakfast outside. Still, he had brought a sheet because the grass was very damp. Realm listened to Nick and Nathalia's fight with a smile on his face.

"You are so very bossy, who do you think you are. My mother?" Nick said as if against attack on a comment Nathalia had made earlier. Realm closed his eyes for a moment and recalled the conversation he had with Nick the day before.

"Realm what about your homework?" Nathalia asked, probably to include him in the conversation. Realm opened his eyes and pushed himself up a little. He looked at her and she watched him closely. "So you haven't started it yet." Guilt-consciously, Realm shook his head, he had not yet started his homework for history. Nathalia sighed and shook her head. "You two are one and the same. Come on and eat and then the two of you go to your rooms to get your books." Realm chuckled and agreed with Nick.

" Alright, mom." Realm quickly ate his breakfast. Before he got up, Nick followed him with out saying a word to Nathalia.

"She can be really annoying at times." Nick said as he entered Realm's room, Realm shrugged.

"I wouldn't know, I've only known her for three days." Realm put a notebook with **History** written in bold letters on the cover, in his bag. He also grabbed a few pens and turned around, Nick standing awkwardly in the room. "Nick are you okay?" Nick looked at him a little startled and nodded. Realm looked closely at him and sighed. He recognized this behavior, according to his mother he had behaved that way before coming out. "Nick you can talk to me, we are friends after all." Nick slowly shook his head.

"It's nothing Realm, and I've been honest with you." Realm sighed, knowing not to pull too hard on Nick. Realm had the suspicion that Nathalia was already doing that enough, but this had to come from Nick himself. Maybe he should say that to Nathalia too. Realm narrowed his eyes and shook his head. No, he couldn't say that to her, because it wouldn't matter.

"Nick sit down, I want to tell you something about myself." Nick looked at him in surprise, but sat down on the bed anyway. Realm walked to the door and closed it. He gasped before turning. "Nick what I'm going to tell you now is personal information and I suspect it won't be a secret for to long, with Selara Crypto sourcing for blood, but I'd like to share it with you." Realm sat down on the bed next to Nick and gasped again. "I believe you've heard of the underground vampires." Nick nodded.

"Yes, that was some crazy vampire family, who thought they were above the law." Realm moved his head slowly back and forth, Nick frowned. "Why are you shaking your head? Are you saying you're an underground vampire?" Realm then nodded slowly.

"Only my version of the story is slightly different."

"GO INSIDE!" MIKAN STRYDER shouted, opening their basement door and gesturing furiously to Realm and his mother Pheobe Stryder. Realm's mother had put her arms around Realm.

"What's down there, Mikan?" That was the question she kept asking his father, but she still hadn't gotten an answer. Realm's father strode over to them and grabbed Realm's mother by the neck.

"I said go in." Realm's mother let Realm go and she was forcefully pushed into the basement. He turned and considered running away, he didn't know his father that way. But before he could take a step, he too was grabbed by the neck, he looked up in fear. His father had an unfamiliar look in his eyes. "You too, son." With the same force, Realm was also pushed into the basement. His father closed the door behind him, Realm heard the clink of keys and the click of the locks. He and his mother were now trapped in this den with his father, and Realm didn't know why. His father pushed him down the creaking wooden stairs, the space at the bottom of the stairs was dark, there was no outside light. Realm found himself at the bottom of the stairs, his feet touching the concrete floor of the basement. His father released him and his mother's slender arm hugged him.

"Realm listen to me carefully." She whispered softly in his ear. "You have to do whatever your father asks you to do, whatever it is. I can refuse him but you can't." Realm felt a clamp around his heart, maybe his mother had an idea what was going on here. Before Realm could ask, the air in the basement filled with an iron scent. Realm didn't know why, but his stomach began to growl. A ball of light fired on and the light illuminated an image that would haunt Realm throughout his life. The basement was filled with ten people, four men, four women, and two children. The people were tied to the wall with chains. Realm's father was sitting next to a young woman, his mouth pressed to her neck. Realm felt his mother tighten. "Mikan, how can you. If the vampire hunters find us they will kill us and not just the two of us. You're putting Realm in danger with this." Realm couldn't take his eyes off his father. His father pulled his mouth from the woman's neck and glared at his wife.

"Are you a real vampire, or are you one of those cowards hiding behind the rules. A real vampire drinks human blood and not such a vague berry." Realm snatched his gaze from his father and looked desperately at his mother. He could see the anger in her eyes.

"Well then I'm not a real vampire, I won't risk my life for a vague idea of yours." Realm gently bit his lip, he had never heard his parents argue before and had to admit he didn't like it.

"Well then you will die of hunger and you son." Realm looked at his father and swallowed, he knew what his mother had just told him. Reluctantly he walked slowly to his father.

"I." He said softly.

"Speak a little louder Realm so everyone can hear you. A real vampire has no fear." Realm started to shake hard, how his father was suddenly obsessed with the words real vampire.

"I'll do whatever you ask me to do, Daddy." He said a little louder this time, his father nodded approvingly and motioned for him to kneel down by the woman.

"Drink from her, son." Realm briefly looked into the woman's eyes, which were filled with fear.

"I am sorry." He whispered softly before biting her on the neck.

REALM SAT IN A CORNER of the basement. His mother lay next to him, her head on his lap. She was weak, Realm didn't know how long they were stuck here. But during all that time his mother hadn't had a drink and that took a toll on her body. Realm had begged her to drink a few times before, but she refused. Realm stroked her red locks and hummed a soft tune, so soft his father couldn't hear it. Because real vampires those not hum, according to him. Realm had stopped himself a few times from asking what a real vampire would do. But he was afraid he already knew the answer and didn't like it.

"Realm come on it's your turn." His father beckoned him to come, Realm watched the group of people on their chains. All adults were no longer moving, his mother had told him they were asleep. Only Realm was sure she was lying, Realm knew all too well that he and his father had killed the adults. His father was kneeling next to a young girl who was trembling with fear. Realm slowly shook his head.

"I'm not hungry, father." That was a lie, his stomach had been grunting for a while.

"Realm." His father's voice was rebuking, but again Realm repeated that he wasn't hungry.

"Realm." This time it was his mother's weak voice. "Listen to your father." Realm stroked her hair again and felt a hole forming in his heart. How could she refuse feedings and he didn't? With a lot of effort she got to her feet and looked him straight in the eye. "Realm your body is not built to be without food for too long. My body can take something." Tears began to pour down her face, and Realm knew she was lying to him again.

"Mother, I already told you, I'm not hungry." Realm's father had walked up to them in the meantime.

"Drink Realm, now." Realm narrowed his eyes and reluctantly sighed, he got up and walked over to the girl who was still trembling like a straw.

"Please Realm, I don't want to die yet." She pleaded as Realm sat down next to her. Realm wanted to say he didn't want to kill her either, but his father was right behind him. Realm leaned toward her neck and was about to sink his teeth when the basement door was kicked in. Quickly, Realm shot to his feet and saw several men and women in black uniforms running into the basement. Realm ran away from the girl, tripping over the legs of a dead man. He fell to the ground with a bang, groaning in pain. He felt a pair of arms grasp him roughly, he squeezed his eyes shut out off fear.

"Be careful with him. He's just a child." Realm heard his mother scream at someone. Realm felt him being carried up the stairs and not much later the cool breeze of the outside air. He opened his eyes carefully, still being held by an unknown man in black. They were outside the house, his mother came through the door. She too was carried by two men, only with a little more care than with which he was held. Realm searched briefly around him, he saw his father nowhere.

"Let my son go, can't you see that he's scared!" The fear in his mother's voice did not reassure him.

"Your son has been arrested, Mrs. Stryder just like your husband. They've broken the law." Said the man holding Realm. Realm looked anxiously at the man's face, it was covered with scars.

"Let him go Lazar. Can't you see that the boy is almost the same age as your daughter." A man stepped forward, Realm could tell by his clothes that he was not one of the men and women in black.

"No one is above the law, Barnier." The man called Barnier nodded.

"We know that, but you can imagine that the boy was forced. We searched the basement and there was no sign of Bloodberry juice or any other type off food. So he was probably forced to drink from the people." Realm felt a grip on him.

"No one, not even this boy is above the law." Realm was put down and the man looked Realm in the eye.

"How old are you?" Realms held up two hands, shaking, six fingers up. "Six years and you know that drinking human blood is prohibited." Realm nodded.

"My father said that real vampires drink human blood and not the juice of a vague berry. I didn't want to drink from the nice people, but he forced me." Tears streamed down Realm's cheeks. The fear of the time in the basement finally came out. "I didn't want to drink, but. But ..."

"That's enough, Lazar. We've already executed the father." Another man in black joined them.

"Let the boy and his mother go." The man Lazar let go of Realm and she ran to his mother. Which was now supported by two vampires.

7

Realm gulped for a moment. He hadn't told this to anyone in so much detail before and it felt good. Maybe Professor Redfang had a point after all. Realm glanced at Nick who had been listening with an open mouth.

"You were just six?" Realm nods, he knew that the fact of his age was not know to the public, that spread this rumor about his family.

"This is the fact that vampires often forget when they tell this story. Also, they forget that I came out of the basement heavily underfed, so just drinking blood for a young vampire really isn't enough." Nick sighed and he got up.

"Thank you for sharing this with me, but I really don't know why you shared this with me?" Realm shrugged.

"I have no idea, maybe I thought if I confide in you. You confide in me." Nick looked puzzled. "Yesterday you said you wanted to tell me something and to be honest you didn't say anything to me. Other than that you are struggling with ADHD, but you are also struggling with something else." Nick's eyes started to spit fire.

"Nathalia said something to you." Realm shook his head. Why would Nick think that Nathalia would betray his trust. In his eyes she was not the person that would not do such a thing.

"No she hasn't told me anything, but I'm not blind."

"I'm not..." Nick stopped in his sentence, then closed his eyes. "I don't know what I am or what I am not, and I wish Nathalia would stop pushing." Realm cocked his head.

"You don't have to say that to me, you have say that to her." Realm got up from his bed. "But I guess you've already told her a few times. Do you want me, to talk to her?" Nick shook his head and sighed again.

"No, it will not make a difference. Why does everyone have to put a sticker on anything?" Realm had no answer for that.

"Shall we go, otherwise your cousin will still grill us." Laughing, the boys left Realm's room.

"Where have you been, are your caves really so messy, that you couldn't find your books and notebooks." Nathalia just sounded a bit irritated. Realm and Nick looked at each other for a moment, then shook their heads.

"It's not that big of a mess, it's an organized mess. That's a big difference." Nathalia raised her arms in the air in irritation and stamped her foot toward the old mansion. Still laughing, the two boys followed her.

"GOOD NIGHT, CURIOUS souls. Nathalia I was already starting to wonder if you were lost, because I have already missed you one whole night." Mister Crypto came out of his office as soon as they walked into the library. Realm looked at her, and she shrugged.

"Don't be surprised, I love to read and a library is a good place to read." Mister Crypto chuckled as he disappeared back into his office. Nathalia walked straight to a table deep in the library, Realm followed her and sat down with a sigh.

"This is indeed a quiet place to read, and do your homework. But it is too quiet for my taste." Nick sat down next to Nathalia and grabbed his books and notebooks from his school bag. Realm did the same with his history notebook and opened it, the virgin white pages stared at him. His pen hung over the paper, not knowing where to begin. He glanced over at Nick, who was asking Nathalia to help him with some calculations, Realm listened to their soft voices. Immediately he wondered why he just found it so easy to share his history with Nick and why he found it hard to write it down. Nick looked up for a moment and saw that he was looking at them. "Realm are you alright?" Realm put down his pen and shook his head.

"No, it's not going to work. I just told you my entire story and now I don't know where to start." Nathalia looked from Realm to Nick and back again.

"Why don't you write down what you told me. Every vampire in Traimora has heard your story, and I understand that you are ashamed of it, especially if they leave out your side of the story. But it's your story, so write that down." Realm nodded slowly. That was a good idea. Nathalia looked at her cousin again.

"Sorry, but am I missing something?"

"Maybe only the fact that your new BFF, is one of the underground vampires. You know, Fathalia, that story of the vampires who actually broke the rules of both the noble families and the vampire hunters by drinking human blood. According to my father who was there when they took the underground vampires above ground, there were a total of six adult corpses and two six-year-old young children..."

"Who survived." Realm said quickly to silence Selara, but the twinkle in her silver gray eyes told him she wasn't done with him yet. Something he really should have known, he had put her on the spot the day before.

"So you don't deny it?" Realm shook his head.

"What can be denied, Selara. That I as a six year old boy was forced by my father to drink human blood and that I am partly responsible for the deaths of six people. That is something I have to carry with me all my life and that is what my father did to me." Selara folded her arms and got a mean but contented smile on her face. She had indeed done her job well.

"Yes if my dad left me after that trauma, it would chase me too." Realm felt a shiver run through his body, what did she mean by that. The vampire hunters had executed him for his crimes, right? Selara had seen the confusion on his face. "Oh wait that was also something my father told me, the vampire hunters had lied to the nobles. Your father fled just after the hunters took you and your weakened mother out of the basement. So your father is still alive."

"Selara that's enough." Mister Crypto had appeared behind her, she turned and shrugged.

"What's up uncle. He has a right to know the truth." Realm could see the anger grow in the librarian, and Selara pretended to be shocked. "Did you and the rest of the staff mean to lie to him. I would have rated you higher uncle." She walked away laughing.

"I'm sorry Realm, I often don't know what to do with my niece." Realm gave him a short nod, and Mister Crypto followed Selara.

REALM LOOKED DEFEATED at his notebook, still virgin white pages. Which would most likely remain virgin white. So his father was alive, at least that's what Selara had told him and how much did he believe her?

"She's lying Realm, why would the hunters lie to you?" Nick said who probably saw him struggling with his thoughts, Nathalia reached out to him and he took it. "Selara lives for this, I'm still amazed that her parents tell her things like this." Nathalia pulled her hand free again.

"Maybe you should ask another noble this, luckily we have members of these families in this building." Nick looked at his niece.

"They're not going to tell him anything, if they haven't done that yet, they never will." Nathalia shrugged.

"You never know." Realm nodded, but he would wait until the next day. Maybe he could get his thoughts together, if he'd slept on it one night.

"Talk to her!" A girl called through the library. "You will never know what she has to say if you don't talk to her!"

"No, Katrina. Let it rest." Another girl strode over to the table where Realm and his friends were sitting. The girl named Katrina followed her. Nick sighed and closed his books quickly.

"Thank you Nathalia for helping me with my math." He glanced at Realm for a moment. "If you're smart, you leave right now." But before Realm could respond, Nick was already on his way to the exit of the library. He looked quickly at Nathalia who shook her head slowly. The girl with frantic dark brown eyes sat down with a loud groan.

"Can you believe her?" Katrina circled the table and sat down next to Realm. She wanted to say something, but Nathalia raised her hands.

"Wait a minute, I'm not a referee. Siobhan did your sister ask for you, again?" The girl with dark brown eyes nodded and grunted slightly. "Well I understand you don't want to talk to her, but you shouldn't get mad at Katrina..."

"She is pushing me towards Ayslin, all the time!" Siobhan shouted indignantly, Realm began to understand what Nick wanted to warn him about. Nathalia looked to and him for help, he raised his hands.

"Don't look at me, I have nothing to do with this and now that I think about it. I promised to call my mother, see you later Nathalia." He closed his notebook and started to get up.

"I won't go out there, if I were you." Katrina said, Realm took a good look at her hair, she had a diadem with cat ears. She had lenses in her eyes to look like cat eyes, he didn't have to guess she liked cats.

"Why should he stay here?" Siobhan asked. "The group outside the library are waiting for the underground vampire. Not for Realm." Realm narrowed his eyes, so Selara had already shared her news with the whole school. Nathalia looked at him with sympathy, she knew how it felt. He nodded slowly and she turned towards Siobhan.

"Siobhan, Realm is the underground vampire." With wide eyes, Siobhan looked at Realm who sat down again.

"It was to be expected, but I had hoped it would remain a secret a little longer than this." Siobhan's mouth opened and then closed again. Katrina leaned back in her chair and examined her razor-sharp nails.

"My father had already told me last week that you were coming, he and your father were friends and he regrets what happened to you and your mother." Realm looked at Katrina in amazement, his father had very few friends and none of them had a daughter his age. Realm frowned for a moment, not that he remembered much of the basement time.

"My father adopted me after your time as an underground vampire." Realm dropped his head into his hands, knowing that the group outside the library would not leave and would most likely follow him all over the grounds until he reached the boys' dorm. Nathalia cleared her throat, Realm raised his head. But Nathalia didn't look at him, she watched mister Crypto walk past their table.

"Mister Crypto?" He looked up, then shook his head.

"Oh no, Nathalia I'm not getting involved in that cat fight." He pointed to Siobhan and Katrina, Nathalia gave him a smile.

"It's not about that Mister Crypto, I can assure you. To be honest, I regret mixing in myself, but what are friends for. They're the family you choose, but hey. I actually wanted to ask is this, is there another exit?" Mister Crypto frowned.

"Different exit from the library, why would you want that?" Realm groaned loudly and bounced his head on the massive wooden table. It hurt, but he didn't want to show this.

"Selara has told everyone who wants to hear, Realm's story. With some adjustments, I'm afraid." Realm looked up, burning the spot where he had hit the table. But he didn't have to look up to hear mister Cleon swear like a boat worker. Before his eyes widened and he looked red-cheeked at the students at the table, as if he had momentarily forgotten that he was standing in the middle of a school building.

"My apologies for my language and unfortunately Realm there is only one entry and exit." Realm thanked the librarian, who quickly left. Siobhan looked suspiciously at Realm. And He saw the burning question in her mind.

"So you're an underground vampire, tell use your side of the story?"

8

Realm didn't know how they got past the vampire crowd, but he did know that he was safe in his own room and they didn't follow him. Something he didn't really expect, at his previous school they had kicked and hit him. Here they hadn't even thrown swear words at his head, they probably just wanted to see a vampire who actually drank human blood and killed his victims. Or if they got the change ask him all kind of qeustions, which he did not wanted to answer. Realm sighed he lay with his back on his bed. The sound of loud music echoed through the halls of the boys' dorm, Realm couldn't remember hearing Nick or Gala say anything about a party. Not that he was looking forward to it, it would present the boys with another oppertunity to ask those feared questions. He rolled over with a loud groan, the spot where his head had hit the table had already left a slight bump. He saw his cellphone light up on the desk, a musical tune trying to chase the loud music from outside the room. Realm got up and walked to the desk. The screen showed his mother's picture and he quickly picked up his phone.

"Hello mom ... Yes, I am doing well and how are you doing? ... Nice, nice to hear that it is going well .... What I shortly ... well I was demolished ... school is going well, of course I only had on day lessons before the weekend started so ... Yes Mom, the food is good here. Still I miss your cooking ... I don't lie ... no really ... I believe I made some new friends. don't know if they think the same ... Their names? Well Nathalia Tomes, Nick Lumina and Gala i have forgotten what his last name was... Yes they are very nice ... Yes I know I'm a little short but my head is a little occupite at the moment ... On a homework assignment for history ... about what? Ehmm, my history. But I am stuck ... Yes exactly ... No you don't have to call the Headmaster, the teacher was there when the vampire hunters took us aboveground ... Mom, by the way, did you hear the rumor that the hunters lied to us ... About father's death ... I don't know what to think, that's actually the problem .. Is good Mom, yes Mom I put on clean clothes. Goodbye Mom ... Goodnight Mom. "And he pushed her away again. He looked outside for a moment and saw that the sky was already turning a light pink, it was time to go to sleep. He quickly changed and crawled under the sheets.

THE SHADING CURTAINS didn't close completely, Realm saw the sun shining through the crack in his room. Several thoughts ran through his mind. Was Selara right, his mother shared Nick's opinion. Why would the hunters and then again the noble families lie to them or hide the truth? Realm tossed under his sheets. Pearls of sweat appeared on his forehead, the urge to go to the toilet only increased, and he got up with a sigh. He grunted when he found his bedroom door locked, something he had done himself. He quickly walked to his jacket and grabbed the key from the jacket pocket. Stomping his feet he walked to the shared bathroom, which was fortunately deserted. He quickly emptied his bladder and rushed back to his room when he saw something in front of his door, it was a red liquid. He walked over carefully, it was too bright to be blood or bloodberry juice. He checked his feet for a moment, because he hadn't felt anything wet when he went to the bathroom. Nothing stuck to his bare feet, which meant that the liquid had only been there at his door since he went to the toilet. The door next to his opened and Nick came out.

"Wow, Realm put on a t-shirt." He said, Realm gave him a grim look.

"I'm sorry, but when I got out of bed I wasn't planning to stay out of me room, at least not for this long." Nick walked slowly over to him and looked at the red stuff in front of Realm's door.

"What is that?" Realm shrugged.

"I really have now idea. It's not blood or bloodberry juice. So my guess is paint, someone thought they were funny." Realm looked at his door, but there was nothing on it.

"Wait a minute, I'll be right back." Nick popped into the bathroom and came out not much later. In the meantime, Realm had stepped over the weird liquid and put on one of his father's old woolen vests. "Well." Nick knelt by the liquid and wanted to touch the liquid, but Realm stopped him just in time.

"Wait a minute, I don't think this is paint. I think this is some kind of acid." Nick looked at Realm's hand on his wrist. Realm gave him a shy smile, then released him. Nick got up and walked to Gala's door, he didn't knock on the door and just walked into the room. Realm heard the thump of Gala's sleepy murmurs and Nick's soft voice telling him what was going on. Nick emerged from the bedroom with a broad smile, a yawning Gala in tow.

"Okay be right back with Professor Blackwood." Gala walked away in a what steady pass, probably half asleep. Not much later he got back with Proffesor Blackwood. She knelt down and looked at the acid.

"Well, Mr. Stryder, at least you paid attention during a chemistry class. This is indeed an annoying and caustic acid, the name of this acid escapes me." Professor Blackwood sat next to Nick in her day clothes, and Gala looked curiously over her at the red acid on the oak floor. "This acid does not affect other material, but causes severe burns if it is in brief contact with human or vampire flesh. If we find out who did this, he will receive a compliment and a high mark for my class. But they need to write about the danger of this acid first." Realm had to admit that whoever came up with this had done a good job. "Fortunately we have cameras in the corridors of the dorms, something your young brain keeps forgetting." Blackwood reached for her purse and pulled out a packet of flour. "Flour absorbs the liquid and neutralizes its effects. This makes it easier for you to clean up." Blackwood explained before she got up and walked away. "Realm I want you to explain to me orally during my lesson tomorrow how you found out that it was acid. For a grade of course." Realm nodded slowly, still amazed that he and his friends had to clean up the mess. But they couldn't argue because Blackwood had already left them.

"HOW DID YOU KNOW?" Nick asked, Gala had conjured up a dustpan, a dustpan and a garbage bag from somewhere. Realm sighed and put a shovel of red-colored flour in the garbage bag.

"It's something my dad taught me before he lost his mind. Crossing out possibilities, like I said. It's too light for blood and bloodberry juice, but paint has a special smell and this stuff didn't have that." Nick rubbed some flour onto the can so Realm could empty it into the trash bag. Gala had excused herself and went back to bed.

"Well I'm glad you paid attention. Because if I had touched that stuff it was literally game over for me. Then I wouldn't have been able to play basketball for the time being, which means that I have to take that damned medication again. Something I don't really look forward to." Realm could infer that the very idea irritated Nick.

"I'm sorry to keep you awake, by the way." Realm sighed, though thoughts of his father had kept him awake earlier. That probably doesn't apply to Nick, who just had to go to the toilet.

"Doesn't matter Realm, but I guess you're going back to what you said before. That this isn't the worst thing you've been through." Realm nodded in agreement, Nick had a point. If Realm or Nick had touched the acid, he didn't really want to think about it. Only the small mention in his thoughts made him nasious.

"I changed schools because of my past. I literally couldn't take it anymore, I was beaten up and called a murderer in the hallways. Something no one have to tell me. I may not have had a choice, I have six lives on my conscience. Not to mention the traumatized children. Harry Graystone, my mother's best friend and our butler. Told us that the two children were housed in vampire hunter families, because their parents were among the victims."

"Have you ever heard from them?" Realm nodded.

"I got a letter from one off them the day I came here, but I just didn't have the courage to open it." Realm emptied the last scoop of flour into the garbage bag and Nick buttoned it up.

"I'll put it in my room and throw it in the container for breakfast. Why don't you take the letter and we can read it together." Realm looked puzzled at Nick, how did he know that he had taken the letter with him? But Nick was already walking to his room, garbage bag in hand. Realm got up and walked into his room, the letter was on his desk. He picked it up with mixed feelings and looked at the envelope with the beautiful handwriting. His door was slammed, Realm looked up, and Nick walked into the room. "Well read it." Realm nodded and tore open the envelope. He read the first few lines with bated breath. "Read it out loud, Realm." Realm tore his gaze from the paper and looked at Nick.

"Alright, I will read it outloud. But let us sit down first." Together they sat down on his bed and Realm began to read.

"Dear Realm,

How strange to start this letter like this, but yes. I heard from my foster parents that you are still struggling with what happened eleven years ago and not that I think it's strange we were both quite young. At least that's what my memory tells me and although I don't remember most of it clearly, I still remember you. I remember how you apologized every time before you bit someone and drank from them and how you tried to stretch it for as long as possible every time before your father forced you again. At least it was clear to my five-year-old self that you were not drinking of your own accord and I have shared this with my foster parents. But when I heard how badly you were being bullied and that it is why you are changing schools, I feel strangely guilty. Perhaps it is not strange to you, because we are both victims of your father's actions. You just as bad as Zack and I, he's fine by the way. He lives on the same street as I am, with a nice vampire hunter family, I had to say hi to you from him, by the way. Nor will he hold you responsible for what happened to his parents. As I write this, he tells me he can still hear the tunes you were humming. If you want to reach out to me or Zack, which is something our foster parent probably won't be too happy about, but we'll do it anyway. I leave our e-mail addresses at the bottom of the letter. Realm take care and hopefully we speak each other soon.

Claire.

clairestakes@hunter.com

z@ck@stakes.com "

REALM LOOKED AT THE letter with watery eyes, and Nick looked at him with a big smile.

"Claire does have balls and when I read her words she is very friendly." Realm let the letter slip from his hands and closed his eyes, a tear rolled down his cheek. Claire and Zack didn't hold him accountable, they didn't hold him accountable. Those were the thoughts that ran through his mind. "Are you crying?" Nick's hand landed on his shoulder, the touch leaving a small tingling sensation. Realm opened his eyes and wiped away the tears.

"I'm not crying, you are crying." Nick chuckled, his hand still on Realm's shoulder. Realm looked at Nick's face and there was some kind of sparkle in his pale blue eyes. Realm's heart skipped a few beats, then quickly looked away. Nick took his chin, then slowly bent his head towards Realm's, until their lips touched.

9

Nick was the first to pull away, what had he done? Realm sat opposite him, his eyes were still closed. A big smile had appeared on his mouth. Nick looked at it and felt butterflies begin to flutter again in his stomach. He had never felt so good and so bad at the same time. What did Realm do to him? Realm opened his eyes emerald green eyes twinkled, Nick got up and began to pace around the room. Before he could speak, Realm had also stood up and grabbed his shoulders.

"Nick calm down." Nick looked him in the eye, how could he calm down? How in soul's name could he calm down? He had just kissed Realm and the urge to do it again was strong. "Nick." Realm said again this time a bit harder. Nick gasped and nodded, still his heart was beating so hard that Realm might heard it.

"By my soul, Nathalia was right. I like men, I also play for the other team." Realm chuckled at his words.

"And how do you feel about that?" Nick looked straight at him again and chuckled.

"Better than I've felt in ages, if I may be honest." Nick saw Realm's face light up, he knew why, it felt good to see Realm like that.

"Well that's good news because thanks to you, I feel better too. Now that I've read Claire's letter." Nick took a step back, and Realm's hands slid from his shoulders. Immediately he regretted it and wanted to step forward, but how long had they known each other? Is it posible to fall in love that quickly with somebody, or was he just in love with the idea?

"I'm sorry I kissed you." Fear became visible in Realm's eyes, Nick immediately wanted to dispel that fear. Was three days enough time to get to know each other? Maybe his parents had thought that too, and Nick knew how that had turned out. Sleepless nights for Nathalia and him and chapped throats for his parents.

"Why do you apologize. I didn't mind." Said Realm lightly, Nick turned and started to walk towards the door.

"Realm thank you for showing me the light, but how well do I know you? Three days is not long enough to get to know someone." Nick walked to the door and put his hand on the door handle. "It's late, I better go to sleep."

"Nick, wait. May I say one more thing before you eat yourself in the next room?" Nick looked over his shoulders, the sunlight coming through Realm's curtains surrounded Realm like a kind of auriol. His heart stopped beating for a moment and the butterflies fluttered restlessly. "Yes, three days is not that long. But that doesn't mean anything and it doesn't have to mean nothing. The kiss I mean. Still, I would like to get to know you better. If you want that too, of course." Nick bit his lip, of course he wanted to and Realm was right if he had walked out of the room he would have showered himself with doubts, something that had now been taken from him. Nick swore briefly, then turned and walked over to Realm. Who let Nick go, Nick took him in his arms and pressed his lips back on Realm's.

WITH A SMILE, NICK sat next to Nathalia in the cafeteria.

"Okay, that's enough. I haven't seen you so happy in ages, so what's going on." Nick was just about to answer her when everyone around them fell silent. Nick looked over his shoulder, Realm and Gala walked into the cafeteria. Gala punched Realm and both ran to the counters. Every step that Realm took was followed attentively and in silence.

"I pity Realm." Nathalia whispered, Nick snatched his gaze from Realm and nodded in agreement. This was the same treatment that Nathalia received when their grandparents had just died. Would he receive such treatment if he came out openly, it was a question he hoped would go unanswered.

"I agree with you Nathalia, I don't even think anyone else bothered to ask him about the whole story." Nick looked around quickly and regretfully, Katrina sat down next to him.

"Not everyone is as curious as you Siobhan. Good evening Siobhan, I saw you running out of the library yesterday. You ran away from Siobhan and myself." Nick nodded.

"Can you blame me, your cat fights and your talent for involving Nathalia in those fights. Is making me sick and since Nathalia does not allow me to say anything about it, well then I will walk away, rather than sit there and listen to the same story, over and over again." Katrina and Siobhan shrugged.

"Realm stayed." Like Realm had any choise in the matter, Nick looked over his shoulder again and saw Realm grabbing a drink.

"I already feel sorry for him, and knowing that he had to listen to you two makes it even worse." The girls at the table started to laugh, Gala was already walking in their direction. But Realm looked around uncomfortably.

"Hey underground vampire, come sit with us." Nick looked back, startled, at Katrina who waved fiercely at Realm. Katrina saw him look and quickly lowered her hand. "What, don't you want him to sit here? Since when have you been a scared tiger."

"I'm not that." Nick hissed, and he saw that Katrina knew were he was aiming for.

"His father and mine were good friends before his father went made. My father asked me if I wanted to watch him and I do."

"By calling him by that nickname...?" He looked quickly at Nathalia, this was the same as he called Nathalia by his nickname for her. Immediately he felt dirty, instead of protecting her, he had thrown oil on the fire. "I'm sorry, Katrina. You don't have to answer that." Realm sat down next to Siobhan and Gala. Slowly the students began to whisper around them.

"Wow this is uncomfortable, it's worse than when I didn't doing my laundry for two months."

"Well Gala, everyone kept telling you that despite the amount of deodorant you put on, you kept stinking." Nathalia said lightly. For a moment there was a dead silence at the table, until everyone burst out laughing. Gala had left them after breakfast to go to his own lessons. Nick kept walking close to Realm, without making too much eye contact. They walked into the library to go to the chemistry room.

"Realm Stryder, Nick Lumina and why not Nathalia Tomes." The Headmaster came out of Mister Crypto's office.

"Good evening, Headmaster." Nathalia said, the Headmaster looked at the three of them one by one.

"Siobhan and Katrina, go to your classes." Nick felt his hackles spring up, he'd never heard the Headmaster talk like that before. "You three walk with me." Nick looked at Realm who shrugged, yet the three of them followed the Headmaster through the school building until they reached the teachers' room.

"Normally students are not allowed to come here, but I will make an exception for today." He opened the door and a woman was standing in the doorway.

"Mom." Realm said and he shot forward. He hugged his mother and she hugged him back.

"Realm, Vance briefly explained to me what happened this morning. Why didn't you tell me when I called you."

"Because I know what your reaction would be and I was right, beside your reaction it happend after you called." Realm let go of his mother. "Mom these are my friends. Nathalia Tomes and Nick Lumina." Nick saw that Realm's mother looked closely at them.

"Greetings." The Headmaster cleared his throat.

"Realm, I asked your mom to come. Because I believe this is something you both should see. Pheobe I asked Realm's friends to attend. Because I want Realm to have a safety net." Realm looked suprised at the Headmaster.

"A safety net for what, Headmaster?"

10

Realm did not know how to describe it, but when he saw that his father was not alone alive. But it was also responsible for the strange acid that smeared on the threshold of his door, it made him nauseous. He got up and started to walk out of the teachers' room. So Selara had been right, the vampire hunters had lied to them, by telling them that his father was dead. Nick followed him and put a hand on Realm's shoulder. The feeling that Nick was close to him comforted him slightly, even though they agreed they were nothing more than friends.

"How is it possible that Mikan could get here on the property?" His mother asked, Realm looked at her in surprise. Why wasn't she angry, she just learned that her husband is still alive? Perhaps she already knew? Had his father approached her yet? Just like his father had done with him and she had figured out on her own.

"I don't know yet, Cleon is looking for the hole in our security right now. Because we patted ourselves on the back with our security and until I saw this." The Headmaster pointed to the image of Realm's father on the monitor. "Well let's just say it took a blow into my pride and even though I'm not a proud man, it still hurts." Nathalia folded her arms and looked at Realm and Nick. Realm looked at her for a moment, but he didn't shake Nick's hand from his shoulder.

"Headmeaster would be wise to not send Realm back to his classes, the news was quite shocking and we can't expect him to keep his mind on the lessons. I'm not pleading for myself." Nathalia said to The Headmaster and he nodded in agreement.

"Go on Nathalia." She gave him a little nod.

"I propose that I am the only one to go back to the scheduled classes and that Nick, assists Realm in processing." The Headmaster looked at them, then nodded his agreement again.

"You're a strange girl, Nathalia Tomes. Any other student would join the group when it comes to missing classes, but you're almost dying to go back to class." Nathalia shrugged.

"It is strange indeed, but you cannot give all three of us a day off. Who will pass the homework on, Katrina or Siobhan?" The Headmaster nodded his agreement again and his face twisted slightly.

"You have a good point in that. Well, Realm and Nick, you are free to do whatever you want. I really hope you will do your homework, but I know it is lost hope. Nathalia go back to your class." Nathalia walked past Realm and Nick.

"The three of us, dinner under the weeping willow." Nick and Realm nodded.

REALM THREW HIMSELF down on his mattress and buried his face in his feather filled pillow. This was rightfully the worst night of the past eleven years, no doubt about that. Realm felt that Nick sat next to him.

"Do I have to ask how you feel?" Realm slowly shook his head, his mother hadn't even looked at him when she left the staff room. She hadn't even said goodbye to him, as if all this was his fault. "Realm do you want me to stay?" This time, Realm nodded, feeling Nick's hand on his back again, Realm's skin under Nick's hand starting to tingle. Realm slowly pushed himself up and looked straight into Nick's pale blue eyes. Realm shared Nick's feelings about taking it easy, but now he wanted him all to himself. Maybe it was better to send him away? Nick slid slightly over and sighed. "Realm is there something wrong?" He whispered softly. Realm wanted to nod, but instead he pushed himself on to Nick and started kissing him passionately. Nick gently pushed him away from Realm. "Realm wait, we would take it easy." Realm nodded and pressed his lips back to Nick, before he took his lips of Nick's.

"Kissing is taking it easy." Nick chuckled, and grabbed Realm by his jacket.

"The The Headmaster was right, we really don't get any homework done." Realm shook his head and before Nick pressed his lips against Realm's. Realm felt Nick take off his own jacket and Realm did the same. Realm felt a smile appear on his face during the passionate kiss. He didn't know how much he longed for this, but when he felt Nick's hands pulling on his T-shirt, the hunger for more began to spark. This went completely against their conversation earlier that day, but he wanted this. No, he needed this. Realm also started tugging at Nick's t-shirt. For a moment they broke the kiss to pull the t-shirts over their heads, then resumed what they were doing.

FILLED WITH HAPPINESS, Realm looked at Nick's head, which rested on his bare chest. Nick's eyes were closed and his breathing was slowly rising and falling. Nick's dyed green locks graced his face. Realm didn't want to disturb the beautiful image, but lunch time was approaching and he could imagine that Gala would disturb their perfect world. Realm didn't want to think about food, or how Gala is going to reject if he found them like this. Carefully he moved his hand to Nick's cheek and slowly stroked away a lock of green, Nick's eyes slowly opened.

"Good morning. Sleeping beauty." Realm said with a smile on his face. Nick slowly pushed himself up.

"How long did I sleep." Realm looked at his phone lying next to him.

"A few hours, which is not surprising we were up pretty late yesterday." Nick nodded and crept up slightly so they were up to eye level. Nick pressed his lips to Realm's, it was a fleeting kiss.

"Thank you for letting me sleep, I think that I need it." Realm nodded and sighed.

"And thank you for, well you know." Nick answered him with a nod this time before throwing off the sheets, Realm watched Nick hoist himself into his clothes. He knew he had to do the same, but he would prefer to grab Nick by the arms and pull him back into bed. Reluctantly, Realm threw off the sheets and got up too, grabbing his pants from the floor and putting them on.

"Realm?" Realm looked up and his heart sank, Nick had a certain look in his eyes. "I wanted to ask you something now that we've had sex. What makes this us." Realm shrugged.

"Whatever we want it to be, weren't you the one who didn't want a sticker on?" Nick nodded slowly. "So why should we do that, Nick I love you and I would like to see where this takes us. But we both have to be open to that." Nick sighed and tried to answer until someone, or rather Gala, knocked on the door.

"Nathalia asked me to bring this to you guys. Am I disturbing you?" Gala entered the room without waiting for an answer, something he and Nick had in common.

"No, Gala." Nick said a little irritated as he snatched the plastic bag from Gala's hands.

"Wow, someone here got out of the coffin with the wrong foot. Well, I'll see you guys later, then." Gala turned and left Realm's room. Realm and Nick sat on the floor of Nick's room with their textbooks around them. They wanted to partially prove the The Headmaster wrong, but the only subject Realm had to do homework for was history. Nick saw Realm stare defeated at his history notebook.

"Your history doesn't start with the basement." Realm sighed and rubbed his temples with both hands.

"I know, but my memories don't go back any further than that. It is like I was reborn in that basement, and all my memories of a free and uncarring childhood were whipped away." He slammed his pen to the wooden floor. "I give up. Because every time I force myself to think about my time in the basement, it's strange when I say I'm afraid I never really left the basement?" Nick shook his head slowly.

"No, no. I don't think that is strange, from what you told me and what Claire told me in the letter. Well let's just say it was a traumatic experience. If you don't mind by the way, may I ask how it feels?" Realm looked at him in surprise, it was not a strange question and it was not that he had not received this question before. Only he never expected to get it from Nick. Realm narrowed his eyes, he was disgusted when he remembered the feeling.

"I can only say it felt strange, as soon as my teeth pierced through a human's skin and their blood poured into my mouth, I could feel what they were feeling at that moment. Their fears and thoughts became my own and I dare not to speak for them, but I think it happend both ways. Maybe I should ask Claire when I e-mail her." Realm felt his body begin to shake and beads of sweat form on his forehead. The last man he'd drank from, a few days before the vampire hunters came to rescue them, was not far from death. "The last person I drank from was a man and I believe it was Claire's father, but regardless. He was very weak when I was forced to bite him and I suspect my last feeding had killed him. I know he was still terrified in the beginning and then it slowly calmed down. Which made me calmer as well." Realm sighed. "I understand why the noble families and the vampire hunters have banned it. It was not a fun experience and not at all when you are that young." He opened his eyes and saw that Nick was writing fiercely, in his history notebook. "Nick what are you doing?" Nick probably finished his sentence before returning the notebook to Realm. Realm examined the ink-black lettering on the once virgin white paper. The paper in somewhat sloppy handwriting bore Realm's story, or the beginning of it. Just as Realm told Nick. "Nick why?" Nick shrugged and crawled over to Realm, now close enough to kiss Realm.

"I saw you were having a hard time so I helped you. Sorry for my handwriting, I was in a bit of a hurry." Realm looked at his notebook again and sighed.

"That's okay and thank you." Realm closed the notebook and set it aside. "Did you really want to know what it was like to drink from a person or did you want to distract me?" Again Nick shrugged and sighed.

"A little bit of both, I think. So where is my reward?" Nick didn't have to ask that a second time, Realm leaned forward and kissed him.

11

Katrina strode down the halls of the girls' dorm, hoping she wouldn't run into one person.

"Dazzlinkat." Katrina cursed and turned around. Behind her was a freshman who looked suspiciously like Siobhan.

"What do you want, Ayslin? And don't say you want to talk to Siobhan." Ayslin walked up to her, her eyes were green instead of brown, but the hair color and height. She really looked like Siobhan, maybe that's why Katrina wanted to help her so badly. Only there was one problem with Ayslin and that was that she wasn't Siobhan.

"Dazz, why wouldn't I go to ask qeustions about my brother. Sorry, I keep making that mistake over and over again. Let me reverse that qeustion. Why not ask about my sister?" Katrina clenched her fist, this was why Siobhan didn't want to talk to Ayslin and she cursed herself for not seeing this before. Katrina remembered well last year, Siobhan had struggled fiercely with her parents not accepting her for who she was, and Ayslin wanted to inflict the same pain. Katrina shook her head, no she could not let that happen. At least not on her account.

"Maybe because you have realized that she does not want anything to do with you and if I am very honest, neither do I." Katrina felt herself boiling with rage and actually wanted to run away from Ayslin.

"Dazzlinkat?"

"My name is Katrina, Ayslin! And I'm tired of hurting my friend just because I'm helping you. Sorry, but I'll pass." Ayslin folded her arms, a cocky look came to her eyes. A look that Katrina had not seen before, not by Ayslin or by Siobhan.

"Well now I know at least for which team you play, you are just as bad as she is." Ayslin didn't have to say a name because Katrina knew exactly who it was.

"I'd rather play for that team, as you and other ignorant idiots call it. Then for your team and if you want to excuse me, I have to apologize to your *sister*." Katrina walked away from Ayslin with her fists clenched. The nerve, who did Ayslin think she was? Katrina stopped walking for a moment and sighed, she was being played and she hurt Siobhan, thinking that she was helping her. Her hands went to the diadem on her head. Siobhan had given it to her last year as a token of their friendship, and what had Katrina done with that friendship? Katrina continued around a corner where, to her surprise, Siobhan was standing.

"Siobhan O'hEaliadthgthe, don't scare me like that in the future!" Katrina put her hand on her chest and took a few breaths. When Katrina looked at her, she saw tears in Siobhan's eyes, her heart sank to her feet. Why was Siobhan crying, was it something she had done? Katrina pushed aside her doubts and guilt. "Siobhan are you okay?" To her relief, Siobhan nodded and her heart began its ascent. "Then why are you crying?" Siobhan said nothing but took Katrina in her arms.

"Oh, Katrina. Glad to have my best friend back. As long as you don't say anything to Nathalia." Katrina nodded and wrapped her arms around Siobhan.

"I'm really sorry where I thought I was helping you. Or at least that's what Ayslin made me think. I'm sorry I risked our friendship." Tears sprang from Katrina's eyes and streamed down her cheeks. Katrina stepped back and wiped away the tears.

"I know your intentions were good, even though it was hurt me. To see you talk to her and laugh, I was afraid that witch ..."

"That witch what?" Ayslin had followed Katrina and stood with her arms folded behind her. "Please finish your sentence if you have the balls." Katrina clenched her fists again, nobody spoke to her best friend like that. Siobhan put a hand on Katrina's shoulder and stepped forward.

"With all the love, little sister. For a moment I was afraid that the witch would take my best friend from me. But luckily my best friend has seen who you really are, so I don't have to worry about that. And I have definitely balls, but nowadays they are in a different place." Siobhan put her hands on her breasts and turned around, grabbed Katrina's hand and walked away.

AS SOON AS SIOBHAN and Katrina were outside, they started laughing.

"Well, we just put your little sister in her place. If only I have done that sooner" Katrina said as soon as she caught her breath, Siobhan nodded in agreement and sighed.

"I can say the same thing, but then again. It is really my sister and putting her in her place is my job." Siobhan let go of Katrina's hand and sighed. "Why were you actually drawn to her? I don't think I ever hid what my sister was like." Katrina looked into the enchanting brown eyes, her heart racing.

"She looked a lot like you in appearance, way too much like you and like Ayslin said I play for the other team." Siobhan looked at her in surprise, and Katrina shrugged. "I liked you before you decided to go through life as a woman and I still like you now, maybe even more." Siobhan smiled, which made Katrina's heart sing. Katrina took a step towards Siobhan and put her arms around her best friend. "Siobhan, I don't care if you feel the same way about me, I really don't care." Siobhan lowered her head slightly and slid her lips past Katrina's.

"Who said I don't feel the same for you." Siobhan whispered before giving Katrina a kiss.

12

Nathalia glanced at her two kissing friends, admitting she was relieved. Seeing Siobhan and Katrina so intimately, it was something different from the cat fights. Gala sighed and sat next to her, he was looking at the sky.

"Nathalia, I'm afraid it's going to rain." Nathalia looked at the dark clouds gathering in the sky, but she saw no sign of rain.

"I think we can sit it until after dinner."

"Let's hope so, because I'm about to die of the hunger." Siobhan and Katrina had let go of each other and sat down with Gala and Nathalia.

"So we just have to wait for Realm and Nick." Siobhan smiled at Katrina, who gave her a smile back.

"Well, I am afraid that we can wait a long time, I think those two are literally stuck together." Gala said as his hand went to the wicker basket, but Nathalia slapped it when it came to close. "Ouch, what you didn't see those two. But when I went to bring them lunch, their hair was all messed up. Especially in Realm's case, which is strange, so I think the two of them had a naked pillow fight." Nathalia chuckled.

"If so, my cousin has finally come out and I am happy for him."

"Who are you happy for, Nathalia." She turned quickly, Nick and Realm had appeared behind her. Nick sat next to her and Realm sat between Gala and Katrina.

"Gala told me he suspects you have had sex, to which Nathalia said if that was the case she was happy for you. So tell us did you have sex?" Katrina leaned defiantly into Realm who leaned back uncomfortably.

"Katrina leave him alone, if they wanted to tell us something they would have done it on their own terms." Siobhan pulled the wicker basket to her and took the plates out of the basket. Nathalia looked at Nick taking his plate and then at Realm both had a special kind of glow around them, she wasn't sure how to describe this. But she could see the happiness and love for each other on their faces when they looked at each other sideways. Nathalia felt her heart fill with the same happiness. That's something she always wanted for her cousin.

NATHALIA CURSED, BUT in the middle of their meal the thick raindrops began to fall from the heavens. Siobhan, Katrina and Gala all offered to return the basket to Madam Valè.

"Why don't you go with the three of you." Realm had suggested, a proposal all three of them accepted. "So finally some rest." Realm sighed, but Nathalia folded her arms. They stood under the thick canopy of the weeping willow tree, so that hardly a drop leaked through.

"Maybe those three give you peace of their minds, but those three are not blind. That story of you two having sex doesn't just come out of the blue and I thought I saw something this morning. That's why I asked the Headmaster to give you guys some time off, but you're probably going to tell me I just imagined it, Nick." She looked at Nick who shook his head with a smile.

"No I'm not going to do that because it's useless. Just amazed me that you know we ..." He didn't finish his sentence and she saw that he was slowly turning red, since when was he ashamed. He didn't know who he was talking to.

"Realms hair that was a mess when Gala came in. That is what gave it away." Realm's eyes widened and one of his hands ran through his perfectly combed hair. When he lowered his hand, he laughed, he looked at her and his laugh was muted. His eyes only grew slowly and his face turned white, Nick took a few steps forward. But out of nowhere, Nathalia felt a hand on her shoulder and a hand on her mouth, a choked cry released from her throat.

"Let her go, creep!" Nick took one step closer. Nathalia couldn't see her attacker, but she heard him laugh. Something sharp was pressed against her throat.

"I'll let her go if you guys come with me without too much noise, especially you son." Nathalia felt her being pulled and Realm nodded. She didn't realize she had been holding her breath, but she gasped violently as she was pushed into the backseat of the waiting car. She moved slowly to the other door, maybe she could slip out of the car through that door and get help. Unfortunately that door opened and Realm got in on the other side and Nick sat on the other side of her. The doors closed on both sides, there was a window between them and the unknown driver. She looked quickly at the doors next to the boys. The car started moving, Nathalia nodded to Nick's door.

"See if it opens." She whispered, and his hand moved slowly to the door. He pulled it gently, but there was no movement. She sighed their kidnapper had prepared himself well and put the child lock on the doors. Nathalia glanced at Realm, whose face was still white. "Realm are you okay?" Realm did not respond to her question. He didn't even blink, they nudged Nick with her elbow. "I'm afraid he's in shock." Nick leaned forward, Nathalia pressed herself against the couch so he could see Realm better.

"Realm?" But even Nick's voice couldn't get him out of his frozen state either. Nathalia put a hand on Realm's arm and then looked at Nick.

"The one behind the wheel is Realm's dad, right?" Nick nodded slowly, Nathalia took a deep breath through her nose. "Well Nick let me be clear, no matter what happens let's not break any laws. Should we be saved by vampire hunters, I don't want to give them a reason to kill us." Nick nodded slowly, his eyes still on Realm.

"You and I are of the same mind, cousin." Nick took her hand and squeezed it gently, she did the same with Realm. Which squeezed back slightly, so he had heard her.

"Realm I know you got out under the death penalty last time, because of your young age. But you're eleven years older now, and the hunters aren't going to be that forgiving, this time around." Realm squeezed her hand lightly again. Maybe he was too scared to speak, afraid his father would hear him. Something she fully understood, his ghost of the past eleven years had returned to bring him back to the source of the fear. Maybe, no not maybe, it was a certainty to her that she would feel the same way if her parents or grandparents came back. Nathalia quickly shook off these thoughts and looked at the dark glass. The glass reflected slightly, she could see her own golden locks and pale blue eyes that she shared with Nick. She felt a bit sleepy, something driving a car always did to her, she bit the inside of her lip. She had to stay awake at all costs and stay strong as she always had. She had to stay strong for Nick, maybe for Realm too.

"Nathalia, are you all right?" She felt Nick's hand on her shoulder, her whole body tingling. She looked at him quickly and nodded. She was not allowed to show weakness, she had to stay strong. Nick scrutinized her, but before he could say anything, Nathalia came up with something. She still had her school bag with her, in the bag there were three filled bottles of Bloodberry juice.

"Nick did you have your bottle with you?" She said a softly as posible. Nick nodded and took the silver flask from his inside pocket, she grabbed it from his hands and ducked for her purse. She unzipped her bag so gently and pulled out one of the bottles.

Gently she poured the juice into the bottle, amazed herself that her hands were steady. She handed the filled bottle back to Nick and she screwed the cap on the bottle. Should Realm's father find the juice in her bag, they still had some juice on hand. With a sigh she leaned back against the couch.

THE CAR STOPPED, NATHALIA let go of the boys' hands. The driver's door opened and was slammed shut not much later. Nathalia looked ahead, her hands clasping her satchel. The door on Nick's side opened and Realm's father was in the opening.

"Get out." Nick got out of the car and turned to face her. He reached out to help her out of the car. She moved carefully to the doorway, then took Nick's hand. She got out and straightened her back, which she did often enough at school. She wanted to get a good look at the area, but she was pushed into a abandoned house; the windows were broke, the outside wood needed more then a good coat of paint. "Keep on walking, girl." She swallowed, staying strong will be dificult with Realm's father around, he genuinely scared her to death.

13

Realm gasped when he saw the abandoned house, it was the same house his father had locked him in eleven years before. Realm gently bit his lip and followed his friends without saying a word. Nick glanced over his shoulder at him for a moment with concern in his eyes, it was not clear about who was he worried. There were two options, Nathalia or he himself, and she put on brave a brave face ever since they were in the car. She most likely felt that she needed to be strong for both of them. Something he appreciated, but not if she had to pay for it. Realm froze for a moment when he saw the repaired cellar door, it was as if he had never been kicked in.

"Realm escort those friends of yours downstairs, I'll be right there." Realm looked over his shoulder and looked straight into his father's dark green eyes. Realm stopped walking and turned to face him. His father had not pressed a knife to anyone's throat this time so there was no reason for his frozen in fear attitude. Something he should have already done with the car.

"No, 1 am not leading my friends downstairs!" Realm's father chuckled softly, perhaps expecting this response from his son. Realm straightened his back as he had seen Nathalia do before. "I will not allow you to put them through the same hell, that you did to me eleven years ago." His father sighed and looked defiantly at his son.

"Well Realm my son, unfortunately I have to tell you that you have very little choice." Realm's voice was a little unsteady, something he hated and he had hoped his father didn't hear.

"And why is that?" His father spread his arms, Realm got a bad feeling about this.

"Well to begin with they are already here, and you are my son, so you have to do what I tell you." Realm folded his arms.

"Never heard of puberty? That is the period, when kids stop listening to their parents." The smile faded from his father's face and replaced it with a dark look that Realm had only seen once before. Realm clenched his fists, this was actually the response he'd been hoping for.

"Realm." His father took a step forward, and Realm released his hand with the clenched fist. He also stepped forward and hit his father on his temple, causing his father to fall to the ground. Realm quickly turned to his friends.

"Run!" They ran out of the house to the car. Realm hoped his father still had the keys in the ignition. Unfortunately, his father had been smart and took the keys out of the ignition. Nathalia looked at it and swore.

"That means that running away is our only option." Said Nick who was already made himself ready for a long run, Nathalia had pressed her lips together. Apparently she had reservations, but she nodded nonetheless. She jumped up and wanted to run.

"Realm!" His father's voice echoed down the deserted street. Realm looked shocked at the front door, his father stood in the doorway. He was holding a young woman, the knife he had previously pressed to Nathalia's throat, pressed to her throat. Realm looked at the young woman and felt his veins freeze.

"Claire?" Realm glanced at Nick, who also looked frozen at the young woman. Realm cursed, his father knew him a bit to well. Realm sighed, I couldn't leave Claire.

"Realm if you run then I will kill her, just as the other blood bags that I collect." Realm squeezed his hands into fists. He looked at Nathalia and Nick.

"Run, save yourselves. He said if *I* run, he said nothing about you two." Nick walked over to him.

"Do you really think that I would leave you here alone? Well, you have no news for you." Nathalia appeared next to her cousin and nodded. The three friends walked back to the house with their heads bowed. Realm stopped right in front of his father's nose.

"I should have knocked you unconscious." His father nodded.

"You should have done that, yes." He pushed Claire into Realm's arms. "Take her with you downstairs." Realm clutched Claire and nodded reluctantly.

THE FOUR OF THEM WENT down the stairs to the basement, the door locked behind them. Realm looked around, there he was back in his prison. Much to his regret, the light was already on and he could see the faces of his father's new victims. There were no young children this time, Realm swallowed, then looked Claire in the eye. The terror of eleven years ago was back.

"Claire I'm so sorry." Claire shook her head, her copper locks flying in all directions.

"Realm just like then this is not your fault either. I was so stupid to think I was safe." Claire got on her own two feet and looked at Nick and Nathalia. "I'm sorry you're here thanks to me." Nick walked up to her and shook his head.

"It's not your fault either Claire, I just have a question is the boy you talked about in your letter here too?" Claire looked surprised at Nick, then at Realm.

"You showed him my letter to you?" Realm nodded, and gave her a thin smile.

"Nick is my... friend." Claire nodded for a moment, then looked at Nick.

"Well Realm, you have taste. But in answer to your question Nick, no Zack isn't here. Realm's couldn't get to him without getting caught." Claire called Realm's father by name, and Realm heard the underlying rage. Realm sighed and looked around the basement, more people were chained than last time. He counted twenty divided into ten men and women. Realm also noticed that there were human food in cans at the door, this time his father had probably thought about keeping his forbidden meal alive. Realm thought about what Nathalia had whispered to him in the car, he agreed. They should not be tempted to drink human blood at any cost. He looked at the door, then at Claire.

"Claire, don't worry that my friends and I will drink. This time I'm stronger, unfortunately that doesn't mean anything to my dad." Claire grabbed his hands.

"Realm, please watch out with your father. He's not the guy from eleven years ago, he's crazier than before. I heard him talk just before he went to get you and the talk was confirmed by the other one here. He doesn't want to only that you eat from us, he also wants you to lie with the females." Realm looked at Nathalia and the other women in the basement. Then he saw that all the women were wearing skirts, the smell of blood entering his nose. Nathalia looked too and then almost crawled into Nick, Realm cursed. He couldn't let this happen, at least not again. Nick put his arms around Nathalia.

"Claire you don't have to be scared before either, at least not in the case of Nick and myself." Claire looked at the other women and Realm looked at the relief on their faces.

"Only you can't protect anyone from your father." Realm nodded, he wished that was possible. But as it turned out before, he had no control over his father.

"REALM WHAT THE HELL are you doing?" Realm looked at the door and saw his father come down, a scorching smell followed him. He probably set the car on fire. "Are you having a whole conversation with your food?"

"Claire is not a food." Realm stood in front of Claire so that his father had to get through him to get to her. "Claire is a friend, just like Nick and Nathalia." Realm's father went down the last steps and glared at Realm.

"Is that right." Realm did not expect the punch to his stomach, gasping for breath he fell to the ground.

"Realm!" He heard Nick calling his name, Claire had ducked after him, her hands on him. She was shaking violently and he couldn't blame her. This time she was not only seen as food, but also seen as a kind of dhampir oven. Realm grabbed her arm, but his father was already pulling on Claire.

"Let her go, son." Realm didn't listen and that was paid for with a kick in the stomach. He gasped again, but still he wouldn't let go of Claire's arm. He was genuinely afraid that if he let her go his father would rape her. He glanced over at Nick, who had been clutching Nathalia, afraid his father would force her to have sex too. Realm looked back at Claire and his dad, just in time to see his dad's foot kicking his face. Realm felt he was losing grip on Claire's arm just before he lost consciousness.

14

With a sigh, Gala walked out of the main building, Siobhan and Katrina followed him hand in hand. They had returned the plates to Madam Valè. Gala looked back for a moment and felt a gaping hole in his heart. After this year, all his friends would be flying out to universities and he would stay here, something he wasn't exactly waiting for. But what could he do about it, nothing. There was nothing he could do about it, as his mother had said at the beginning of the school year.

"Then you shouldn't have thrown your hat at it." Worst of it all, she was right. But she was also the first to admitted that he had a little too much on his mind last year. With his father suddenly standing in front of him. Gala shook these thoughts out of his head, enjoying the time he had left with his friends.

"Gala, if you don't mind we will go back to our dorm. The teachers literally and figuratively buried us with homework..." Gala was no longer listening. Homework? Yeah right. Those two planned to follow in Nick and Realm's footsteps. Gala looked at the weeping willow and was slightly surprised that it was deserted. Normally Nick and Nathalia would have waited for them, maybe they also had too much 'homework'. Gala rolled his eyes and sighed, but what was Nathalia's excuse. Gala walked towards the tree and was surprised to see that the sheet they had eaten on was still on the ground. He knelt down and took it. It was the quilt that Nicks and Nathalia's grandmother made when Nathalia moved in with her. It was meant to comfort Nathalia after the loss of her parents, not knowing that she herself was not having long either. Nathalia had finished the quilt with her own hands, and Gala knew one thing for sure. Nathalia would never just leave this quilt behind. Gala looked around for a moment, Katrina and Siobhan were not yet in their dorm.

"Siobhan, Katrina!" The two girls looked up and he motioned for them to come. Reluctance was drawn on their faces.

"What's up Gala, we already told you..." Siobhan began, but stopped when she saw that Gala was holding Nathalia's basket. "Nathalia would never let this here ungaurded." Gala looked at Siobhan.

"Take this up to Nathalia's room and see if she's there. I'll go see if Nick and Realm are in theirs. Let me prepare myself."

"For what?"

"In case I interrupted a naked pillow fight." He said with an unconvincing smile on his face. Gala ran into the dorm and stormed to the stairwell.

"Slow down, Galakrond." Alex-Lucas blocked his way.

"Move over, Barnier." Gala squeezed past him. "I need to see if Realm and Nick are in their rooms."

"And why if I may ask?" Gala normally had no patience for this upholstered noble, but perhaps he could use his help.

"Because yesterday there was a strange liquid in front of Realm's door, at first we thought that it was a sick joke from onw of the students. But then Nathalia told me over lunch that the acid had been applied by Realm's presumed dead father. Just now I found Nathalia's basket ungaurded at the weeping willow and she, Nick and Realm were nowhere to be seen. So fill in the rest of the puzzle yourself." Gala ran up the stairs ,and was not to his surprise that Alex-Lucas ran after him. "You look in Realm's room and I'll take Nicks." Alex-Lucas nodded and ran to Realm's door. Gala jumped into Nick's room and much to his fear it was empty, he turned and Alex-Lucas was behind him.

"Stryder's room is also empty and I've already checked the bathroom." Gala's stomach formed a knot.

"This is very wrong. I have to give Vincynt some water." Gala quickly ran to his own room, followed closely by Alex-Lucas.

"You have a snake in your room? Do you know that this is against the rules?" Gala nodded and sighed.

"Best kept secret at the academy, at least until now." Gala opened the terrarium and picked up the stone water bowl. He pushed the tray into Alex-Lucas's hands. "Fill it with water, but first remove the algae with your fingers. Then I will do the rest of its care." Alex-Lucas was still amazed that a snake lived in one of the rooms. Gala quickly cleaned the loft with a scraper and a damp cloth before Alex-Lucas entered the room. Followed by Katrina and Siobhan, Alex-Lucas handed Gala the water bowl and opened his mouth to speak to the girls.

"Yes we know we are not allowed to come here without the permission of a teacher. But Gala, Nathalia is not in her room or in the bathroom." Katrina said quickly, Gala cursed. "What's going on in your head?" Gala looked at Katrina and swallowed.

"I'm afraid Mikan Stryder hasn't forgotten his tricks yet." Alex-Lucas sighed.

"We have to tell this to a teacher." Gala nodded and looked at Katrina, who had a certain kind of look in her eyes.

"What is it?" But before Katrina answered, she pulled her phone from her inside pocket. "Katrina?" She raised her hand to silence him.

"Let me, just put my magic to work." Her finger ran across the screen. "A car got fire near where Mikan first built his den. I bet my cat-ear headband collection that he's back there." Katrina looked at

Alex-Lucas. "But to make sure, the three of us are going to take a look."

"That is prohibited!" Opposed Alex-Lucas, Katrina shrugged.

"Not so prohibited as kidnapping and drinking human blood, but that didn't stop Mikan Stryder. Besides, me and the boundaries of the law are no strangers to each other. Listen carefully, Barnier. If you haven't heard from us when the sun goes down, alert the suits."

"The suits?" Katrina sighed, and rolled with her eyes. Gala needed to constrain himself not to laugh.

"The vampire hunters, stay focused, Barnier." Katrina turned and walked away. Siobhan and Gala looked at Alex-Lucas and both shrugged. "Are you two still coming?" Katrina called out through the halls. Gala and Siobhan ran out of Gala's room.

IT FELT STRANGE TO be outside the iron gates of the academy. Katrina was behind the wheel of a car, Gala had no idea how she got it, and if he was honest, he didn't want to know either.

"Okay, we're almost there. The fire was two blocks away, but the abonded shack as my father affectionately called it is around the corner. I park the car here." She parked the black car in a tight alley. "Gala, Siobhan give me your phones." Gala did as she asked, but wondered why she needed their phones. "I'll put a lost and found app on your phones and we'll leave it here, just in case. I'll take mine with me, so my father and the suits can find us. If necessary." She leaned over to the glove box. "This box is fire resistant and can only be opened with a key that only my father and I have. So don't worry about your phones." Katrina muttered as she put the cell phones away and locked the glove compartment. Gala was relieved, so Katrina hadn't stolen this car. It was her own car, but what was it doing so close to the school? Perhaps that was a question he should ask another time.

"How do you know all this?" He asked. Katrina looked over her shoulder and gave him a mysterious smile.

"You don't want to know." Gala and Siobhan pushed a weathered yet well-stocked container in front of the alley, concealing the car. Katrina nodded approvingly to their work and motioned for them to walk with her. Gala nudged Siobhan and she leaned slightly towards him.

"Do you know how she knows all this?" Siobhan shook her head.

"No, all I know is that Katrina grew up on the street before her father took her in. I guess you need these things on the street." Katrina glanced at them and gave Siobhan a smile. For a moment, Gala wished he had this too, with someone. He pushed aside the hollow feeling in his heart, he was here to find his friends. That was his job and that of the girls. Katrina stopped in front of an abonded house, if this was it Gala could understand why Katrina's father called it a abonded shack. A fresh coat of paint is not going to help this house, to look as good as new.

"I have a bad feeling about this." Siobhan said before walking into the abonded shack.

15

Realm groaned, his head felt like a herd of elephants had been dancing through his brain. He wanted to bring his hands to it, but he couldn't move his hands. He slowly opened his eyes, the artificial light from the single bulb of light stung his eyes. Where was he and how did he get here? He was not in his room at the academy, that was for sure, or else a naked Nick would most likely have layed against him.

"Realm?" Nick's soft voice startled him. The memories came back like an explosion, something that did not help to get rid of the headache. "Realm you are awake, good." Realm looked around, it took a while for his world to take shape and color. He raised his hands again, but again his hands didn't touch there. The ring of a chains echoed in his ears, he looked in surprise at the chains on his arms.

"By my soul?"

"Your soul has nothing to do with it, trust me." Realm's head shot to the side and he looked straight into Gala's emerald eyes. Which gave him a thin, yet warm smile. "Do me a favor and leave a note with it next time. I was kidnapped by my crazy still alive father." Realm sighed.

"By my soul, Gala what are you doing here?"

"He's not alone." Realm leaned forward and saw Siobhan and Katrina sitting. Realm cursed, he wasn't worried enough about those who were already here. "You can say that again." Katrina said lightly and Realm did as she asked. "Amen." Realm felt a smile appear on his face, something that was very painful. So the smile quickly disappeared.

"So you are finally awake. Nice then you can tell me how it is possible that these three found us?" His father walked into the room, Realm laid his head against the stone wall.

"I really have no idea, *old man.*" He omitted the word father, the man standing before him was not his father. The vampire hunters hadn't completely lied eleven years ago. "Maybe you left a trail after all. Did you ask them, I did, but I got no answer." Realm suspected Katrina and her father had something to do with it, but he didn't tell Mikan that. Mikan sat down next to him.

"If I were you I would concider your words carrefully. Son." Mikan emphasized the last part of his sentence, Realm shrugged.

"Why would I do that, you're kidnapping me and four of my friends. You're breaking the law again and basically forcing us to do the same. Now you've chained three more of my friends to the wall. Have I forgotten something, oh yes. You knocked me out. Thanks to you, for the first time in eleven years, I'm glad I don't have a mirror at hand." Realm heard Gala chuckle softly, Mikan glanced sideways at Gala and nodded.

"I should have known you were weak, your mother was weak and I regret I couldn't get that out of you." Mikan got up and walked over to Nick. "Your boyfriend here is just as weak as you, you with your filthy way of life. I did hear what that girl said about the two of you." Realm shrugged.

"Well then I'm not a *real* vampire, just like my mother and you know what old man. I'm proud of it!" Realm's voice buzzed against the basement walls. That way everyone could hear it, Mikan looked surprised for a moment and then anger took over again.

"Well in that case, where did I leave that Tomes girl." Realm's breath caught in his throat, he glanced at Nick, who also stiffened.

"Oh look, there is the frightened boy, again. So he's still there, good to know. Maybe I'll have her after my meal." Mikan walked away. Realm glanced around. He hadn't noticed this before, but he didn't see Nathalia, Claire and the other people anywhere.

"We're in another room." Nick said in a muffled voice, the fear that Mikan would harm Nathalia was clearly great.

"I'm sorry Nick, if I had known he..." Realm swallowed his words, he would have known that was the problem. Why had he challenged Mikan, Realm cursed and hung his head in shame.

"Uhm, Reallm what did your father mean I'll take her?" Siobhan asked softly, Realm sighed.

"The way you think he means it Siobhan, and don't call him Realm's father. Because I really can't imagine that someone like that could bring someone like Realm into the world." Realm looked at Nick in amazement, he could understand his fear of Nathalia. But to talk to Siobhan like that, Nick went a step too far. Nick sighed and nodded to Realm. "I'm sorry Siobhan. I'm worried about Nathalia." Realm reached out to try to get his hand to Nick, but the ringing of the chains and the chains themselves just wouldn't let it.

DOES ANYONE KNOW WHAT time it is? "Katrina asked out of nowhere. Realm looked at her in surprise.

"Quarter over the edge of the pisspot, how should I know that. I'm not wearing a watch." Nick said, he came forward a bit. "That's what any sane person started doing when the mobile phone was invented." Katrina stuck out her tongue at him.

"Haha, very funny. I practically peed in my pants." Katrina straightened her back. "Mr. Stryder!" There was no response. "Mr. Stryder!"

"What!" Mikan walked into the room, flushed, a drop of blood still on his chin.

"I'm sincerely sorry to interrupt sir. But I really need to pee." Realm was amazed at the polite tone Katrina used, this was the first time she used this tone, Mikan looked at her in surprise.

"Why would I bother, pee in your pants for my part." Katrina gasped, startled.

"Mr. Stryder I hope you don't mean that, do you?" Realm had to admit and he would if anyone asked him, Katrina was a damn good actress. If he hadn't known her well, he frowned for a moment, at least he hoped he knew her well. But he would almost believe her, almost. Realm glanced at Mikan, who was a little defeated.

"Weluhh."

"Mr. Stryder, please may I use your water closet. Maybe I can be of service to you afterwards." Realm's eyes widened, he glanced at Siobhan, then Katrina again. Mikan smiled too willingly for Realm's taste, and he walked over to Katrina.

"Well then go ahead." He untied her, but still held her just to be on the safe side as they walked away.

"Please don't tell me Katrina just offered herself to that man, judt to go to the toilet?" Gala asked and Realm looked at the door through which Mikan and Katrina had just disappeared.

"Gala I wish I could." Nick fired an entire landing curse. Unfortunately, the one it was aimed at was not present in the room.

"She sacrifices herself, by my soul I wish I wasn't stuck." Nick started pulling the chains, replacing the swearing with the loud ringing.

"Nick!" Siobhan's voice was just above the ring, it worked. "Katrina, is a smart girl she knows what she's doing. She asked Alex-Lucas to give us until sunset, if he hadn't heard from us then he would warn Katrina's father and the vampire hunters."

"They don't know where we are. It could be days before they find us." Siobhan chuckled softly, yet Realm could see a glimpse of fear.

"Do you think so low of our Katrina so low?" Nick slowly shook his head.

"Katrina Link, is a woman in a million." said Nick and Gala, at the same time. A loud explosion echode through the space. They all switched looks, was this there rescue?

"Sorry can you two repeat that, I am afraid I did not hear you with all that noise." Katrina walked into the room, followed by two vampire hunters. Realm didn't know them, but they got the same look in their eyes. The hunters released Realm and the others.

"You are free, so go outside." Realm rubbed his wrists, he saw that the others did the same thing. Gala leand towards him.

"Is it wrong to say that I am missing your old man?" Realm nodded, and walked towards Nick.

"Yes Gala, that is wrong." Gala nodded and walked with Siobhan to the stairs. Nick looked at the hunters.

"My cousin was also here. Did you see her?" One of the hunters looked at him.

"We do not know, if you go upstairs, you can see it for yourself." Nick looked at the man, anger was burning behind his eyes. Realm laid a hand on Nick's shoulder.

"Lets go outside, and see it for ourselves." Nick nodded.

"If uncle Abraham was here I would have got an answer right away." Realm didn't know who uncle Abraham was, but he may figure that out when they are outside.

16

Realm had clung on to Nick, worried he would disappear if Realm let go of him. They walked outside the house.

"Nick, Realm!" Nathalia's voice reached them above all voices, Realm bit his lip when he saw her run. He let go of Nick with one hand to catch Nathalia, her cheeks wet with tears. "I'm so glad to see you in one piece." She took a step back and looked at Realm. "For the most part then." Realm made a painful smile on his face.

"I'll ask Nick to get all my mirrors out of my room for the time to being." Nathalia laughed through tears.

"Maybe that's a good idea." Nick laughed with her and Realm wrapped his arms around her once again.

"Nathalia, did you see uncle Abraham?" She shook her head, Nick cursed. "I had hoped that he was here." Realm wanted to ask who in soul's name uncle Abraham was.

"Stryder!" Realm slowly shrank, that was the voice of vampire hunter Lazar. Realm let go of Nick, but then began to stagger on his legs.

"Maybe I should hold you." Nick said, and Realm nodded gratefully. Lazar appeared in front of Realm, his angry eyes seemed to burn through Realm.

"Stryder send your friends away, they will be questioned in a minute." Realm slowly shook his head and sighed.

"Nick Lumina is the reason I'm still standing, so if you don't mind. I'd rather keep him with me." Lazar looked as if he didn't like it at all, but sighed.

"I thought you learned your lesson the first time we where here. But now I find you here again. With your father, again." Realm straightened up, with Nick's support.

"Would you say I did this on purpose. Mr. Lazar this morning before the sun came up, my friends and I were eating quietly. Under a weeping willow behind the iron gate of my school, after dinner three of my friends were going to bring back the plates that we used. Then a man decided, a man you had pronounced dead in front of a six-year-old, to threaten my friend here with a knife. My friend here Nick Lumina is Nathalia Tomes' cousin and we had no choice but to follow Mikan's orders. When we got here, I tried to fight him. But when we found out my dad was holding Claire and others. I had no choice tham to stay, my friends here decided to stay with me. But no none of us was here by choice. Except Mikan Stryder. "

"And I!" Katrina called to them as she passed by. Realm sighed.

"And Katrina Link apparently. But that's my story and I'll stick with it." Realm felt his head spin and his stomach growled violently. Realm put a hand on it and Lazar followed the hand with his eyes.

"Do I have to ask what happened to your face? Did that girl hit you black and blue when you tried to assault her?" Realm's blood began to boil, Lazar went too far, and this time there was no fellow vampire hunter to call him back. Realm was too old for that, this time. Realm glanced at Nick and he nodded in agreement, as if he was thinking the same thing as Realm.

"Lazar if Claire was a boy who looked just as good as this boy right here next to me! Then maybe I would have been tempted. I have this decoration from Mikan Stryder when I wanted to protect Claire from him! I don't doubting it that she will tell you the same thing and if you'd like to apologize to me and my friends. We'd love to go back to our school cafeteria. Because we're longing for a good bloodless meal from Chef Madam Valè." Realm stepped aside and Nick followed.

"Mr. Stryder, we're not done here yet!" Realm looked over his shoulder.

"We are definitely done, you should have done your job. You should have cut that madman down and not lie about it. If you have to point out a culprit, start with yourself first." Realm pointed to all the vampire hunters who surrounded him. Vance Dracul was in between the group.

"Lazar, let my students go. If you have more questions, you know where to find them." Realm walked to the the Headmaster, and by his souls what was he glad to see him.

REALM SAT AT THE CAFETERIA table with his friends, everyone sat in silence and ate their soup. The Headmaster walked into the cafeteria and sat down at their table.

"I'm not going to talk about you three." Vance looked at Realm, Nick, and Nathalia. "I honestly believe you had no choice to go with Mikan Stryder. I must confess that I am ashamed of that at the moment." His gaze went to Katrina, Siobhan and Gala. "I actually wanted to talk about the three of you, how could you be so stupid!" Realm glanced at his friends across the table. Katrina looked straight at the Headmaster.

"I'm not stupid, I knew exactly what I was doing." The Headmaster narrowed his pale purple eyes and Katrina looked back at her soup. "What, I knew exactly what I was doing, otherwise you would never have found us." She muttered softly.

"That may be Katrina, but why couldn't you have done this on your own? If you knew so well what you were doing. For example, did you know that Mikan raped the women in that dungeon?" Katrina slowly shook her head.

"No, I didn't know, Headmaster. I didn't know at all, until Mikan threatened to assault Nathalia. That's why I..." Katrina fell silent as the Headmaster's eyes widened.

"You offered yourself yo him? By my soul, Katrina." Katrina shrugged, but Realm saw that she was ashamed.

"I could have lived with it, Headmaster. At least it was by choice." The Headmaster got up and swore. He put his hand over his mouth and clearly cursed again. He walked back and forth for a moment, then sat down again.

"Katrina, Katrina you really don't value yourself so much. I have to tell your father this and to be honest I don't know if I can. Because I don't know if I should be disappointed in you or proud because you wanted to sacrifice yourself for someone else." He said with a sigh. Realm reached out to Katrina along with Nick. Katrina took them.

"I'll tell my father myself. I'm sorry, Headmaster."

"Katrina Link what do you have to tell me?" Everyone looked up and a hefty man in a suit was standing in the cafeteria. Katrina let go of Realm and Nick's hands, and she got up and walked over to her father. She had put her arms behind her back and spoke softly.

REALM WAS HAPPY TO be on Nick's bed, Nick was next to him on his head on Realm's chest. Nick was already fast asleep, but Realm was strangely wide awake. Perhaps it was because he had already slept all day, thanks to his father's kick in the face. One of the reasons he wasn't in his own bed. With a sigh, he gently played with Nick's green locks. Realm had actually hoped a good naked pillow fight would tire him out, but unfortunately for him, it had only given him more energy.

"Realm?" Nick opened his eyes slowly. "If you can't sleep then do your homework." Realm chuckled for a moment and stroked Nick's hair.

"Nick should anyone ask, you're the smartest of the two of us." Nick pushed himself slightly up and pressed his lips to Realm's.

"As if anyone will ever believe that." He said when he interrupted the kiss. Realm slithered out from under Nick and pulled on his underpants.

"Maybe you have a point there." Realm sat on the floor and picked up his history notebook. It seemed so long ago that Nick had written in there. Realm opened the notebook and reached for his pen, took a deep breath and began filling the virgin white pages with black ink.

17

Realm limped through the gray corridors of the old mansion, history notebook in hand. The candles hadn't even been lit and the other students were most likely still lying in their beds, somewhere he should have been. But he couldn't wait for his wounds where healed to submit his homework. Realm ran the library in Mister Crypto's office was closed. Strangely, Realm enjoyed the stillness and tranquility that lingered in the hallways, perhaps because it was now still and quiet in his mind. He strode to the history room, the door was open and seemed to welcome him. It was different from the first time he entered this classroom.

"Realm Stryder, what a surprise. After your adventure I didn't expect you until next week." Realm nodded and walked on into the room. Professor Redfang looked at him with a friendly smile.

"Oh all I can I say, that I couldn't sleep and that's why I made my account of my own history." He held up the notebook, Professor Redfang beckoned him to her desk and he limped slowly towards it. He put the writing on the wood.

"I confess, the first part was written by Nick. But I did the rest myself." Professor Redfang opened the notebook.

"I recognize Nick Lumina's sloppy, yet legible handwriting. Thanks for your honesty, but Realm can I ask you something?" Realm nodded. "I remember well that you were taken aback when I gave you this assignment last Friday. Does that have anything to do with what you went through as a little boy?" Realm nodded again.

"I think the six-year-old boy never really left the basement until he was forced to go through that hell, again." Professor Redfang nodded and sighed.

"The words escape me if I have to express, I was there the first time you came out of the basement. You were so emaciated then, I was the one who urged Jorin Barnier to intervene. I'm sorry I contributed the trauma. "

"Sorry to say it, professor. But you actually showed me that I was still in the basement, you don't have to apologize for that. I just have to thank you for that and apologize for my response. " Professor Redfang chuckled.

"You are not the first teenager to dislike homework and you will not be the last." Realm nodded and sighed.

"Good to know, well then I'll see you in a week. I hope the swelling in my face has gone." Professor Redfang nodded and Realm stumbled out of the classroom.

"So you took your time." Nick was waiting for Realm outside the classroom. Realm chuckled for a moment and sighed.

"I don't know what Mikan did to me but. My leg is having a hard time with it." Nick bit his lip gently, he spread his arms. Realm looked around quickly.

"Are you sure? Nick nodded and he took a step forward so that Realm would have to take one step less. Realm put his arms around Nick."

"Well, I'm out of the closet, Traimora just has to live with it." He said a little louder than he probably intended. Still, Nick had a big smile on his face. Realm enjoyed his bright smile and sharing in Nick's happiness.

"Nick can we go to the infirmary, maybe the best doctor has a painkiller." Nick chuckled and nodded.

"Of course we can."

REALM LIMPED NEXT TO Nick who walked slowly and carefully, Realm had been given some painkiller from a doctor whose name he had forgotten.

"Two overworked muscles, well that's what happens when you don't exercise." Nick joked. Realm chuckled slightly.

"As if exercising is so healthy for you." The two walked past the library just as Selara Crypto came out.

"By my soul. That they allow your *leeches* in the school and Nick why are you so attached to that Realm?" Nick looked at Realm and shrugged slightly. Realm cleared his throat.

"Well to answer your first question, we didn't do anything wrong. Mikan Stryder was the real culprit." Nick nodded in agreement.

"And why am I holding Realm so tight, use your silver eyes. Realm limps and then I better help my boyfriend where I can." Realm looked at Nick in amazement, did he hear right?

"You put a sticker on it." Nick shrugged again and Realm looked at Selara.

"I think those were your questions. Please excuse us." Nick carefully pulled Realm along and Realm limped to keep up with him.

"To my soul where is it going with our school." They heard Selara say. Realm smiled at Nick and looked back.

"Only count Dadrick Ventila will know." Said someone in the dark, that someone slittered away before Alex-Lucas turned the corner with Nadia.

"Please, Lucas. Not all chair's of the student council are filled and Nathalia Tomes is a perfect fit." Alex-Lucas nodded slowly.

"You are right, you may tell her this after our lessons." Nadia clapped in her hands.

"As you wish."

1

The car stopped right in front of the iron gate of her new school, it seemed somewhat uninvited. But Velika had learend to look passed that. Because behind that same iron fence stood an very old mansion. Her mother turned in her chair, the belt tiedend on her neck.

"Well here we are." Velika saw the tears in her mother's eyes. But she rolled her eyes, she knew her mother better than that. Why else would both her parents accept a job abroad and dump her at this boarding school.

"Are you sure we don't have to come in?" Her father's head immediately turned to her mother.

"If we do that, we will arrive too late at the airport." Velika sighed, she hadn't expected anything else from him either.

"It's okay mom, I don't have to be held by my hand anymore." She unbuckled her seat belt and opened the door, while getting out she reached for her pink shoulder bag that her mother had given her when they told her about their plans.

"You will find the rest off your stuff in your room. Velika I warning you. I do not want any calls from the Headmaster." Velika slammed the car door in reply to her father. What was he thinking, she had an outstanding reputation in her school record. She hoisted the bag onto her shoulder and put her hand on the cold iron gate. She had to hold her pink beret with her other hand so that it wouldn't blow away. She pushed open the gate and walked through it, the car moving away from her. She watched it for a moment, her father hadn't even said a proper goodbye to her. She was used to it by now, but it still hurts. She walked through the gate and locked it behind her, ahead of her was a shell path leading to the old mansion. Next to the path were neatly trimmed hedges and a green lawn beyond. She walked down the path, the shells cracked under her feet, she saw none of the other students even though it was the middle of the day. She stopped at the large wooden doors, this was not her first time changing schools. After the last time, she'd begged her parents to wait until she graduated, but as usual, they hadn't listened to her. She put her hand on the wooden door and pushed it, much to her surprise it went with great ease.

THE DOOR CLOSED BEHIND her, her mouth dropping open. There was a small corridor behind the door, but a library was visible through a large marble arch. Velika walked into the large room in amazement, the bookcases lined up in several rows next to each other. Two spiral staircases in the corners of the room led to a balcony with more bookcases. In the center of the room were desks with computers.

"A feast for the eyes, don't you think?" A man came from a small office that she hadn't noticed before. The man reached out to her.

"You must be the new student, Velika Lazar. If I'm not mistaken." She looked at the man and took his hand. The man had medium-length dark hair and soft gray eyes.

"You are not mistaken, sir"

"Cleon Crypto, Librarian of the Red Tempest Academy. Unfortunately, the Headmaster is busy for a while so I am your welcoming committee, just come along to my office." Mister Crypto beckoned with his head and walked to his office without waiting for her answer.

"Here I have your uniform and the key to your room." He walked out of his office, completely amazed that she hadn't followed him. She quickly went over to him.

"Sorry." He shrugged and handed her the clothes.

"There are pants to alternate it, and now I show you your room." Mister Crypto motioned for her to come along and this time she did as she was told. He took her through the small hallway that led further into the school. Until they got to a door, he pushed it open. It led out where three other buildings stood.

"The building in the center is for the teachers, the building to the right of the teacher residences is the boys' dorm and the other is for the girls. Your new home until you graduate, of course. " Velika looked at the building on the left. She still hadn't seen any of the other students.

"Mr. Crypto, where is everyone?" He checked his watch and sighed.

"Hopefully, most of them are still in the kingdom of dreams." Velika frowned in surprise, they were sleeping?

"It's the middle of the day?" He nodded.

"Red Tempest Academy is a night school, which means that our campus only comes to life around seven o'clock in the evenings." Velika looked at him in shock. Her parents had not told her this, but now that she was thinking about it her parents didn't share any information on this school at all. "Fortunately, it is a Sunday and you have one more day to adjust before your lessons start tomorrow." He walked into the girls' dorm and held the door open for her. The commonroom was filled with paper strings and plastic cups. Music was still softly heard from an unknown place, Velika looked at the man next to her. There was a big smile on his face, however a feeling off discomfert crept up to her.

"Ignore the mess that will be cleaned up before the sun comes up. At least I hope." He stepped over a cup without paying any further attention to the mess.

"HERE WE ARE ROOM 55, in other words your room." Mister Crypto turned the key in the lock and gave the door a hard shove, which jammed. "Someone should take a look at that, but welcome home." Mr. Crypto stepped aside and let her walk into the room. The room was not large, it had an empty bookcase, a single bed with no bedding, a desk and a wardrobe with a mirror on the door. "The shared bathroom is at the end of this corridor, just like the toilets." Velika turned to him and he pointed to the left. She nodded and he bowed slightly. "Then I will leave you, Velika Lazar. Come by my office for your lessons and I will give you books." That was all he said before he left her alone. There were several boxes on the floor, which her parents had probably had delivered. Velika slipped the pink shoulder bag off her shoulder and walked over to it. With some force she opened one off them, several pink items became visible. Velika shook her head, it soon became clear to her that her mother had picked these things out for her. She went to the wardrobe and saw that new pink bedding was there, still in it's seel. She grabbed these and pulled the plastic off. She made her bed and then started clearing out the boxes. She was just putting a white plush rug on the floor next to her bed when there was a slight knock on the door.

"A moment." Velika quickly folded the empty box and put it on a pile. She walked to the door and pulled it open with some force. A boy in school uniform stood at the door, wearing an old-fashioned collar around his neck. He bowed his head slightly.

"Miss Lazar, my name is Alex-Lucas Barnier. Chairman of the student council and I am here to welcome you to our school." Alex-Lucas came up and looked straight at her now.

"Thank you, Alex-Lucas. I wish I could say I'm happy to be here." Velika saw that he looked at her in surprise, and she shrugged. "Family drama. Do you want to come in, I have to warn you, it is a small mess." He studied her closely, then shook his head.

"That is not necessary, I will see you again during our lessons. Or durring one off the meals." Velika nodded and he walked away from her door, she took a few steps outside and watched him go to the stairs. She looked around in amazement to see if any other students were already up. But she was on her own again, with a sigh she walked back into her room and continued unpacking the boxes. The boxes kept getting emptied and her room filled with awfull pink stuff. As she folded the last box and shoved it under her bed. There was a knock on the door again.

"It's open!" The door opened slowly, a young woman in school uniform entered the room.

"By my soul, Lucas was right you're a *Candy Cane*." Velika shrugged and looked closely at the young woman. She had long red hair, and gold rings in her ears.

"Well, I have to make do with it. My mother still doesn't realize that I am no longer her little girl." Velika stepped forward and held out her hand. "By the way, I am Velika Lazar." The woman took her hand with a firm grip.

"Nadia Dracul, my father is the Headmaster here." Velika let go of Nadia's hand.

"I can say what a nice man, but then I would be lying. I was received by the Librarian."

Nadia shook her head with a sigh.

"Sweetie, sit down. I have the feeling that you walked in here without having any idea where you really are." Velika frowned for a moment, but did as Nadia had said.

"What do you mean, I know this is night school." Nadia raised her hand to silence her.

"Well Sweetie. That's only half the story. The Red Tempset Academy is a boardingschool for vampires." Velika laughed, Nadia had to joke. But unfortunately Nadia didn't laugh with her, so her laughter died away.

"You're not serious, are you?" Nadia opened her mouth and her teeth that Velika had only seen in horror films became visible. Just in time, Velika suppressed a cry of fear.

VELIKA JUMPED OFF THE bed and her beret fell from her head to the floor.

"This simply cannot be true." She began to pace the room. "Actually, how could it be otherwise with parents like mine." She only increased her pace, until suddenly she froze and turned to Nadia. "Wait, why are you telling me this?" Nadia shrugged.

"I like many in this school, are trying to live next to the humans. But there are also vampires, how can I put it nicely, like to play with their food. By the way, it is illegal to drink human blood. So here you have nothing to fear." Velika hung her head.

"Where are the times when I was just weird because I was new?" Nadia did laugh and she also got up from the bed.

"Come on, get changed into your uniform, I'm starving." Nadia walked to the door. "Hey like I said, I'm the Headmaster's daughter, if you need something ask me." Velika quickly changed and put a pair of pants under her white T-shirt. She combed her hair and put it in a tight ponytail. She picked up her beret and threw it in the wardrobe. No more pink for her, just blue and blood red. She straightened her jacket and opened her room door. At least there was more life in the hallways than when that strange boy was at her door. She looked around for a moment, where was Nadia. A few girls walked up to her.

"Oh look what we have here, a lost ugly duckling." Velika straightened her back, vampire or no vampire, she would not allow someone to talk to her in that way. The girl whom had called her an ugly folded her arms. "My name is Ivetta Stardust and this is my girlfriend Lucinda Mask." Velika shrugged.

"And that should tell me something. I'm sorry ladies, but it doesn't." The two looked surprised.

"Not that it is necessary, Velika." Nadia appeared next to her, her arms folded. "You two need to clean up your mess from last night. Lucas has seen the mess and so has Mr. Crypto. So I suggest you better get to work." Ivetta and Lucinda looked at each other, then dashed out of the hall. Nadia spun around on her axis. "Great now that I have everyone's attention. A few things before breakfast. Velika is not like us, she is human. So that simply means that she does not know our ways, so be patient with her." Immediately the hall filled with a buzz. Nadia looked stern for a moment until she looked at Velika again. "Well, as I just said, I'm starving. Will you go to the cafeteria with me?"

2

Alex-Lucas Barnier, that should have told her something. His families name has commanded respect for centuries, but that weird girl in her pale pink outfit clearly had no idea. Velika was not impressed with him. The sun stung his eyes, so he should have brought sunglasses. But when he heard from Mister Crypto that the new student had already arrived and that he had missed her, he had to go to the girl's dorm. He still hated the clutter that littered the common room, but that wasn't why he was there. He was there to greet the new student. He walked into the main building, this was ridiculous. Because she was too early, he was late for the student council meeting. He walked into the library and almost bumped into Mr. Crypto.

"I'm sorry, Mr. Crypto." Which immediately dismissed the apology

"It doesn't matter Alex-Lucas. Did you greet the new student?" Alex-Lucas nodded with a sigh.

"I have, but now I'm late for the meeting." Mr. Crypto motioned for him to calm down.

"Relax Alex-Lucas, the members of the council will not mind if you are a little late. Do you want to talk about what borders you." Alex-Lucas sighed.

"It's the new girl, she didn't know who I was at all. I saw that in her eyes, my family name has commanded respect and fear in our

171

world for years. But she looked at me sheepishly eyes as if the name meant nothing to her at all." Mr. Crypto nodded, slowly.

"How do you feel about that?" Alex-Lucas looked at the man in surprise.

"What do you mean?" Mr. Crypto gave a short laugh.

"Don't forget my family name does the same as yours, and my familie is the only noble house still walking the old ways. But like with your family, the girl had no idea and I found that refreshing. Not once when a new student arrived at my shrine has such a breath of fresh air come through it." Alex-Lucas lowered his head.

"My brother would immediately tell her where her place was. But I was just amazed, no suprised." Mr. Crypto nodded.

"The reason why Velika Lazar does not know who we are, is because she was not born in our world." Alex-Lucas's mouth fell open.

"She's human!" Mr. Crypto nodded.

"When Vance got the call from her parents, they made it clear that they had already approached every boarding school in the country and that the Red Tempest Academy was their last hope. Of course Vance accepted her, he has been trying to mix our two races for years and now he has done it." Alex-Lucas felt his blood boil, this was a place set up for vampires. So that they could study safely, without feeling the so-called breath of the blood bags, as some vampires call them. This was simply wrong.

"How does the Headmaster think this is going to end? The students will not hurt her there are rules set up to prevent that. But every time someone comes to visit the school, she will be in danger." Mr. Crypto shrugged.

"That's not a question I can and do not want to answer, but you weren't late for the meeting."

Alex-Lucas cursed and continued into the library.

———— ⟨⟩ ————

AT THE VERY BACK OF the library wass a small room that had been set up for the student council, the other members were already waiting for him. He quickly opened the door and entered the glass cubicle.

"Forgive me for being late, a new student has arrived this afternoon and as you know it is my job as Chairman to welcome her." In the glass cubicle was a round wooden table with the school logo engraved on it. He sat in the free chair and looked around for a moment. Most of the members of this council were members of a noble house, one of the pillars of their community. A young woman with long red hair leaned forward slightly.

"A new student, father has not said anything about that. Who is she and what does she look like?" Alex-Lucas sighed.

"I'd rather not talk about it, Nadia." But Nadia did not give up that easily.

"Come on Lucas, give us the info. You know I won't stop until you give it to me." Alex-Lucas looked around the table and sighed. The request for more information was on everyone's face. He slumped slightly and dropped his shoulders.

"Her name is Velika Lazar, she is seventeen. In the senior year, just like most people here at this table. What I have seen from her room is she great fan of the color pink." Nadia narrowed her eyes.

"Lazar, that name doesn't sound familiar to me. Where does she come from?" Alex-Lucas shrugged and sighed.

"No idea where she comes from. But it maybe true that you never heard of her familie name. It's not a vampire name. She's human." Most of the members jumped from their seats. Of course it was Selara Crypto expressing her displeasure.

"How can the Headmaster allow that? How can my uncle welcome her, with open arms?" Alex-Lucas shared her view, but still gave her the gesture to calm her down.

"What I got from your uncle, Selara. Didn't the Headmaster have much choice, the girl's parents approached every boarding school in Traimora. As for your uncle, you also know that he is seen as the white spider of your family." Selara grunted, but sat down anyway. Nadia reached for his hand and touched it lightly.

"Someone has to protect her, Lucas. If I saw your reaction when you came in here. Does she know nothing and ignorance in our world is dangerous." He sighed and then looked at her.

"And you definitely sign up voluntarily." Nadia nodded.

"I am the daughter of the Headmaster and it has been a while since I took someone under my wing." He nodded, that might have been a good idea. Nadia was right, ignorance was deadly.

"Okay then, Nadia watch over the *Candy Cane*. Well, since everyone is shocked by my news. I hereby close the meeting."

ALEX-LUCAS GOT UP AND started to walk away.

"Lucas, by the way, maybe it would be better if your brother doesn't know." He clenched his fists. It was indeed better that Nirrox did not know, but there is still a danger with that.

"Nadia, the Bloodmoonball is almost here. Nirrox has let me know he would be there." Nadia turned her head away from him, he heard her swear.

"I know why you hate him, but are you still angry about it." Nadia rolled her eyes.

"You really asking me that? He traded me in for, what was her name again. Colette Mask? "

"I'm sorry, I should not have asked." Nadia nodded.

"Well then I'll just go to the new girl. To look like she's really as awful as you claim." She walked through the door and he watched her go. She greeted Mr. Crypto as she passed his office and pulled out her green sunglasses from her small purse.

"Barnier! You're not serious I hope! That child has to get out of here!" Selara stood next to him, her raven-black hair hanging down on her back, and the golden frame of her glasses sparkled in the candlelight.

"What do you want me to do about it, Selara. This is up to the school council and I have no doubt they agreed. At least the majority then. " Selara folded her arms.

"My parents are on that council and I can't imagine them."

"You should ask your parents that, Selara. But Nadia is right, Velika is here so we have to help her adjust." Selara shook her head and folded her arms.

"She can't expect any help from me, Alex-Lucas. That is up to Nadia and you." She dropped her arms and left the cubical, he looked at the others.

"Does anyone want to add anything to that?" The others shook their heads, but he saw the doubt on everyone's faces. "If you think I agree then you are wrong. But she's here, let's just treat her like any other student." Some nodded and left the glass cage one by one. As always, he was the last to leave the glass cubical.

"IT LOOKS LIKE THE NEWS of a human being in our midst didn't fell well." Mr. Crypto came out of his office. Alex-Lucas lowered his head.

"That was to be expected." Mr. Crypto nodded and sighed.

"My niece didn't even look at me when she walked by. Something that is not uncommon." Alex-Lucas shrugged.

"As you said before the meeting, your familie is still walking the old ways." Mr. Crypto nodded and sighed again.

"By the way, is there a good book I can read?" Mr. Crypto nodded.

"If you didn't know, we have a library full. But what you ask is, can I recommend something to you?" Alex-Lucas nodded and Mr. Crypto shoved a book into his hands. Alex-Lucas read the title.

Family History of Lazar

He held it up.

"What is this?"

"She maybe a human but her family has a rich history, her line leads back to the royal family of Narinor." Alex-Lucas's eyes widened.

"The royal family of Narinor, but that was the land ruled by my family?"

"That is correct, good to know that you paid attention during my lessons." He turned and straight in the eyes of Professor Redfang.

"Professor Redfang." The woman nodded and turned her attention to the book in his hands.

Narinor was run by two houses. The house of Lazar representing the human inhabitants of the land and the house of Barnier representing the vampires. Unfortunately, this system did not survive and the kingdom fell. By the way, this school is located on the old border between Narinor and Traimora." Alex-Lucas pressed his lips together and was actually amazed at how much this interested him. He lifted the book.

"Thank you for the history lesson Professor and thank you for the book Mr. Crypto." He left the library, but paused around the corner.

"What are you doing Cleon?"

"He should know Lynede, it's his family history too."

"That Lazar girl, this is no coincidence and you know it too. She is the last of her line and suddenly she is here on the doorstep. "

"That's what I say Lynede, the Lazars joined the vampire hunter a few years after the first war." Alex-Lucas had heard enough and walked on. He had to agree with them, this could not be a coincidence. For a moment his brother came to his mind. His grip tightened around the book with a light blue leather cover, the color of her eyes. He shook his head, he couldn't think about it. If his brother had anything to do with this she might be in danger and he couldn't do anything about it.

3

The stream of women passed through the doors of the girl's dorm, Velika walked past the two girls who were busy cleaning up. Velika stopped for a moment, Nadia looked at her in surprise.

"Uhm, Ivetta and Lucinda." The two glared at her.

"What do you want?" Velika shrugged her shoulders.

"Well why don't you come along for something to eat and then I'll help clean up." The two looked at each other in surprise. Nadia put a hand on Velika's shoulder.

"That's very nice of your Velika, I assume these good-for-nothings will respond to your request." The two glared at Nadia, but nodded at the same time.

"Of course, we will. Velika, thank you for your offer." The two dropped the bags and walked with the rest of the house. Nadia sighed.

"That was nice of you, even if they don't deserve it." Velika shrugged again.

"I'm new and that's why I know I'm being looked down upon. And I really don't feel like making it worse." Nadia nodded.

"You have a good point there, I will come every hour to see if it goes well. But when I notice that they let you do all the work." Velika smiled and shrugged.

"Then you put your wounded pride aside and help me clean up." Nadia shook her head with a sigh.

"Was it that clear?" Velika nodded.

"You don't have to tell me, but please let's go to the cafeteria. I'm also starting to get hungry." Nadia nodded and laughed, she wrapped her arm around Velika's shoulder.

"Oh Sweetie, I think we're going to be very good friends." They walked into the cafeteria laughing, the smell of freshly baked bread entering her nose. Velika's stomach immediately started to growl.

"Wait it is evening, why does it smell like eggs and freshly baked bread here?" Nadia laughed and shook her head.

"Oh Sweetie. How green you are in this world. In your eyes it is evening, in the eyes of the vampires it is morning. So we have breakfast and no we don't drink blood here. Vampires only stat drinking blood from the age of eighteen. But most of us prefer bloodberries and even if we don't. It is against the law to drink human or animal blood." Nadia led her past the buffet.

"Take the pancakes with caramel sauce, the red sauce is Bloodberry sauce and I can't imagine you'd like that." Nadia herself took a plate with the Bloodberry sauce, while Velika took the other. As a drink, Nadia put two mugs under the hot chocolate machine. "You like chocolate, don't you?" Velika nodded while Nadia took syrup, Velika could guess what kind of syrup it was. Nadia picked up the full mugs on the trays. "Oh my friend Lucas is alone." Nadia nodded her head at the strange boy who was at her door this afternoon.

"I thought his name was Alex-Lucas, so why do you just call him Lucas?" Nadia walked to the table.

"That's because I've known him for years. We almost grew up together. Always to the same school and that is why I do not call him by his full name." They stopped at the table, Alex-Lucas sat with his thoughts in a book that seemed vaguely familiar to her.

"HEY BOOKWORM, DO YOU mind if we sit down." Nadia didn't wait for an answer and just sat down. Alex-Lucas sighed.

"I do have a choice Nadia, apparently not. Velika Lazar please, sit down." Velika nodded and sat down. She reached for her mug and warmed her hands.

"Has Nadia already told you what we are?" She looked at her mug and nodded slowly. Still not knowing what to make of her new sitatation.

"She has, and my brain is not sure whether it is a joke or not." She looked at Nadia. "Sorry." Nadia shrugged.

"I can well imagine that it is a bit difficult to comprehend. Hé Lucas." Alex-Lucas nodded and closed the book he was reading. The gold letters sparkled in the dim candlelight.

"I can understand, but I have to warn you. There are families who have a kind of natural hatred for your race. A few members of these families have already spoken out loudly that they would rather see you leave. They don't care how. That aside I am Chairman of the student council and I am responsible for your safety." Velika nodded and took a sip of her chocolate.

"I'll do my best not to make that task more difficult." He pushed the book over to her.

"Your presence makes it more difficult." Velika read the gold letter on the cover.

"I thought I already recognized the book, but what are you doing with my family history?" He looked at her intently.

"Have you ever read the book?" She shook her head.

"I tried once, but then my father came into the room and pulled the book from my hands."

He patted it.

"Read it and it explains why your father didn't want you to read it." After these words he got up and walked away. Nadia pushed the book closer to her.

"This book comes from our library. What was it doing there?" Velika shrugged, how could she know that closely. "Well I think he is right. But let's eat before you do the cleaning. I'll pick up the boxes from your room. Then they can also be thrown away immediately."

"The are laying under my bed." Nadia nodded and took a sip of her hot chocolate.

THEY ENTERED THE COMMON room, Ivetta and Lucinda were already busy.

"I'll see you later, you two." Nadia pointed to Lucinda and Ivetta. "Behave yourself, she is so nice to help you. Something you don't deserve in my opinion." Ivetta nodded, but Lucinda sighed.

"Nadia, I have nothing to do with what is going on between you and my cousin." Nadia shook her head.

"You introduced Nirrox to Colette, I know he didn't love me enough. But you are therefore part of the problem." After those words, Nadia stormed away. Velika picked up a garbage bag and threw in the first plastic cup.

"Looks like I missed an interesting party." Velika saw Ivetta nod, but Lucinda looked at her.

"Who do you think you are, or who we are? Are you really thinking because you help us, that we going to treat you differently now? "Velika shook her head.

"Of course not. But you have only thrown this party. But I don't see the others who participated in the party helping you. In my opinion that is just unfair, I have to live in this building. Whether you like it or not. And I like to see it as neat and tidy as posible." Lucinda was just not satisfied with the answer.

"That's why you help us, don't make me laugh."

"Lucinda, she's helping us and let it pass." Ivetta threw a few cups into the bag.

"No Ivetta, I will not *let it pass.*" Lucinda threw down the garbage and walked to Velika, she grabbed Velika by the neck and squeezed it. "I'm disgusted by people like you hiding behind someone else." Velika didn't want to scream in pain, but she dropped to her knees "See how weak you are. You don't eat enough bloodberries." Lucinda let go of her.

"Didn't you hear, I'm not a vampire and I'm not hiding behind anyone." Lucinda looked at her in amazement.

"You are human? What are you doing here?" Velika shrugged and sighed.

"That is a question that unfortunately I cannot answer. My parents chose this school for me because they have a new job abroad." Reluctantly, Velika picked up the garbage bag, then released it to pick up the broom in the corner. "I don't really want to talk about it." She started sweeping up the confetti and other junk. Ivetta picked up a duster and dustpan and wiped it up. As Nadia had said she came after an hour to check that Ivetta and Lucinda were still helping Velika clean up. In her hands she held the boxes from Velika's room. Ivetta just brushed up the last bit of debris and slipped into the garbage bag.

"Wow it is really a record, the common room cleaned up in an hour." Nadia's gaze darted over Velika and lingered on her neck.

"By my soul." She walked to Velika and she immediately wanted to cover it up with her jacket. But Nadia pulled it down. "Who did this, Velika and please don't protect them." Lucinda stepped forward alone.

"It was me, I was pissed off at a particular vampire and I aimed it at her. Only then did I learn that she was human." Nadia walked to Lucinda, but Velika jumped in between.

"Let it go Nadia. It's just bruises." Nadia's pink eyes lit up with rage.

"Sweetie, she could have easily broken your neck."

"But I didn't, or did I." Velika was pulled out between the two by Ivetta.

"That was a nice attempt, but those two have been flying around the neck since Nadia's boyfriend broke up with her and run off with Lucinda's cousin." Velika sighed.

"It was Ivetta Stardust, right?" Ivetta nodded. "Can you tell Nadia I went to the library. I have to pick up my textbooks." Ivetta nodded and Velika left the common room.

THE NIGHT AIR CAME with a welcome kind of chill, she had not realised it was that warm in the building. Or that came from all the cleaning. Velika reached for the elastic that held her hair together. She pulled it off and her light blonde locks danced around her face and neck. No one else had to see the bruise. Several students sat on a rug in the grass, reading or working on their homework. One group caught her eye, they were sitting under a whipping willow. It was a group of three man and three woman, they were laughing about a joke one of them made. They had no form of light with them, so she assumed the vampires could see in the dark. Or the moonlight was enough for them.

"Have you read the book yet?" Startled she looked next to her, Alex-Lucas walked next to her. Her lips pressed together and shook her head.

"I helped clean up the common area. In addition, according to Nadia we have been working on it for less than an hour." He frowned for a moment.

"I also did not expect that you would have read the entire book in an hour. But at the very least I expected you would have read something. But unfortunately." She stopped walking and looked straight at him.

"I'm sorry, but I assume you saw the common room when you came to my room. It was a mess and when I saw Ivetta and Lucinda working together, I decided to help. I'm sorry I let you down by being human." She saw her still contained outburst startling him, but she shrugged and walked away.

"Velika please wait." Velika felt him take her arm, but she pulled it free.

"No Alex-Lucas. I'm not waiting. I'm going to the library to pick up my school books and then I'm going to read that stupid book." Velika walked into the main building, only turned around at the library to her suprise Alex- Lucas hadn't followed her. She went straight to the librarian's office and patted softly against the open door, the man shot up from his chair.

"By the grace of my lost soul, Velika you scared me." She couldn't contain her laugh.

"Well, in the movies, you kind of do that with us. So." He nodded in agreement.

"Don't believe everything you've seen in movies. Most are based on lies, some on truth but that is not my story to tell. If you caught me drift." She nodded.

"I try to stay awake. If only I had taken coffee instead of hot chocolate." The Librarian nodded and smiled.

"I hear you, wait here and then I will go and get your books. Why don't you get a good book, I have bookcases full." She nodded and as he slipped past her. She watched him go until he disappeared between the bookcases. She sighed and walked over to the first bookcase she saw, her gaze moving over the leather covers.

"Here."

4

Velika let out a cry and Alex-Lucas winced.

"Do you have to scream like that?" She immediately covered her mouth and shook her head. Alex-Lucas had the book in his hands again.

NADIA CAME RUNNING after Velika had run away, with the book in her hands.

"What are you doing with that?" He pointed towards the book and Nadia sighed.

"It was still in my bag. I would actually put it in her room. But I got into a heated argument with Lucinda. That I lost sight of her." Alex-Lucas growled softly, Nadia looked at him closely. "What's wrong with you?" He growled again.

"That girl she is really impossible. Maybe I was a little rude to her."

"And she's tired." He looked surprised at Nadia and she sighed.

"Really Lucas. The child is literally training herself to our hours. Something that is not easy. You know where she is, bring her the book and a strong espresso." She shoved the book into his hands, then walked back to the girl's dorm.

ALEX-LUCAS WAS STANDING in the library, with the book and a mock filled with coffee. Velika gasped.

"I'm terribly sorry, but you really scared me." He shrugged and held up the mock.

"Now we are at the same level, Nadia told me you might need this." She took the coffee mock and opened the cap.

"Hmm the smell alone, is enough to wake me up." She screwed the cap back on and nodded at the book.

"Then let me install myself somewhere so I can read." He gestured to a row of tables set up between the bookcases. She nodded and he pulled back a chair.

"Please sit down." She sat down and he pushed the chair back on. She opened the book slowly and poured out a mug full of the black stuff. He meanwhile had another book off the shelf, one. With a sigh, he sat down opposite her. While Alex-Lucas was sitting there, he occasionally looked at Velika.

"Barnier, we need to talk." He looked up to see Selara approaching him. With a sigh he closed down his book.

"What is it Selara?" The girl plants a hand on the table.

"I called my parents and the news about the *monstrosity* is also news to them. So what the Headmaster did, did not even pass through the council." He sighed and sat back a bit, with a slanted eye he looked at Velika. Who sat listening in silence.

"Selara, let it go." Selara shook her head.

"Let it go. This goes against the principles of our race. Or have you been sleeping during history." He shook his head.

"No, I have not. But I do know that the lessons we receive are written from our point of view. Today I read a book from the point of view of a human family." Selara sighed.

"If Nirrox could hear you now. You're starting to sound like my uncle. But seriously, Barnier, the Headmaster can't really do this, we could just put that *monstrosity* out on the street and not have to feel guilty. Do we care that she had nowhere else to go." He looked again at Velika taking a sip of her coffee.

"Selara, I am afraid that unfortunately we have nothing to say about that. Yes we are part of the student council. The reason we can not force her out is in our name, student, and I just think it's ridiculous what you're saying. You can't put someone out on the street." Selara now also looked at Velika.

"You say something about it." Velika gave a smile he did not know yet.

"Like what. I think to be honest everything has been said on this subject. But I have a little question Selara, did you bother to talk to that *monstrosity*?"Alex-Lucas could imagine Selara's astonished look.

"Why would I?" Velika simply shrugged.

"Well, maybe you wouldn't have the whole conversation just in front of her, or ask her opinion on this subject." He heard someone laugh out loud and he knew it was Mr. Crypto, who immediately appeared from behind the bookcase. Alex-Lucas turned back to Selara.

"Selara, I think you've said enough for today." The girl did not move, but kept staring at Velika, the fire of hatered burned in her eyes. Velika paid her no attention and simply had her nose in the book again.

"Selara, you can go." Selara only woke up when she heard Mr. Crypto voice and did indeed back off. Mr. Crypto put the stack of books on the table.

"MASTERFUL IF I SAY so myself. Velika you played my niece masterfully." Velika shrugged and sighed.

"That was not my intention. You already warned me there would be opposition. But now that I've heard it with my own ears, it doesn't make it any easier." She looked at him and he felt strange. He was one of the vampires who was against it, but hearing Selara talk like that made him feel sick.

"Well, if this bothered you at all, wait until you meet her father at the blood moonball." Already on hearing the name of the party, his stomach turned.

"Is your brother coming too?" Mr. Crypto nodded.

"He comes every year, because he sees it as his duty. Why are you looking at me like that, oh wait Nirrox is coming too. Nadia would like that." Alex-Lucas shook his head.

"No she won't, because he's taking Colette." Alex-Lucas looked at Velika, who took another sip of her coffee. She had probably already heard this, but he was not 100 percent sure if it came from Nadia. She turned to Mr. Crypto.

"Mr. Crypto, is there a quick guide to what I need to know about vampires and their customs among my textbooks?" He himself had not expected this question, why did she ask about it. Mr. Crypto shook his head.

"I have a number of books, I will get these for you. But Velika I have to warn you. Our ways are not learned in one day." Velika nodded but tapped the book with her family history.

"I think I have little choice."

AFTER MR. CRYPTO, HE, Alex-Lucas, offered to help her with her books. They both walked down the path to the girl's dorm with their hands full of books.

"Velika, I know you are going to retire to your room for the rest of the day. But if you have any questions, feel free to ask Nadia or me. We are happy to help you." Velika nodded and gave a grateful smile.

"Thanks, Alex-Lucas." Why did he feel a little lighter.

"No problem and please call me Lucas. Just like Nadia does." She shook her head.

"I'm sorry, but I don't know you well enough for that." He wanted to agree, but she opened the door to the girl's dorm with great difficulty. They walked up the stairs and then down the hall to her room. As soon as she opened the door, the soft pink met him. She walked into the room and put the books she was holding on the desk. "I put them in my bookcase after lunch." She turned and he walked into the room a little uncertainly.

"You still have some time before lunch starts." She looked at the pink clock that hung above her bed.

"Can you put the books on the desk so I can view the titles?" He nodded and watched her review the titles. She took the bottom book from its stack and set it on the first shelf in the bookcase.

"Velika, what are you doing?" She didn't look up and went on with what she was doing.

"I like neat and tidy. Another of the reasons why I helped with the big cleaning in the common room. I put the books I have in alphabetical order and with a little post-it. I mark the books that are not intended for school." He saw with wide eyes that she was doing what she said.

"So are you saying that your room is still organized like this after a few days?" She nodded without looking or blushing.

"My dad doesn't like clutter and let's just say that if my toys weren't put away at the end of the day, he would throw them away. My mother then bought a replacement, but I soon learned that I should clean up after myself." He frowned for a moment, then looked around the room.

"So your favorite color is pink?" He wanted to change the subject, but to his surprise she shook her head.

"No, my favorite color is blue. The same blue as this uniform. My mother wanted a daughter who she could dress and used to panic when I showed up in a blue dress when we went shopping together. Just like with my father, I learned to adapt and now I am known as the *Candy Cane*. The only regret is that I love berets but the only one I have is soft pink. What those not go well with this uniform."

VELIKA PUT THE LAST book in its place when there was a knock on the door. Nadia opened the door carefully.

"Oh, Lucas I wasn't expecting you." Alex-Lucas looked at her, she had a strange look in her eyes.

"What is it?" Nadia opened the door all the way, to his shock it said in large red letters.

MONSTER.

"Is that blood or Bloodberry?" Nadia smelled the letters.

"Bloodberry." He looked at Velika who looked at her door in disgust. "Don't worry after lunch we'll clean it up." Nadia's voice filled the room. Velika nodded for a moment and then walked over to Nadia.

"Let's go and have something to eat." Surprised, he followed the two women, it didn't seem to affect her. They walked into the noisy cafeteria, but as soon as Velika stepped over the threshold, the noise was silenced. The three of them walked past the sandwich buffet. They looked around the cafeteria with trays filled with food and drink. All the tables were taken, suddenly a hand raised at one of the tables.

"Velika, Nadia and Alex-Lucas come and sit here." He knew the girl, it was Ivetta Stardust. They walked to the table and sat down at it. "Come on, Lucinda. Where should they sit then. Everyone is acting so strange now that Velika is here and they haven't even bothered to get to know her." Lucinda didn't look dirty at Velika, but at Nadia. Who leaned closer to Ivetta.

"Did you see Velika's door?" Both girls shook their heads. Ivette looked at Lucinda, who forgot to look dirty.

"But we can go now and look at it, we're done eating anyway." Lucinda got up and Ivetta followed. Nadia took a bite of her sandwich, with a satified grin on her face.

5

The morning came early, or to be fair the evening came early. The knock on Velika's door buzzed through her room. Nadia entered without knocking again.

"I didn't think so. Come on, get up." Nadia pulled the covers off Velika. Still half asleep, she looked at the clock, which indicated five o'clock.

"Okay okay. I'm awake." Velika swung her legs over the side of her bed. Her pale pink pajamas made Nadia shake her head.

"Oh Sweetie. I know you told me about your mother. But that has really gone wrong." Velika shrugged and sighed.

"I've lived with it for seventeen years, so I'll survive. In addition, I am forced to wear something else." With those words she walked to the closet where her school uniform was already hanging on a clothes hanger.

"Sweetie, just take your reserve with you." Velika nodded and put her spare uniform in her bag, which was already full of pens and notebooks. With a sigh, Velika put on her shoes, ready for her first day of school. Nadia nodded and walked to the door. Velika was surprised when she came back from lunch yesterday and the door had been scrubbed clean. Nadia suspected Ivetta and Lucinda for cleaning. The two of them walked to the cafeteria, this was the first time she had been there since lunch. Nadia had brought her a plate of freshly roasted meat yesterday. But now her nose filled with the smell of freshly baked sausages and eggs.

"On Monday we have a Narinor breakfast with sausage, beaten eggs and white beans in tomato sauce. Or in Bloodberry sauce. Coffee?" Nadia already walked to the coffee machine without waiting for her answer. In the meantime, Velika picked up the plates and some toast. Nadia looked at the signs with a nod of approval.

"And you picked the beans with Bloodberrie for me." Nadia put the coffee on the trays and picked up hers. "Let's see if Lucas managed to keep a table free." Ivetta and Lucinda arrived a little later.

"Thanks for my door." said Velika, Ivetta shrugged.

"It was nothing, I didn't see you at dinner." Velika gave her a smile, Nadia sighed.

"I brought her a plate of food yesterday, she was so caught up in those books that it was imposible to break her out of it." Alex-Lucas looked at her.

"Was that your study of vampires or your family history?" Nadia looked at him in surprise.

"Study on vampires, what did I miss?" Her surprised look went to Velika who shrugged.

"I would like to know more about your customs, but in answer to your question Alex-Lucas it was my family history. I read the whole book yesterday." Alex-Lucas nodded in agreement.

"Beautiful then I would like to speak to you after the lessons, you Nadia too." He got up and walked away. Nadia looked at Velika, who looked at her plate.

"Okay what was that about?" Velika looked at Ivetta and Lucinda.

"My arrival at this school entails more than just the fact that I am not one of you."

THE BELL RANG AND EVERYONE got up.

"We have chemistry from Professor Blackwood. Am I correct?" Nadia nodded.

"We're in the same class. Just follow me and you will automatically end up in the right classroom." Velika hoisted her pink school bag on her shoulder and followed Nadia.

"Thank you, Nadia for taking me under your bat wings." Nadia shivered.

"I hate bats, but no problem." They were almost at the door of the cafeteria.

"Hey *monstrosity*!" Velika did not want to respond and walked on. Suddenly she felt a hot liquid hit her. It burned through her clothes, she bit her teeth together so she wouldn't scream but the tears of pain shot to her eyes.

"Selara, what's wrong with you." Ivetta's voice filled the cafeteria. "This is already dangerous if you do that to one of us." Lucinda had apparently run to the kitchen, now carrying a pitcher of cold water.

"I'm sorry, but I have to get the heat out of your clothes." She poured the jug over Velika, but left a little bit in the jug.

"She doesn't belong here, Stardust, and I want to make that clear to her." Nadia stepped forward but was stopped by Lucinda. Who still held the jug with a layer of water in her hands.

"By throwing hot Bloodberry juice all over her?" Velika turned, her uniform clinging to her body. Never in her live she felt this filthy, but as soon as she looked at Selara, Lucinda poured the last bit of water over Selara and then turned to Nadia.

"You go to class and tell the Professor what happened. I'll take her to the infirmary. I think it would be better if Dr. Krauss looked at her back." Nadia wanted to argue, but Lucinda shook her head. "Believe me, I could miss a lesson." With those words, Lucinda took Velika's arm and pulled her along.

"LUCINDA MASK, WHAT are you doing here and what happened to the new student?" Lucinda briefly explained to the doctor what had happened. In the meantime, Velika looked around the infirmary. The dark stone arches dividing the space into smaller spaces. A large candelair hung from the ceiling and the candles on the colossus were lit. Where the arches ended, racks of dark red curtains ran. "Then I'll write a note for both of you, Miss Lazar, can you please take off your jacket and blouse?" Velika looked at the man, who immediately understood why she had doubts. "Don't worry, there's nothing I haven't seen yet." She nodded, still uneasy. Still, she did what the doctor asked her to do. She turned her back to him and he hissed. "It's a good thing Lucinda put it out with cold water. Otherwise, this would have looked very different. " Velika looked at Lucinda.

"Can you check my bag to see if it's still clean on the inside?" Lucinda nodded and picked up the pink bag on the floor. She unzipped it carefully.

"It's clean inside. Ah that's why you asked, there are clean clothes in it. Smart." The doctor pressed something cold against her back. She ducked from it.

"Oh, I'm sorry, I should have warned you. This is ointment that will help your skin heal."

She nodded, then looked back at Lucinda, who had pulled a cloth from somewhere. She gently wiped the juice off, but sighed.

"I'm afraid this won't go out. What a beautiful bag without it." Velika raised an eyebrow and sighed.

"It is a bit too fussy for my taste, but it was a new bag." Lucinda looked at Dr. Krauss.

"Hopefully you will report it, right? This is not only an almost mutilation of a fellow student, but the destruction of property. Yesterday Ivetta and I scrubbed Bloodberry juice from her bedroom door." Dr. Krauss opened his mouth.

"He doesn't have to, because I can see it with my own eyes." A man with dark red hair and pink eyes walked into the infirmary. He looked a lot like Nadia.

"Good to have you here, Vance. The hot liquid got through her clothes onto her skin, lightening the burns. That is also due to Miss Mask's quick response here." Vance nodded.

"I heard that, also from the last bit that went over the head of the perpetrator." Lucinda shrugged.

"Selara deserved it, Headmaster. And unlike her action it will not leave a mark." He nodded.

"That is correct, but still you know better. We'll talk about that another time, Lucinda." He turned his attention to Velika.

"Velika Lazar, we finally meet. But I wish it would be under better conditions. I called Selara's parents and her father is on his way. Oh he is already here." Velika pursed her lips. There were three grown men in the infarmary and she sat only in her bra on one of the beds.

"Okay Vance, what should I see?" The Headmaster pointed to her.

"That Draven, that's what you have to see." Velika looked over her shoulder and felt the man's eyes sting her back.

"Is that the new student my daughter called about yesterday?"

"She is and before you say it. I am under no obligation to have student at this school approved by the council. I was approached by her parents and the other boarding schools in Traimora had no place for her, and yes I checked their story was correct. But we're not talking about that, we're talking about abuse. I have been approached by several students and staff that Selara has thrown hot Bloodberry juice against her." Selera's father sighed and rubbed his eyes.

"You should have walked this through the council, with the whole story. What do you think I am heartless, I will not leave a child on the street and I will say that to the council. But what my daughter has done is going too far. How is she doing." He did not ask the question to her but to Dr. Krauss who repeated his statement.

"Draven, then there is another point. Her clothes and bag were destroyed by this joke." Selara's father nodded and sighed.

"I'll pay for it, Vance. What lesson does my daughter have. I have a heartfelt word to speak to her." Lucinda got up.

"Mr. Crypto, unfortunately I cannot prove it." She picked up her phone and showed him something on it. "There are a number of students in the girl's dorm who have often heard Selara say this word. This was around lunch yesterday." The man's green eyes darkened.

"Thank you Lucinda Mask." He stormed out of the infirmary. The Headmaster leaned his head towards her.

"Headmaster Dracul, can I ask you something?" The Headmaster nodded.

"Go ahead." She swallowed.

"Was it because no one else wanted me or my family history that gave me a place in your school?" Headmaster Dracul sighed.

"So you know about it. Don't worry Velika. I will not use it against you." He walked away and left her without an answer.

6

Alex-Lucas paced through the glass cubical, Velika had dropped out of class after Selara's stunt and he was strangely worried about her. The door of the cubical opened and Velika entered with Lucinda.

"Lucinda what are you doing here?" The girl with her silver hair sighed.

"I am here because Velika asked me. Don't forget I'm on your side." Velika looked at Alex-Lucas.

"She told Selara's father about that message on my door." He nodded and sighed.

"Then I can certainly expect Ivetta too?" Lucinda nodded and the Nadia entered the room, followed closely by Ivetta. Immediately the two sat down, Nadia in her usual place. He cleared his throat and put his hands together on the table.

"If you three want to know a little more about what Velika and I are discussing here. I suggest you read the Lazar family history." With those words, Velika put the light blue book on the table and then looked at him.

"You tell me because even though I've read it, I still can't quite get it." He nodded and sighed.

"Velika is the last of the Lazar line, a line that actually goes back to the ancient kingdom of Narinor. You know from history lessons that my family ruled there, but that was only half of the royals and the other half, the human half, was ruled by the Lazars."

"My family and a falling out between our families led to the first war between humans and vampires." Alex-Lucas nodded.

"I think it is no coincidence that the last of the Lazar line ended up at this school." Nadia's lips pursed.

"Are you saying my father is up to something?" Alex-Lucas shrugged, but Velika nodded.

"Maybe not immediately, but something is definitely going on." Lucinda nodded.

"He said don't worry." Nadia looked at Lucinda and sighed.

"So we have no idea. What is going on, but that something is going on is clear. Let's agree that no one and I mean no one outside of this group should know." With those words, Nadia got up and walked to the door. "Velika, come along, I have your homework and you have to finish it tomorrow. Lucas, can I ask you to bring us dinner?" Velika got up and followed Nadia. Selara entered immediately.

"Okay, Barnier we need to talk. You two traitors turned away." Alex-Lucas shook his head.

"There is no need for them to go, because I have nothing to say to you. After that stunt you pulled." Alex-Lucas wanted to leave the loft but she blocked the door.

"What do you mean, I only did what a good vampire would do." He straightened his back.

"Maybe, but Velika is a student here. As a student council member, it is your job to protect every student. That was the oath you took and you broke this oath." He pushed her out the doorway. "I don't really care what your motivation was." He leave with Ivetta and Lucinda.

"Why do I only see now that you are a weakling?" He turned to Selara.

"I'm not weak, just unlike you, I made the effort to get to know her and those two traitors as you call them. Did the same, even though it was slightly forced because Velika helped them clean." Ivetta and Lucinda stood next to him with folded arms. "So learn the facts before you judge, because right now you are the only *monstrosity* I know." With those words he turned and walked away from Selara.

"Take that back!" But he didn't respond, he greeted Mr. Crypto who came out of his office.

ARMED WITH PAPER BAGS filedl with food, Alex-Lucas walked to the girl's dorm. Nadia and Velika were studying in the common room. Ivetta and Lucinda ran up to their room to get their books.

"The ladies persuaded me to join this study group." He put the bags down by the dark red sofa.

"This is for all of us?" He nodded, this was the third time he had been here in a very short time. He did not like to come into the girl's dorm, even when a party was being held. It was different from the communal areas in his building. The rooms had the same soulless wallpaper that hung in the bedrooms, but the decoration was different. The dark red sofa's were closer together, the black rug underneath created a warm and cozy corner. With the boys everything was more apart, more on its own. He grabbed a black bean bag from the corner and put it down by the sofa. In the meantime, Ivetta and Lucinda had returned and fell on the sofa opposite Nadia and Velika. "Okay ladies books away first dinner and then we move on." He looked sternly at Nadia, who closed her book with a sigh.

"Alright. Arithmetic was not agreeing with me anyway." He bent down to the loud creaking of the bean bag, but took the food from the paper bags. He handed it out and the first bites were taken in silence.

"Did I see Selara at the glass cubical when Velika and I left?" He nodded.

"She wanted to talk." Lucinda looked at him for a moment and sighed.

"He gave her a taste off her own medicin." Nadia snorted.

"I like to believe that, but tell Lucas." He sighed.

"She thought I was weak because I hang out with Velika and not really on her side. Then I told her that she was the one who was weak since she violated her oath to the student council."

"And most important of the whole story he has said literally. Because right now you are the only *monstrosity* I know." Ivetta happily finished his story. Nadia looked at him in surprise and he nodded.

"Nobody calls me weak." Nadia nodded in agreement, he looked at Velika who had not touched her food during the conversation.

"Velika are you okay?" Startled, she looked up and nodded. As proof, she immediately put a bite in her mouth. But when she swallowed the bite, she stared at it again. "Velika, if you are not hungry you should leave it." The words didn't seem to get through. He looked at Nadia, who shrugged. Ivetta sighed.

"Are you homesick, Velika?" She looked up again, startled, then back to her food.

"Maybe a little. By the way, thank you for what you said to Selara." Nadia put an arm around Velika.

"You know what let's keep on eating and dive back into the books. Before Lucas has to go back to his own building." Alex-Lucas checked his watch, he had a few hours left. But they continued to eat and threw the paper plates in the trash.

VELIKA SCRIBBLED SOME sums in her notebook while Nadia chewed the back of her pen. Ivetta talked to Lucinda about their history paper, which they would write together for convenience, and what did Alex-Lucas do. He cracked his head over a Pisoen text. Several female students gathered in the room, but for some reason it didn't get too busy.

"Lucas, are you getting through that texst?" He shook his head in exasperation.

"I really do not understand that we have to learn a language that is no longer spoken or written." Nadia handed him her dictionary.

"You shouldn't make it more difficult for yourself than it already is. You know that we can also use a dictionary during the tests." He sighed and opened the book. It was indeed easier, but he would never admit it out loud.

"Chairman?" He looked up at a young girl standing behind him.

"Can I help you with something?" The girl with black hair and soft green eyes nodded, he just couldn't think of her name. So he looked to her neck were a golden pendant hang, on the pendant stood a feather, the symbol of the Ombre family.

"My friends overheard your conversation with my cousin." He bit his lip for a moment, she was the daughter of the Cleon's sister. Brienna Ombre.

"What about that?" Brienna took a step forward, standing right in front of him now.

"Are you going to put her out of the council?" He sighed and shrugged.

"It's not up to me, Brienna. That is up to the entire council. But remember when she joined the council she vowed to protect all students from outside and inside dangers. She broke this oath and so the other members and I will have to consider her cause." Brienna nodded, then looked at Velika. Who was still doing her math homework.

"Thank you Chairman." She started to walk away, but he took her arm.

"Brienna, do yourself a favor and don't get involved. I am not saying this for myself or for Velika, but I am saying this because it is not a pleasant situation to be in between." He let go of her arm and she nodded.

"I'll pass this message on and then I'll be done with it, thank you." Alex-Lucas looked at Nadia and she indicated that she had heard.

"It is indeed something that we have to consider. I'll call a meeting at one. Should Selara invite or not?" He shook his head.

"She may come, but she will not enter that glass cubicale." Nadia nodded and reached for her phone. He checked his watch and sighed.

"I better go, otherwise I'll break the rules and be on trial tomorrow." Velika looked up and he pointed to Nadia.

"She will explain it to you." He put his books together and got up. "I'll see you at breakfast."

Ivetta and Lucinda gave a quick wave and Velika nodded with a thin smile. He walked away before getting a response from Nadia. When the outside door closed behind him, he looked shocked at the man standing in front of him. The man gave him a mean smile.

"NIRROX WHAT ARE YOU doing here?" His brother looked shocked.

"What am I doing here? What a strange question. You are my little brother and I heard strange reports about a person who was between you." Alex-Lucas straightened his back.

"There is indeed a person here at school, those reports are true. But I'm sorry brother I have to go to my building." Alex-Lucas walked past him, but Nirrox took his arm.

"Watch out my brother, don't get too attached to your toy." Alex-Lucas pulled his arm free.

"Don't threaten her Nirrox, or do you want to feel Nadia's revenge?" Nirrox shivered for a moment.

"I say what it says, brother. Sweet Dreams." Nirrox walked away and Alex-Lucas cursed. Whatever was going on, his brother was most likely in the middle.

7

T he chemistry class was almost over, Velika quickly picked up the last composition, strangly engough this class looked more like a cooking class.

"Miss Lazar." She raised her head. "Can you sit down after class, there are some things I need to discuss with you." Velika gave the Professor a smile.

"No problem, Professor Blackwood." She hadn't told her to ring the bell yet. Everyone got up, Nadia turned around.

"I'll wait for you outside the classroom." Velika nodded gratefully, but now she was really alone with the Professor. With long black hair hanging in a braid down her back. The white rag coat made the woman's face paler than it already was.

"Miss Lazar, I know you missed my class under special circumstances. I've read the report and I actually agree with Dr. Krauss. How is your back?"

"It stings. Nadia Dracul helped me put some of that healing salve on it this morning." The Professor nodded and walked over to the table where Velika was sitting.

"Well the homework you submitted is nothing to criticize, not something suspected from a human?" Velika shrugged. "But that is it for now, you have to be on time for your next class. I see you tomorrow." Velika got up and walked to the door. What a strange conversation, she actually expected to get extra homework. She took another look at the lab before leaving it. The entire space was divided into two parts, the practical part and the theory part. Which she had been on for the entire 45 minutes today. As Nadia had promised, she was waiting outside the classroom, together with Alex-Lucas.

"What did she want?" Velika shrugged.

"She wanted to know about my back." Alex-Lucas looked surprised.

"I have to tell you something. I should have done that at breakfast. But when I left you yesterday, I ran into my brother." Nadia grunted.

"What was he doing here?" Alex-Lucas sighed.

"He wanted to warn me, I shouldn't get too attached to Velika. Or how he put it into my toy."

Nadia hissed.

"Glad to know he hasn't changed anything. But that means that you were right when you said it was no coincidence." They were standing in front of the room when the Professor from that class came out.

"Are you three still planning to come in?" The woman resembled Professor Blackwood like two drops of water.

"We are sorry, Professor Redfang." They entered the classroom and sat down at the still empty table.

"Good, glad I have a full class." Said Professor Redfang as she took her place at the front of the classroom.

"I'm not going to bore you today with one of my boring lessons. You are going to give presentations in the groups you are in now. A week from now. And yes this is the presitation. It must be about the first war between vampires and humans."

"You mean the one in which the people chased us from Narinor?" It was Selara's voice that echoed through the room. Velika looked at the Professor who looked annoyed.

"That's just the beginning of that story, Selara. I understand that your family likes to make you forget the rest. But there is more and I want to challenge you to delve deeper into the subject." The Professor looked at Velika. "And maybe someone will surprise us with a different point of view."

ALEX-LUCAS LEANED FORWARD.

"She literally gives us a license to find out what's going on." Nadia nodded and sighed.

"It sounds like nobody is holy anymore." Alex-Lucas shook his head.

"Thanks to her I know that something is going on because I heard a conversation between her and Cleon." Nadia clenched her fists.

"Was that before or after he gave you that book with Velika's family history?"

"Afterwards." She sighed.

"And why am I only hearing this now?" He raised his shoulders.

"The three of you are already busy discussing things, I would like to write down a topic at the end of the lesson." Velika looked at the Professor Redfang and then looked at her friends.

"I think we already have a topic. Am I right?" Alex-Lucas nodded.

"We want to talk about the two ruling families of Narinor." Professor Redfang nodded.

"I thought so. Good choice."

"What that is not really the subject of the first war!" Professor Redfang folded her arms.

"It is indeed, Selara. It is thanks to Narinor's two ruling families that the war started. Maybe if you had paid attention during my lessons, you would have known that." Velika did look over her shoulder this time, simply to see the surprised look on Selara's face. And that was a good excuse for the classroom that was full of posters about history. One of the photo's featured a young woman with light blue eyes and light blond hair. It reminded her of someone, she just didn't know who.

Meanwhile, Alex-Lucas and Nadia were busy talking about the division of labor.

"What do you think Velika?" That brought back her attention.

"I'm sorry, I wasn't there for a while. By the way, may I ask you a question, who is the young woman on that photo over there?" She pointed to it, and the others' gaze went there too. Alex-Lucas was the first to respond.

"I don't know, but she looks a lot like you?"

THE BELL RANG TO INDICATE that the second class of the day was over. Everyone got up and pushed out. Velika also got up, but instead of the door, walked out to the poster to have a closer look. The woman did indeed look a lot like her, only there was no text on it.

"That's Vanessa Lazar, the last Queen of Narinor before war broke out. Her husband King Mathéo Lazar's death was the beginning of the first war. She fled to Traimora with her children. But I think you already knew that story?" Velika nodded.

"It's strange learning about this part of my family history." Professor Redfang shrugged.

"It may be, but it is your history. Did you know that Vanessa was a patreon of Count Dadrick Ventila, the founder of this school. I think she also gave him some diaries before her death. I can whip these up for your presentation, if you want." Velika nodded.

"That would be wonderful." The Professor looked at the clock.

"You better go to the cafeteria, otherwise you will miss lunch." With those words she walked away from Velika. Velika walked into the cafeteria, her eyes searched for her friends who waved at her.

With a smile she went straight to the table, where Nadia pushed a bowl of noodles towards her.

"I didn't know which flavour you liked, so I took chicken." Velika sat down and told the other what she had learned. "That's great, with those diaries we get a little more insight into the war." Alex-Lucas also nodded.

"I think my ancestor also had a number of records about the war. In the free hour I will call my father to ask if he can have them delivered." He looked at Nadia."The danger is that Nirrox will bring them." Nadia looked at Lucinda who looked at her bowl.

"Let him hope he doesn't see me. I would like to give him another scar on his other cheek."

Velika almost choked on her noodles and Nadia nodded proudly.

"Something else by the way. Next week it is also the Bloodmoonball." She pointed with her fork at Velika. "Tonight after the meeting, the two of us are going to look for a dress." Velika looked at her with wide eyes and shook her head.

"Isn't that the ball that symbolizes the end of the first war?" Nadia nodded, Velika looked at Alex-Lucas who looked amused and then again at Nadia. "I don't think it's such a good idea." Nadia sipped her juice.

"And why not." Velika sighed.

"Maybe because I'm human, Nadia. It's an annual reminder that the vampires lost the war."

Alex-Lucas eyebrows shot up.

"You did your homework, but that doesn't mean you weren't invited. As long as you are a student at this school. Maybe it is best if you just join the others." Velika finished the last bit of soup and put down her bowl. She wanted to fight again.

"Hey Chairman, what do I hear. There is a meeting and I have not been invited!" Selara walked over to their table and planted her hands on it. "What nonsense is that, I'm still a member."

Alex-Lucas nodded.

"That's right, you are indeed still a member of the council. But we are going to hold a meeting based on your behavior and you, like the others who have to appear before the council, cannot be there."

"My behavior?" Selara put a hand on Velika's shoulder and squeezed it. The nails bore into her flesh.

"Selara lets her go. And yes your behavior." Alex-Lucas got up, along with Nadia. But Velika was the one who responded, taking Selara's hand and tearing it away from her shoulder. She turned and got up.

"I'm going to the library for homework. Perhaps Professor Redfand found Vanessa's diaries."

She picked up the bag she had borrowed from Nadia.

"Why would Professor Redfang give you the diaries of Count Ventia's patreon?" Velika shrugged.

"Well if you really want to know, Vanessa Lazar is my ancestor. Maybe you should get off your soapbox and accept that I'm here in school. Because you probably wouldn't have been here without her." Velika straightened her back and was almost out of the cafeteria.

"You lie that you burst."

"She doesn't and I have the proof here." Lucinda's voice echoed through the silent cafeteria. Velika turned to see Lucinda take the light blue book from her bag. She opened it and flipped through it.

"Here is the family tree of the Lazar family. Here is Vanessa with her husband Mathéo and at the bottom is Velika. She is the last of the Lazar line." Selara looked at the book and then at Velika. Velika shrugged and turned back.

8

Alex-Lucas looked at the members of the council one by one.
"I know this is a difficult package. Not often have we had
to decide the fate of someone on the council. But the council's job is
set, and each of us has taken the oath. Selara broke this oath by
throwing hot Bloodberry juice over Velika. Something that could
have ended much worse. What we can all read in Dr. Krauss's
medical report. Some of you will feel that Nadia and I are favored
because we associate with Velika. That's why the two of us have
decided to hold back from the vote." He looked at Nadia for a
moment, who nodded in agreement and then took the word.

"I would also like to emphasize that the damage that Velika's
clothing and bag has already been compensated, so we do not look at
that. Some have probably also heard rumors that Selara is responsible
for smearing Velika's door. However, this has not been proven, so she
is not justified for that. Are there any uncertainties I need to clarify?"
Alex-Lucas nodded when no one spoke and stood up with Nadia.

"Nadia and I will leave you alone and let us know when you are
done. We are somewhere in the library." Together they walked out of
the cubical, but almost ran into Lucinda and Velika.

"We got some food for the council." The girls both held up two
paper bags.

"Of course we didn't know how long the meeting would last."
Nadia took the bags and put them on the table.

"In other words, discuss it while enjoying a stew." She nodded to the members and closed the door behind her.

"Our bag of food is included with the homework." Velika pointed to the table where Ivetta was already sitting with her nose in a book, while she was chewing something. He walked over and took a plastic container with his name on it from the bag. He sat down next to Ivetta. He opened the container and his nose filled with the scent of mashed potatoes and the lightly salted gravy. His mouth was already filling up. He poked it and took a bite. Velika sat across from him and opened one of the many diaries that surrounded them. He quickly swallowed his bite and took one from the stack.

"Well I think we need more than a week to dig through all these." Ivetta looked up and shook her head.

"Lucinda and I have decided to focus our paper on the same topic. We have already gone through it with Professor Redfang and she thought it was a good idea." Alex-Lucas laughed and shook his head, a few days ago this would not have been possible for him. He preferred to work alone.

"I HAVE A DELIVERY HERE for Alex-Lucas Barnier." Alex-Lucas had predicted it, and yet he was astonished to hear Nirrox's voice. In the corner of his eye he saw Nadia stiffen. He turned to see Nirrox walking towards him with a huge box. With a heavy blow, he put it on the table and panted.

"Here are the diaries of our forefather." Nirrox looked at Velika. "And who is this beautiful appearance?" He reached out to her and she took it.

"I am the toy." Nirrox withdrew his hand.

"Ah. What an honor to finally meet you. Velika Lazar." Nirrox then looked back at him.

"I thought you had a meeting, by the way." Alex-Lucas nodded.

"I have, it is a meeting to decide whether Selara Crypto can stay on the board or not." Nirrox frowned.

"Why shouldn't she stay?"

"What is that to you. When I last checked, you were no longer here at school." Nirrox looked at Nadia for a moment.

"Oh Nadia, I hadn't seen you. How are you?" Alex-Lucas took another bite of his stew, because this could take a while.

"Selara attacked a student, which breaks the council's code." It was Lucinda who intervened, Nirrox looked dubious.

"That is indeed against the council and if a member of the council gets away with it, it causes loss of face. We can't have that. But why are you two too close?" Once again it was Lucinda who gave him the answer to his question.

"Selara has attacked Velika with hot blood berry juice and since Nadia and your little brother are interacting with Velika. Are they too close to it."

"Why are you telling him this?" Indignation drenched Nadia's voice. Lucinda looked at Nadia.

"So that we can get rid of him faster. Do you really think I liked it when he left you for Colette? Who says he doesn't do the same to her." Nirrox raised both hands.

"Wait a minute, do I also have a voice in this conversation?" Lucinda and Nadia looked at him.

"No." They said in unison. Nirrox nodded.

"Clearly. Well then I'll go. Velika Lazar again an honor to meet you." Nirrox walked away, Nadia breathed a sigh of relief.

"I'm sorry if I was a little blunt with you, Lucinda." Lucinda shrugged.

"As if I wasn't used to it yet." Alex-Lucas put his empty bowl with food on the table. "And I'm sorry Nadia, but I learned my lesson last time." Velika closed her book and got up, easily unfolded the cardboard.

"Well those are indeed a lot of dairies, but we have to give it to our ancestors. At least they wrote it down by date, to make it as easy as possible for us." She took a book out of the box and showed the gilded numbers. "All we have to do is put them together."

THEY WERE JUST BUSY when the door to the glass cubical opened.

"Alex-Lucas, Nadia we have made a decision." Velika nodded.

"You just go, we'll finish it here. And if you are not back yet, I will already divide the years. In this way we distribute the work fairly." Alex-Lucas sighed and nodded in agreement. He walked into the glass cubical with Nadia. The plastic plates were neatly stacked, ready to be thrown away. Alex-Lucas and Nadia sat down, the one who had taken over in their absence got up. The girl with golden hair cleared her throat.

"Chairman, Nadia. We will wait a while for Selara. Because I thought it would be better if she also heard our verdict right away." Alex-Lucas nodded.

"That's good Nathalia. It was only important that she was not here, during the trail." They did not have to wait long, immediately when Selara came in the tension could be cut by a dull knive. Nathalia looked from him to Selara. He knew there was some bad blood their, but he knew that it wouldn't cloud her judgment.

"Selara Crypto. The Chairman and Nadia Dracul did not attend the meeting. So they hear our judgment along with you." Selara nodded.

"I've seen them sitting in the library, along with the *monstrosity*. So what have you decided?" Nathalia looked shocked for a moment.

"Selara Crypto, when you attacked Velika Lazar we were all present in the cafeteria. So we all know you're guilty of that. With that you have broken your oath. That is why we have come to the decision to expel you from the council. But that won't be your only punishment. Because we just heard that you don't regret your actions by calling Velika Lazar *monstrosity* to our faceses. We have also decided that you are not welcome at the Bloodmoonball." Alex-Lucas looked at Nadia and her eyes were wide. It was a severe punishment, no one has ever been excluded from the Bloodmoonball.

"You can't do that. My father is present at the ball." Nathalia raised her hand.

"We have already spoken to him, together with the Headmaster and they both agree with us."

Alex-Lucas was amazed at that and Nadia was also amazed. He could see that in her face. Selara stamped her foot.

"This conversation is not over yet." Alex-Lucas now got up and turned to Selara.

"It is, since it has already passed the Headmaster. So with that in mind I will end this meeting."

THE OTHERS OF THE COUNCIL got up and walked past the dumbfounded Selara. Alex-Lucas did not feel sorry for her when he passed her last. He walked to the table where Velika was still sitting. The number of diaries had shrunk, but that was also because Lucinda and Ivetta had disappeared. Nadia picked up a sheet of paper and pointed to it. It was probably a list of annual numbers and Velika let them choose which one they wanted. Velika made a note of what he could guess in the list. Nadia's name, and Nadia grabbed the stack of books.

"I'll see you in my room when you're done." Velika nodded and Nadia left the library. Alex-Lucas walked up to Velika.

"And which ones are left?" Velika handed him the sheet of paper.

"Only the year before the war and the one after the war are over. The others have the years during the war. Unfortunately we don't have much choice, but which one do you want?" He sighed.

"I don't know, it seems cool to know what happened beforehand. But actually the one after the war sounds more seductive." She gave him a warm smile.

"That is not an answer to my question." He sighed.

"Tell Me Something I Do not Know." He tapped the date after the war and scribbled his name.

"Those books are at the end of the table. Mine are here." She pointed to the stack of two in front of her.

"Mr. Crypto has just put the other diaries in his office. As long as we get it out of there that morning." He glanced at the office at the entrance of the library. A faint flame lit the space behind the frosted glass windows. Alex-Lucas walked to the end of the table and picked up the two diaries. "Well then it is time to go to my room. And time for you to pick out your dress for the ball."

She groaned as she picked up the two diaries. But had a smile on her face from ear to ear.

"I better go before Nadia pushes me into her room." With those words and the diaries in hand, she left him alone. He shook his head with a big smile on his face. Why did she make it so easy and difficult at the same time. He walked out of the library and waved to Mr. Crypto, who stuck his head out.

"Alex-Lucas. I want to get the box out of my office by tomorrow. Do you hear me." But Alex-Lucas heard him faintly and walked on.

9

With a sigh, Velika put the two diaries on her desk. The two books were very similar. They had the same gilded numbers on the covers, which were of the same color. She had been surprised the others had more diaries at their disposal, while Alex-Lucas and she only had two. And from the same persons, Vanessa Lazar and Armand Barnier.

"Velika, are you coming?" Nadia stood in the opening of the open bedroom door. Velika shook her head and walked over to her friend.

"Alright then." She closed her bedroom door behind her and walked to her room with Nadia. For that they had to go down the stairs to the first floor. Nadia immediately opened the first door and motioned for Velika to follow her.

"I know it's not as sweet as yours, but this is my place. Welcome." Veliak followed Nadia inside, her eyes instantly caught by the amount of clothes that seemed to flow down the closet. The various books that were in different places except in the bookcase. Posters of various boy bands hung diagonally on the wall, the bed looked as if it had just been slept in.

"And what do you think of it?" Velika opened her mouth, but immediately swallowed her opinion. Because she didn't want to hurt her new friend. Nadia probably saw the answer on her face.

"Just say it, it's a mess. But it works for me. Lucas told me you can't really stand junk. So I've already made an attempt to clean it up, but that didn't really work out." Velika pursed her lips.

"Well, I'm here to pick out a dress, so let me see what you got." Nadia laughed.

"Have you gone mad? I really won't let you walk in one of my rags. No Sweetie we are going to pick one out." Nadia went to her desk and picked up her laptop.

"Online?" Nadia nodded and opened it, immediately the white wall behind Nadia lit up.

"Sit next to me." Velika stumbled over clothes to the bed. Nadia opened a few tabs to online stores where she said she visited a lot. But immediately Velika noticed that Nadia's taste was slightly different from hers.

"Okay what were you thinking about?" Velika gave her a smile.

"You know when I was little, my mother and I often watched those old black and white movies. In those films, the women always wore long dresses." Nadia sighed and shook her head.

"Then we'll look at that." Nadia clicked away from the short skirt dresses and pressed the buttom of long dresses. Unfortunately, those dresses were not to Velika's taste either. "I have to go to the porcelain throne." Nadia handed Velika her laptop and left the room herself. Velika sighed and closed the many tabs. Her mother swore to an online store where she got all of Velika's clothes. Velika typed in the name of the store and the webshop immediately showed a whole list of clothes, with the mouse she went to the picture of a dress with a long skirt. She clicked it on and immediately filled the screen with dresses, which she used to dream of.

"AND HAVE YOU FOUND something yet?" Nadia came back into the room, flapping her hands wildly.

"I think so." Velika turned the laptop over to Nadia, who looked closely at the dresses.

"That online store I did not know yet. But these are indeed beautiful dresses, Velika." Nadia crawled next to Velika again, then pointed to one of the dresses. "That one, that's your dress." Nadia was right, it was a light blue dress without sleeves. Nadia clicked on the dress and read the description.

"Looks like it comes with a gold-colored belt and two straps that I can wear on the upper arm." Nadia looked at her and nodded.

"We will then order that one. Lucas doesn't know what happens to him when he sees you like this." Velika looked surprised at Nadia, what did Alex-Lucas have to do with this? She shook off these thoughts, then got up.

"I better go back to my room, then I can immediately start with one of the two diaries." Nadia nodded and ran her hands across the keyboard, but said nothing.

Velika walked into the hallway where her room was, the door was wide open. At the end of the hall she saw someone running away. The only recognition she had was long raven-black hair. Velika quickened her pace and looked into her room, she gasped in shock and immediately covered her mouth. From the doorway she saw that all her books had been thrown across the room. There was a pool of red liquid over the floor and her bed. Her clothes were smeared with it, she didn't dare to enter the room. She dropped her hand and took a few steps inside. A cry of disgust and terror left her throat.

"What is going on?" The voices filled the hall. Velika felt her stomach tilt. She turned and staggered out of the room.

"Velika, what's wrong?" Lucinda walked up to her.

"By my soul. It looks like you have seen a ghost." Velika shook her head, it wasn't a ghost, she had preferd that.

"Luc, her room!" Ivetta's voice echoed in her ears. She stepped outside and sat against the wall next to her door. She watched Ivetta and Lucinda enter her room.

"By my soul!" Both came out of the room, Lucinda already had her phone pressed to her ear.

"Hello, Headmaster Dracul. You must now come to the girl's dorm. There is something you must see." The other students looked at her in surprise as Ivetta knelt next to her.

"Velika would you like a glass of water?" She slowly felt her head nod. Her stomach was still turning, the rest of her body felt numb.

"LUCINDA MASK, WHAT in my soul's name is so important?" Velika watched the Headmaster walk past her. As she sipped water.

"Velika's room, Headmaster." The Headmaster entered her room, but the man did not stay long.

"Velika Lazar, do you know who was responsible for this?" She shook her head. No all she saw was the glimpse of raven black hair.

"I'm going to take pictures of your room and then have teachers take it away."

"What should the teachers take away, father?" Nadia appeared in the crowd.

"I'm sorry, but as a student council member I need to know?" Headmaster Dracul sighed.

"A snake, Nadia. Someone has soiled Velika's room with snake blood and left the poor creature on her sheets." Velika heard the disgust going down the hall.

"Who says she didn't do it herself." Of course it was Selara's voice that rose above the group.

"Who knows, she can act very well." Nadia shook her head.

"Velika has a form of obsessive neurosis. She was totally uncomfortable when she arrived in my room." Lucinda and Ivetta looked at each other for a moment, they understood that it was also one of the reasons Velika had helped them clean up the communal space. Headmaster Dracul nodded and sighed.

"Velika, unfortunately I have no room left until this is resolved. Also not in theboy's dorm so there is nothing for it but to take you to my rooms." Velika looked at him in surprise, but he was already crouching.

"Do not worry." Nadia shot past her father into Velika's room.

"Father, I will soon get one of my nightwear for her to sleep in. Fortunately the diaries are unharmed. "Nadia came out of the room with the two books. "Father, the snake on her bed. It's a king cobra, the symbol of Barnier." Headmaster Dracul nodded and pulled Velika to her feet.

"Nadia, I'll see you with that nightwear."

VELIKA HAD RECEIVED almost nothing from her walk with the Headmaster. All she knew was a door slammed behind her.

"Velika how are you feeling?" Velika was shaking violently, she had never felt so miserable. But not a word left her throat, there was a knock on the door. "That will be Nadia, with some nightwear for you." He walked to the door and opened it, it was indeed Nadia. She heard her voice faintly. "Nadia, I'm making an exception for Velika. But you know the rules." She heard the squeak of the door as it closed. She saw him squat on his knees and hand her the nightclothes. "I'm in the other room to get you a blanket and a pillow." She took the clothes and he came up and walked away. She change quickly but still numb. And sat back on the couch when the Headmaster entered the room. "I put it here, I sleep in the room next to the office. If you need anything, I'll hear it."

Velika took the pillow and blanket and made a place to sleep. Only every time she closed her eyes she saw the bloody snake on her clean sheets. The sunlight peeked in through the dark red curtains. Velika got up slowly and walked to the curtain. She opened it slowly and let the light caress her face. How she missed it, the sun.

"Vanessa, what are you doing here?" Startled, she turned around. A man with white hair stood behind her. She recognized the man from somewhere.

"I'm sorry, but I'm Velika." The man took a few steps back, startled.

"Vanessa, you are acting weird. What are you doing here? You are dead and so am I." Velika looked at the man, but the man faded before her eyes. She frowned for a moment, who was that man. He knew Vanessa.

"Velika, I heard voices." The Headmaster ran into the room, wearing the same clothes as when he left her. Velika looked at him in surprise.

"There was just a man here. With long white hair and red eyes. He kept mentioning Vanessa." Headmaster Dracul looked at her with wide eyes.

"Did he call you Vanessa? As in Vanessa Lazar?" Velika quickly thought of the poster in the history room, which looked so much like her. Her jaw dropped. This couldn't be true.

"Wait was the man from just now Count Ventila?" She felt her head grow light.

"Velika!" She felt her legs give way under her body. Her body slowly turned black and before her world turned black the image of the king cobra lying dead on her bed flashed before her eyes.

10

A lex-Lucas ran to the infirmary, why hadn't Nadia called him. He slowed down when he got close to the door, he entered the infirmary.

"Ah young Lord Barnier, what can I do for you?" Alex-Lucas straightened his back.

"I am here for Miss Lazar. Doctor Krauss."

"Alex-Lucas?" Velika's voice sounded so happy, but how can she be happy after what she had been through. He walked in the direction of her voice. She was at the very back of the room, the dark red curtain shaded her a little. But as soon as he walked around it, he looked straight into her blue eyes. The dark blue bags adorned her face and her light blond hair looked a little dull. She was holding one of the two diaries.

"Velika, is this through the snake or through the sight of the Count's ghost?" She looked away from him, so she was ashamed of something. Was it her OCD or was it something else. And why did he care so much?

"That snake was a real disaster. I've never felt so nauseous. I don't know if you've seen pictures or gotten a living image from Nadia's words. But nothing quite like reality. As for that ghost, it was strange rather than scary. We knew he knew my ancestor, but in which way I wonder."

Alex-Lucas's mouth fell open, he had also learned that in Vanessa's diaries yesterday. Worst of all, love was only one-sided.

"Count Ventila was mabye in love with the human queen, but Vanessa had already given her love to someone else. My ancestor Armand." Velika held up the diary.

"I know that. He gave her this diary. That's why they look so alike." Alex-Lucas went to the bed and sat on it. She looked away from him again.

"Velika, I might be one of the first to notice your OCD and I'm sorry I passed it on to Nadia. But I know what her room looks like and let's just say I didn't want you to see it on his Nadia's." He saw her bit her lip, so Nadia had not cleaned up her room.

"Alex-Lucas do you know what kind of snake it was that bleed my new sheets?" He nodded, so it was the picture of her room. He was afraid to say that he had seen the mess and that he had cleaned up the mess together with Nadia and the other girls from the building. The only one who shined in her absence was the one he suspected of causing this damage, Selara Crypto.

"AH, I SEE THAT YOU have a visiter, Velika." Vance Dracul also came running, Alex-Lucas could see from his face that he was shocked. Alex-Lucas could understand why, one of his students passed out before his eyes after describing seeing the founder's ghost.

"Alex-Lucas, I want to thank you and the rest of the female students for cleaning up. But the reason that I came heree is that, I found out who the culprit is. With the permission of the school council, I have installed security cameras in every dorm. Just for the safety of the students and their belongings. And these cameras captured the culprit. I've already called her parents."

"Who was it?" Velika asked before he could do it. Vance sighed.

"Selara and because she continues this behavior. I see no other option than to suspend her."

Alex-Lucas nodded in agreement.

"Lucas. We washed her sheets, but the blood cannot be removed even with cold water." Nadia also entered the room. "Oh good morning father. I didn't know you were there too." Vance gave his daughter a smile.

"Not for long. I have such a meeting with Draven Crypto and his wife. Actually, I want those pictures you took of the room, Nadia." Nadia nodded and took her phone from her purse.

"Here father, I made as many as possible. By the way, do you want someone from the student council to be there?" Vance sighed and nodded.

"Actually, I wish all three of you could be there. But in Velika's case that seems unwise." Alex-Lucas nodded, but Velika shook her head.

"I want to be Headmaster Dracul." She pulled the covers lightly so that he had to get up. She got up, he looked at the nightwear she was wearing, and he recognized it as the pajamas Nirrox had given Nadia. Velika stood next to the bed, but staggered a little on her legs. Still, he admired her persistence. Vance was just not convinced, he folded his arms.

"I do not know."

"Father, I think it's important that Selara's parents see what this stunt has done to Velika. Obsessive neurosis or not, seeing an animal bleeding out on your bed will not do anyone any good."

PERHAPS THAT WAS THE argument that convinced the Headmaster, because not much later they were in the glass cubicle. Mr. Crypto had set up a television in the room while the Headmaster was busy on his laptop. He probably got everything ready for the meeting. Alex-Lucas leaned towards Velika.

"Are you sure you're okay?" She nodded, but his fists clenched. He could clearly see that this was not the case. Why did she keep herself up and why did this interest him so much? The glass house door opened and Draven Crypto entered. The woman he had with him was undoubtedly Selara's mother. She had the same fire in her eyes as her daughter.

"What is this Vance and why are these kids here?" Vance got up.

"Draven, Velicia please sit down." The woman named Velicia looked at her husband and he nodded. They sat down next to Nadia.

"I asked Cleon if he wanted to bring your daughter in too. Ah there they are already." The door opened again and Selara entered with Mr. Crypto.

"Selara, sit next to your parents and we can start." Selara did as she was told, and Vance moved to stand next to the television, which was now connected to his laptop.

"I'll charge you guys first see why we're here." The television switched on, from the corner of his eye he saw that Mr. Crypto was holding a remote control. Immediately the photos of Velika's room became visible. The snake on the pale pink sheets marked the most. Selara's mother made sounds of disgust.

"Vance may I assume this is Velika's room?" Draven's voice was so quiet, as if he knew what was coming. Vance nodded.

"That's right, Draven. And as you know, a few years ago I installed a camera system in the hallways of the dorms for moments like this." Alex-Lucas saw Selara stiffen. It felt good to see her so shocked. The television switched to the security footage. The colors of the images were black and white, but they were bright. Selara entered the corridor of Velika's room with a living snake in her hands. The animal squirmed violently, the good feeling he had disappeared when he saw the images of the living animal. He looked aside for a moment and saw that Velika turned white. He took her hand, giving him a thin smile. Selara walked into Velika's room, not much later she came running out of the room. Without the snake, later Velika herself came into the picture. Who stood petrified in the doorway of her room for a moment, but then walked in anyway. She had probably screamed because the doors of the other rooms flew open and the other girls came out of their rooms. But his eyes were not on the other girls, who came out of their rooms in their nightwear. His eyes looked at Velika, who came trembling from her room and collapsed next to her door.

"That's enough." Draven broke the silence, rage in his voice. Alex-Lucas looked at the man, who was flushed with rage. Draven turned to his daughter. "Wasn't smearing her with hot Bloodberry juice more than enough? Wasn't it enough to be banned from the Bloodmoonball? You really had to shame your mother and me even more." Selara did not look at her father.

"But father, she doesn't belong here."

"That is not for you to decide. Selara! That's up to the Headmaster! Who doesn't even have to tell you why we are here! I have read Velika's file after you informed me of her presence and judging by your stunt you have read it too!" Alex-Lucas looked at Velika who was as white as fresh snow, even her pale blue eyes were dull.

"I have indeed read her file, father." Velika stiffened for a moment, Alex-Lucas looked at Vance who now also looked at her.

"Alex-Lucas, get her out of here and take her back to the infirmary." He just nodded and pulled her to her feet.

"No, Barnier leave her here." Alex-Lucas shook his head.

"Can't you see how she's doing, Mr. Crypto. She is whiter than snow." Draven nodded once and looked at Vance.

"This meeting is over then, I assume Selara is suspended." Vance nodded.

"She is indeed, Draven. Human or not Velika is one of my students and is therefore under my protection. Just like everyone else. That is why unfortunately I cannot allow one to be tortured like that." Draven raised his hand.

"You don't have to explain yourself, if the roles were reversed I would have done the same. How long?" Vance looked at Selara.

"One month. I have already consulted with the other staff members and I have the homework here for that month." He held up a list and handed it to Draven, who nodded at the list.

"I'll take her to the car, Velicia, you pick up our daughter's personal belongings." Velicia Crypto nodded, then looked his way.

"VELIKA LAZAR, THAT is your name, right?" Velika was still in his arms, but nodded bravely. "I will make sure that everything that was in your room is replaced. My husband's family may have walked the same old ways that my daughter walkes. But I hat how my daughter treats people like you, or like me." Nadia got up.

"It is mainly the materials made of fabric that can no longer be cleaned, even with cold water. I have literally tried everything." Velicia nodded.

"Thank you for your honesty, Nadia Dracul." Nadia shrugged.

"It wouldn't be fair to let you pay for more then what is damage beyond repear." Alex-Lucas watched Vance's chest grow. But he felt that Velika was getting weaker.

"Headmaster, I'll just go then." He nodded and he walked out of the glass cubical supporting Velika. As he walked her through the halls, he felt that she was getting weaker.

"Lucas!" Nadia walked next to him and took Velika's other arm.

11

Velika woke up on one of the beds in the infirmary. She slowly scrambled up. She hadn't seen them right away. But Nadia and Alex-Lucas immediately rushed to bed.

"Easy." Nadia pushed her back down."You have literally been under the sail for a night. So you shouldn't rush it." Velika looked at them in shock. Had she missed another day of lessons. Velika did not make a good impression. She frowned for a moment when she had missed those lessons and they, Alex-Lucas and Nadia, had not left her side. Then they would also have missed those lessons, this has to stop otherwise teahers will think she is a bad influacne.

"How are you feeling?" Alex-Lucas took her hand, she looked at it in surprise. Why did her hand tingle so much?

"I feel a lot better than before." Alex-Lucas sat down on the bed again and Nadia joined them, crossing her arms.

"I understand what you mean, after Selara was banned from the Bloodmoonball, I actually expected her to withdraw and lick her wounds. But no, Selara Crypto just goes the extra mile. Selara's mother was here an hour ago, she wanted to give you this." Nadia showed a bag containing nightwear and sheets. "I told her that pink is not really your favorite color. But that you feel more comfortable with some blue in your life." Nadia handed the bag to her. "You know what Velika, I am starving. Get dressed and then we will see if the cafeteria is still open." Velika nodded and Nadia tapped Alex-Lucas on the shoulder. He nodded and got up. As fast as she could, Velika changed and neatly folded the nightwear she had worn. She also made the bed.

"Velika, are you ready?" Velika looked at the bed and nodded.

"Yes I'm coming." She ran around the curtain where her friends were waiting.

"You sure left that bed tidy." Nadia got a nudge from Alex-Lucas. "Ouch, Lucas that hurt. I meant it as a compliment, there are few people who are as decent as Velika. I didn't know how neat you was, until you explained me how she organized her books. It is awesome. Maybe I'll try it too."

"I won't hold my breath until that day." Nadia looked surprised at Alex-Lucas and shrugged.

"By my soul, was Lucas Barnier joking?" Velika put a smile on her face, it felt good to see her friends so relaxed. It was something different, but in a good way.

THEY WALKED INTO THE cafeteria, the cafeteria staff was already cleaning up. The cafeteria lady, Mrs. Valè, came their way.

"By my soul there you are, I already missed you three. Sit down and I'll bring your food to you. And you girl." She pointed to Velika. "You get an extra scoop, from what I understand you haven't eaten anything all day." Mrs. Valè disappeared and they sat down. Velika sighed, her stomach started to growl violently. Alex-Lucas was the first to laugh and Nadia followed him.

"Well, I think your stomach agreed with Mrs.Valè." Velika felt her cheeks glow, but she smiled along with the other. Mrs. Valè stood behind them with three plates in her hands.

"It was nothing, Mrs. Valè. We had a little moment of peace and quiet." Mrs. Valè nodded and put the plates on the table one by one.

"Well, I had some white rice left with egg sauce in sweet and sour sauce. Enjoy your meal. And you girl eat your plate completely, it's good for you." Velika nodded and put a bite in her mouth in response. She loved how her mouth filled with the flavors of the food.

"By the way, I have almost finished the diaries of your ancestors. That ancestor of Lucas is the one who killed Vanessa's husband, that was something I did expect. But to read it in his own words, that was something else." Alex-Lucas looked briefly at Nadia and then at Velika.

"Where was that, Nadia." Nadia reached into her bag and took out the book.

"Here, but that was not the strangest thing. I went through Vanessa's diary and was amazed that she was not even mourning the death of her husband."

"It's probably because she loved someone else." Nadia looked surprised at Velika and she nodded.

"Don't get me wrong, but in the days of Vanessa and Armand, people didn't get married for love. That is only something of the present tense. In their day, your parents chose whom you married. Vanessa probably saw her husband for the first time at the altar. I don't know if it happened before or after. But Vanessa fell in love with another man, Armand Barnier and from what I probably understood from her stories, he was most likely the father of her two boys." Nadia looked at Alex-Lucas.

"Armand Barnier was married, right?" He nodded.

"He was married to Lady Helena. With whom he also had two sons and a daugther, but what Velika said is true. We used to marry not out of love, but out of duty. But I still think that the murder of Vanessa's husband sparked war between our two races." Nadia looked at the book in her hand.

"So it was not for the throne of Narinor, but for the hand of a woman." Alex-Lucas nodded and Velika looked at her now empty plate. Was it strange that all the talk of war made her hungrier. Nadia sighed and put the diary back in her bag.

"So weird." Alex-Lucas nodded and shrugged.

"All I know is that, Armand introduced Vanessa to Count Ventila. Count Ventila livedu in Traimora and he offered Vanessa protection. Something Armand couldn't, because he was the enemy." Nadia's face twisted.

"That's just sad."Alex-Lucas nodded again, then rose from the table. He piled the plates on top of each other, Velika watched him go to the kitchen.

"Velika, Velika are you still there?" Nadia took her hand, she looked at Nadia in alarm.

"I'm sorry, I was distracted for a moment." Nadia nodded.

"I saw that. But what I said was, we better go to our building. You may have slept all day, while I have been stuck in those diaries." She got up and walked past the kitchen.

"Lucas, I am taking Velika to our building. I'll see you tomorrow, hopefully we'll have a normal day then." Alex-Lucas was standing with a tea towel in his hands.

"I hope so too. Hopefully we will get a good day of sleep now." Nadia nodded and took Velika's arm.

"I hope so too. See you tomorrow and don't make it too late." Nadia pulled Velika with her before she could speak.

"WHERE WAS THAT GOOD for?" Velika squeezed her arm out of the main building.

"Well, I don't want to say that history repeats itself. But I think you are slowly falling for Lucas." Velika tilted her head slightly. Thick gray clouds were already gathering above their heads.

"Not at all." Nadia sighed.

"Really you two are even more stubborn than donkeys." Velika started to walk a little faster, the first raindrops were already falling on the ground. "Velika come on, I've known Lucas almost all my life and I see him coming to life around you. Before dinner he made a joke, I never heard him make a joke before. And I really mean *never.*" Velika raised her arms and folded them over each other.

"That may be the case. But I don't really want to talk about it." She opened the door to the girl's dorm and entered. She shook the little rain from her hair.

"Why not. We are friends right, and as friends we can talk about boy's." Velika sighed.

"I am going to take a shower." Said Velika before she ran away from Nadia, who of course was right. You could talk about boys with friends, but for some reason she didn't want to talk about Alex-Lucas. She entered her room and saw that there was a new carpet. As she opened her closet to get a towel, she saw that they were gone. They were also distroyed, and there were alos no towels in the bag with new bedding and nightwear. Nadia entered the room.

"No towels?" Velika closed the wardrobe and shook her head.

"Nope, but you already knew that. And Mrs. Crypto didn't get me replacements for the ones I lost." Velika held up the bag, Nadia sighed and shrugged slightly. She came to talk about Alex-Lucas, Velika could see it in her eyes. "I don't want to talk about Alex-Lucas, because I have no idea how I feel. I don't know that since I've been here at school." Nadia went to the bed and fell on it.

"Please tell me why that is, I am all ears."

"Wait a second." Ivetta and Lucinda also entered the room. "Before you say anything we just walked by and heard you girls talk." They sat down on the bed next to Nadia. "Now you can begin." Velika closed her door so that she could shut out the world outside her room.

"What shall I say. From the moment I got here, it has been made clear to me by Alex-Lucas, that some vampires prefer me to leave immediately. But I have nowhere else to go, so I am basically stuck between two worlds. I'm a human in vampire school, if it wasn't enough just to be the new girl. Then I also learn that my ancestors were involved in a war, were I initially knew nothing about. In the four days I've been here, my door has been smeared with Bloodberry juice, Bloodberry juice has been thrown all over me, whoever was responsible for it read my file and took advantage of it. Should I continue, or are you getting the picture?" Nadia shook her head.

"No you don't have to, but those it help?" Velika nodded and then dropped to her knees, immediately the three sitting on her bed shot forward. She raised her hand.

"It's okay, the tension leaves my body this way." The three nodded, but were not completely reassured. Velika scrambled to her feet.

"Can I borrow a towel from one off you, until I have new towels. I promise you will get it back washed." The three looked at each other and laughed and Velika couldn't help but laugh with them. Ivetta jumped off the bed and left the room, she returned not much later with two white plush bath towels.

"Here." Still smiling, Velika took the towels.

"Thank you, Ivetta. Then I just go under a hot water, because I feel very dirty."

Ivetta nodded and beckoned Lucinda.

"We have to do our homework. We'll see you tomorrow." Lucinda nodded as she got up, Nadia also got up.

"I also take a shower and then I come here for some vampire tutoring." Velika nodded and put one of the bath towels in the wardrobe.

"I'll see you later, then."

12

Alex-Lucas dried the last plate and hung the brightly colored tea towel back where it belonged.

"Thank you, young master Barnier." Mrs. Valè stood behind him, he shrugged and sighed.

"It was only three plates and you were kind enough to let us in anyway." It was Mrs. Valè who shrugged.

"The poor girl had not eaten all day, it would be irresponsible of me not to feed her. Since I like the girl, she might be here for a few days. But always gives me a warm smile when she sees me. I know she's not one of us, but if I were your Alex-Lucas I wouldn't let her pass you by." He wanted to open his mouth to ask what the cafeteria lady was talking about. But closed his mouth again. She was right in the few days that Velika was here, it had not been really boring for a moment. Of course it had been at her expense, something he wished he could turn back.

"As you said, Mrs. Valè, she is human." Mrs. Valè shrugged.

"In the days before the first war it was quite normal for vampires and humans to interact in a romantic way. You probaly know the story of Sediana Lumina and Abraham van Helsing. Anyway, it's time for you to retreat to your own room. The sun does not stop for anyone." Ofcourse he knew that story, Nick Lumina told that one during history. He was quite proud that his ancestor stayed in the mansion as refugees, before they went to Narinor. Nick even told them that he and the rest of his family had still contact with the van Helsing family. Alex-Lucas sighed, so much history.

ALEX-LUCAS ALMOST SCREAMED a curse when he got outside, it was raining cats and dogs and there was no other option then to run towards the boy's dorm. The feeling of his clothes on his body didn't make the situation any better. He walked through the somewhat cluttered common room, his mind brought him towards Velika. She would clean this mess up without a second thaught, and he would help her ofcourse. He walked through the arch that led to the badrooms. He came into the hallway that lead down to his room, he always was glad that his room was on the ground floor. So that he didn't have to run up or down all those stairs every day. He opened the door and walked in. The posters of possible universities hung neatly in a straight line on the wall above his bed, but that was the only neat thing about his room. He stepped over the sheets of his bed, trying to remember why they were by the door. But it escaped him. He opened his wardrobe and pulled out a black bath towel. He needed to get out of the wet tacky clothes and he would worry about the mess in his room later. It felt like a new person when he got back, the warm water had done him good. It had driven thoughts of a certain girl from his mind. But these thoughts immediately came back when he saw the clutter in his room. What was this feeling, he used to look past the mess and sit at his desk to do homework. Only now he felt a great urge to clean, with reluctance he bent down to the sheets by the door and threw it back on his bed. At least that was something that even his untidy self could not comprehend. The floor was covered with dirty laundry and paper notes. With a grunt he plucked it from among the laundry and placed it on his desk. The only place in his room that was not covered.

After a while he let himself fall onto his bed with a sigh, the silk black sheets surrounding him. The floor of his room was empty, only the basket his father had given him to put his laundry in. was now bulging. He sighed again. That was a problem for the weekend or most likley tomorrow, he grabbed one of the diaries from his nightstand. He could tell from the graceful handwriting that it was one of Vanessa's. His eyes slid over the words, but his brain didn't take them. He closed the book and laid it back. He was done for today. he wrapped the black silk blanket around him. Before closing his eyes, in his dream she was waiting for him.

HIS ALARM CLOCK WOKE him from that beautiful dream. Still, he couldn't ignore that jealous thing, he knocked off the sheets and walked to the bookcase where his alarm clock was, he pressed the red button as hard as he could and the alarm stopped screaming. Alex-Lucas took breathed of relief as he stretched. He had to admit that he had slept well, the dream was slowly lapping into the background. The person who played the lead however was etched into his memory. He wondered how it was possible. That someone he had only known for a few days could have such an impact on him. He got himself dressed, it would be another school day, at least that was the plan. He looked at his wardrobe, there was a chain with a gold pendant. His family emblem, a kings cobra, was engraved on the pendant. He reached out to it, his hand touching the cold presious metal and his thumb ran across the rippled surface. Every vampire had one and where suposed to wear it at all times, it was a sign of respecting your family, as quick as he could put the pendant around his neck. He heard several voices in the hall indicating that the other boys were also awake. He closed his wardrobe door and reached for his bag, which still contained the books from yesterday. He had already done his homework in the infirmary when he was watching over Velika with Nadia. Now that he thought about it, it was strange that both Dr. Krauss and Headmaster Dracul had allowed them to stay. He hoisted his backpack onto his shoulder and took it to his bedroom door. But when he pulled it open, he immidatly wanted to close it once again.

"My little brother. My apoligize for disturbing you once agian. But father sent me, he had heard that you did not show up in your lessons yesterday and that you were in the infirmary all night. So he wanted to know how you are doing?" With a sigh, Alex-Lucas pushed Nirrox aside.

"I'm fine, tell father that as Chairman of the student council, I was worried about one of the students." He walked past him, down the hall.

"What is that all! You are missing lessons, because you are worried about some girl? Little brother, you are not going to hear the ending about that." Alex-Lucas sighed.

"It wasn't just *some* girl, Nirrox you know that as well as I do." Nirrox narrowed his eyes.

"You don't mean that, Alex-Lucas Barnier. I warned you not to get too attached. But of course, my words fall opon death mans ears when a man starts to fall in love." Alex-Lucas clenched his fists, how eager he wanted to punch his brother.

"You know what big brother, if I were your Iwould have run away. Nadia still hasn't forgiven you, for what you have done to her." Nirrox shrugged.

"I'm not afraid of her and I never will be." Nirrox's hand went to the scar on his right cheek, but did not move away from Alex-Lucas.

"Right, well I need to go."

"ALEX-LUCAS!" NIRROX was still by his side, when he heard his name. Her voice stopped his heart beating. His ancestor would have had this with Vanessa too. He watched her walk their way. "Good morning Mr. Barnier. How nice to see you again." Nirrox bowed to Velika and Alex-Lucas rolled his eyes.

"The pleasure is entirely mine, Miss Lazar. I heard about the unsavory incident in your room, are you all right?" Velika looked at Alex-Lucas and he shook his head, no he told Nirrox nothing.

"I thought father had sent you to see if I was okay? But if you already knew that it was not me, but Velika that was in the infarmary bed. What are you doing here?" Nirrox sighed and put an arm around Velika's shoulders.

"Did you hear that, my little brother doesn't trust me. How lucky you are that you are the only child. But now that I say it. Your father would have been very disappointed to learn that your mother couldn't have any more children." That was it Alex-Lucas had heard enough. He lashed out at Nirrox and punched him in the stomach, Nirox collapsed and gasped. "I deserved that." He said between gasps of breath.

"Get lost, Nirrox. I don't really want to see you again until the Bloodmoonball. If father wants to know something about me, he will know where to find me." He grabbed Velika's arm and gently pulled her away from his brother.

"I'm sorry you had to see that. But my brother is justifiably impossible." She nodded and didn't even look back.

"Nadia saw you two from the window of our building and she ran ahead. But I was just not that fast." Alex-Lucas laughed.

"I can say that I am very happy with that. Nirrox started to get on my nerves." He let go of her arm, but immediately regretted it.

"You know, he just insisted again, that I shouldn't get too attached to you." Velika sighed.

"I'm afraid everyone around us knows more than we do." He nodded.

"And I'm afraid they are right." Alex-Lucas and Velika entered the main building. But after the doors closed behind them, she grabbed his arm.

"I'm not afraid of it, Alex." Alex-Lucas eyes widened, she only called him by one name. Something he never expected to hear from her. The only one who did that with ease was Nadia, and they known each other for years.

"You should be." He said, but she shook her head.

"No, I shouldn't. Otherwise I would be afraid of you. And for what I feel and after I let everything out yesterday, under pressure from the girls. It is not you that I am afraid off, but it is what we are going to reprecent." He listened to every word.

"So what are we going to do we do now. History is repeating itself, with us and the worst part is both our species are still hostile to each other. So nothing has changed since Armand and Vanessa." She burst out laughing.

"Oh, your only concern is our species. Not the fact that we may be distant relatives?" He shrugged his shoulders. That was not so strange, his parents were also distantly related.

"I can live with that." Togheter they entered the cafeteria, almost everyone's eyes immediately shot towards them.

"Hehe finally." Nadia's voice echoed across the space, his gaze turned to her. Nadia had a big smile on her face, next to him Velika sighed and walked to the buffet. He followed her and occasionally looked up to the cafeteria. He had the feeling that every student was staring at him.

"What are they waiting for?" She leaned towards him and he sighed. So she had noticed it too.

"Maybe they expect a kiss or something." Velika sighed again and shook her.

"This just goes to show, vampires and humans are exactly the same." He pursed his lips and nodded.

VELIKA AND ALEX-LUCAS walked with their trays to the table at which their friends stared expectantly to them. Lucinda just put a piece of a chocolate-covered waffle in her mouth.

"I saw how you punched your brother, may I compliment you for that." Lucinda said after emptying her mouth. He looked at her and she looked at him with twinkles in her eyes.

"Yes I was fed up with him. He kept insulting me." Velika took a quiet sip of her coffee, but put the mug down with a bang.

"Get out of here with the question." Nadia nearly snapped.

"So you are an item then?" He looked at her.

"We just talked. Nothing has been decided yet." Their mouths fell open, Nadia almost jumped out of her skin.

"Come on, you can't be serious. You just talked, about what? Everybody with eyes can see that you are in love!" He motioned for Nadia to adjust her volume slightly, but everyone had already heard her and Velika nodded.

"Don't forget Nadia, we've learned the first war between our species. Begun with an affair between Armand Barnier, crown prince of the vampire throne, and Vanessa Lazar, queen of the human throne in Narinor. We can assume that Vanessa's husband discovered it and therefore openly attacked Armand. That is something we cannot and must not forget." Nadia sighed.

"Well, you know how to turn the mood into something gloomy. But you must be right." He nodded slowly, looked at his plate.

13

Why did it feel like the rest of the week had flown by? Maybe, because nothing strange happened. Velika had not been attacked by flying food or drinks, and had not received any unexpected presents on her bed. She breathed in the night air as she stared at the stars on her back. Next to her was Alex, he had his nose hidden in a book. She enjoyed this moment of tranquility, Nathalia was so kind to point out this place under the weeping willow.

"Hey lovebirds!" She came up with a sigh. Nadia ran their way.

"Goodbye, rest." Alex sighed, closing his book. Nadia dropped herself down on the sheet. She had one of the diaries in her hand.

"Finally I have found you." Velika rolled her eyes. Nadia should have known that they would not have sitting in plain sight, everyone had decided their relationship was the talk of the school. Even though there was no real mention of a relationship. All she and Alex have done is talk about it. Much to the annoyance of their friends.

"What's wrong Nadia?" Alex looked at her intently. Nadia sighed, but a smile was not far from her face.

"I have two things, number 1 the dresses have been delivered so Velika has to come with me to try hers on. Second, I found out something in Vanessa's diary. There is a secret page in it but it is written in Pisoen." Velika was now completely focused.

"In Pisoen, have you already translated it?" Nadia nodded.

"Long story short, it is indeed what we already suspect, Vanessa's husband discovered the affair and planned to destroy it, by killing

Armands bastards. As she described it, Armand had no love for his wife, but would commite murder before he saw his childeren hurt and we already know that he did just that." Velika looked at Alex and he closed his eyes.

"This is a juicy story that we can tell during our presentation, who doesn't love a good love story with a tragic ending." Velika snorted through her nose.

"We only have one problem, unfortunately we don't have the point of view of Lady Helena or Mathéo's. Or the point of view of Count Ventila. So in other words the other side of this story."

Nadia sighed.

"You have a good point there. It is indeed a shame that we have no diaries of those three." Alex rebounded.

"Wait a minute, Lady Helena was not a Barnier by birth. She came from the Redfang family." He got up from the sheet. "I'm going to find something out, why don't you two try on those dresses." He ran away before she could answer him.

"WELL I HOPE HE FINDS it, what ever it is." Nadia helped Velika fold the sheet.

"I hope so too, but Nadia you didn't have to look for us. I have told you where we were." Nadia nodded, but shrugged.

"To be fair, the dresses were already in, before you left the girl's dorm. But when I found that secret page and translated it, I really couldn't wait anymore." Velika took the books under her arm and Nadia the sheet. Together they walked from the wheeping willow, to the girl's dorm. Inside Nadia turned to Velika.

"I'll get the boxes with the dresses and then come to your room, as my room is really a mess. Didn't really had time, or rather a lag on motivation, to clean it up." Velika watched Nadia and shook her head. Before climbing the stairs to her room. As she entered the hallway Lucinda and Ivetta just walked out of their rooms in their red dresses.

"Velika what do you think?" Ivetta made a round. The red fabric of both dresses, which looked a lot alike, showed nicely on their skins.

"It really suits you. Our dresses are also in, we will try them on." Ivetta's smile just widened, and she jumped up and down.

"Really, you have show them to us." Lucinda took hold of Ivetta's arm.

"Calm down Ivetta. Please calm down." Velika chuckled for a moment. How much had changed in a week.

"I'll discuss it with Nadia." She opened her door and entered the room, carefully putting the sheet in the laundry basket and putting the books at their proper place in the bookcase. It was strange this room felt so much more like a home than any of the rooms in which she had slept. Maybe because the pink was interrupted by small breaths of blue.

NADIA ENTERED THE ROOM without knocking, perhaps it was because she had no hands left to knock. The two boxes containing the dresses were large. Velika quickly walked past Nadia to close the door. Who put the boxes onto the plush rug.

"Here they are. Okay, let's see, this one is yours and this one is mine." Nadia got up with the box that had been on top of the stack and pushed it into Velika's hands. With the box in her hands, she walked to her bed and opened it. The soft blue satin fabric glistened slightly, she took the dress out of its cardboard wrapping and held it in front off her. While she looked at herself in the mirror. "Wow it is really beautiful, Velika, put it on." Velika quickly took off her school uniform and carefully put on the dress. When she looked at Nadia she saw that Nadia was doing the same. "I thought it came with a gold belt and bracelets?" Nadia looked in the empty box, had missed something? As she ran her hand through the box, there was a knock on the door. Nadia opened the door and Lucinda was in the doorway, with a small box in her hands.

"This was just delivered." Lucinda handed Nadia the box. "Nadia, that dress looks really beautiful on you. But that's no surprise, emerald green suits you so well." Nadia shrugged.

"Thank you, I think." Nadia closed the door just before Lucinda's nose, looking confused at Velika. Who looked back confused.

"Why did you do that?" Nadia shrugged.

"I really have no idea, but I think here are your belt and bracelets." Nadia gave the box to Velika, she immediately opened it and it were indeed the belt and bracelets. She quickly put on the belt, only the bracelets were a bit too wide. "Wait I think those bracelets should be a bit higher." Nadia was already raising one of the bracelets until it could go no further. Velika nodded and did the same with the other one. Nadia stepped back and nodded her approval. "Velika." She looked at herself in the mirror and gasped. She had worn dresses before, but this was something completely different."Wait, where is your phone. Then I can take a picture." Before Velika could do anything about it, Nadia already had her phone in her hands. "Come on, your mom will love this, even if you don't wear pink." Velika bit her lip gently, but still posed. She heard the click of her camera. "So there go the photos." Velika reached for her phone, but Nadia kept it from her. There was another knock on the door. Velika reluctantly forgot her phone and walked to the door, opened it and was surprised to see that it was Alex. He looked at her with an open mouth, his eyes moving from top to bottom.

"You look really beautiful. I just have to think about my suit." He scratched his ear.

"Have you achieved what you want to achieve?" Nadia's voice broke the spell. Velika looked down the hall for a moment but Lucinda and Ivetta had disappeared.

"No, Professor Redfang was pleasantly surprised that I asked about it, but according to her, Lady Helana's diaries had not survived the war, if she had any dairies at all." He looked again at Velika.

"I'll just go to my own room, being ashamed of my suit." He quickly walked away from the door and she looked after him in surprise.

"He has got it bad." Velika looked at Nadia who took off her dress again. "Well, we still have a few days before the ball." It wasn't long before Nadia was back in her school uniform. And tucked the dress back into the box. "I have to thank you by the way, I also bought my dress from the online store as yours and I have to say that it looks better on me than all my previous dresses. Well, I'll see you at dinner." Nadia picked up the box and took it to the door and disappeared.

VELIKA ALSO TOOK OFF her dress and hung it on a clothes hanger. She sighed as she pulled her jacket back over her blouse. There was a knock on her door again.

"A moment!" She quickly put on her skirt and then ran to the door. She should have known, Alex stood for it. "Did you actually go to your room to think about your suit, or did you wait for Nadia to leave?" She stepped aside so he could enter.

"I actually went to my room, I ordered something and I actually wanted to save it for the ball. But when I saw you in that beautiful dress, I decided I wanted to give it to you now." He had a box in his hands and he gave it to her. She opened it carefully, the inside was covered with a dark cloth. On the fabric was a pendant made from gold, with a symbol of a rose engraved on it. "The vampire families all have a symbol that is distant from their times in Narinor. But since your family is from the same country, I took it upon myself to find your family's symbol." She looked at him with a smile for a moment and then again at the symbol on the pendant, it was a rose. She took the pendant out of the box, there was a small gold chain attached to it.

"It's beautiful, thank you. Can you help me." She handed him the pendant, he took it as she turned around. He carefully hung the pendant around her neck. The cold precious metal hung on her chest. With a smile she turned back and looked straight into his icy blue eyes. He was so close, she took a small step back and immediately regretted this action. "Thank you for for the pendant." She clasped the jewelry with her right hand. He nodded briefly as he studied her. She felt her heart beat faster.

"Alex?" He took a step forward and put his arms around her. Gently he pulled her closer and pressed his lips on hers.

14

Velika hadn't pushed him away, Alex was the one who broke the magic moment.

"I'm sorry I went a little too far." She shook her head, looking into his eyes. Her heart was beating so heart that maybe he heared it. She wanted to say something to him, but the noise in the hallway distracted her. Her room door was closed. "I think it's time for dinner." He released her and nodded.

"I think so too." This is the one time that she could skip dinner and kiss him one more time. But Madam Valé would come to the girl's dorm to get her, after that she had not eaten for a whole day. The cafeteria chef took it upon herself to watch over her meals. He did one more step back, so they had no other choice then to go to diner.

Alex-Lucas

UNFORTUNATELY FOR THEM, the weekend was drawing to a close and he was getting ready for an exhausting week. But than Professor Redfang entered the classroom.

"A very good evening, as you know there will be the Bloodmoonball tomorrow. And I have heard from several ladies that their dresses have been delivered. That's all sweet and nice. But don't forget that tomorrow is for your presentations." Alex-Lucas looked interested at Professor Redfang, where did she want to go with this speech? "Last week I heard that some of you ended up in some kind of rabbit hole. Once you discover one fact, you are eager to learn more. However, I would rather have your presentation end with you not knowing the rest because the trail of knowledge has become cold or you didn't find the rest of the trail, than having you rush it off. Remember this presentation hold 2/3th of your grade." Professor Redfang looked at their group and nodded they at her. So that's what she was going for, the fact that they are indeed looking for more voices in their story. Velika leaned forward, he and Nadia looked immidatly towards her.

"Maybe it is better that we focus on what we have now." He nodded slowly, they will find those voices. Only they will not find them in time.

"Would you like to share something with the class, Miss Lazar?" Velika shot to her feet, and shook her head.

"I'm sorry Professor, I consulted with my group about what you just said." Professor Redfang nodded.

"That's a good thing, because I think you're the ones who fell down that figurative rabbit hole." He looked at Velika, who nodded.

"She just indicated that she wanted to focus on the information we have now. Instead of looking for more voices in our story. Professor." He said, Professor Redfang walked to their table.

"That's a really good idea." She walked away from them, then turned back to the class. "In the light of the Bloodmoonball, tomorrow is history your first and only lesson. Also a small warning because you are in your senior year is this presentation for all other teachers and students. Yes this is the presentation of your nightmares." Suddenly a voice of indignation rose from the classroom, though he remained silent. He cursed anyway, until he felt Velika's soft hand on his. He looked into her light blue eyes and nodded. They could do this, even though they had a unique topic.

NADIA CLEARED HER THROAT and he looked at her.

"We can still work on the presentation, let's make an action plan. I got a summary from Ivetta and Lucinda so we actually have what we need." He nodded and sighed at the same time, Velika took all her notebook and pen.

"Look, I want to see that." Startled, he looked at the Professor, who pointed to their group. "They don't complain, they immediately put their heads together and come up with a plan of action." He quickly looked around the class where everyone was staring at them and stood up.

"I'm sorry to say this guys. But these presentations are given around this time every year, so to be honest I don't understand where all the commotion comes from. So stop complaining and get to work, we all have one more day to work on this. So let we all use this time to do so." He sat down again and the murmur rose again, but he paid no attention to it. He looked at Velika who assigned them a subject. Nadia nodded, then picked up Ivetta's and Lucinda's summary and read it carefully.

"As I read it here, the two good-for-nothings have done a nice job. Here are not the big battles, but rather the small battles and then from two points of view. From what I received in class, the other groups have already chosen these big and bloody battles." She handed the summary to him and he nodded.

"I only have a request Nadia, don't call Lucinda and Ivetta good-for-nothings in front of the entire school." Nadia shrugged.

"I can not promise anything."

THE LAST BELL OF THE school day rang and everyone made their way to the cafeteria for dinner. Alex- Lucas waited in the music room, Velika, as always, carefully put her sheet music away. Today,

Professor Le Rouge had complimented her on her singing voice and Professor Le Rouge never gave a compliment lightly.

"Ready?" Velika walked his way with a big smile. He reached his hand out to her and she took it. "Nadia just suggested that we find a quiet place after dinner to go through the presentation again." Velika nodded.

"To be on the safe side, let's take Lucinda and Ivetta with us. So that we can practice in front of the public." He burst into laughter as they walked down corridors.

"I don't think Nadia had that in mind. But I agree with you. Our best option is to go through it carefully with the audience." She let go of his hand as they entered the cafeteria.

"No, no." Lucinda looked at her in surprise, fowlding her arms. Alex-Lucas was not surpised that Lucinda took the lead in defending Ivetta and herself.

"And why not, we helped." Nadia's pink eyes narrowed and almost spit fire towards Lucinda.

"Because, Lucinda Mask. I want to go through it once without prying eyes." Velika shook her head and stepped between the two.

"Nadia, don't get me wrong. But I think it is better if they are there. They know what we are talking about, they can actually steer us in the right direction when we get stuck." Nadia narrowed her eyes.

"Alright then." He had stayed aloof from this discussion, but when he saw Ivetta look at him, he knew that the topic of the conversation would soon change to another topic.

"What's it Ivetta?" He tried not to sound tired, something he really needed to work on. The girl bit her lip gently and sighed.

"Well Alex-Lucas, I actually wanted to ask you something. My father comes to visit at the prom and I know you prefer to dance with Velika all evening. But would I like one dance from you?" He almost choked on his drink, this was a question he hadn't expected. He wanted to say something, but Lucinda was ahead of him.

"I thought you were going to dance with me all night?" Ivetta looked at the empty plate in front of her.

"That was before I knew my father was coming. You know he won't accept it, Lucinda." Alex-Lucas raised his hand before Lucinda could respond.

"If that's what you really want, it's an honor." He looked at Lucinda, who looked away angrily. Velika took Lucinda's hand.

"When Alex dances with Ivetta, I am going to dance with you." Lucinda looked at her in amazement.

"Would you do that?" Velika nodded.

"Sure we're friends." He looked at Nadia, who was listening to the conversation with wide eyes.

"Wait a minute, rewind." She pointed from Ivetta to Lucinda. "You two have a relationship?"

Ivetta and Lucinda nodded together. "Well then I learned something new." Velika looked at him and reached out to him. He picked it up without thinking too much about it. "Wait a minute, you two too!" Nadia hit the table. "I was already wondering how you got that pendant. Thank you for letting me know." He shook his head.

"I think you're the only one who didn't realize it yet, you can't blame us for Nadia." The others around him laughed and Nadia nodded in agreement.

"There you have a point, Lucas." After dinner they walked to the glass cubicle, which was deserted to Alex-Lucas relief. Velika discussed the sequence again with Nadia. As he turned to Lucinda and Ivetta, who was still arguing about the dance question.

"Let it go, Lucinda."

"No, I won't *let it go*, Ivetta. I love you to much for that. You can't always listen to your father."

"I know that all too well. But Lucinda , but after my mother died. He is all I got left."

"You got me, Ivetta." Maybe he should stay out of here, but if those two keep going. They couldn't practice their presentation.

"Ivetta, Lucinda is right. Maybe it's time you were honest with your father. And if he loves you he will understand, maybe not right away but in time he will. And Lucinda you know better than anyone what a big step it is, coming out to your loved once is scary, give her some time." Lucinda folded her arms.

"You are right." Nadia came to his side and nodded.

"Well when you are done bickering then weare ready to begin." Ivetta and Lucinda sat down and they started the presentation.

AFTER VELIKA SAID THE last sentence. He already knew that their presentation was rock solid, there was nothing wrong with the story and the facts.

"This sounded so good. I dare to say with certainty that you will run off with the highest grade." Ivetta bounced up and down in her chair.

"Calm down Ivetta, that will say that is was not bad, for our first try. But from what I've heard, the others also have solid topics." Lucinda nodded slowly before she opened her mouth.

"It could be, Nadia. But those are all topic's we've heard several times before. You have something new and fresh, and I'm not talking about Velika." Ivetaa nodded in agreement. "And you complement each other masterfully. It is because I know what you are going to say, otherwise I would not have noticed that Alex-Lucas had forgotten something." He nodded and sighed.

"Thank you for emphasizing it, Lucinda." Who shrugged indifferently.

"Hey, I'm just stating what I noticed." Nadia sighed and started cleaning up their stuff, before Velika could do it.

"The most important thing is that we know it. Then I suggest that especially the ladies come with me for a girls night. Because if you don't know yet, the ball is tomorrow night." He shot into the air.

"What a pity that I cannot participate with you. But then I am not a lady. Whill you are doing each others nails and hear. I better go iron my suit. Now that I know that two ladies want to dance with me, I have to live up to their expectations." Nadia punched him.

"Very funny Lucas. You iron something I have to see that." The others got up laughing and left the glass cubicel, except Velika. Who put her arms around him, he lowered his head.

"Then I will see you tomorrow." He nodded and pressed his lips against hers. And she pushed hers against his.

"You know that this space is made of glass, right." Grunting, he broke the kiss and Nadia raised her hands. "I'm just telling you." Velika gave him another kiss on the cheek before running after Nadia.

15

"Hmm, this red nail polish looks best with your dress, I think. What do you think Velika?" Nadia looked away from Ivetta's hand, at Velika who was busy blowing her nails dry. Nadia had decorated them with light blue nail polish with gold accents.

"The dress is very dark, maybe it should be a shade darker." Lucinda looked at the nail polish jars and gave Nadia the color that she had in mind. Nadia looked at it and nods. She was already unscrewing the cap when Ivetta cleared her throat.

"Wait a minute, you two have forgotten someone in this conversation." Lucinda and Nadia looked at each other for a moment.

"I don't know who." Velika started laughing, this was typical Nadia. But it suprised her that Lucinda played along.

"Ivetta which color do you want?" Velika asked, Ivetta nodded to her.

"Thank you for asking my opinion, Velika. It goes on my nails so I want to have a say about which color goes on it." Nadia sighed and closed the cap.

"You're right, which color do you want?" Ivetta glanced at Lucinda.

"If you can, you can decorate my nails with the first red you picked out. It fits best with Lucinda's dress." Velika smiled softly, it was so typical Ivetta. "And I have some nail stickers of masks in my room." Nadia nodded in agreement and Ivetta got up from the sofa,

Lucinda who got curious was one step behind her. Nadia looked at her for a moment before they laughed. The girls' night had started so well in the common room and they weren't the only ones doing it. There were groups all over the room, busy with each other's hair or nails. Velika heared Nathalia, Katerina and Siobhan discussing diferent hairstyles. It felt so normal, maybe it was normal. Her new normal.

"SO TELL VELIKA WHAT'S on that pendant of yours. I know that all members of a vampire family have one. I have one too, but what does yours say?" Velika took the pendant and looked at the rose. With a ribbon behind it.

"According to Alex, this is the symbol of my family." Nadia came up to her and examined the pendant carefully.

"He really loves you." She said when she let go of the pendant. Right away Velika saw the pain in her friends eyes. "I wish his brother loved me so much when we were together. Don't get me wrong, I know Lucas is not Nirrox. He was the one who stood up for me after I attacked Nirrox. It was one year ago tomorrow and when I saw him kissing Colette Mask." She shook her head. "I lost myself for a short moment, but that moment was just enough. She was a year older than him, and went to another school. But he was all over her. Actually, I should have been kicked out of the student council just as Selara. But all the members of the council, besides Nirrox, decided not to do that to me. Nirrox was then Chairman of the student council just like Lucas is now and he was rightfully pissed off. But when he wanted to go against it, literally all the female members stood up for me. It felt good, not that it satisfied me. But still..." Velika looked at Nadia.

"You really loved him." Nadia's eyes felt with tears and she nodded slowly.

"I still love him. Every time I see him I hope he will take me in his arms and apologize." Velika took Nadia in her arms, who broke completely. She looked carefully at the other girls in the room, who looked at Nadia with empathy.

"I don't know him or Colette well. But I know one thing, he was fool for letting you go." Nadia really burst out into tears, Ivetta and Lucinda ran into the room.

"Nadia whatis wrong?" Ivetta asked, Lucinda walked over and sat down on the sofa next to Nadia before looking at Ivetta.

"It's been one year." Ivetta hit herself in the head and also walked to the sofa.

"That is true and those two will be there again this year." Lucinda put a hand on Nadia's shoulder.

"Nadia I spoke to my cousin over the weekend and begged her not to come. Then she had the guts to tell me that it was not going to happen, because Nirrox had proposed to her that same evening and they are going to make the announcment at the ball." Nadia stopped sobbing and looked startled at Lucinda.

"So not only did she steal it from me, she wants to smear it on my face." Lucinda nodded and sighed.

"I've been walking around this knowledge all day long, not knowing how to tell you this." Nadia took Lucinda's hand.

"Thank you for telling it me."

VELIKA RUBBED HER HANDS, she was nervous about the presentation. They had been approached by Professor Redfang durring breakfast with the news that they were last group.

"Lucas stop with passing or you'll leave a groove." He grunted at Nadia.

"Why are we not allowed to see the presentations of the others, then at least we have something to do." Nadia rose from the chair in the history room.

"You know why it is. In order not to be distracted." Velika walked to the poster with Queen Vanessa on it.

"I hope we honor their story." She felt Alex hand on her shoulder, it felt comforting and she relaxed a little.

"That is really the least of my worries, but I believe we will." The classroom door opened and Professor Redfang entered.

"It's your turn, are you three ready?" Velika wished she could answer that. Unfortunately, not a word came out of her throat. She hoped it was temporary. Nadia nodded to the Professor.

"Give us a minute." Professor Redfang nodded and left them alone for a moment. Velika and Alex walked over to her. "Okay, let's take a breath. Because we are nervous as fuck. We can do this, because we already gave the presentation yesterday. If we keep that in mind, we will be fine." Velika looked at her, she burned with confidence and she nodded.

"We can do this." They walked to the gym where the rest of the school was already waiting for them. Velika stood behind a platform with a microphone. She cleared her throat, she felt her whole body tremble. Yet she opened her mouth.

"The first war between humans and vampires, that's the topic that has been going on all day long. One presentation after another has been about the bloody battles and their aftermaths. But where this gruesome story begins is often only a vague story. A story that we would like to clarify for you." She walked away from the microphone and Alex took his place.

"We delved into deep history with the diaries of our two protagonists. Queen Vanessa Lazar and Crown Prince Armand Barnier of the kingdom of Narinor" The whole hall was silent as he spoke of the love story and the murder of King Mathéo Lazar, which was the start of the war. When Nadia took over and talked about how both sides led their armies, in the big battlefields but also the small battles. She could see from some of the students that they were on the edge of their seats. Now it was her turn again.

"The war turned the vampires into real refugees, while humans quickly wrote off their enemies as a bad memory. Something you see in bad black and white movies, nothing more than a campfire story. Yet this war will never completely disappear from the memory of the actual families. This school was built on the border of Traimora and Narinor and funded by Vanessa, who had been expelled from her homeland. And felt guilty for what she and Armand had done. Something that they couldn't turn back. But their story is one of many, a story of how it started. But not about how it ends because their stories continues with us, today." She took a breath, then stepped back. She glanced at Alex who nodded, there was a moment's silence. So quiet she was afraid everyone could hear her heart beating in her chest, untill Professor Redfang got up and clapped in her hands. The rest of the school followed suit. Nadia let out a little cry of relief and she fell into Alex his arms.

AFTER A SHORT MOMENT, Professor Redfang took the stage.

"As usual, the graduate students have had one week to prepare these presentations and, as usual, the bar is set high. I have discussed the grades with the other teachers. Which I'm going to announce to the class tomorrow, except for one. The one with the highest grade and that is the group of Alex-Lucas Barnier, Nadia Dracul and Velika Lazar. With their beautiful presentation about two of their own ancestors." Velika swallowed for a moment. They had the highest grade, she looked at her classmates who all nodded in agreement. Nadia leaned towards her.

"I'm curious what it is?" Velika held her breath.

"This group has a 9.5 for their presentation." Nadia shrugged, and she looked at Velika.

"That's a shame, just under ten. But we were not far from it. " Alex looked at her in surprise and pinched her softy in her arm.

"That's the highest grade ever given for a presentation, Nadia." Nadia's eyes widened and her jaw dropped.

"Are you serious." He nodded, Velika looked at him in surprise. What those that mean?

"That means we have broken a school record..."

"Which means that we end up hanging with our faces in the library." Nadia finishes his sentence. Mr. Crypto has already stepped forward with a camera in his hands.

"Can the three of you stand together a little better?" Nadia pushed Velika in the middle of the threesome.

"Perfect. Say bloodcheese." They repeated after him, the flash blinded Velika for a moment. She flashed with her eyelashes to clear her vission. "Wonderful, congratulations on your performance." Lucinda and Ivetta shot past him.

"I told you so!" Ivetta jumped up and down excitedly.

"And then we are going to get ready for the ball." Lucinda smiled and grabbed Ivetta's shoulder.

"Calm down, yes you said it. As far as the ball is concerned." Lucinda fell silent and sighed.

"I'd rather not think about that yet."

"Students, may I have your attention, please. I know it's a bit short for the ladies. At least that's what my daughter is trying to tell me. But you now have the opportunity to withdraw, while the teachers and I will transform this room. See you tonight. Oh Nadia, I want your first dance of the evening to be with me." Nadia covered her eyes with embarrassment and sighed.

"He just can't resist."

16

Alex-Lucas straightened his old-fashioned collar and ran again a comb through his hair just to be on the safe side. His inky black suit and white shirt exuded a classic look. Something he liked, he looked at the clock. It was almost time to go to the girl's dorm to pick up the girls. With a sigh he opened the door to his room and started to leave the room. But stopped in the doorway, he had forgotten something. He looked around the room for the last time until he saw the small box on his desk. It was a bracelet that he ordered, at the same time as the necklace. He walked quickly into his room and grabbed the box from his desk. And left his room for the last time. As fast as he could, without running, Alex-Lucas walked to the girl's dorm. At the door he paused and ran a hand through his hair before pulling the door open. With a sigh he walked into the shared room, where several women in their dresses were waiting for their dates.

"Finally." Nadia got up from the sofa and her dark green dress rose just above her knees. "I thought you forgot about us." She walked over to him and put a hand on his shoulder, but he didn't payed any attention to her. His eyes were on Velika in her light blue dress. Her hair was in a kind of tail that was held together with a golden cord. The gold pendant he had given her hung around her neck. There was a gold band around both of her upper arms and a gold belt completed the outfit. "Yes, yes. I agree, she is a stunning."

Nadia patted him on the shoulder and he walked over to Velika. Who received him with a warm smile.

"That dress suits you better than I can remember. It is a custom as a member of a noble house to give something to the lady when he takes her to the Bloodmoonball. I know I've already given you the pendant, but I hope you'd like to wear this anyway." He handed her the box and held his breath as she opened it. Lucinda and Ivetta looked over her shoulders.

"Wow, it's a bracelet with the Barnier family symbol." Ivetta's disbelief was evident and he knew why. Velika looked at him in surprise.

"Alex, I don't know if I can accept this. With this you promise yourself to me, in fact you are proposing to me." He lowered his head slightly. So Velika had read about the custom, and she also knew the meaning of it.

"That is indeed the purpose of the practice and I understand your reluctance. But let me tell you something. Before you came here to school I was frozen, I wasn't really alive. I got up eat something, studied and went to bed, the only highlights of my week, were the student council meetings on Sundays. But then you came and I started to live, I started to look forward to the next night when the sun would go down and I would see you again." Alex-Lucas had looked straight at her when he gave his speech, he saw tears spring to her eyes. He took her face and wiped one of the tears from her cheek. "So will you do me the honor of accepting the symbol of my family?" She nodded slowly as the next tear ran down her cheek. He breathed a sigh of relief.

"If you want to help me put it on?" He nodded and took the delicate gold bracelet from the box.

"Well, I'm glad I witnessed that." Nadia took him out of the spell.

"Now your brother is not the only one with 'good news.'" Alex-Lucas nodded and offered Velika his arm who took it.

"Well shall we go then?" Nadia nodded and walked to the door, he followed her with Velika by his arm.

THEY WALKED THE PATH that led to the main building, classical music echoed through the corridors. It got louder the closer they got to the gym. Nadia opened the double doors with flair and then entered the room without looking.

"Ah. there is my beautiful daughter." Vance Dracul walked up to her and took her in his arms. "You are stunning, your mother would have being proud." Nadia embrased Headmaster Dracul, with a little tear in her eyes.

"Thank you father, is he here?" Vance shook his head.

"No and I don't want a repeat of last year." She released him and nodded.

"I just can't make any promises." She turned to Ivetta and Lucinda. They snickerd, behind there hands. "Come on, let's go to the drinks." Nadia left her father with them. Velika stepped towards the Headmaster.

"Headmaster Dracul, rumor has it that Nirrox will announce his engagement to Colette." Headmaster Dracul looked first towards her and then towards him.

"He's up to something?" Headmaster's voice was louder than he himself expected, quickly he looked around before his gaze was set on them. Velika looked at him and nodded.

"That's what Nadia meant by, good news. Colette told Lucinda." He sighed.

"It sounds like something my brother would do. Headmaster keep an eye on your daughter."

Headmaster Dracul nodded and walked over to Nadia and the other girls. Alex-Lucas looked at the young woman at his arm. "Shall we go to the dance floor then?" She gave him a smile.

"As you wish, my prince." With a broad smile he escorted her to the dance floor, where several couples were already circling. Out of the corner of his eye Alex-Lucas saw Vance waltzing across the dance floor with Nadia and Lucinda drumming Ivetta with her. Velika looked at the two of them and laughed loudly.

"Looks like those two are having a good time, at least until Ivetta's father arrives." He nodded and sighed.

"If you don't want me to dance with her, tell her." Velika shook her head and put her head on his chest.

"I don't mind, by the way if you dance with Ivetta, I dance with Lucinda." Again her head, he was so lucky that he had found her. Without her he would have hang against a wall, watching how Nathalia in her long light purple dress was dancing with Gala. Or how Siobhan in her black dress that bleeded in a rainbow of collors at the bottum was wrapped in Katerina's arms. Katerina was wearing a dress made from white and red fabric. Now he could understand their fun, because now he was part of it.

THE MUSIC STOPPED FOR a short moment, it was a small break between songs so that vampires could change dance partners or simply catch their breath. The doors flew open and Nirrox entered the gym with a beautiful woman on his arm. The woman was tall and had silver-blonde hair, her dress was long and light red.

"Colette Mask." Said Velika softly, will gently dragged him towards Nadia and Headmaster Dracul. Nirrox just looked around, and from his smile Alex-Lucas saw that he was going to use this brief moment of silents.

"Friends, please don't stop on my account. But now that I have everybodies attention, I have good news. Last week I proposed to this beautiful woman and she accepted my hand in marriage." Velika let go of him for a moment and took Nadia's hand. Out of the corner of his eye, he saw Nadia's eyes fill with tears. Headmaster Dracul put an arm around his daughter.

"It's going to be okay, that guy simply doesn't deserve you." Velika turned her attention to him.

"Maybe we should bring his attention to us." Alex-Lucas nodded and gave her a kiss on the cheek.

"Well my brother, may I be the first to congratulate you." Alex-Lucas took a step forward.

"I just have to say that this announcement is a year late." Velika stood next to him along with Nadia.

"Did you hear it, by the way? My group and I received the highest mark ever for our presentation."

Nirrox nodded.

"I have that, father is proud of you. He literally wished that mother were still there to see it." Alex-Lucas spread his arms.

"Well, he must also be proud of his eldest. You're getting married!" Nirrox straightened his back.

"I did not say that father was not proud of me. He only wished I would marry a noble. But yeah." Nirrox kissed Colette's hand and she leaned forward to whisper in his ear. Nirrox accompanied Colette to their group. Nadia stopped where she was.

"Who is this beauty here. Oh by my soul it is the last Lazar." Nirrox looked at Colette. "Wait you two don't know each other yet. Colette Mask this here is Velika Lazar." Velika bowed her head slightly and Alex-Lucas cleared his throat.

"Velika Lazar, this here is my brother's wife-to-be, Colette Mask. Lucinda's cousin." Now Colette bowed her head.

"It is an honor to finally meet the last Lazar princess. I've heard so much about you, but never before about your beauty." Velika tilted her head slightly.

"I've heard a lot about you too, Colette Mask. Only they weren't friendly words." Colette's gaze immediately turned from her to Nadia.

"That was to be expected. But what a beautiful pendant. Can I see it?" Before Velika could answer, Colette already had the pendant in her hands.

"This is the symbol of the Lazar family, a rose. Well, it suits you. A pretty flower but you have to look out for the thorns." Colette let go of the pendant. Velika straightened her back a little more.

"Now I see were those negative words are coming from." Colette gave her a dirty look and Velika shrugged. Alex-Lucas took Velika's hand from which the bracelet hung.

"Velika, that was not really nice of you. Good thing now that we've got this over with. Will we return to what we came here for." He gestured to Mister Crypto who was behind the DJ table. "Give the music some water." Mister Crypto nodded and the music echoed once again through the gym. Alex-Lucas then looked at Headmaster Dracul pulling Nadia away. Lucinda danced off with Ivetta. He then turned to Velika. "Where were we?" Velika nodded and let him take her back into the dance.

THE NEXT SONG WAS ABOUT to start when Nirrox lightly tapped Alex-Lucas shoulder.

"Little brother, I'm sorry but cmay I?" Alex-Lucas looked at Velika.

"Well that's not up to me, it is. That is up to the lady herself." Velika straightened her back, he could see it in her eyes that she really didn't. She looked at him instead.

"Is Ivetta's father here?" He nodded and moved his head towards the man standing under the basketball ring.

"He is now looking furiously at his daughter. I have keep my promise." He walked away to Ivetta and Lucinda and gently tapped Lucinda's shoulder. Who looked at him in amazement.

"Ivetta's father is here." Lucinda looked past him and nodded.

"I'll go and look for Velika." He turned and saw that she was already walking towards them.

"I'm dancing the next dance with Nirrox. I'm sorry Alex, but he didn't want to take no for an answer." He nodded and took Ivetta's hand.

"Shall we then?" Ivetta nodded, but looked at her father for a brief moment. She gently bit her lip.

"Alex- Lucas, if it is not to much. Can you help me after this dance? I want to be honest with my father. It is not fair to keep him in the dark." Alex-Lucas nodded.

"Before Velika came here I would have said no. But now you are one of my friends Ivetta, in other words of course you have my support." Velika laid a hand on his shoulder. "I mean our support." She nodded in aprovel.

17

The music stopped a little too quickly, to Velika's liking. With a sigh, she took a step away from Lucinda.

"Well then it's my turn now, I think." Velika turned with another sigh, Nirrox was behind her and she nodded politely.

"You are right. Nirrox Barnier. Just give me a moment and I'll accompany my previous dance partner to her friend." But when she turned towards Lucinda, but she had already walked up to Ivetta, who was walking with Alex to her father. She shrugged and turned back to Nirrox.

"Well what we you waiting for?" He took her hand and waltzed her across the dance floor. "I just wanted to thank you for what you did for my little brother." She looked away from him and bit her lip.

"He always had it in him. So I haven't done much." Nirrox laughed.

"That's a good joke, you have to remember it. But I mean it *princess*. My little brother has surrounded himself with members of his own kind, which is something to celebrate. Maybe I'll see you at my wedding next week." She looked at him.

"You're getting married next week, isn't that a very short engagement?" He raised his shoulders.

"Maybe, but I like Colette. I must confess that I feel guilty towards Nadia and the way things ended between use. But she just wasn't the one."

"You most know, she still loves you." His eyes widened.

"What did you say?" Maybe she shouldn't have said that biut Nadia was her friend and she hated how Nadia was feeling.

"I said that Nadia still loves you. With all her heart, maybe you should have a good conversation with her before you get married. Because now you just keep hurting her, and I believe that is not your intention." He looked away from her and at Nadia.

"You are probably right. I don't want to hurt her anymore than I already did." She felt a little lighter, maybe she wass wrong about him.

"But speaking about your wedding, I'm sure I'll be there." He looked at her again and she pointed her head at the bracelet. It glistened on her wrist, his gaze went to it.

"Isn't that the symbol of my family?" She nodded.

"And you don't have to tell me what that means. I love your brother with all my heart and if I have to let him go because it is better for him I will." Nirrox ice blue eyes sparkled.

"I told him not to get too attached. But now that I talk to you I can already see why that didn't work out." She bit her lip gently, this was not the response she expected. Nirrox had probably seen this.

"Don't worry, I'm not the one to be afraid of. That role is more for my father. But unlike myself, my little brother has given his hand and heart to someone of a noble bloodline."

THE MUSIC STOPPED, he let go. She looked aside and saw Alex standing, Nirrox put a hand on his shoulder.

"What am I hearing now? I am not the only one who has bound himself to a woman." Alex nodded and took her hand.

"That's right brother." Nirrox shrugged.

"History repeats itself, but I hope it ends better for you than for Vanessa and Armand. You know how their story ends, don't you?" Alex pulled Velika closer to her.

"Vanessa was literally burned on the field on which this gym was built. The honorable Count could not protect her as Armand had hoped. Rumor has it that the Count has never forgiven himself and is still wandering around this school, looking for Vanessa. Now I hear you think, what happened to Armand? Well they burn away on the firepile next to her. That's what we're celebrating here today, the deaths of two traitors." Velika's eyes widened and Alex's grip around her tightened slightly. She looked away from Nirrox and looked at Professor Redfang, who looked away in embarrassment, so she clearly knew about it.

"Oh you have never been told that andyou still got a nine and a half for your presentation? What a remarkable development." Nirrox took a few more steps back, then took Colette's hand.

"I'll be back my Angel of the Night in a minute." He kissed her hand and then walked over to Nadia. "Headmaster Dracul, can I talk to Nadia?" Headmaster Dracul looked at his daughter and Nirrox again.

"You can, but I also want to hear what you have to say." The three of them walked out of the gym.

VELIKA LOOKED AT ALEX, who watched his brother and the Draculs in amazement.

"What did you say to him?" She lowered her eyes.

"I told him that Nadia still loves him despite what he did to her. But that was after he told me his wedding is next week." Alex nodded and sighed.

"So you urged him to talk to her. That might be wise for both of them."

"Do you think?" They both turned to Colette. And nodded.

"Yes, Colette. I think so. I see that my brother loves you a lot more than he loved Nadia. But even you wouldn't want Nadia to spend the rest of her life hating you for what you did to her, would you?" Colette folded her arms.

"I don't know, but since Nirrox leaves me no choice, I just have to deal with it." Velika sighed and wanted to walk away until Colette grabbed her arm. "You sure think you are quite something, *princess*. But you are nothing more than food that is played with." Velika tore her arm free.

"And you direct your insecurities towards me. So what makes it you?" Colette reached for her again, but was herself grabbed by the arm by Lucinda.

"Colette, what do you think you are doing?" Lucinda let go of Colette, Colette tilted her head slightly and a small smile appread on it.

"Ah, my self righteous cousin. I hadn't seen you. How is your GIRLfriend?" Lucinda shook her head.

"Glad to see that you will not change anytime soon." Lucinda addressed Alex and Velika.

"Ivetta and I have decided to go back to the girl's dorm, as the conversation with her father was also going so smoothly. I actually wanted to ask you if you wanted to come with us?" Velika glanced at Alex who nodded.

"The party is a bit ruined. Colette I'll see you on your big day."

VELIKA WALKED TOWARDS the entrance of the gym with Lucinda by her arm. When these flew open, Velika's father was walking through the doorway.

"Father?" He didn't look at her, several men entered the gym behind him. "Father, what is this?" Her father still didn't look at her.

"Where's Headmaster Dracul!" He grabbed something from his back, to her horror it was a crossbow. Loaded and well, he looked across the room and his eyes fell on Lucinda, but also the bow. "Well where is he?" Velika took a few steps forward.

"Headmaster Dracul is talking to a student. father." Only now did he look at her, but there was no trace

"Well that's nice then. Since that leech is a noble." Velikas looked at him in surprise.

"What are you talking about, father?" Her father put his finger on the trigger.

"You have nothing to do with that. Velika." She stepped infront of Lucinda, so that the crossbow was aimed at her. He wouldn't shoot his own daughter, would he?

"Well, since you are attacking my school with whoever these man are and aiming a crossbow at my friends. I think I have the right to know." Her father laughed.

"That is the Lazar fire in you. Maybe you are not quite a failure after all. These men behind me are all men of our family. And we are here to finish what our ancestor King Mathéo Lazar failed to do. Eradicating the vampire race." Velika looked at her father, her heart felt hollow.

"What?"

"You heard me, daughter. I sent you here so you could learn more about our history and deduce the vampires. Something that has succeeded masterfully. I must confess with pride." The hollow feeling grew, she had never had a good relationship with her father. But that he would use her like that was just nauseous. "Why do you look at me with such disdain, daughter? Did you really think I would just send you to a leech school, without a good reason?"

"It was founded by Vanessa Lazar, our ancestor. So it is also my school. And King Mathéo was not our ancestor, Crown Prince Armand Barnier was." Her father shook his head.

"I knew you're weak. Maybe that's my fault. But you may gain strenght in time. Men aim your arrows at the Barnier boy!" The others did as he said.

"Father, please don't do this!" But her father aimed his bow at Alex. Velika ran towards him until a shot of pain shot through her body.

"No!" Alex's voice buzzed in her ears as she sagged. "Velika!" He knelt by her, pulled something out of her back and held the arrow from her father's bow in his hands. "How can you, she is your flesh and blood!" His eyes filled with tears.

"Richard, what have you done!" Her mother's voice buzzed around the room. "My little girl! Men of Lazar, take that fool."

"Lara, that's your husband!" said one of the men, Velika couldn't see which one.

"And that's my daughter! My flesh and blood as that leech called her. So do what I tell you before I lose my patience with you." Velika heard her father scream. She wanted to see what was happening, but her vision blurred. "Well what are you standing there now. Is there a doctor in the room. My daughter is bleeding out here."

18

Alex-Lucas walked back and forth like a madman. Dr. Kraus had denied him and the rest of the group of friends access to the infirmary. Nirrox sighed and held Colette's hands. Nadia held her father's. Every so often she asks him if he can go inside to have a look. Something that Vance contradicts.

"If I go in, I'll distract Dr. Krauss. Nadia." Ivetta sat on the floor, her eyes flushed, with Lucinda rocking her back and forth.

"Okay, Alex-Lucas, calm down!" Nirrox released Colette's hand and took hold of him.

"Doctor Krauss is doing what he can, but you have to be strong for Velika." Alex-Lucas shook his head.

"I should have been there, I should be the one in there fighting for my life. That carzy man aimed at me, and she, without thinking jumps..." He couldn't finishes his sentence, Nirrox came towards him and laid a simple hand on his shoulder.

"This just goes to show how much she loves you. She told me during our dance that she loves you so much that she will let you go if necessary." Alex-Lucas eyes filled up with tears.

"Did she say that?" Nirrox nodded and pulled him into his arms. "She has that little brother. She has."

"NIRROX WHY IS YOUR brother crying like a baby?" Immediately Nirrox released him.

281

"Father, what are you doing here?" Alex-Lucas swallowed his tears and looked at his father, with long black hair tied back with a cotton ribbon. His green eyes were much different from his own and Nirrox's eyes. Their father planted his fists in his hips.

"Don't talk nonsense, son. When I heard of the Lazar family who entered the school and opened fire on one of my boy's, I dropped everything at the hostpital and came straight this way. Only here I see that both my boys are fine, so Nirrox inform me." Nirrox told that Velika jumped for Alex-Lucas, their father nodded.

"Your brother is right, Alex-Lucas. That is a sign of love that characterizes the Lazars. Queen Vanessa was safe within the walls of this school, but when she saw Armand being led to the firepile. She sacrificed herself, because she couldn't bear to life without him. She left her children with Lady Helena, whom she raised as her own." His father looked at the closed door. "Well, let me help the good school doctor." Their father walked past them through the doors of the infirmary. Alex-Lucas looked at Nirrox.

"I guess you didn't know the part of Vanessa's sacrifice either?" Nirrox shook his head.

"Nope. Otherwise I would have told you." Colette put a hand on Nirrox shoulder.

"I'm a doctor in training so I'm going to see what I can do to help." Nirrox nodded and Colette also disappeared into the infirmary.

"They are going in without permission of Dr. Kraus, why are you not going in father?"

"I am not a doctor or one in training, Nadia. I am an overrated teacher." Nirrox sighed and pulled Alex-Lucas with him to the wall.

"Father and my future wife are now with her, what you are going to do now little brother is sit and get some rest." Alex-Lucas did as he had said and saw how his brother now turned to Nadia. "Nadia I know we haven't finished our conversation, and the most important thing hasn't even being said." Alex-Lucas looked at his brother in surprise, why did he choose this moment to talk to Nadia? "Shall we sit down, all we can do is wait. So we better finish that conversation." Nadia nodded and sighed.

"Nirrox, you know how I have felt for the past year." Nirrox sat down next to Alex-Lucas and Nadia across from him.

"I know Nadia and you should know that I regret it. I should have talked to you before the ball. My feelings for you were never really that deep as seemingly your feelings for me. And what can I say, when Lucinda introduced me to Colette, I immediately knew she was the one." Nadia hung her head.

"By the way, do you want to know why I was so angry with you?" He shook his head.

"Yes, I betrayed you. I was kissing another woman. " Nadia picked up her bag and reached for it.

"That was only part of the story." She took out a box. "When I went looking for you I wanted to ask you something." She opened the box and a simple gold ring with the symbol of the Dracul engraved on it.

"Oh, Nadia. I really didn't know I was so deep in your heart." Nirrox looked at him. "Did you know?" Alex-Lucas shook his head, but then nodded.

"I '*borrowed*' one of your rings for the size. She only dind't say for what it was. I taught it was for your birthday." Nirrox looked puzzled.

"By my soul, how could i being so blind." Nadia closed the box and a tear escaped her eye and rolled down her cheek. "Nadia, if I knew what you were up to, I would have talked you out of it." Nirrox took Nadia's hand and sighed. "I am very, very sorry Nadia. I don't know what else to say." Nadia pulled her hands free.

"Have you ever loved me?" Nirrox lowered his head slightly.

"Yes I loved you, but not in that deeply. Not in the sense that I would say yes to your question."

"So you used me?" Nirrox looked straight at her.

"No, I never used you, Nadia. Like I said I just didn't love you enough. Not the way I love Colette. Or Alex-Lucas loves Velika." Alex-Lucas knew he was serious, Nadia looked away from him.

"It's easier to think you've used me. Than you didn't love me enough." Nirrox gave her a smile that she did not see.

"I understand what you mean."

ALEX-LUCAS DIDN'T KNOW when it happened, but it was certain that he had fallen asleep. His head leaned against Nirrox's shoulder. As the doors of the infirmary flew open, Velika's mother stormed out. Tears were in her eyes, his heart stopped beating.

"Mrs. Lazar?" He got up and walked to the woman with long blond hair and light blue eyes, she looked a lot like Velika. The woman looked at him and gave him a watery smile.

"You're the boy my daughter risked her life for." He nodded.

"I would have done the same for her, ma'am. But how is she?" The woman burst into tears. He shook his head and looked through the open doors at his father. Who was washing his hands, his father looked up and beckoned him.

"Alex-Lucas come here son." Although his heart still wasn't beating, he walked slowly into the infirmary. Until he stood with his father.

"Father please tell me she's still alive."

"Alex?" Her voice was weak, his heart started to beat again as he walked up to her.

"Velika." Her pale face and her shaky arm startled him as she reached out to him. He grabbed it as quickly as he could and got as close to her as possible.

"Son, now that you are here, I want to tell you what is going on. Velika Lazar lost a lot of blood, the point of the arrow was poisonous.

And that's why it took so long. But to our great regret we have to say that Velika doesn't have much time left." Alex-Lucas squeezed Velika's hand gently.

"Father please tell me it isn't. I just found her, in this lifetime. I am not ready to lose her, again." His father put a hand on his shoulder.

"I would love to tell you what you are wanting to hear, but then I would be lying to you and that is the last thin that I want, and what you need." His father sighed. "There is only one other option, it is a risky procedure." Alex-Lucas looked at his father.

"What is it?"

"We could give her vampire blood, but that would mean she's slowly turning into one of us. But I have to warn you, if her body doesn't accept the blood then it's the end of the story." Alex-Lucas looked back at the woman on the operating table.

"She is not yet eighteen, what does her mother say?"

"She thinks that the choice is yours, especially since you two are engaged." Alex-Lucas looked at Velika and swallowed, it was not his choice either. It was her life, her choice.

"What do you say?" He preferred to keep her with him for as long as possible. She opened her mouth.

"I say why not." Why didn't her answer surprise him. She has proven herself several times that she was stronger than she looked.

"Are you sure?" His father walked around the bed and looked her straight in the eye. And she nodded., a small smile appeared opun his father's face. She had earned his respect.

"Well, let's get started. Alex-Lucas you will be the donor so sit here in this chair."

His father patted the chair next to him. Alex-Lucas did as his father said.

"Can you take off your jacket and shirt?" It was Colette who asked this of him, he shrugged.

Not much later the red liquid ran through the thin wire to her veins. She herself had fallen asleep. Colette had given him a Bloodberry juice to keep up his strength. While he drank it, his father put a hand on his shoulder.

"You are strong my son, just like your grandfathers. Alex and Lucas who you are named after. But take your rest." Alex-Lucas put the empty cup on the side table and closed his eyes.

19

The voices were weak, or was Velika the one who was weak. That was something she wasn't sure, but she could distinguish Alex's father's voice from her mother's.

"The acquisition of blood seems to be catching on. Your daughter has a strong soul Lara Lazar."

"Tell me something I don't know, leech." Velika felt the hate from her mother's voice on her skin.

"Come on Lara we are almost family. Your daughter is engaged to my youngest son and according to our traditions he can take her last name. Which means the Lazar name doesn't end with her.

"So you finally have our name in your hands. Something you allways wanted."

"Come on Lara, don't forget who raised your forefathers. You should know that we don't want to include your name. But this was the only way to save your daughter." She heard her mother sigh, something took her hand.

"You are right Jorin Barnier. But you also know that the rest of my family will no longer accept her. She has already been looked at with a slanted eye for being a girl, but now she will be disowned for being a vampire and will never be accepted by the vampires for being once human. She is littarly stuck between both worlds."

"There you have a point, Lara, but I'll do what I can to protect her. You have my word." The grip on Velika's hand strengthened.

"I know that." Then the grip slackened and the hand holding hers let go.

"Lara, where are you going? She will be waking up soon, will you not say goodbye."

"I can't, Jorin. I can't say goodbye to her. It will hurt to much."

"She's not dead, she's still alive."

"She is dead in the eyes of my family, in their eyes Richard shot his own daughter and she died on this table. Which means that I am not allowed to see her anymore."

"You can always see her, that hasn't changed."

"Jorin I cannot go against the believes of my family, take good care of her." A door closed and that was the end of the conversation, Velika's closed eyes stung with tears.

"Hopefully you caught all that?" The voice of Jorin Barnier, the father of Alex and Nirrox, sounded very close now. She nodded with difficulty. "This doesn't mean she doesn't love you anymore."

"I know, it's not nice to hear it." She slowly opened her eyes and looked straight into his green eyes, although the color was different from Nirrox and Alex's. She could immediately see that the man was their father.

"Well Velika Lazar, I will then pay Vance a visit and tell you that whatever happens to you. He needs to contact me. You will be under my protection until my death and then under that of my sons. You are the daughter my wife has always wished for, but never got." He walked away from the bed.

"Mr. Barnier?" He turned to her, the look in his eyes soft and warm.

"What is it?" She gave him a smile.

"Nothing special I just wanted to thank you." He nodded and bowed slightly.

"It's no trouble at all. Princess Lazar."

VELIKA HAD DOZED OFF again, because when she opened her eyes again, Alex had disappeared from his place. Nirrox satin the chair instead.

"If you are wondering where my brother is, I have to report that I sent him to his room. The poor soul couldn't even move his little pinky anymore." Velika slowly scrambled to her feet, causing Nirrox to bolt to her feet to push her back into the pillow.

"Not so fast, *princess*. Your body is still heeling from the poison and your transformation. So give it some time." Her stomach immediately started to grunt and Nirrox looked at it in surprise.

"Well you haven't eaten anything since the ball and you've been under for three days so that your stomach is protesting so loudly doesn't surprise me." She sighed.

"Is it Friday?" Nirrox nodded and a smile appeared on his face.

"Don't worry about your lessons. They did not start again after the attack on the Bloodmoonball. Most parents have temporarily removed their children from school. Even though your mother has promised that the Lazars will stay away from the academy." She sighed again, this time with relief.

"I don't know whether to be happy or ashamed, what were they doing here anyway?"

Nirrox sat down again.

"They were invited by Vance Dracul. He's been trying to find a way to bridge the gap between humans and vampires for ages." Velika narrowed her eyes, Nadia might have told this a few times already.

"Now I feel guilty." When she opened her eyes she saw that Nirrox was looking at her with a tilted head.

"Why, if I may ask?" She looked at her hands, which were trembling violently.

"All vampires that I have met, have been so open, there are a few exceptions ofcourse. And my family throws a spanner in the works with that wonderful idea." Nirrox had risen again and was now taking her hand.

"Your father probably misunderstood the invitation." She nodded, against her better judgment.

"Ah, you are awake." Velika looked up. Jorin entered the infirmary, followed closely by Colette.

"How do you feel?" Colette put the back of her hand on Velika's forehead, who shrugged.

"Hungry but otherwise good." Nirrox laughed.

"You should have heard her stomach, my Angel of the Night. It growled at me like an angry mama bear." Velika felt her cheeks flush.

"Nirrox don't tease her that much." Nirrox immediately stopped laughing and lowered his head slightly.

"As you wish, father." This made both Colette and Velika giggle. Jorin picked up a table and rolled it over to Velika's bed.

"Velika, I have brought two kinds of food with me." He put a plate of chips on the table. "As you can see, this are fries and the red sauce is Bloodberry sauce. Then I also have this simple." He put a cup of red juice on the table. "You should actually drink the juice, but the fries can run off a bit. Because you have transformed from human to vampire, at the age of seventeen. I don't knowin what stage your body is in right now. As you undoubtedly know, a vampire's body repels human food by the age of eighteen and we completely transition to blood berry juice or plain blood." She nodded and desperately grabbed some fries from the plate and dipped it in the sauce. She quickly put it in her mouth, feeling a little uncomfortable when three pairs of eyes followed each movement intently. Velika let on off the fries float infront of her mouth.

"Mr. Barnier, have you heard anything from my mother?" Jorin Barnier, almost bursting with tension, nodded.

"She sent me an invitation to your farewell ceremony. With a friendly request not to take you with me." Valika took a bite of the fries, the iron taste of the sauce dominating her mouth. She swallowed it and waited a few seconds before reaching for the cup of juice.

"I won't ask why that is. Are you going?" Jorin nodded and relaxed slightly.

"If you want me to go, I'll go. It is a day after the wedding on a Wednesday." Velika put a few more chips in her mouth and looked at Nirrox and Colette.

"I almost forgot about that. Sorry." Colette gave her a smile.

"That doesn't matter, you had something else on your mind, like. O I don't know, staying alive." Velika frowned for a moment, why was Colette so nice to her? "I'm sorry, by the way, I was pretty awful to you at the ball. That cannot be justified, but I am going to try it anyway. Nirrox often unintentionally talks about his time here at school and with Nadia. When he went to talk to her that night, I was afraid that he would go back to her. I was frustrated and I took that out on you."

"Do I really talk about Nadia that often?" Nirrox looked puzzled at Colette and she nodded.

"Which is not surprising since you two grew up together. That's something you shouldn't forget about Colette. Although my son chose you, he still has a past. In addition, I am glad that he talked to her. From what I understood, Nadia planned to propose to him until she found you two. So you can understand how she felt." Velika saw Colette look in surprise at Nirrox and she nodded.

"It also surprised me, we had never really talked about it. But the air between use is cleared now, at least I think so." He looked back now to clearly not comfortable with the subject. "Are you done eating, you know what Colette why don't you sit here and keep Velika company while I go get us some drinks."

"So now that we are alone, what did you want to talk about?" Velika gave Colette a smile.

"Well, since you are about to get married, what about the dress and flowers. You know the usual stuff. Maybe I'll borrow some ideas from you." Colette laughed.

"You won't get much out of me, because my mother has planned it all. And since I will become miss Barnier it will be a big party, with a lot of fuss." Velika started to chuckle.

"Then tell me what your dream wedding looks like." Colette sighed.

"It's actually quite simple. A ceremony in the presence of friends and immediate family. A simple white dress. I know, it's pretty boring. " Velika shook her head.

"That's not it. Do you have a picture of your dress?" Colette nodded and reached for her phone.

"That was all I had a say on." Velika looked at the photo of a simple dress that looked a lot like her ball gown. Only this one had sleeves.

"It's beautiful." Colette sighed.

"To be honest, I picked this one when I saw your dress." Velika shrugged and gave Colette a smile.

"Glad I was able to help with that."

"I AM BACK, SO WHAT have you talked about? Wait, let me guess, the wedding and the dress." Nirrox entered and placed two cups of juice on the table.

"Father is talking to Dr. Krauss. Poor man, it mustn't be easy to have a famous doctor in the infirmary. Anyway, back to the wedding. It is a vampire tradition that the female member of grooms' family is witnesses for the bride. Since that female member of my family has died, that was not possible. But you are engaged to my little brother and my father has offered to be your guardian. These are all reasons that make you eligible for the job." Colette nodded in agreement.

"The only thing Nirrox forgets to say is that it is also a tradition after a woman is asked to be married, that she get married as soon as possible. Preferably a few weeks after the proposel." Velika looked at Colette and shook her head.

"No, I know where you want to go with this. But it's your big day." Colette looked at Nirrox and he nodded.

"Colette has been grumbling for a while about her mother, who wants to turn her big day into a spectacle. Just because she marries a noble." Colette nodded in agreement.

"My mother wouldn't mind adding another bride to that ceremony." Velika sighed.

"I want to talk to Alex about it first if you don't mind." The couple nodded and Velika was afraid that even when Alex said no, they wouldn't have a choise.

20

This is not what Alex-Lucas expected, yet he stood next to his brother at the altar. Alex-Lucas was surprised when he entered the infirmary a few days ago and Velika told him what Nirrox and Colette were up to. Actually it made sense as it was indeed tradition, but Velika hadn't fought for her life to get married so that sher could get married after three days. His brother pierced him in the side with an elbow.

"Don't worry, you're probably not the youngest to ever take the vow of everlasting faithfulness." Alex-Lucas pushed Nirrox slightly.

"That's not what I was thinking about, but you're probably right in that area." Nirrox chuckled for a moment.

"You should have been there when Colette introduced Velika to her mother and told her you asked her." Alex-Lucas chuckled with him.

"Velika has tried as best as possible to describe it."

"What are you laughing about?" Their father's question chided them, and the chuckles died away.

"I was just talking about Colette's mother and how she almost snapped with excitement when she heard there was another bride in attendance." His father nodded and almost chuckled himself.

"That was a funny sight indeed. But straighten your backs, because the brides are coming." Their father had not yet spoken when the wedding march had already started by the orchestra. Alex-Lucas looked around quickly to push the nerves aside. The ceremony took place outside the school on a large field. They were surrounded by trees covered with Spanish moss and wires with lights were hung between the moss, to give it a fairytale feeling. Several members of his own family and that of Colette sat on the wooden chairs. And some friends from school.

"Alex-Lucas, stop dreaming and look at your bride she is absolutely stunning." Nirrox hissed through his teeth. Alex-Lucas did as his brother said and looked at Velika, his heart stopped beating and he had to do his best not to let his mouth drop. Velika was wearing a simple dress without sleeves. On the skirt hung a transparent fabric that dragged on the floor. Her hair was the same as at the ball, she had gold rings in her ears. Around her neck she had a white chocker and the pendant he had given her. In her hands she had a bouquet filled with red and white roses. She had a smile on her face from ear to ear. But what suprises him even more that Nirrox had the time, Because Colette also looked very enchanting. His father put a hand on his shoulder and that awoke him from his thoughts. Alex-Lucas took a quick step forward and reached out his hand towards Velika.

"I Alex-Lucas of the Barnier family offer you my hand to Velika of the Lazar family."

He came up and saw in her eyes that she had forgotten her lines, he formed the words with his mouth and she nodded.

"I, Velika of the Lazar family, give my hand to Alex-Lucas of the Barnier family. Thank you." He nodded and took her hand.

"No problem." Carefully he pulled her along and his brother walked forward and repeated the gesture. When they were both in place, his father cleared his throat.

"Friends, family. I am here before you with these two couples so that they can take the vow of everlasting faithfulness before our very eyes. But before we start I want to know one thing Alex-Lucas, my son. You are the second of my line and therefore you can take your bride's last name." Alex-Lucas nodded, Velika and he had already talked about this.

"With your blessing, father, I take the name of the Lazar family." His father nodded.

"You have my blessing. Well now the vow of everlasting faithfulnes. Colette Mask and Nirrox Barnier go ahead."

"Bone from my bone, flesh from my flesh. I am yours and you are mine. I will honor you in your strength and assist you in your weakness. Until the end of time." Colette and Nirrox said in unison.

"Wonderfull." His father took over. "Well now Velika and Alex-Lucas now it's up to you."

"Bone from my bone, flesh from my flesh. I am yours and you are mine. I will honor you in your strength and assist you in your weakness. Until the end of time."

"Again, wonderfull. May I have the rings of our ring lady?" Alex-Lucas looked up at Nadia from her chair. In her hands she held a white pillow with four rings.

"Nadia from the Dracul family, give the rings of everlasting faithfulness to Nirrox Barnier and Colette Barnier." Nirrox and Colette took their rings from the pillow. Nirrox took Colette's left hand and put the ring to her ring finger.

"With this ring I accept you as my family. Colette Barnier." And he put the ring on her finger. Colette then took Nirrox's left hand and held the ring to his ring finger.

"With this ring I am joining your family. Nirrox Barnier." Nadia nodded, Alex-Lucas saw the tears in her eyes. She turned to him.

"Nadia from the Dracul family, give the rings of everlasting faithfulness to Alex-Lucas Lazar and Velika Lazar." Velika took the rings from the pillow. Velika took his left hand and held the ring to his finger.

"With this ring I accept you as my family. Alex-Lucas Lazar." With a lot of effort she slipped the ring on his finger, he even had to help her. With a broad smile on his face, he took her left hand and held the ring to her ring finger.

"With this ring I am joining your family. Velika Lazar."

"Then I will declare you husbands and wifes. My sons kiss your brides." His father didn't have to say this twice. Applause arose as he pressed his lips to Velika's.

CONGRATULATIONS!" IVETTA ran to them and flew into Velika's arms. Lucinda followed her friend. Velika hugged Ivetta back.

"Thank you." The two girls let go and Ivetta stepped back. She looked at Alex-Lucas uncertainly and he spread his arms so that she could jump into his too.

"Okay, that's enough. Ivetta. " She immediately let go of him.

"We are sorry, unfortunately we did not have time to buy anything. So we owe you one." Lucinda took Ivetta's hand.

"Come on let's go." Lucinda carefully pulled Ivetta with her. Velika took his hand and sighed.

"Too bad my mother couldn't see this." He nodded.

"I will go to the ceremony with my father tomorrow, then I will take today's photos." She squeezed his hand gently.

"Thank you." He could see that she wanted to come as well, but she knew that she couldn't and he hated to see his new wife like this. Hopefully she could enjoy the rest of their day together.

THE NEXT MORNING ALEX-Lucas stood outside the gate to wait for his father. He was holding the light blue photo album in a light brown paper package. His father's black car stopped in front of him, the backseat door flew open and Nirrox poked his head out.

"Get in, little brother. We are a bit late already. Which is my fault." Alex-Lucas got in and the car pulled away. "What is that?" Nirrox pointed to the album.

"I promised Velika that I would give her mother our wedding album." Nirrox frowned slightly.

"How do you get that album so quickly? Colette and I needed to wait a month to see ours." Alex-Lucas shrugged slightly.

"Nadia, who else is capeble to get things done quickly. She and I believed that every mother should have the chance to see her daughter in white." A slight smile appeared on his face. He watched his father look at him from the rearview mirror.

"You were right about that, my son." It didn't take long for his father to park the car. "We are here. I don't have to tell you that we will be the only vampires after Vance. So behave. " Nirrox groaned a little.

"Father, we are both married men." His father nodded.

"I know that, but that doesn't change your behavior. Nirrox." Before Nirrox could respond, their father got out of the car. Nirrox looked at him and he shrugged. Before he got out of the car himself. He followed his father next to Nirrox as he walked into the room.

"Mr. Barnier, thank you and your sons for coming." Velika's mother walked over to them.

"Lara, it was really no problem. By the way, I did what you asked for." Her mother nodded a little.

"How did she react?" His father shrugged.

"She took it like an adult, with saying that she understandand, not showing the pain that it those to her. But on the other hand, she was completely exhausted yesterday." Her mother tilted her head slightly. Alex-Lucas stepped forward and held out the album.

"If you see this madam, you will understand what my father means." She took the album and took off the paper. She opened it, on the first page was a picture of Velika in her wedding dress.

"You two are married. My little girl, she looks so beautiful. "

"Lara, let's get started." Richard, Velika's father walked up to them. Alex-Lucas couldn't hide the shiver that went through his spine. This was the man that tried to shoot him.

"Richard look." She held the album out to him, he looked for a moment, then closed it.

"Don't fill your head with delusional human ideas. Our daughter died a week ago while protecting this boy." He pointed to Alex-Lucas."What are those leeches actually doing here?" Lara straightened her back.

"I invited them, Jorin is now her guardian until she is eighteen." Richard glared at his wife. Tha hatered was clearly visable.

"What do you want me to do thank him. You're crazy woman."

"Not as crazy as a father who shoots his own daughter, I think." Nirrox said bit. Their father wanted to argue, but Nirrox shook his head.

"No father. I don't want hear that I have to behave. I don't care that he talks to us with such disdain. But I do care if he speaks with great disdain about his own daughter." Lara nodded and looked straight at her husband.

"Nirrox Barnier is right, Richard. We are here because our family wants to believe that Velika is dead, because of your actions. So you can only put your hand into your own bosom. Well, let's get started. The sooner I can put my nose back into this wedding album."

THE CEREMONY WAS SHORT but sweet. With a few speeches from the family, Velika was simply talked out of their family. In the end, Vance Dracul took a place behind the microphone, Alex-Lucas had not seen him before he did that.

"Velika Lazar, like any new student, she was looking for her place in my school. In a way I was proud of the strength she showed when she found this strenght, and I had hoped she would keep that place for the rest of her term. Yet her human life came to an abrupt end, much to my regret. Still, I want to compliment her parents for their hard work. They raised a strong young woman, something that as a father I would be proud of." Alex-Lucas knew this was a sneer in the direction of Richard Lazar. After the service, Lara got up and walked over to Alex-Lucas.

"May I?" He nodded and she hugged him.

"Take good care of my little girl and thank you for the album Alex-Lucas Barnier." She let go off him and he gave her a soft smile.

"Lazar, I have taken my wives family name." A watery smile appeared on her face. She opened her mouth to say something to him...

"Lara, what are you doing with that *leech*." Richard grabbed her, but she pulled herself free again.

"If he's a *leech,* then what are you? I lost her thanks to you." Richard pointed to him. "Don't blame him for your own shortcomings, yes she jumped infront of him. But that was because she loves him. You pulled the trigger after all." Richard dropped his finger. Alex-Lucas briefly looked between Velika's two parents.

"Mrs. Lazar, don't worry. I'll do my best to make her happy." He bowed for a moment, then walked past the two.

"What does he mean by that?"

"My son means that he will do his utmost to take care of his wife." Alex-Lucas was surprised that it was his father who said it and not Nirrox. "And if you want to excuse me. I have go and bring him to her, it is not healty for newly weds to be sepereated for long." Alex-Lucas couldn't hide the smile that appeared on his face and this smile stayed there until he was in the car. "I am proud off you two. You stood your ground, even against my wises." Alex-Lucas and Nirrox looked at each other, with mouths wide open. Did there father just said he was proud of them. "Do not get used to it." Siad his father before he started the car.

THE CAR STOPPED IN front of the school gate, Alex-Lucas looked at it. The gate that tried to keep the outside world out of the school. Two weeks ago, his bride had been in her parents' car. Getting ready for the unknown adventure that awaited her.

"Well little brother, what are you waiting for, go to her." His brother almost pushed him through the door.

"Give me a moment Nirrox." He took a breath before opening the door and got out. His father hit the horn before driving away.

"Welcome back." He looked straight into his wife's light blue eyes. He nodded and took her hand.

Curse of the Ancestors

1

Kailey wakes up with a cry, a shiver ran through her spine. Her heart was still beating in her throat and her whole body was covered with a layer of sticky sweat. Kailey pulled her hands from under already thin sheets and examined them closely, there was no blood as she had just seen in her dreaming. She slowly shook her head, to keep her mind clear. No, it wasn't a dream it was a nightmare, a nightmare she had to live with for the rest of her life. The door of the room opened and two young men came in, one with dyed green hair and another with black and crimson hair lights. The latter lingered in the doorway while the green-haired one walked over to Kailey. He carefully sat on the edge of the bed.

"Kailey, are you all right?" Kailey looked at him in surprise. Nick was only one year older than her, but with that look in his eyes she would estimate him older. She nodded fleetingly, but he already knew it was a lie.

"It was just a nightmare, I'm sorry if I woke you up." She glanced at Realm who shook his head.

"Kailey, you don't have to apologize for anything, what happened to you. Let's just say it's still pretty frightening."

"You mean that Alexandra tried to kill me." Nick pressed his lips together, Kailey knew it was a touchy subject, he was a vampire and she was a member of a vampire hunter family that strangely has the same ancestor as Nick. But that never hurt her relationship with cousin Nick, as she'd called him. "Don't forget Alexandra was my best friend and I did what I could to prevent..." Nick took her hand and squeezed it gently.

"You don't have to tell me that, Kailey. Of all the hunters I know, the van Helsing family isn't really known for being bloodthirsty vampire killers. So don't worry." Kailey pulled her hand lose and sighed, Nick looked at his boyfriend, Realm and then looked back again at her. Kailey also looked at Realm for a moment, she had heard his story from her father and if she was honest she would had condemned him. But now that she knew him and heard his music, her opinion of him had changed completely.

"Nick, maybe we can talk about this tomorrow. She had a nightmare, just like we've had. She need's to live with her trauma and it doesn't help if we, like two worried parents are keep floating away from her." Kailey struggled not to laugh, it wasn't what Realm said, but the way he said it. He took a few steps into the room and bumped into a cardboard box, hissed and released a curse. "I'd be happy if those night vision rumors turned out to be true, and I can't wait for these boxes to be gone." Kailey's smile faded and her demeanor darkened.

"Realm." Nick reproved and Realm raised his hands. Kailey forced a smile and looked at Realm.

"It's okay, I know he didn't mean he wanted me out. But I can't say I'm looking forward to going to vampire school. I know it's a good school, but it won't take way that I will be surrounded with..."

"Leeches, Vamps, bloodsucking demons. How many other names do vampire hunters for our kind?" Said Nick and she shrugged, she never listened to that kind name calling. She look at Realm again, she had stayed in their small apartment after her father told that she was changing schools, that was even before Alexandra attacked her. The assault on Kailey's life and the fact that she had to take Alexandra's life to save hers hadn't changed her father's mind.

"I think Realm is right. I really need some more sleep. Tomorrow I'm going to a new school full of new challenges." She tried to sound cheerful but they didn't look convinced. But they left the room nonetheless, Nick closed the door with one last worried look. Kailey laid down on her back, looking up to the white plastered sailing. It was not difficult to geuss what was on her mind. Alexandra and the Red Tempest Academy. Before her father had told her she would go to the Red Tempest Academy, she was a student at the Hunters Conservatory, a school for the future generation vampire hunters. But after what happened with Alexandra she didn't want to go back to that school either. She closed her eyes and sighed, maybe vampire school wasn't so bad idea after all.

A SOFT KNOCK ON KAILEY'S door let her know it was time to get up, she hasitated for a moment this was her last night's sleep. The Red Tempest Academy was a night school, slowly she got up and stretched out. Kailey's gaze went through the early sunlight-lit room, her gaze caught on the garment bag containing her school uniform. Realm had picked it up for her the day before, so she could try it on and to her great regret it was the perfect fit. Both Nick and Realm had told her that she had to wear this uniform every time she left her dorm, what a retarded old-fashioned custom. Still, she went to the garment bag and unzipped it. Another knock on her door, this time it was a ferm one.

"Come in." Kailey pulled her ponytail straight and looked from the mirror to the door, which opened slowly, Nick entered the room.

"Hey Kailey, did you get some sleep?" Kailey couldn't help, but to hear Realm's words about worried parents in her head.

"Yes, father." Nick looked pained, but still laughed. He walked farther into the room and sat on her bed.

"Yes, yes. I know, I act more than a parent than a peer." Kailey walked over to him and sat down on the bed next to him. "It was nice to have you in my apartment, which is not build for three young adults."He sighed and looked at Kailey "Still, you wish that it was not necessary." Kailey nodded slowly.

"But Nick, you and Realm welcomed me with open arms at the beginning of the summer, my parents could have sent you to your parents too." Nick's face twisted slightly, and Kailey knew why. In the family it was known that Nick's parents had fierce arguments and that only the vampire's customs kept them from a divorce. Nick had explained it to her a few times when they were younger, and yet she had to admit that it sounded strange to her. Her parents had being divorced, because her father believed in the peace between vampires and human, and her mother did not. Kailey sighed, feeling a bit down thinking her parents split up, it was time for another topic. "So, one which time are we going to your school?" Nick smiled at her, noticing the change of subject.

"It's no longer my school, I graduated last year. Remember?" Kailey nodded. "But Realm asked me the same thing this earlier and I was thinking we will bring you there after lunch." He took his eyes off her and looked at the stack of boxes in the room, which had been there since she came to stay with them and hadn't been opened either. "Are you sure you have everything?" He had asked that question several times, Kailey knew why. Last year he met Realm and finally came out of the closet, but as soon as he took the step. He, Nathalia and Realm were kidnapped by Realm's lunatic of a father, Mikan Stryder, who had miraculously escaped the hunters, *again*. Later that year, Velika Lazar, a human girl and friend of Kailey's, joined thevampires of the Red Tempest Academy and the school was attacked by the Lazar family during the annual Bloodmoonball. Velika was shot by her own father while trying to protect her boyfriend, Alex-Lucas Barnier. Kailey could rightly understand that it had left a everlasting impression on the now eighteen-year-old Nick. She slapped her bare legs with her flat hands. Right away she wished that she had not done that, she felt her bare skin burning under her hands.

"Yes Nick, like I told you before. I have everything and if I don't have something I have my father's permission to order it online." Nick was visibly unconvinced, Kailey always praised herself for her patience. But even that had it's limits and it slowly came into view. "Nick." He blinked a few times and gave her a thin smile.

"Come on, let's have breakfast. Then you can listen to Realm when he talks about his music education again. Or again about that song that he recorded, you know the one that has being on the radio a view times." Kailey sighed, she knew which song Nick meant, but she was not sure if that was an improvement. Yet at the same time they got up and left the bedroom. Realm was already waiting for them at a small round table. There were three plates on the table, Kailey looked in surprise at the plate on her place. There was a small white box on it, she looked at Nick who was not hiding his smile well. She sat down and pointed to the box.

"What is this?" Realm chuckled.

"That's a little white box." Kailey sighed and picked up the box, carefully opening it. In the box was a gold chain with a gold pendant attached to it. The pendant was engraved with a tiger, the sign of the Lumina family. She frowned at the piece of jewelry, which looked old, she looked at Nick with a small frown.

"Why are you giving me a family pendant? You're not proposing to me, are you?" Nick laughed and shook his head.

"No, by my soul, Kailey that is... why would you ask me...? You know what never mind. Kailey do not forget that we are family somewhere at the bottom of the bloodline and this pendant symbolishes that." Kailey carefully took the jewelry out of the box and held it up. Nick was right on the bottom of the bloodline they were family, which meant she had vampire blood somewhere far away. "In addition to what it symbolishes, this pendant belonged to our common ancestor, Sediana Lumina." Kailey looked at Nick from the hanger and pressed her lips together. Did she deserve this pendant? Nick had probably seen the doubt on her face and got up. He held out his hand and she handed the pendant over to Nick. "Kailey, you've got the white tiger's blood in your veins. If you're cornered, you'll fight back. That means in my humble opion that you deserve this pendant." Nick said as he hung the pendant on her. The cold precious metal felt strange, yet she felt a weird sense of pride.

"Thank you." She said when Nick was back and he gave her one short nod.

"No problem."

2

L eo got out of the car with a big sigh, it was Sunday evening and the first lessons of his senior year were due to start tomorrow. According to his sister, this feeling would never be forgotten, the strange mixture of relief and despair. Leo's gaze darkened slightly as he remembered his beautiful sister. Who could have predicted that she could no longer be there and all because she had been murdered by a vampire hunter. No, she wasn't a vampire hunter yet, she was the daughter of hunters and according to his parents one of the better hunter families. But that couldn't say anything about their daughter who had killed their own daughter in cold blood. Leo felt his blood boil in his veins.

"The little lion cub has returned." Leo had walked through the iron gate of the school and hadn't looked back. Galakrond stepped out of the shadows into the dim sunlight, the boy with his half-shaven haircut looking a little to serious to Leo's taste.

"Well it had to happen, Gala the summer will not last forever." Gala nodded in agreement and sighed.

"I'm sorry about Alexandra." Leo clenched his fists if he needed to hear that one more time, he didn't know what to do. Leo strode past Gala to the main building, which provided further access to the rest of the Academy. "Leo, you should know that Kailey..." But Leo didn't listen and walked into the main building without saying a word.

He slammed his bedroom door, it looked exactly as he had left it. Except for the thick layer of dust. He threw an old weekend bag on the bed, immediately thick cloud of dust rose up. As fast as he could, he ran to the window and slid it open, maybe he should get his room cleaned up before this school year started. He was slightly horrified at the idea, but which other choice did he have. Head bowed and shoulders slumped, he walked to the cleaning shed, where he pulled out a bucket and some dusters. With that in hand, he walked to the bathroom to get water.

THE SCHOOL YEAR HADN'T even started and his laundry basket was already filled. Leo cursed that the rooms were not cleaned during the holidays, but according to his parents it was to give the students a sense of responsibility, something he didn't see. With the full laundry basket, he marched down the steps of the boy's dorm to the laundry room. To his relief, the laundry room was quiet, probably the other boys hadn't forgotten to bring their laundry home. Something Alexandera teasted him with when the where at home. Still grumbling, he put the laundry in the machine, when he turned the machine on, he gave his thoughts free reins. He was not surprised that his thoughts led to Alexandra, as it had been lately. He tried to remember her last words to him, but unfortunately, as always, he couldn't remember them. The washing machine's bell rang, and he bent down to take out the laundry. He came up and looked out the window, to his surprise he saw Realm and Nick strolling the grounds. Both had a cardboard box in their hands, and Gala was dancing around them like a young puppy. His hands were noticble empty, but Leo didn't pay much attention to the three man. His attention was grabbed by the young girl that followed the three man. Her brown hair was caught in a tight ponytail, he had seen her before. He sourced his mind, hoping that he could remember her. A thought struck him, he knew where he had seen that girl.

"What is she doing here?" he asked no one in particular. The group walked to the teachers' dorm, which had been expanded to Leo's surprise. Why didn't he noticed that before? Maybe he was too much in his own world and now the person who killed his sister walked the school grounds. The anger flared up like a flame that had never really been extinguished. He pressed the button on the dryer and left the laundry room. What was her name again, he was sure his parents told him. But just like Alexandra's last words, he couldn't remember and that was her fault.

THERE WAS A KNOCK ON his door and before Leo could answer the door opened. Realm entered, Leo lay on his unmade bed. He had dumped the weekend bag in the wardrobe.

"What are you doing here?" He snapped at Realm. Realm looked around the room and shrugged.

"Maybe I'm here to see how you are doing. Because, I haven't seen you since the funeral." Leo frowned for a moment, was Realm at the funeral? Then a speck of memory returned to him. Realm was there with her. Leo got up, his blood still boiling.

"It would be better if you leave." But Realm didn't move a mussle. "Are you deaf, I don't want to see your face here anymore. Not yours and Nick's, not now that you've got involved with her."

"With whom, Kailey." Leo's eyes widened, Gala had already mentioned her name earlier. "Leo, I can say by now that I know Kailey very well. She's been living under my roof all summer to get her used to vampires. I have heard her scream every night, because she was plagued by a nightmare."

"That's a good thing, I feel a lot better now that I know she is suffering."

"Leo, Alexandra attacked her. She had no other choise." But Leo didn't butch, he had heared that story all summer. But he didn't believe it.

"That's what she says."

"Yes that is indeed what she says, and I believe her. I have seen her wounds and I hear the fear in her voice when she speaks about that morning." Leo rolled his eyes, likehe cared. He would never see his older sister again, and that was Kailey's fault. Realm had seen this and he sighed. "You know what Leo. I can see you are filled with anger, but don't forget you are not the only one feeling Alexandra's loss." Leo wanted to throw a nasty comment at Realm's head, but Realm already turned away from him and left the room. He knew well that he was not alone in feeling Alexandra's loss, everyone adored her. Not only because she was nice and warm, but also because of her beauty. He was all too often amazed that they were brother and sister by blood. That's why it was so hard for him to comprehend that his sister would attack someone out of nowhere. A knock on the door startled him from his thoughts, but no one entered this time around. Leo walked to the door and pulled it open, there was no one standing there, but what he did see was a basket with his laundry. Someone and he already suspected who, picked it up and delivered it to his room. Leo grabbed the basket and took it into his room.

3

Nick put down the last box from the car into Kailey's dorm room. He looked around briefly and frowned. Kailey looked around too, not knowing what or who Nick was looking for.

"Kailey do you know where Realm is? I haven't seen him in a while." Kailey frowned, too, and shook her head. No, she hadn't seen him since they brought the first boxes to her dorm room. Nick left the room and almost bumped into Realm.

"Wow, it's like we never left." Realm walked into the room. "We met each other several times in the corridors of the boys' dorm." Realm pointed through the window at the building next to hers. "Only this building was then only for the teachers and that was only one year ago." Realm looked around in surprise. "And you have your own bathroom, do luxury. We didn't have that, didn't we Nick."

"Realm where were you?" Nick tried to sound strict, it just didn't work. Realm turned to him, with a brought smile on his face. He had noticed Nick's failed atempt to sound sturn.

"Who me? Well my beloved Nick, I went to see Leo Cormwell. I wanted to know how he was doing. You know about who I am speak, you know Alexandra's shadow?" Kailey stiffened for a moment and looked at Realm with wide eyes. She had heard from Alexandra herself that she had a little brother, but not that he went to school here. Kailey glanced at Nick, who quickly looked away. Did he kept this from her, her hand went to the pendant that hung around her neck. So that is how much he trusted her, he didn't had the guts to tell her, that she was going to school with the younger brother of the person she killed.

"How is he doing?" Kailey was surprised by her own question and Realm looked at her in surprise too. But he looked outside te window to the boy's dorm.

"Well it would be better if you avoided him, Kailey." Kailey nodded that was all the information she needed and could she blame him? She shook her head slowly, no she couldn't.

"Well it's time for us to go or Vance will keep us here, for another year. Kailey heard the forced joke from Nick. He took Realm by the arm and pulled him gently, but surely, out of the room. "We'll come to vistit you when our own collage schedules are convenient." Kailey waved at them, and as they walked the path back to the main building, she had to hold herself back not to run after them.

KAILEY JUST UNFOLDED the last off the boxes, when there was a knock on her door, Kailey's door was open so at least whoever knocked had manners. She looked at the person in the hallway, Kailey straightened her back and straightened her uniform. The girl in the doorway let out a scream that startled Kailey.

"By my soul, you are Kailey van Helsing. Descendant of the most famous vampire hunter Abraham van Helsing. Did you know that your ancestor grew up here." Kailey raised her hands and motioned for the girl to calm down. But that was a futile effort. "I'm sorry, but I'm just so glad to finally meet you. I'm also new by the way, I'm only not a vampire hunter kid like you and the others in this building. But they had no rooms left in the girl's dorm so they gave me instead a room in this dorm. What am I lucky that my room is next the room of a van Helsing. Among all those vampire hunter kids, you already make me feel a lot safer. But when I told my mother this exciting news, she told me that you killed a vampire girl from this school last summer, but I assured her that if it were you wouldn't hurt me because we're friends." Kailey's eyes widened and she raised her hand.

"Wait a second, will you rightly claim that you want to be friends with me. Even if I killed someone of your kind?" The girl who had not yet introduced herself nodded violently.

"Sure why not, silly?"

"I'm a trained killer of vampires and you want to be friends with me, who's crazy here?" Kailey's hand went to her pendant and she sighed, maybe she was a little too hard. This girl was nice and what was she doing, she snapped at her. "I'm sorry the last few months have been agonizing and I don't really think I'm ready to make new friends. But having said that, at least tell me your name? We are neighbors after all." The girl raised her hand to her mouth in alarm.

"Oh, I turned on my rattle without introducing myself. How embarrassing and so me. My name is Alexia from the Crystal family." Kailey nodded.

"Nice to meet you Alexia. But if you don't mind I have to clean up these boxes."

"Oh I don't mind. I even wanted to suggest that I help you with that. I already threw mine away, so I know where the trash cans is." Kailey forced a smile on her face, but the feeling that she was not getting rid of Alexia anytime soon weight heavily on her mind.

"Sure, why not." While Kailey bent down to pick up the boxes, Alexia walked into the room to help her with the boxes.

"Why did you actually kill that vampire girl?" Kailey dropped the boxes she was holding out of her hands. Alexia had seen this and gasped in shock. "I'm sorry, sometimes I talk without thinking. This was one of those times." Kailey picked up the boxes, again and sighed. This will be a long schoolyear.

KAILEY WAS HAPPY TO be able to close the door to her bedroom, she'd managed to shake off Alexia at the trash cans just outside their dorm building. Kailey knew she would get attention for what happened last summer, but she had thought in the negative way. She had definitely not counted on a bouncing ball and flapou like Alexia, who almost praised her for her actions. With a sigh she looked around her room, everything in this room smelled clean and new. Something that would be over after a month unless she kept it tidy. It was strange to see all her things out of the boxes after months. She had packed them in the beginning of the summer after her father told her she was going to this school. He advocated the idea that vampires and vampire hunters should interact from an early age in order to understand each other better. Her mother had disagreed with him, which is why Kailey was staying with Realm and Nick so they could fight it out undisturbed. But Kailey doubted her mother would ever understand her father's logic. These thoughts ran through her mind when her phone rang, she took it from her breast pocket and saw her mother's name on the lit screen.

"If you speak about the Count Dadrick Ventila, there he is." She picked up the phone. "Hey mom... Yes everything is fine here, my dorm room is tidy. I even have a private bathroom, according to cousin Nick that's a rarity... Cousin Nick took good care of me mom... Yes, they had human food... No, Mom for the umpteenth time Realm doesn't drink human blood. He's not his father. Mom I'm a van Helsing and if our family doesn't set a good example who will do it? Yes I sound just like my dad I know. Don't want to say he's wrong... Yes Mom... I'll be careful... Mom I just saw it's almost time for breakfast here... Yes I'm going to catch up tonight... According to Cousin Nick they have good coffee here... That's okay Mom... Talk to you later Mom..." With a deep sigh Kailey hung up the phone. For a moment she doubted who she was trying to convince, her mother or herself. With another sigh she opened her bedroom door and almost bumped into Alexia.

"I'm sorry, I wanted to ask you to go for breakfast?" asked Alexia. Kailey forced a smile on her face again. Why did this girl want to be around her so badly? Was she so warm and inviting without even knowing it.

"Sure, why not." She shouldn't have said that, because Alexia let out a scream again. Several doors opened and vampire hunter children put their heads outside their doors. To see what was happening.

"Is everything okay over there?" asked one of them. Kailey raised her thumb and the vampire hunter kids retreated.

"Alexia let's agree that you don't turn into a guinea pig again." Alexia nodded violently and jumped slowly up and down. Immediately, Kailey doubted Alexia was going to keep this agreement. Plagued with doubts, the two walked the corridors of the brand-new dorm.

4

Leo walked to the cafeteria with his head and shoulders bowed, it was time for breakfast. It felt weird walking around the academy without Alexandra by his side, but that would have been the case anyway. He entered the cafeteria and without looking up or down at the counters overloaded with food for breakfast, without thinking he picked up a cup of Bloodberry Coffee and a few sandwiches with an unknown topping. He will find out what is on there when he put his teeth in them. He sat down at one of the few empty tables and began to eat reluctantly.

"Well wounded lion cub, I heard you were very kind to Realm earlier." Leo looked up and sighed when he saw Gala sat down opposite from him. "But Realm is not the person who would keep it against you. At least as long as you don't lock him up in a basement and force him to drink blood." Gala took a sip his coffee.

"Well Galakrond, he's just as bad as his father. Since he brought her into his house." Gala lowered his cup of coffee slightly. Leo had visibly hit a nerve. Gala had actually met Mikan Stryder so he knew better than Leo. Gala was part of the rescue part that tried to save Realm, Nick and Nathalia Tomes. But instead of rescue anybody they got caught themselves. It was thanks Katrina Link's quick thinking that they were found by the Suits.

"You mean Kailey van Helsing, did you know that she and Nick have the same ancestor Sediana Lumina who married Kailey's ancestor Abraham van Helsing the third, after the first war. The van

Helsing and Lumina families are therefore intimately linked. That is one of the two reasons why Kailey was staying with Nick and Realm during the summer."

"Gala, all good and well. But what good is that information? I just don't care what her family history is, all I want to know is why she's here? I thought we went to vampire school?" Gala slammed the now empty mug onto the table top.

"This is still a vampire school, but the Headmeaster wanted to bring vampires and vampire hunters closer together. Especially if you take last year into account. The two groups were rightly diametrically opposed and my grandfather even feared for a second war. Something no one wants in the long run." Leo reluctantly had to admit that there was some truth in Gala's werds, no one was waiting for a second war between the humans and the vampires. But what did Kailey have to do with it, she was a murderer, so what was she doing here? Those thoughts were hunting his mind, especially when the door of the cafeteria opened and Kailey van Helsing walked in. Gala had probably seen him tighten up and looked back. "Ah, if you want to excuse me. Nick asked me to help her where I could." Leo glared at Gala. Why was he helping a vampire hunter children. Leo had heard rumors before the beginning of the summer that Gale was dating a Claire Coltman, one of Mikan Stryder's victims and an orphan raised by the Suits. But when he heard the rumors for the first time, he'd pushed them away. Gala didn't wait for his answer and walked over to Kailey. Another girl with short blond hair was very close to Kailey and almost dived into her when Gala appeared before their noses.

LEO WATCHED WITH EAGERNESS as Gala led the two past the counters filled with food. The door to the cafeteria opened again and the rest of the vampire hunter children walked into the cafeteria.

Gala waved to them and motioned for them to come, maybe he wanted to help them too. Reluctantly, Leo had to admit it was smart, Gala only had to explain it all in one go and then he could relax. Leo's eyes darted from the group of hunter children to Gala and back. A young woman with copper-red hair and snow-white skin strode toward him, Gala spread his arms and embraced the young woman. Leo caught the name Claire vaguely, so she was here too. What a surprise, not? With a sigh and filled with anger, Leo watched as Gala started his story again, Leo could have finished his breakfast quickly and left the cafeteria. Sadly, though, he had to admit he was curious about most of the vampire hunter children, just not in Kailey. In the meantime, the vampire hunter children had all grabbed a tray and reluctantly grabbed some food. Leo's eyes fell on Kailey, she seemed so comfortable. Probably because, as Realm and Gala had told him, they'd stayed with Nick and Realm all summer. But she was also surrounded by her own kind, she might have felt his gaze because she was looking at him. His heart stopped beating for a moment, he glanced at his tray with his breakfast. But not before his eyes fell on her neck, she had a pendant around her neck. Why did she have a pendant around her neck, it was something vampires did to recognize each other in pre-war times. Gala had told him she was descended from Sediana Lumina, maybe it was passed down through the generations. Or maybe-, the thought ran away from him like a mad hare, Leo ate his leftover food and wanted to get up.

"LEO, STAY A LITTLE longer. My friend." Gala came up with the whole group of five vampire hunter children, she was one of them. "I want to introduce you to Red Tempest Academies newest students. Beside all the new freshmen od course." Gala nodded to the young woman with copper hair. "You have heard the rumors about my girlfriend here, this is Claire Coltman." The young woman gave him a shy smile and sat at the table with him. Gala introduced the other vampire hunters children to him, but he heard none of their names. Leo's eyes were pinned to Kailey, who didn't sit across from him. She didn't look straight at him, maybe that was a good thing. "And if I'm honest I don't know who this is." Leo ripped his gaze off Kailey and looked at the girl who pointed to Gala. It was the girl that he noticed before and in the group of vampire hunter children, she was sticking out like a wingless bat.

"I am Alexia Crystal." She said when she sat down next to Kailey. "I don't belong to the Blacks." Leo saw some vampire hunter children look at Alexia in amazement, but Leo had to admit that the Blacks sounded better than vampire hunter children. It referred to the black clothes their parents wore on missions. Leo looked out of the corner of his eye at Gala, who also nodded in agreement, but Claire looked at him in surprise.

"The Blacks?" Gala quickly explained what Alexia meant by that, and when he was done, Claire also nodded in agreement. "It indeed sounds better then vampire hunter children." The other 'Blacks' nodded to. Leo returned his gaze to Kailey and her neck. He tried to find out what symbol on the pendant was, but the jewelry was old and the family symbol had faded slightly.

"Kailey." It was Alexia, his eyes went to her. "I also noticed earlier that you are wearing a vampire pendant, one worn by a member of every family." Kailey's hand went to the pendant and Leo saw the uncomfortable smile on Kailey's face.

"My Cousin Nick gave it me earlier today. He says it belonged to my ancestor Sediana Lumina." Alexia let out a high-pitched scream and moved closer to Kailey, Leo felt a faint smile appear on his face as he saw the discomfort on Kailey's face. Meanwhile, he cursed Nick Lumina, why had he given the pendant to this killer? What did it matter that she was a distant relative of him. He stood abruptly up, everyone looked at him in surprise.

"I've finished breakfast, so I'm going to the library to get my textbooks." He wanted to explain why he did what he did, but what should he say. "It's not you, it's her." It might have been his right to say that, but it didn't seem polite to him. Or he didn't feel like explaining why it was because of Kailey. He walked to the door that led to the rest of the school and glanced over his shoulder at her. She looked at him too, this was going to be a long and difficult year.

5

Kailey and Alexia walked the already full cafeteria, the space was made entirely of gray stone. In the corner of the room were counters loaded with food and various drinks.

"Kailey." Kailey looked up in surprise to see Gala, a friend of Nick and Realm's, approaching her. Gala had already visited Cousin Nick durring the summer, and he had to promise Nick several times that he would take her under his batwing. A promise that he intended to keep.

"I was wondering were you where, after Nick and I put down the first boxes. The two of you diseapered." He looked shocked.

"I didn't disseaper. I need to see if my snake was adjusting to his new/old home." He smiled but he already had to know that she was not buying it. "Come on, I'll explain our cafeteria, take your friend with you." Kailey wanted to say that Alexia wasn't her friend, but if she was honest, she didn't see the point. They followed him and he explained which dishes were for human consumption and which were in riched with Bloodberries. "Oh there are the other vampire hunter children, I will also explain to them how or what." He began to wave to the group that had just entered the cafeteria. Kailey looked at the group, she wasn't surprised it was just a small group. Not everyone shared her father's faith. She recognized a number of faces from here old school. A girl that she knew all to well, beckoned the group to follow her.

"Hey Kailey." said Claire when she was close enough.

"Hi Claire, it looks like your parents changed their minds." Claire shook her head and got a sneaky smile as she walked over to Gala who put his arm around her.

"I just gave them little choice." Gala cleared his throat and started the story again.

WHY GALA CHOSE TO LED the group to Leo's table that was still mystery to her, there was enough room in the cafeteria. But she didn't want to isolate herself, at least not more than she already did in her own mind. At one point Leo got up and hurried out of the cafeteria, the guilt that plagued her all summer reappeared. But the feeling was stronger, because she had seen the pain and hatred in his eyes.

"Okay that was strange, what did he suddenly have?" asked Zack a guy she kwen from her previous school, glancing around the table, his gaze fixed on Kailey. "Kailey, do you know more about it?" Kailey quickly took the last sip of her coffee. Maybe she can slip away.

"I'm just going for a refill." She started to get up, but Alexia grabbed the mug from her hands. There goes her chance.

"I will get it for you." Alexia was gone, before Kailey could say anything to stop her. With a sighed, she looked at her food, although she was hungry, the sandwiches did not look appealing.

"Kailey van Helsing?" Zack wouldn't let go, Kailey sighed.

"That was Leo Cormwell, the younger brother of Alexandra Cormwell's. You know the vampire girl I killed last summer." The color faded from Zack's face, Claire's amber eyes flashed as she looked at Gala. Who lowered his head ashamed. He probably hadn't thought this through, something Kailey couldn't blame him for. Why should he take her into account, she should have just sat down somewhere else. Alexia put the mug in front of Kailey's nose and sat down next to her again.

"Thank you." Kailey muttered softly and picked up the mug. She wasn't thirsty, just the feeling to have something to do calmed her, all was it just a little.

KAILEY FOLLOWED THE group of Blacks like a lost person, Gala explained at each classroom which classes were being given there, it was only not that difficult to guess there was a sign above every door. Vaguely she heard the surprised expressions as the group entered the library, but the miracle strangely left her cold. Her thoughts were too much with Leo and Alexandra, because Alexandra always bragged about how warm her younger brother was, and that she thought he was a handsome boy. Something Kailey had to agree on, Leo was indeed very handsome. But she had felt nothing of that warmth, not that she deserved his warmth. She robed him of his sister, so why should he be nice to her.

"Kailey are you all right?" asked someone. She didn't know who, but she came back to the group with her thoughts, and saw that everyone looked at her. Kailey forced a smile on her face and nodded.

"I'm sorry, my thoughts were elsewhere." A number of Blacks were satisfied with this answer, but Claire walked towards her. She grabbed Kailey's arm as the rest of the group moved on. Kailey gave her a questioning look, but Claire shook her head, then looked at the group, which was still within earshot.

"Kailey, what's really going on?" Kailey looked at Claire in disbelief, did she really have to ask?

"Alexandra's younger brother," said Kailey reluctantly. Claire opened her mouth for a moment and then closed it when she nodded.

"Is it because of the cold shoulder, or is it because of the cold shoulder and that he is so incredibly handsome." Kailey raised her hand to the pendant, feeling a little insecure. The later weighted heavely on her mind, but she was responsible for Alexandra's death. "Kailey stop blaming yourself, I admit it's strange that Alexandra attacked you from nowhere. Everything seemed so normal when I left you two on the beach." Kailey sighed. She remembered the early morning on Red Tempest Beach as well as the events that followed. Alexandra was over the moon when she heard that Kailey was attending Red Tempest Academy, she'd even joked a few times that she would pair Leo and Kailey over the course of the summer. Something Kailey wasn't exactly looking forward to, but the rest of the summer didn't come, at least not for Alexandra.

"I'm going back to my room, see you later." Kailey turned and she left the library. Her hand was still on her pendant. She missed Alexandra, what she wouldn't give to hear Alexandra's warm voice sound one more time. She almost bumped into someone, but stopped just in time.

"YOU CAN WATCH WHERE you walk, murderer." Leo's cold voice cut through her like a knife, and she knew that she deserved this. No matter how much she missed Alexandra, it was nothing compared to whatever Leo must feel. She wanted to say how sorry she was, but what could she say?

"I'm sorry Leo." That was a dreadfull excuse and she knew it. She didn't have to look at him to know that this made him only angrier.

"You're sorry, come on. Do you really think I believe that, do you really think I would ever believe you?" Kailey hung her head slightly. "And what was that just now, you who happily sat down at the table and proudly told you that your stupid Cousin Nick, a traitor of his own race. Gave you that." Leo pointed to the pendant under Kailey's hand. Kailey felt something other than shame and sadness, nobody spoke that way about Cousin Nick.

"I can't believe my ears." She knew that he was hurting, but that was no excuse.

"What don't you believe?" He looked with hate to her.

"That's the brother of Alexandra, who calls a vampire who works so hard for the cooperation between humans and vampires, *a traitor*."

"How dare you speak about my sister, especially in that sense." snapped Leo at her. But she didn't care about his feelings, not anymore.

"I can say the same to you, you insulted a member of my family, and then I have to listen to it in silence. I'm sorry, but then you have the wrong van Helsing in front of you. Besides, I don't care whether you like me or not. I know what happened and Alexandra knows what happened, the only problem is..." She swallowed the last words and didn't know why. Kailey had said those words out loud several times, why was she swallowing them now? Leo had probably seen her doubt, it was an opening he could have used to place a verbal attack. But he didn't, he grunted softly and then walked past her, as if their conversation had not taken place. Kailey squeezed her eyes shut, she felt tears sting her eyes. She only let them out when she was safe in her bedroom.

6

The sunrise slowly turned the sky red, something that was visible in the water of the Red Tempest Sea. The three girls sat on the pale pink sand of the beach looking at it with admiration, they had seen it several times and this was only the beginning of summer. The girl with copper-red hair sighed, her hair color was even redder than usual.

"Kailey, don't you know how lucky you are. You go to Gala's school and even though I've begged my foster parents, they won't let me go." The brown-haired girl began to laugh and lay on her back.

"I'm not saying I'm lucky, but as a van Helsing it is my job to walk the delicate balance between vampire hunters and vampires. By my soul, I almost sound like my dad." Now all three girls laughed. The girl with ebony black hair was the first to recover from laughter and sighed.

"I go away from that school and you go in, why is life so unfair." Kailey slowly pushed herself up and chuckled. Alexandra had said this a few times since hearing that Kailey was attending Red Tempest Academy. "Well then I have all the more reasons to come visit, of course I can not live too long without my little brother and now that you are also at that school..." Kailey rolled her eyes, Alexandra would come up with the idea again to play match up between Kailey and Leo. "And now that the two of you are in the same school, it makes my job only easier."

"Alex, leave her alone. As far as I know, Kailey has never met Leo." Claire, the girl with copper red hair, gave Alexandra a playful push. "And when was the last time a vampire married a vampire hunter. To my knowledge, Kailey's ancestors were the last ones." Alexandra gave a playful push back.

"The last was a week after Bloodmoonball, when Velika Lazar married Alex-Lucas Barnier."

"Velika Lazar was not a vampire hunter, even though she comes from a vampire hunter family. She never came to the Hunter's Conservatory." Said Claire. Kailey nodded, she knew Velika from preschool and they stayed in touch with her. She did not know that the Lazar family was a vampire hunter family at the time. And when she found out, she heard from her father that Velika didn't know about the vampire's or werewolfs. Her father didn't know why that was, but Kailey needed to keep it a secret from Velika. "By the way." Started Claire, bring Kailey back to the beach. "Have you heard that her parents gave a farewell ceremony. Her father rejected his own flesh and blood." Kailey looked at Claire who was apparently still amazed at the fact and if Kailey was honest it surprised her too. She had been to Velika's farewell ceremony, Velika's husband was already there at that time, this was the first time she saw a noble vampire. She admired Alex-Lucas for being in the hunter's den.

"Well to be honest Velika's dad is a strange man, don't forget I was there when he stormed the ball and shot his own daughter." Kailey had heard the story how Velika became a vampire several times, at the Hunter's Conservatory. But they were never as colorfull as the first hand account of Alexandera. Alexandera looked at her watch. "Anyway, Claire I think it's time for you to go home." Claire nodded slowly and stood up. Since the fall, Claire's foster parents have been extremely careful with her. It had taken an awful lot of effort for Kailey to persuade them to let Claire take her to the beach. Claire nodded and got up.

"I know, lets go shopping later this afternoon. It is then bright daylight so my parents need to be crazy to think that anything could happen to me." Alexandra started laughing.

"It is fine by me, but a quick question. Will your boyfriend joining use?" Claire turned slowly red and Kailey started laughing.

"I love to meet Gala, Cousin Nick and Realm always talk about him. But alright Claire time to go otherwise that shopping trip is not going to happen." Claire sighed and turned around.

KAILEY GAZED AT THE water.

"Kailey?" Kailey tore her eyes off the calm sea and turned it on Alexandra. Her breath caught in her throat, Alexandra's honey-colored face was completely gone. Her enchanting blue irises were surrounded by red circles. "Kailey, can you give me my bag." Kailey reached for Alexandra's bag on the other side of her. With a heart that beat like a horse's hooves galloping on a race track, she handed the bag to her friend. Alexandra reached in and pulled out a bottle with Bloodberrie juice. She put the bottle to her mouth as quickly as she could and drank in large gulps. Kailey had never seen Alexandra so eager, not for food or for the bloodberry juice. But to her horror the juice didn't do much, Alexandra's skin remained gray and her eyes remained surrounded by red. Trembling, Kailey got up, but fighting with her fear she stayed where she was.

"Alex?" Her voice trembled violently, she had been around vampires all her life and she knew what they could do. But she had never really been afraid of them. Alexandra lowered the empty bottle.

"Kailey, get out of here." Those were the words Kailey needed, she grabbed her bag from the sand and ran as towards her car in the deserted parking lot. Her heart raced in her throat and the red small car slowly but surely came closer. Kailey felt her feet leave the soft

ground and her pace accelerated slightly on the hard asphalt. Her
hand reached into her bag looking for her car keys. But as always
these were on the bottom, she let a curse fly. When her hand lost
grip on the key ring. Instead, her hands fell on her small crossbow,
something her mother told her to always carry with her. The weapon
was made of the strongest material in Traimora and the stake
contained an acid that would catch fire if the stake hit the flesh of a
human or vampire. Kailey had reluctantly agreed to the time then,
vowing to herself she would never use it. Maybe she had been a little
too naive, Kailey blinked for a moment. She had stopped running,
why had she stopped running? She glanced over her shoulder.
Alexandra was nowhere to be seen, fear of her best friend crept over
her. She quickly resumed her way to her car until she was almost
there. She finally had the keys in her hands and had already removed
the remote lock from the door. Kailey reached out to the vehicle,
suddenly out of nowhere she felt a push in her back. She hit the red
metal with a bang, then fell on the asphalt.

KAILEY TURNED IN SHOCK, Alexandra standing above her
with a look in her eyes that Kailey did not know. Kailey tried to get
up, but Alexandra knelt by her. Laying her hand on Kailey's chest.
Kailey gasped, since when was Alexandera this strong.

"Oh, no little blood. You can't get rid of me that easily." Even her
voice wasn't even hers, it was hoarse and gave Kailey goosebumps.

"Alex, it's Kailey. Why are you doing this?" Alexandra blinked a
few times and a look of recognition appeared, albeit temporarily.

"Kailey, use your crosbow." Kailey swallowed, she'd told
Alexandra about the weapon. Just so she wouldn't be surprised when
she found it in Kailey's bag. "Please Kailey I can't control myself."
Alexandra reached for her own throat, with tears in her eyes she saw
the struggle in Alexandra. She had no choice, she didn't know how,

but she already had her crossbow in her hands. She aimed it at her best friend, her heart racing.

"Do it!" That wasn't Alexandra's voice, but Cousin Nick's. She blinked for a moment, now Nick was bent over her. His eyes surrounded red and face gray, his vampire fangs turned out menacingly. "Then shoot you murderer!" Kailey narrowed her eyes and fired.

KAILEY FLEW UP SCREAMING, panting heavily she glanced around the dark room. Where was she, where was Cousin Nick? Her whole body was covered with pearls of sweat, her breath heavy. Slowly the memories came back to her, Alexandra was dead and Cousin Nick was in his apartment with Realm. Kailey threw off the sheets and got out of bed. She went to the sink and poured some water on her face to wash off the sweat. She did not dare to look in the mirror above, because she already knew what she would see a white face with dark blue bags under her eyes. Lips pressed together, she walked to the window and paused for a moment, peeking through the curtains. It was not even night, it was midday, a strange concept that the campus was so deserted and quiet at this time of day. Her eyes fell on an old weeping willow; Nick, Nathalia, Realm and even Alexandra had told her stories about the old tree and how they picnic there under the stars. Her breath caught, Alexandra stood in front of the tree. With her gray skin and reddish eyes, but after a few blinks Alexandera was gone. Kailey's heart started to race again, was this also part of the daymare? Because Alexandra couldn't be here, she was dead and her blood was on Kailey's hands.

7

The sound of his alarm went off a little too early for Leo's taste, but that was nothing new. He reached out to grab the object, to his surprise the annoying thing wasn't there. He lifted his head slightly from his feathered pillow and was irritated to see that the alarm clock was out of reach on his desk. It had been a tip from Alexandra at the end of the senior year. Since she could no longer call him every day, he put a small smile on his face and got up with a groan. In a curse and a sigh he changed his clothes and made his way to the cafeteria. The school year was really about to begin and there was nothing he could do about it. His backpack weighed heavily with the books he needed for the lessons. Was he imagining things, or was his backpack lighter last year? With this though on his mind he entered the cafeteria, he was one of the first students to attend. His gaze moved over the other students and his eyes caught on Kailey's face. Who looked even paler than she did the day before. She had her hands clasped around a coffee mug, she looked anxiously around the cafeteria. He could see the dark blue bags under her eyes, she had tried to cover it up with a layer of make-up, but it didn't work. He still could see them. Had she looked so bad the day before, he wondered? He quickly tried to shake these thoughts out of his head. Every time something bad happened to hear, she deserved it.

"By my soul, she looks like hell." Claire had appeared next to Leo, concern plagued her face and voice. Leo grunted slightly and Claire looked at him intently. "Leo I think there is something I must tell you." Leo shook his head, there was nothing he needed or wanted to know, not if it had anything to do with Kailey. He wanted to walk away but she grabbed him by the arm. "I was there Leo." He froze, what was she talking about? "I was there that morning when Alexandra attacked Kailey. I left a little earlier, because I had to be home on time. But I went back, because I forgot my phone in Kailey's car. I saw how kailey was thrown against her car. I heard Kailey try to talk to Alexandra, but it was no use. Out of nowhere Alexandra begged Kailey to end it, Alexandera was afraid hat she might hurt Kailey. Leo do you understand, Alexandera chose death above hurting a friend." Leo clenched his teeth, why did she tell him this?

"You are lying." Claire shook her head slowly.

"Why should I lie about that, Kailey doesn't even know tha I was there. I told this to my parents and they told the other vampire hunters. But no one else knows, except for you now." Leo grunted, then looked at Kailey who shivered. What was Claire trying to do? He didn't know, but he felt sorry for Kailey. He wanted to shake his head. No, she still pulled the trigger. She still killed Alex, she still was a murderer. "I heard her scream Alex's name during the day. I almost got up from my bed." He wanted to shrug, he didn't want to hear how much Kailey was suffering. He was suffering to but it seemed that Claire didn't care about him at all. "Leo, Alex and we were friends and in Kailey's case I can say with certainty that they were best friends. Hate her all you want Leo, but if you're looking for someone who misses your sister as much as you do. Look no further, you've found her." Leo wanted to respond, but Claire made her way to Kailey and sat down with her. Leo looked at the two girls, Alexandra had told him a few times that she was friends with some Blacks, but he was sure she had never mentioned names. Or had she? He couldn't remember, his shoulders stooped, he sauntered over to the coffee maker. He needed that on this emotional morning.

"If you're looking for someone who misses your sister as much as you do." Claire's words haunted his mind, she had a point why would she lie about it. She knew that he would give her the cold shoulder too. But still she told him anyway, He quickly glanced over his shoulder and looked at the two girls again, Claire applied a little more makeup under Kailey's eyes.

WITH A FILLED COFFEE mug in his hand and a tray of Narinor breakfast in the other, he walked over to the table where Kailey and Claire were sitting. If he were to believe Claire, something he reluctantly and surprisingly did. Then Kailey had told everybody the truth about Alexandra attacking her. Yet there were so many questions buzzing in his mind, questions he wanted answers to. He knew who could answer those qeustions. The one person he blamed for Alexandrea's death. Kailey looked puzzled as he sat down. Claire had indeed done a better job with the makeup, those blue bags were almost invisible unless you knew were to look.

"Good evening. By my soul you look terrible." The insult was out before he even bothered, but why should he turn his heart into a murder pit. She was still responsible for Alexandra's death whether Alexandra attacked her or not. What thinking person had a crossbow in her bag when she went out with friends.

"Good morning, or evening whatever you want to call it. I see you slept well?" Kailey didn't seem to need much sleep to respond fervently. Or this just made her comments a bit more fiery. He took a bite of his beaten egg, it could have been slightly more salt for his taste. But he didn't feel like getting up and get some more salt. Bit will provide an opportunity for her to get up and disappear and his questions will not be answered. "Leo what are you doing here?"

"I eat my breakfast. By my soul, have you slept that badly? Or did you get up from the coven with the wrong foot."

"I'm going to grab some food and some more coffee." Claire gave him a disgusted look before she left, but still she left so he could fire his armada of question towards Kailey. And maybe she had a small shred of hope that Kailey and he become friends. He wanted to roll with his eyes, that seemed a bit unlikely.

"Kailey," He started. "Let's say that I believe you and my sister attacked you. The only trouble I have is that you were in you own words good friends. Why would she attack a good friend?" Kailey let out a sigh and her head fell into her hands.

"I really have no idea, one minute there was nothing wrong. Alex sent Claire home, so she wouldn't get in trouble. We enjoyed the sunrise and the change of color on the water for a while, when Alex came for her bag asked. I gave her that and she drank very eagerly the Bloodberry juice away, something I've never seen her do." Leo had to admit neither did he. Alexandra didn't like the taste of the Bloodberries.

"And then?" He looked impatiently at Kailey, he wanted to know more. No he needed to know more.

"And then, she told me to run. Something I did, I got into the parking lot where my car was and..." Leo saw Kailey started to shake, pearls of sweat appeared on her forehead. Leo felt his stomach turn, this interrogation made Kailey visibly ill. But was what she told him the truth? He needed to know more, but did he wanted to pay the price for this knowledge.

"Kailey?" He got up and walked around the table. What was this, he was concerned. But why she killed Alexandra, she deserves everything that made her feel ill. He shook his head was he out of his mind. Alexandra wouldn't have wanted this for him or her best friend. Leo touched Kailey's shoulder and she fell towards him, he was shocked. He looked at her closed eyes, she lost concuncions. He glanced up and saw that Claire was already heading their way, her hands were filled with coffee and food. "Claire, she has to go to the infirmary!" other Blacks who just entered the cafeteria looked alarmed towards them, Zack ran to help Leo lift Kailey. "Thank you, Zack." Zack nodded.

"Do not worry about it. Kailey is a friend." Leo sighed.

"Cousin Rhain is going to love this." Zack looked at him. "He is the school doctor and married to my blood cousin Fern." Zack shook his head.

"You vampires are really a strange bunch."

LEO DROPPED HIS FACE in his hands, Cousin Rhain had asked him through a lot of questioning.

"Did she eat enough? Did she get enough sleep?" He could have guessed the answer to the enough question. All he had to do was look at Kailey's face. But still he asked Leo all those questions.

"Sleep you only have to whip away the make-up to see that she didn't get enough. But I didn't see her eat. She had a cup of coffee when I entered the cafeteria." Cousin Rhain looked at him.

"I am not going to ask how you are feeling. I am going to give you something about the headache." Leo lowered his head, it was a still a wonder to him how Cousin Rhain knew how he was feeling. "Please sit down, I will be right back." Leo sat down and sighed. He didn't want to stay here but there was something kept him there, and it was not only what Cousin Rhain would give him for the headache. But what was it? For a result on Kailey's condition, for more answers? For a moment he couldn't remember. He felt responsible for what happened to Kailey, he had only thought about what he wanted. He didn't think about Kailey.

"Leo Cromwell, in souls name. Why aren't you in class?" Headmaster Dracul entered the infarmary. Leo jumped up from the chair.

"I um." Cousin Rhain, shook his head when he looked past the curtains. He disseapered for a moment but walked then towards them.

"Leo, take this in here." Cousin Rhain pushed a green pill into his hands. "That will help against your headache. In response to your question, Headmaster, Leo Cromwell took the van Helsing girl to the infirmary. But was dealing with a headache himself, so I asked him to stay here."

"Alright, well Leo take that pill and go back to class. And thank you for helping Kailey." Leo nodded and put the green pill in his mouth, and he rushed towards his first class. He was not sure if it was the right move, but Headmaster Dracul told him to go and he will be crazy if he wouldn't listen to the Headmaster.

8

Leo had not received much of his first lessons and even less of what was said at lunch. His thoughts were in battle with each other, he wanted to hate Kailey so badly that it hurt. But he felt so horrible about what happened to Kailey. He kept seeing her white face, the dark blue bags under her light gray eyes. The pearls of sweat on her forehead as she struggled to keep her hands still. Her falling unconscious when he touched her. Leo swallowed, the green pill that Cousin Rhain had given him had not helped much. The headache that first nibbled on his mind, started to feel like a horde elephants dancing in his head.

"Hey lion cub, how are you?" Leo looked up, he was still sitting in the cafeteria. While the lessons were already started, which was against the rules. But what good were those lessons if the information went in one ear and out the other. All what he thinks about is Kailey. He even forgot about Gala. "Leo, wake up!" Gala put a hand on Leo's shoulder and shook him violently from side to side.

"Can I be alone for a moment, with my own thoughts?" Leo sighed, Gala stopped shaking and sat down next to him.

"Not if you are skipping lessons. Do you know what punishment is for that?" Leo rolled with his eyes. Could use this, Gala made his headache worse. Unfortunately, Gala hadn't Cousins Rhain gift to see inside Leo's head. He just want Gala to go away.

"No and neither did you, because no one had missed a lesson without a good reason. But whatever it may be Gala, I'm happy to take it." Leo rested his elbows on the table and dropped his head into it. Could he trust Gala, maybe it those not matter if he trust Gala or not. He needed to talk to somebody, normally he would go to Alexandra. "I thought at the beginning of today that I was so sure of my case. Kailey is responsible for my sister's death, she pulled the trigger on her crossbow. But when I saw her like this this morning, sick and weak." Leo shook his head slowly. "It's partly my fault that she's now in the infirmary. I wanted answers to my questions so badly, I almost forced her to explain it to me in detail. While I watched with open eyes what it was doing to her." Gala put his hand back on Leo's shoulder and squeezed it gently.

"Leo let me tell one thing that I have learned about Kailey during the summer. She is not stupid, she understands that you wanted those answers. She wanted for you to find some shred of piece. But the real question that is on your mind right now. Have you become wiser?"

"What?" Leo looked puzzled at Gala.

"Have you become wiser from Kailey's answers?" Leo slowly rocked back and forth. That was a good question, one that he had asked himself several times since the lunch break.

"Yes I have more information, but at the same time so many more questions. It's just like that snake creature from the old legends, you chop a head his slippery body and two more grew in its place. Do you know which one I mean." Gala frowned for a moment, lost in thought for a moment.

"That's a good one, I wouldn't know the name of the creature. But I understand what you mean." Leo dropped his head back into his hands and let out a deep sigh.

"Why has everything become so damn difficult." His head started to throb, talking to Gala helped him in some way. But it was not enough to work away the headache, or the heartache. "Thank you Gala, for listening. But are you not to late for class?" Gala looked at the great clock above the door and cursed.

"I need to go. And do not worry about what you just said. It will stay between you and me." That was good to hear. Leo watched as Gala ran towards class, and maybe it was time for him to see Cousin Rhain again.

LEO SAUNTERED SLOWLY to his room, he had no appetite. That didn't mean he hadn't eaten, it just wasn't much. During dinner he had avoided Claire and Gala's worried looks. He hadn't heard from the teachers yet, but he was sure he would get punished tomorrow. Something he wasn't looking forward to, but it was his own fault. He stayed away from classes and without a note from the doctor. After Gala left he didn't go towards the infirmary like he planned to, instead he thought that some fresh air would help him. But to his regret it had not helped him at all it made it only worse. Now he entered his room and his heart leaped to his throat. Alexandra was sitting on his bed with a big smill, her whole body bloody and her skin ashen. Her beautiful eyes surrounded by red circles. What was this, Alexandra couldn't be here she was dead. Leo started to scream, but quickly covered his mouth with a hand. Because when he blinked his eyes, the image of Alexandra was gone. His bed was exactly as he had left it. He took that breath a few times, were these the same images Kailey saw when she closed her eyes. No wonder that she didn't sleep well. Immediately he was taken over by a wave of pity, his stomach made a few figurative somersaults. He pressed his hand more tightly against his mouth to keep his stomach contents down. It was no use, he turned and ran to the shared bathroom. He almost bumped into Gala.

"Leo?" Leo didn't stop running and he heard Gala coming after him. "Leo what's up?" Leo shot into a toilet cubicle and vomited.

That had to be an answer to Gala's question. "I'm going to the cafeteria to get you something to drink. I will be right back." Leo wanted to argue, but the next load made was ready to leave his body. This was only possible, but because of the stress there was no other explanation. He came out of the booth coughing and spluttering, his stomach was empty, there was simply nothing left in it. He stumbled to the door, where he was met by Cousin Rhain.

"By my soul. Leo, you look like hell. It's a good thing your friend sent for me." Cousin Rhain caught Leo and dragged him back to his own room. Leo closed his eyes for a moment when they got close to the doorway.

LEO GROANED SOFTLY, his stomach twisting and his ears ringing.

"Lay still, Leo." Cousin Rhain's voice was steady and calm. Leo carefully opened his eyes and immediately regretted it. "I'm sorry, I should have said it. Lay still with your eyes closed. You and that van Helsing girl are one and the same. Both keep thinking too long until it makes you sick." Leo wanted to roll his eyes. Cousin Rhain knew him for the moment he was a babe, he should know him by now.

"I saw Alexandra on my bed, dead." Leo heard Cousin Rhain tighten.

"Was this before or after you got sick?" Leo opened his mouth, then closed it again. If he was ill before he saw her, he no longer suffered from major headaches.

"I had a major headache." Leo turned his head away from the light and opened his eyes. He looked straight at the doctor. "One of the reasons I didn't go to classes." Cousin Rhain nodded and looked over Leo, his nose told him he wasn't in his own room, and the shuffling behind him made him believe he and Cousin Rhain weren't the only ones in the room. Leo could guess who was behind him.

"I'm sorry I didn't report it, Headmaster." A loud sniff through the nose told him he had made a good guess.

"Don't worry about that now, Leo Cromwell. Make sure you get better first. By my soul, the year has only just started and I already have two students who are sick with stress. If this continues I can join you guys, I'm really getting too old for this."

"Don't be a nag Vance, these students were stressed out before they got here. You know that as well as I do. From what I've heard about Kailey from Nick Lumina and Realm Stryder, she's been sleeping badly since the attack and been plagued with nightmares. She herself told me that she has seen Alexandra under the weeping willow." Leo opened his eyes wide. The infirmary was still turning, but he shot up nonetheless. Kailey had seen Alexandra too, how could this be. Immediately he was pushed back into the cushions. "I said stay down, if you do something like that again I'll tie you to the bed." Cousin Rhain looked at The Headmaster. "I honestly believe it is not wise to keep these two on school grounds. They were both connected to Alexandra and we still don't know what happened to her."

"What are you suggesting. That I'm already barking these two. Rhain this school has been in the spotlight because of last year. From both the noble and young vampire parents, as well as that of the vampire hunters. That's why I started opened the school for those vampire hunters kids."

"The Blacks." Leo said weakly, he hardly recognized his own voice.

"What do you say?" The surprise was evident in the Headmaster's voice.

"The students have renamed the vampire hunter children the Blacks. Because of their parents' uniform."

"The Blacks, I have to admit that it does roll better off the tongue. Anyway Rhain, what are you suggesting." There was a moment of silence, to a soft breath from someone who was sleeping further up in the infirmary. Leo guessed it was Kailey and he knew he was with her.

"I suggest you send them to Nirrox, Vance. He's been researching what happened to Alexandra almost all summer and I know he's desperate for more information. What these two can give him."

"But their lessons?" Said the Headmaster, but Cousin Rhain shook his head. He was not going to change his mind about this.

"Can they catch up or do their homework there, Vance their health comes first and you always thought the same way. At least before Velika came here." The Headmaster groaned, Leo actually wished he didn't have to hear this. Kailey was lucky, she was sleeping.

"You are right, send a message to Nirrox and Colette. I will let their parents know that they are not in school, but they are in safe hands." Leo heard the Headmaster walk away and Cousin Rhain let out a deep breath.

"I wish you hadn't heard us."

"You and I together, Cousin Rhain. You and I together."

9

Kailey sat what defeated in the cafeteria, Dr. Krauss had told her she had slept all night and day, and she had to admit that she was feeling much better. Still, something kept gnawing at her, when she woke up. Leo was also in the infirmary. His skin ashen, she had run out of the infirmary almost in panic. But Dr. Krauss had assured her that there was nothing serious about it, just that he, like her, was beating himself so much up about Alexandera's death that also he became ill. She sighed and a cup of tea stood on the table in front of her, her hands surrounded the warm cup. The fragrant fumes teased her nose slightly, only she couldn't make up what the sent was. Maybe it was because she was a little hastened of taking a sip. Leo was sitting across from her. Also with a cup of tea in his hands, the good doctor had advised against coffee for the time being and they listened to him like good students, that they want to believe they are.

"Kailey." Leo's voice was shaved. His skin was still a bit gray, but since he woke up his normal color returned. "I'm sorry truly about yesterday." It felt like she'd been punched in the stomach, he actually thought it was his fault. She shook her head and grabbed his hand, which he pulled away quickly. "I could see that you were not doing well and yet I forced you to answer my questions."

"It's not your fault, I could have kept my mouth shut too. Or ask you to go away. But it would not have mattered at the end. I was not doing so well before I came here. I should have asked Cousin Nick to bring me to the hospital or a doctor." He nodded slightly, did he agree with her that was something she didn't expect. There were two weekend bags standing next to the table. Headmaster Dracul had told them they were being temporarily housed with old student of his and that students wife. Kailey didn't had to geuss who the student was. She had heard from Velika that her brother-in-law Nirrox was looking for Alexandera's illnes, as he described it.

"Colette Barnier is a licensed doctor and she will take charge over your medical conditions." That is what the Headmaster had told them, but Kailey had seen him fight with his own words, something she understood all too well. After what happened last year with Cousin Nick and his friends, and of course with Velika being shot in front of the students and some noble guests. The school was under amount of pressure. That was why her father had sent her to this school, to show off how good the school was. Now she was failing him by being to messed up to attend this school. She looked again at Leo, what was going through his head? She didn't know and she doubted if he wanted to share it with her.

KAILEY DIDN'T KNOW how long they were sitting there for a man with long light brown hair to enter the cafeteria, his icy blue eyes were twinkling in the dim candlelight.

"Kailey van Helsing, what an honor to finally meet you." The man strode over to them, when he got close to them, Kailey noticed the scar on his cheek. "Your ancestors Sediana Lumina and Abraham van Helsing, saved mine ancestors on the night my forefather Armand Barnier killed the human king of Narinor. And now I'm here to serve you and now we are full circle. What do you say?" Kailey had only seen Nirrox Barnier once before and that was during Velika's farewell ceremony. But she hadn't the change to talk to him, and maybe it was for the best.

"Barnier why do you always need to be that dramatic. Kailey and I where waiting for what seems like hours." Leo got up from the table, but Nirrox shook his head in disbelief.

"It remains a mystery to me to this day that you and Alexandra are related. But drink your tea first, we have the time." Kailey looked at her tea and put it to her lips with a faint smile. She hoped, but that Nirrox didn't always do this. She took a sip and a cry went through the cafeteria.

"Kailey!" Quickly, Kailey put her mug back on the table, just in time. Alexia wrapped her arms around Kailey and all what she want to do is push her away as hard as she can. There was an up side by her leaving the schoolgrounds, she would have some time off from Alexia. "Kailey please don't ever startle me like that again. I was justifiably terrified! I didn't hear from you all day, I needed to hear from others that you collapsed."

"Alexia, can you let me go." But it was no use, Alexia had her a little too tight in her grip. "Alexia, I can't breathe!"

"You don't have to shout, I heard you the first time." Still, Alexia let her go and looked at her somewhat ashamed. "But I mean it, you scared me." Kailey wanted to say she was sorry, she couldn't say it. She didn't mean it so way should she say it? To make Alexia happy, she shook her head. But that didn't stop Alexia. "Have you eaten anything and oh, I'm sorry. Did I disturb you?" Alexia turned her gaze to Nirrox, who shook his head.

"Not at all and from which family are you? I do not recognize the symbol on your pendant." Nirrox searched his eyes for Alexia's gold pendant.

"The Crystal family, Mr. Barnier. We just moved to Traimora, so it is no wonder you do not recogonize my families crest." Kailey saw Nirrox look dubious, but it was only for a moment. "Well..." Alexia took a few steps back and started to walk away. Kailey could kick herself, but Alexia was so nice to her, maybe it would be better.

"Alexia." It was on her lips before Kailey regretted it, or maybe it was not so good idea after all. "You do not have worry, but I'm leaving for a while."

"You are leaving, where are you going?" Alexia looked from Nirrox to Kailey and back again. "Kailey?" Kailey sighed, this was her one fault. Now she had to see it through.

"I'm going with Nirrox Barnier for my health. His wife is a licensed doctor." Alexia's lips tightened slightly and something strange shot her eyes there. Only Kailey could not decipher what that was.

"Well your health is important. I hope you take good care of her, Mr. Barnier." Alexia turned away from them. Kailey was still amazed at Alexia's reaction, it bordered on the cold side. Very different from what she showed the previous days.

"What an interesting girl, but please, drink your tea. My Angel of the Night is waiting for use." Kailey did as she was told and drank the stuff in big gulps.

"It is maybe heartwarming to know at least one person misses you. But I agree with Barnier, Alexia Cristal is a strange girl." Kailey couldn't argue with that. She got up and picked up her weekend bag. Without saying a word or glancing at the two men, Kailey left the cafeteria.

KAILEY TOOK A DEEP breath as she stood outside the academy's iron railings. She hadn't known how trapped she felt when she walked through the fence with Nick and Realm a few days before today. But now that she was out of it again, she had the feeling that she could breath without feeling trapped.

"Well let's go then, my Angel of the night is waiting for us and I hate to keep her waiting too long." Said Nirrox while he opened the door of a black car and motioned for Kailey to sit. Did he know that he said the same sentence earlier in the cafeteria? Kailey nodded vaguely to him and got into the car. She had the back seat to herself because Leo sat down in the passenger seat next to Nirrox. Nirrox started the car and they left the Red Tempest Academy behind. During the entire ride not a word was spoken and that was a good thing. Kailey had nothing to say. She was still a bit tired and yet the gears in her brain didn't stop. Dr. Krauss suspected that this would continue until there were more answers about Alexandra's death. She could only hope that he was right. Kailey rested her head against the blinded car window. It was cool compered with the heat outside the car. Or she was suffering from a fever? Who would say, Nirrox's wife would be her best geuss. Vaguely she caught a soft tune coming from the radio, she recognized the song. Wasn't that the song that Realm wrote and bragged about? She frowned and tried to catch the rest of the song, but it was too soft. She didn't want to ask Nirrox if the music could be louder.

Kailey didn't know how, but she had fallen asleep. Her eyes opened again when the car stopped moving.

"We are home sweet home, as my father and most likely my little brother would say." Nirrox got out of the car, Leo glanced over his shoulder at her.

"Kailey..." It looked like he wanted to say more, but he opened the door and disappeared into the night. With a sigh, Kailey followed him and together they followed Nirrox up the stairs that led to the four-story mansion.

"Enter." Nirrox pushed open the red wooden front door, as she walked past it she saw that the door was engraved with the Barnier family's coat of arms. But her mouth really fell open, a crystal chandelier lit up the wood-clad hall. On the walls hung several green banners with the Barnier emblem embroidered in gold, the king cobra. On the wooden floor was a dark red carpet that led to the rest of the house. Next to the front door were two huge vases filled with tiger lilies, the entire hallway smelled was filled with their light sent. Leo passed her, clearly not enchanted by the pomp and circumstance of the hall. With lips pressed together, she followed Leo and Nirrox to the rest of the house. Nirrox led them down the hall to the sitting room, which again took Kailey's breath away. This room was also covered with wood, in the four corners of the room were again large vases with tiger lilies. In the center of the room, three benches surrounded a black marble coffee table. The benches were covered in dark green velvet, the backs of which were propped up with gold studs, which seemed to sparkle softly in the dime light of the candlesticks that were hanging on the wall. Why vampires loved candlelight so much, she might never really understand. A woman sat on one of the benches, she was holding a leather-bound book. She didn't look up as they entered the room.

"Angel of the Night, I have returned with the younglins." The woman looked up and slammed her book shut. Kailey felt something she had only felt when she was around Alexandra, a twinge of jealousy. It was not very incomprehensible, Colette Barnier had a smooth white skin and silver blond straight hair. That hung perfectly on her back, her dark green eyes matched the color of the sofas very well.

"Hi Colette, good to see you again." Leo muttered as he sauntered over to the couches, carefully sitting down on the expensive cloth without waiting for an answer.

"Well Leo, it is indeed good to see you. Especially since you haven't changed a bit." The coolness in Colette's voice was clearly audible. "It really is a mystery to me that you and Alexandra share the same blood." Kailey had to agree with Colette, but Alexandra could give someone the cold shoulder if she wanted. She made her way to the benches but paused, when she noticed that Colette looked at her and gave her a warm smile. "Kailey van Helsing, I suppose. Please, these benches are not there for decoration." Kailey smiled and sat down. "Well let's get started right away." Colette looked at the two.

"My Angel of the Night, let them catch their breath first. They just got here." Nirrox came back into the room, Kailey hadn't even noticed he had left. In his hands he had a tray filled with tea cups.

"That may be true my love, but the sooner we have all the information. The sooner these young souls can go back to school, were they belong." Kailey pressed her lips together, Colette Barnier had a point. But something in her immediately told her that they will not leave here anytime soon. Colette looked at Leo, who bowed his head slightly. "Let's start with you Leo, you saw Alexandra before she went to the beach. So tell me everything and then I really mean everything."

10

Leo didn't know why his time with Alexandra before she left the house was so important, but still he gave Colette Barnier all the information he could give.

"What's the last thing she said to you?" Colette asked him, writing her notes down in a notebook. That was a good question, he was still thinking about it a few days ago, but he had just been forced to remember every simple detail. So this came a bit easier than before.

"See you later lion cub, I now have an appointment with your future wife." Kailey, who was sitting across from him, looked at him in shock, why was she so surprised. Maybe she knew the girl Alexandra tried to pair him with, he frowned. "Wait a minute, Alex has been teasing me for a few years now that she would pair me up with one of her friends. She said it again that night, Claire and you were on the beach with her. Alex is not the person that separates couples..."

"She was talking about me, Leo. She couldn't stop talking about it, even that night she joked about it." Leo shook his head, of all the girls Alexandra could pair him with. He glanced at Colette, who had turned her attention to Kailey. Kailey was apparently already expecting the question and immediately started talking about how they sat on the Red Tempest Beach, the jokes that were told between nose and lips. The plans she made for the summer. Leo struggled not to smile, it sounded just like his sister. She always wanted to know what came next.

"You only live once." That was her standard line, when he said anything about it. His smile faded into nothingness. What he wouldn't give to hear her say this one more time?

"Her skin was gray and her irises had red circles." Kailey continued, and Leo gasped. The image of the dead Alexandra on his bed immediately came to mind. "She drank her Bloodberry juice in big gulps but it didn't help. She told me to run and I was afraid of a vampire for the first time in my life. I couldn't find my car keys in my bag. Alex easily caught up with me and she pushed me against my car. I tried to talk to her and for a moment seemed to get through to her." Kailey swallowed, Leo saw her wet eyes, she was at the part Claire had told him about. About Alexandra begging Kailey for her death. "Alexandra knew about the crossbow in my bag, my mother wouldn't let me out of the house without it." Her whole body began to shake again, like it did when she told him this. "When she wanted to attack me again, I pulled the trigger and, and..." Colette reached out to Kailey, but Kailey ducked from it. Like a skittish animal running from a possible predator.

"Kailey, can you tell us again, what Alexandra looked like?" Kailey nodded slowly, even though it was a small, short nod. She echoed the dullness of Alexandra's skin. "Can you give me an example?" Kailey nodded to Leo.

"Alexandra had exactly the same complexion as Leo, maybe a little darker. But just before she..." Leo felt in his own stomach turn, he could hardly imagine how difficult it was for her to find the right words. "Her skin was just as dull as in the last bad vampire movie Vladimir Dracul starred in." Nirrox sprang up and stormed out of the sitting room.

"And the bottle of Bloodberry juice, did she bring it from home?" Kailey and Leo nodded, just like seemingly Kailey's crossbow, his mother wouldn't let them out of the house without a bottle of bloodberry juice. Colette nodded and wrote it all down. "Dr. Krauss told me you were having trouble sleeping and that you had seen Alexandra." Leo stiffened again, he had heard this from Cousin Rhain, but now he was eager to hear what Kailey had to say about it.

"She was standing by the old weeping willow, opposite my bedroom window." Leo swallowed, Alexandra was always waiting for him under that willow. Colette looked at him.

"Dr. Krauss said the exact same thing about you, Leo." Leo reluctantly told what he had seen in his room, Colette pursed her lips. "Well how much I would like to send you back to school, it doesn't seem wise to do so. I will show you your a rooms, where you can put your things and then I think Nirrox has some answers for us."

AFTER SEEING THE WONDERS of the hall and sitting area, Leo found the guest rooms were a bit disappointing. The walls were covered with pale blue wallpaper, which goes perfectly with the bed linen and sun-blocking curtains. There was wood on the floor, seemingly all over the house, of a kind that Leo did not know. Leo set his weekend bag on a plain wooden desk. He would love to lie down on the neatly made bed and close his eyes. Although he had slept a bit in the infirmary, it wasn't enough to kill the headache that was torturing him. But Colette had made it clear to him that he was going to pick him up later, he stifled a yawn. To stay awake he walked out of the hall, the lady of the house had simply pointed to the door next to his and then muttered something about a bathroom. He got the feeling that Colette didn't like him that much, which was a good thing. Because he didn't like her either, Alexandera didn't like her either. She always said that Nadia Drucal and Nirrox were made for each other. He opened the door and closed it again immediately, just before a cry nearly burst his ears.

"Sorry." The door was pulled open and Kailey appeared in the doorway. With a towel wrapped around her, her light gray eyes fired.

"Never heard of knocking!" He raised his hands and deliberately did not look at her, her brown hair was wet like the rest of her body. But it wasn't because she was wet, but her towel hung a little too low.

"Yes, I have heard of that. By my soul, I retire to my room. We will continue talking when you are dressed." He heard her about to say something, but he slammed the door. He leaned against the door, his heart pounding hard against his chest, and he felt his cheeks slowly turn red.

"By my soul she had never heard of a lock on the door." He grumbled to himself, he swallowed. The image of her wet hair and half-naked body would not leave his mind. Not that he wanted to go away, the dark blue bags under her beautiful eyes had disappeared, he stiffened. *Beautiful* eyes? Well, he reluctantly had to admit that they were indeed beautiful, he had even discovered that they had a shade of green. He slapped his face with a flat hand. "That's your sister's killer." He said to himself.

THERE WAS A FIERY KNOCK on his door.

"Leo!" Her voice was filled with rage, he got up slowly and carefully opened the door.

"Are you dressed?" Kailey didn't answer him but pushed herself into the room. She was wearing light jeans and a light pink T-shirt. The light pink T-shirt that once upon a time belonged to Alexandra.

"Well?" Leo pressed his lips together, it suited her better than Alexandra's. "Leo, where are your thoughts and don't say to me." She raised her hand threateningly.

"That T-shirt, it suits you." She looked at him in amazement and he was also amazed with himself. He had just complimented her and he meant it. "I'm sorry, I forgot for a moment that Mrs. Barnier told us to share the bathroom. I should have knocked and you should have locked the door."

"I would have locked the door, but there is only no lock." She said harshly, but there was a hint of uncertainty in her voice. She clearly didn't know what to do with his compliment.

"Hmm, no lock. We'll hang a towel on the door handle from now on." He tried to sound light-hearted, but he knew he couldn't quite make it. Kailey nodded slightly, before Leo knew their eyes hooked and something in him wouldn't look away. His heart began to beat violently and something in his stomach began to flutter, hoping he had not become ill again. Leo took a step forward, they were now very close together. He put a pair of hands on her shoulders, but did nothing.

"Kailey," what was he doing? She was still the murderer of his sister, but she was also Alexandra's friend. "I just wanted to tell you that I forgive you." Kailey's light gray eyes with a shade of green began to twinkle, tears already appeared in the corner of her eye. He raised one hand to wipe away the first tear. "I'm sorry it took me so long." She slowly shook her head and closed her eyes for a moment. Leo didn't know what he was doing, but he pressed his lips against hers. Gently he pulled her closer and slid his lips past hers. A knock on the door drove them apart.

"I'm sorry to interrupt, but I need you downstairs." Nirrox stood in the doorway, Leo felt his face begin to glow. Nirrox eyes were amused, Kailey hurried past Nirrox and Leo followed her. "Looks like Alexandra's plan to get you together worked." Leo wanted a furious look at him, but Nirrox was right, Alexandra's plan to get the, together seemed to work and he didn't know if it was a good thing.

11

Kailey felt that her cheeks still glowed after the kiss. Her hand reached for the pendant she didn't know how or why, but the cold metal calmed her a bit. Something what was quite welcome in a mind buzzing with strange, or not so strange thoughts. Leo had just walked into the bathroom, while she was under the shower and when she wanted to confront him about it. Only instead of telling what an idote he was, she kissed him and most important fact was that he kissed her back. Or did he kiss her and was she the one who kissed him back. She honestly didn't remember. Her heart was already starting to slow, but it didn't help to clear her mind. They entered the library, Colette was already standing behind a desk, the wooden top of which was hidden under a pile of leather-bound books. Kailey could see where they got the inspiration for the room. It looked suspiciously the same as the library at the Red Tempest Academy, and she had to admit that it looked impressive. The bookcases reached towards the ceiling, the rows of books that completely filled the shelves. Under the desk was a dark green carpet, in the middle of the library was a large dark green vase containing tiger lilies. Someone really loved those flowers, Kailey couldn't blame them, they were very pretty.

"Nirrox, I'll keep them busy. Alex-Lucas and Velika can be here any moment." Nirrox nodded and left the library again. "Leo, I thought I heard someone scream. So what did you do?" Kailey struggled to control her face. She looked at Leo who folded his arms.

"Why do you assume I did something, what happened to innocent until proven guilty?" Colette gave him a stern look. "Anyway I confess, totally forgot you told us that we needed to share the bathroom. I walked into the bathroom without knocking. Still, the whole scenario wouldn't have happened if there was a lock on the door." Kailey could no longer contain her smile and began to chuckle softly, something she hadn't done since Alexandra's death. Kailey saw Leo glance at her and wink at her. Something that made her cheeks glow again, or they still glowed, she didn't know for sure. She only hoped that Colette wouldn't see it.

"Well, the scenario would also have been prevented if you had your ears checked." Said Colette a little bit angry. Leo raised both his hands up, like he was surrendering.

"In my defense I have slept very badly and I am hungry. So I apologize that I am not functioning to completeness." Kailey's soft chuckle began to turn into a true smile, which she kept muffled behind her hand. This is what Alexandra meant, Leo could turn a serious conversation into a play. "Anyway, are we waiting for your other guests or is there a reason we were called here?" Colette's eyes burn with rage, and Kailey fought to control her laughter even more.

"That's exactly what I was wondering." Kailey turned behind her was a younger version of Nirrox, Alex-Lucas, and next to him an all-too-familiar face.

"Velika!" Kailey runned towards her and gave her a hug. Velika gave her a warm smile and sighed.

"It's been too long, Kailey, and I'm sorry." Kailey shook her head slightly and bit her lip gently. Alexandra and she also invited Velika to come to the beach that day. Only Velika had to decline their invitation, she was not feeling that well. Something Kailey fully understood. Velika had only turned eighteen a view days before the summer started and her body could no longer tolerate human food.

It was normal for vampires to get a little sick during that transision. Nirrox appeared behind Velika and cleared his throat.

"Well if everyone wants to take a seat on the prepared chairs, I want to tell my younger brother and his lovely wife why they are here." Everyone did as Nirrox had asked, Kailey had not noticed before that there were a circle of chairs. She sat in the chair closest to Leo and Nirrox took his place in the middle of the circle. "Well, after hearing Kailey van Helsing's story, with some extra detail. I went looking for a possible condition in this library and I regret to say that I'm still searching." Kailey looked at Leo, who was clearly about to say something, but Nirrox paid no attention to him. "But I have no doubt that the answer is somewhere in these books. That's why I called you Alex-Lucas. Because I can't go through all the books on my own and Colette has her hands full with these two young souls." Then he pointed to Leo and her.

"Kailey, are you sick?" Velika looked at her in surprise. Kailey nodded slowly, and she sighed. But before she could explain what was wrong with her...

"Kailey and Leo both suffer from a great deal of stress. That resulted in too little sleep and nightmares, which in turn lead to hallucinations." Said Nirrox, and Kailey narrowed her eyes.

"Hallucinations? I wouldn't call the things we've seen hallucinations. Kailey saw Alexandra under the old willow, where Alexandra normally was waiting for me in the early evenings. I saw Alexandra laying on my bed with ashed skin and red eyes, just like how Kailey described her. A describtion I only heard a few hours ago." Leo was right in Kailey's opinion, also she couldn't call it hallucinations.

"Leo Cromwell, the brain plays different games with us. There is no other logical way to explain what you two have seen." But Velika shook her head.

"I'm sorry to say it, Colette. But I think if I am honest, that I am agreeing with Leo. There is no logical explanation in either case. Kailey seeing Alexandra under the old tree and Leo seeing her in a sees form that he has not seen before." Velika looked at Leo for a brief moment. "I actually had a one-on-one meeting with Count Dadrick Ventila when I slept in the Headmaster's office, last school year. He thought he had my ancestor Vanessa in front of him. But it doesn't matter, my guess is that both Leo and Kailey have experienced the same thing."

"Alexandra's ghost?" Said Kailey and Leo, at the same time. Velika answered them with a simple nod, Leo looked at Kailey. In his eyes stood the same question that went through her mind as well. Did they really see Alexandra's ghost and if so, why was she hunting them?

NO ONE SAID ANYTHING at dinner, but Kailey didn't have to guess what was on everyone's mind right now. Velkia had painted a clear picture of her encounter with the Count Dadrick Ventila's ghost. But this didn't mean that Kailey and Leo had experienced the same thing. Kailey bit on her lip, why would Alexandra hunt her? She begged Kailey to kill her, at least that is what she remembered. She sighed, from the corner of her eye she saw that Leo looked at her. Another question popped up in her mind. Why would Alexandra hunt Leo in soul's name? He did nothing wrong, or did he? She sighed again, maybe if they find the answers about what happened to Alexandra, then maybe they will find those answers too.

After dinner, Kailey slipped into the garden. The early fall night was still warm for the time of year. The garden, like the main floor of the house, was enchanting, the various shrubs bore no flowers. Something they would probably have in the spring and summer, at the back of the garden was a pond where several fish were swimming around. A black marble bench stood on the shore of the pond. Kailey sat down with a sigh, a few late fireflies drifted through the yard. She knew that she could sit here and let her thoughts wonder off. But she didn't know if that was such a smart idea.

"Kailey?" Velika had come after her. "Are you okay?" Kailey shook her head slightly. It has not been going well with her for a long time, she has only managed to hide it for so long. Velika sat down next to her and sighed. Neither said anything until Velika started to chuckle. "Kailey do you remember our conversation after I graduated from the Red Tempest Acadamy." Kailey immediately chuckled and Velika continued. "I told you that vampires were real and that Alexandra was one of them." Kailey nodded.

"Yes, I remember your face when I told you that I already knew that she was a vampire." She fell silent for a moment and sighed. "By my soul what do I miss her. There are so many things I want to tell her. She was right." Velika took her hand.

"That is nothing strange, Alexandra had a talent for being right most of the time. But what was she right about, this time?" Kailey glanced quickly over her shoulder to make sure Leo wouldn't be behind her.

"About Leo and me." Velika's smile widened by the second and Kailey shrugged.

"Yes, yes. I know. It was stupid of me to argue, with her for so long." Both fired in a short, yet sincere laugh. Only Kailey's laugh stopped, a little too quickly. "Velika do you really think Leo and I saw Alexandra's ghost." Velika sighed.

"Kailey, since last school year my mind has been open to everything, even ghosts. But know this that what Colette suggested may well be possible." Kailey nodded, her hand reaching for her pendant. "May I see it?" Velika pointed to the pendant and Kailey nodded. "The Lumina Crest, the White Tiger. Did Nick gave you this" Kailey nodded, her gaze on the pendant around Velika's neck.

On it stood the Lazar Crest, two roses in bloom. Kailey stood up with a deep sigh.

"I better go to sleep. Nirrox may have turned Alex-Lucas and you in personal assistants, but that doesn't mean I'm gonna sit on my butt and do nothing." Kailey did not wait for Velika's answer and went back to the mansion.

12

L eo smiled faintly when he heard her laugh. Reluctantly he had to admit that he enjoyed the sound and that he would hear it more often. He saw that she stood up and started to walk towards the house, quickly he ducked into a dark corner so that she wouldn't see him. What should she think of him, in two days he went from a resentful person, to someone who pressed his lips to hers. His heart began to gallop when he thought about the kiss. He sighed, then stepped out of the dark corner. It was foolish to hide from her, they were bound to see each other every day locked up in this mansion.

"Kailey?" She looked at him in surprise. "Sweet dreams." She gave him a genuine smile, something he had never seen on her before.

"You too, Leo." He wanted to nod, but she was already walked away from him. He heard Nirrox laugh and Leo faintly caught a comment directed at him. But he didn't hear what was said and if he was honest he didn't care. It was better to follow Kailey's lead and go to bed, he mumbled something about needed the rest and disappeared. Again a comment from Nirrox headed his way, but again he didn't hear what it was.

Kailey's room door was already closed when he got upstairs. She probably was changin into her night clothes or she was already a sleep. He shook his head he needed to stop thinking about her, or he would go mad. Maybe a cold shower will do the trick, quickly grabbed the towel from the chair in his room. Not much later he came back into his room, the shower indeed helped. He couldn't stop shivering until he had enough. His hear was still a bit wet, but that would dry up when he was fast a sleep. He was about to get into bed when he heard a scream from across the hall, without thinking about it, he shot out of his room and into Kailey's. She sat upright in bed, her body covered in pearls of sweat. Her eyes were filled and her cheeks wet from tears. In the distance he heard voices from the others while they ran up the stairs. He stuck his head out the door and saw Nirrox ran first around the corner.

"It was a nightmare." Nirrox immediately stopped running and nodded. Leo walked further into Kailey's room and sat on the bed. Tears streamed down Kailey's face.

"It was you, this time I shot you." She whispered, he didn't know what she meant. Still, he took her in his arms and pulled her towards him. She buried her face in his shoulder. The sound of her sobbing was heartbreaking, but for her he would endure it. "Make it stop, make the nightmares stop. I can't take it anymore." A lump formed in his throat.

"I would like nothing more than to take them away." He turned his gaze towards the door, Colette stood in the doorway with a cup of steaming tea in her hands.

"Let her drink this, it will help her sleep." They put the mug on the desk and left the room.

Kailey had finished the cup of tea, her eyes were dry but her cheeks were still wet from her tears. Leo pushed her gently into the pillow.

"Try to get some sleep. If you need something, I am across the hallway." He started to get up, but she grabbed his arm. He felt that she was still shaken up, he did not know what she had seen in her dreams and he did not want to ask her about it until she was ready. But she radiated genuine terror.

"Stay." Her voice trembled so badly that he could not refuse her. "Please stay with me?" He motioned for her to move a bit, which she did and he lay above the covers next to her. No matter how cold it would get during the night or day in this case, he would stay above the covers. He put an arm around her, her breathing calmed down a bit. Her body was shaking, but it was noticeably less.

"I'll stay as long as you want me to stay." He whispered in her ear.

LEO DIDN'T KNOW WHEN it happened, but it was certain that he had fallen asleep. He woke up next to her, his arms wrapped around her like some sort of barrier against the bad dreams. Her breathing was still steady, a sign that she was still asleep. He wanted to pull his arms back, but he was afraid of waking her if he did. The door opened softly, he turned his head slightly and saw Nirrox lean over him with a meaningful smile that said enough. Leo wanted to punch him in the face, only to get rid of that smile. But then he would wake Kailey, and that was the last thing he wanted.

"She wanted me to stay." He whispered, Nirrox nodded.

"Sure, lion cub and I see you are rightfully suffering." Leo grunted slightly and glared at him. "But at least she got some sleep and something good in my opinion. But I do not know what my Angel of the Night has to say about this." Leo sighed deeply and looked away from Nirrox. He shared this opinion with Nirrox, even though he would never admit it out loud. Kailey moved in her sleep and Leo felt himself stiffen, he could stay like this forever. Altough his arms felt into sleep. But to his regratted her eyes opened and this moment was over.

"Good evening!" Nirrox wanted to make it clear that he was still in the bedroom. "My Angel of the Night, actually sent me upstairs to wake you up. And you make my task so much easier when you two decided to share this room." Kailey rolled with her eyes before she met Leo's gaze.

"Glad we could be of service, Nirrox. We will get up and get dressed." She clearly wanted him out of her room. Leo looked at Nirrox who got the hint.

"I will see you two later then." And he left the room. Leo pulled his arm back and pushed himself up. His whole body felt a little stiff, but maybe that was because he was not used to sleep like this.

"Thank you." She said softly, and he forget his stiff body in an instant. "You could have left as soon as I was asleep, but you stayed the whole time." He gave her a warm but a small smile.

"I could have done that, but I fell a sleep before I could think of doing so." She started to laugh, which sounded like music to his ears. "It wasn't a problem Kailey. As long as we're here we can do this, but when we get back to school. Well lets hope that you will not me anymore." She nodded to indicate she understood what he said, or what he didn't say. With a deep sigh and great reluctance he got up and trudged into his own room to change.

THE TWO OF THEM WALKED downstairs, the Barnier and Lazar family were already gathered in the library.

"Good evening, did you sleep well?" Colette did not hide her sarcasm. He gave her a friendly smile, because he didn't trust his mouth.

"Thank you for the tea, Mrs. Barnier. Because of that and with the presence of Leo, I slept a lot more peacefully." Kailey walked with her back straight to the desk where Velika was already sitting, her nose hidden inside a leather-bound book. Leo wanted to join her, but his way was blocked by Colette.

"I will allow this, only because it helps her sleep. But know that I am not happy about it." She gasped to say something more.

"By my soul, Colette. Come from that soap box of yours. it's allowed at the Red Tempest Academy. If I think if you wanted to say something about sex or something like that. I can report that nothing happened I was on top of the blankets. But I have to say that you really need to do something about the heating in those rooms. I almost froze to death." Colette had narrowed her eyes, but Leo walked away from her and sighed. Slept on top of the blankets one day and he was immediately suspected of being a pervert. He cursed softly, what did Colette think of him? Leo picked up a cup of tea from a silver tray and sat down on the chair next to Alex-Lucas. Who looked at him for a moment. "Leave it out of your mind, Alex-Lucas. Your sister-in-law have said enough." Leo took a sip of his tea and grabbed a book from the ground.

"All I wanted to say is that you are right about the heating in those rooms. It is really criminal." Leo started to laugh, softly. Velika had changed the once stiff Alex-Lucas. Leo's gaze went once more to Kailey. Would she change him too?

13

Kailey didn't know how many days they'd spent in the library at the Barnier mansion, but she slowly began to suspect that the answers they were looking for must be deeply hidden. Her nightmares were some what diminishing, she only didn't know if it was because of Colette's special tea or the presence of Leo. How still lay above her sheets, but she finally got him so far that he would get his own sheets to sleep under. She would know what was responsible for her good day rest, but she didn't want to take the chance to put it to the test. With a weary sigh, Leo closed his book and got up with a groan. Kailey could hear his muscles pop.

"I'm going for a walk in the garden, if have being sitting too long." He said quickly when he saw Colette's narrowed eyes.

"My angel of the night, the lion cub is right. We are here quite a long time." Leo took this as his opportunity and walked to the door that led to the garden. Kailey put a bookmark between the pages and closed it softly.

"I'm going to get some fresh air too." And before anyone could say anything about it, Kailey ran into the garden. She only breathed a sigh of relief when she reached the pond at the back of the garden.

"Looks like you fled the study session too." Leo had his back to her, probably not seeing her, but hearing her coming. "By my soul, I have done more reading here then I have done during my entire school carrier." Kailey started to chuckle, she could say the same thing.

"Yes, the chair is great. Just not for more then a few hours, otherwise your butt turns into wood." Now both of them started too laugh, a welcoming sound in Kailey's opinion. A fresh breeze blew between them, taking with it a few red-colored leaves. Autumn had finally decided to set in, bringing with it the discoloration of the leaves and chilly winds. Kailey shivered slightly, she should have put on a coat. Leo had heard her teeth chattering. He took off his vest and wrapped it around her.

"I know we live in a doctors' house, but that is gives you not the excuse to get sick." She shrugged lightly, she had come to appreciate his presence very much and in moments like this saw his warm side. A side that Alexandra always bragged about. Kailey only wished that Alexandra was here to see how the two of them were growing. But of course she was not here, she was death.

"The same applies to you." She said under her breath. He raised his shoulders.

"I'll be fine."He said without giving it a second thought. She gave him one of her rare genuine smiles and he took her in his arms. She closed her eyes and rested her head against his chest. Her ear against his chest, she heard the pounding of his heart and she sighed. She wanted this moment to last for ever.

"Hey lovebirds the Headmaster is here to check on you two, what should I tell him that you are to busy!" Nirrox's voice echoed through the garden and Kailey sighed.

"May I kill him?" Kailey looked at him questioningly, and then shook her head laughing.

"No, you can't kill him. Because if you do that, that means I can't kill him." They started to laugh and with hands entwined they walked back to the house.

THE HEADMASTER WAS waiting for them in the sitting room, Leo and Kailey immediately went to the couch and sat down like they had done on their first day at this house. The Headmaster sat uncomfortably on the last and free couch. He looked at them intently with his pale pink eyes.

"Well, Kailey, to be honest. You look way better than the last time I saw you." Kailey gave him a forced smile and glanced at Leo, who nodded in agreement.

"Thank you, Headmaster Dracul, I have to say that I feel better too." The forced smile faded and she crossed her arms slightly. It seemed as if a cold gust of wind was blowing through the room, she shivered, it even came through Leo's warm vest. Kailey saw Leo looking around too and she did the same as the candle flames did not flicker.

"Is something wrong?" Asked the Headmaster. Kailey's eyes meet those of the Headmaster, who sat unmoved. Had he not felt the cold wind? Leo got up and then sat down next to her, just as he put an arm around her. Her heart stopped beating, she heard him gasp for breath. Alexandra appeared on the couch where Leo had been sitting a few moments ago, her skin ashen and gray and her irises completely red, not just surrounded by red. The Headmaster has most likely seen the fear on their faces, as he also looked at the coach. Only it was clear he didn't see anything, which annoyed Kailey slightly. A mean smile appeared on Alexandra's face.

"He doesn't see me the poor wretch, the blood traitor." Kailey shivered again, Alexandra's voice was so cold that it left goosebumps on Kailey's arms. "But what do you expect from someone who wants peace between vampires and humans." The smurk on Alexandera's face was one that Kailey didn't recognize."And you Kailey, do you want peace between our two races?" Kailey leaned against Leo. She was talking about a Second War and that was exactly what Kailey didn't want. "Wait a minute, you two? Ah, now I see it. You two finally figured out that I was right, little lion if you want to protect her. You need to turn her into a real vampire. It should work, if you take her blood history into account." Kailey got up and wanted to ran out of the sitting room. She couldn't here this for one more second. But Alexandera blocked the doorway.

"You can't escape me, little blood. Even if you kill me, wait a minute you've already tried that." Kailey put her hands over her ears, she didn't want to hear Alexandra's terrible voice anymore. "Admit it Kailey, you want nothing more. You want to be a vampire, just like me. Just like Leo. You're jealous of Velika, she turned into one of us."

"Leave me alone!" Kailey fell to the floor, tears streaming down her cheeks. Her whole body was shaking. "I'm sorry that I killed you, but please leave me alone!" Leo appeared next to her and took her in his arms.

"She is gone."

"What in souls name is wrong with you two?" The Headmaster didn't hide his anger mixed with a level of worry. They walked back to the couch supporting each other, Colette and Nirrox entered the room. Probably because they heard Kailey shouting and then the question of the Headmaster.

"We saw her." Leo turned his attention to Nirrox and Colette. "She was so clear, as we see you two and not only that." He let her sit, she trembled violently and clung to him. "She spoke to us this time."

"Who was here, who was talking to you? I was sitting here and I didn't see or hear anyone!" The Headmaster was not hiding his confusion. It was clearly that he wanted some answers.

"Vance, calm down. They're talking about Alexandra, seemingly she is still haunting them. Leo, I want ask Kailey this, but seeing her like this, it doesn't seem wise. What is your sister saying to you?" Asked Colette, with a honey sweet voice. This was the first time that Kailey heard this voice from her. Leo told them what Alexandra said, word for word. Leo sighed, Kailey saw that there was a question on his mind.

"Why would the forbidden act work on Kailey?" Leo looked questioningly at Nirrox, who cleared his throat slightly.

"It is believed that the forbidden act has a higher chance of success if a human already has vampire blood in his or her system. Even though it is very thin. Take Velika for example, she is from the Lazar family and it has been proven that Armand Barnier, a vampire, fathered Vanessa's children. So which means she had vampire blood in her veins before my father and brother performed the forbidden act on her. Kailey is of Lumina bloodline, that is no secret. So it is likely that it will work on her two. Only it is called the forbidden act for a reason." Kailey jumped up and bit her lip a little too hard. She tasted the iron, which made her sick. Alexandra was right, she was slightly jealous of Velika. She covered her ears and narrowed her eyes, she had to get out of this house and quickly. She ran out of the room, down the hall to the front door. She needed to get out of this house, she needed to go to a place were she could think. And there was one place that popped into her mind.

The Red Tempest Beach.

14

The sound of the waves racing to the pale pink beach filled Kailey's ears. She sat on the grainy surface and watched the water slowly fade under the morning sun. It seemed so long since she'd shot her best friend here, but it hadn't been more than a few months. Her heart had been pounding in her throat all the way here, she hadn't told anyone where she was going. She also had nothing with her, her mother would justifiably be terrified if she knew this. Kailey exhaled and dropped her head into her hands, tears streaming down her cheeks and dripping into the pale pink sand.

"You are jealous of Velika, admit it." Kailey tried to push Alexandra's words out of her mind. But she kept hearing them, over and over. *"You are jealous, because she is one of use."* It was if she was listing to a broken record. Kailey shook her head. She wasn't jealous of Velika, not in the way Alexandera suggested. On the contrary, she was very happy for Velika. Velika looked so happy and Kailey wanted that too. She wanted to be happy with Leo by her side, she wanted his lips on her lips and his arms around her. That's what she really longed for, not to become a vampire.

"It is so beautiful here, if there were no more you would almost forget. Almost, but not completely." Kailey had felt Alexandra before she appeared It was only not the same way as in the Barnier Mansion. No gust of cold wind, only a tingle on her skin. Kailey glanced sideways next to her sat Alexandra as she remembered her. Her best friend, her support and anchor who desperately tried to link her to Leo.

"Kailey," Alexandra sighed, "what are you doing here?" Kailey frowned, what was Alexenadera talking about. They always came here if they needed a break from real life. "Kailey, go back to the mansion. You'll be safe there."

"Safe from what, Alex what are you not telling me?" Kailey asked, the fear that she felt at the begin of the summer came back. Alexandera opened her mouth to say something, but instead of words. She gasped. Kailey didn't know what was happening. Ghosts were a new territory for her. Alexandra reached for her throat, it looked like if she was choking, or being strangled. Kailey looked at her best friend in surprise, what was going on here?

"Kailey, run." Same warning as before, but this time Kailey didn't run. Alexandra reached out to Kailey and then Kailey saw what her friend was fighting. A silver cord ran tight around her neck.

"Alex, what's that?" Kailey reached towards the cord, but she burnt her hands while she touched it.

"Oh that. Just a trick to keep her in line." Kailey froze, that voice, normally so high and loud. "She's a tough one, she keeps trying to fight herself. So yery annoying. And I could say do not touch it, but I can see that I am a bit late for that." Kailey turned slowly, Alexia behind her. She had the same silver cord in her hands as on Alexandra's neck.

"Alexia, what are you doing with her?" Alexia's mean smile chiseled on her face widened. Kailey wanted to punch that smile from her face, so badly. But she needed answers.

"Like I said Kailey, I'm keeping her in line."

"Why?" That was the one thing she really wanted to know. Alexia always looked so innocent, so why those she need to keep Alexandra's ghost in line?

"You would like to know that, but do not worry. There will be plenty of time to explain it in full detail." Kailey frowned for a moment, enough time? Why would Alexia have enough time? Suddenly she felt a strike on the back of her head, the sand disappeared from under her feet and her world turned black before her head hit the ground.

"TIE HER UP TIGHTER, Alexia. We wouldn't want to lose this one, like we lost the other." Kailey opened her eyes slowly, her head pounded and her vision was blurred. Something tightened around her wrists.

"If I tighten it even more, the blood cannot flow freely. Master Mikan." Alexia's slimy and happy voice was back. Kailey shook her head what happened to her? Wait a minute, did Alexia just say Master Mikan? Mikan as in Realm's father, Mikan? Her sight came back slower than she would have liked, to her horror there was an IV stuck into her arm.

"By my soul, what's going on here?" Her voice was shaved, a red liquid shot through the IV to her arm. Was that blood? Who's? Were they preforming the forbidden act on her?

"Well what does it look like?" Kailey looked aside and saw that Alexia was sitting next to her, the same IV in her arm. "You are in transition to become one of the strongest vampires in history." Kailey looked at Alexia wide-eyed. "This time we'll win, we the *real* vampires will win." Kailey felt her stomach turn, she was talking about war and she wanted to recruit her.

"I don't know what you're up to, but vampire or not I'll never be one the side of the *crazy* vampires." A laugh from a dark corner was released, the laughter was empty and vague. A man stepped into the dim light of the single orb of light.

"What fire and what courage, you are truly a Lumina, more than that weakling you call Cousin Nick. But do you actually think that I am giving you much choice in the matter." Mikan slowly shook his head, Realm had his eyes. But that's really all. "No, I'mdoen burning my hands on the same fire over and over again. Your dead friend helped us pretty well with an ancient spell and I have to say I'm in love with the result." The image of the silver cord around Alexandra's neck flashed to Kailey's mind. What was he up to and why did he want her? She might have vampire blood in her veins, it wasn't noble blood like Velika's. A shudder went through her, they didn't want a noble, they wanted a vampire hunter by their side, one with a good name. The spell that Mikan was talking about would most likely not work on hunters only on vampires, dead or alive. Kailey tried to fight the chains on her wrists. She had to fight, this madman was not allowed to win. Her father fought to maintain this so breakable peace, that is why he sent her to the Red Tempest Academy. "There is no point in resisting little tiger, the transition has already begun and if you resist too much. Well then it will kill you."

"Well then you now know what I will choose." This time Alexia laughed, but it was not that happy girlly laugh. That Kailey so hated, no she hated this evil laugh even more.

"You really are a dumb muscle are you? When you die, the vampire hunters will take revenge on the vampires. So however the out come from this day, a war will come. You better lean in and relax a little." Kailey looked puzzled at Alexia, why was she doing this? She didn't even have to guess Mikan's reason, she knew the man wasn't sane, but Alexia was always so friendly and cheerful. "Are you really guessing at my motives, let me help you with that. I do this because I firmly believe that we vampires are better than humans. We live longer, are smarter. Or at least some off us."

"That depends on who you ask." Kailey said bit. "What do your parents think about this?" Alexia simply shrugged.

"If you are so eager to die, you can ask them yourself. Ask them for forgiveness while you ad it, because thanks to your parents they are no longer alive." Kailey bit on her lip the crust from which she bit too hard was still there, but this time too her tooth went through. She had to find a way out, because although they hate to admit it. Alexia and Mikan were right, when she dies here, the vampire hunters finally had their excuse to start the Second war. She looked around in amazement, where was this actually? She'd heard enough stories from Cousin Nick to know she was in the same basement that he was one year ago. Kailey swore if anyone knew who had kidnapped her then she was easy to find, but the problem was. She had stormed out of the mansion, without telling anyone were she was going. Tears stung her eyes, but she didn't want to cry. Not here where these fools could see her.

KAILEY DIDN'T KNOW when she fell asleep, all she knew is that a the tingling on her skin from Alexandra's presence, woke her up.

"Kailey, it's me." Alexandra didn't have to say that, but it was kind of Alexandra to warn her this time. "Hang on. I've let Leo know where you are and with whom. He just needs to convince those stocked up Barniers to take the right precautions." Kailey wanted to nod, but she was feeling nauseous.

"Alex, I don't feel very well." Kailey got those words out of her mouth, without throwing up. Alexandra's ghostly hand touched Kailey's

"I know Kailey, your transformation is almost over. In a little while you will be a vampire just like Velika. We just need to prevent you from getting under that dammed spell." Alexandra's voice was so warm, it comfert her al was it just a little. Kailey knew that Alexandra was right, she couldn't become a puppet.

"Alex, I miss you. I'm sorry." Kailey wanted to say those words for months, and she no longer could hold them back. Alexandra gave her one of her famous warm smiles.

"Kailey, quit blaming yourself. You had to shoot me, we both know it, I forgive you and now do what I tell you. When they cast that spell on you, stick to your own thoughts, don't doubt them for a second. Do you hear me, not for one moment. Think about Leo and how much he loves you." Kailey nodded slightly, she would do her best.

"Tell your brother to hurry up. Because doubting myself and others has become my second nature." Alexandra answered with a short nod and disappeared into thin air.

15

L eo was almost startled to death when Alexandra appeared in front of him, he was lying on his side on Kailey's bed and almost dozed off when she suddenly sat on the edge of the bed.

"Lion cub don't be afraid." Said Alexandra softly, he rolled with his eyes. It was not that he was talking the ghost of his sister, o wait that was excellently what he was doing.

"By my soul, Alex you can leave that in the future." Alexandra rolled her eyes and sighed loudly, she looked different. Her skin was no longer gray and dull, and her eyes were no longer red.

"Kailey doesn't scare them easily, because she knows immediately when I show up to her. But then again Kailey is a vampire hunter so she is trained." Squinting her eyes, she pulled the face she used to pull when she forgot something. "By my soul, I am so empty head. Leo, Kailey is in danger. Realm's crazy father took her to that creepy basement. He's going to make her a vampire, before you ask, he wants to make a vampire army for the Second war and Kailey is the perfect soldier."

"Alex, are you saying?" She raised her hand and sighed.

"Do you really want to ask questions now, get from that lazy ass of yours and go to the bunch of royals downstairs. Kailey needs you. Let Nirrox search for the Curse of the Ancestors, then he will find what he has been looking for all along." She looked at the door. "I have to go Leo, I'll let Kailey know that you know where she is. But you have to hurry, she's running out of time." And she disappeared into thin air.

"Never thought I would say this, but ghosts are handy spies." He jumped off the bed and ran barefoot through the mansion.

"THE CURSE OF THE ANCESTORS was what Alexandra told you. By my soul that explains a lot and that's probably why I hadn't thought of that before." Nirrox grabbed an old, worn book from the cabinet and opened it, the cover cracked violently and a thick cloud of dust rose from the yellow pages.

"I've never heard of this curse before." Colette said, looking at the Headmaster, who for some reason was still at the mansion. But Leo was not going to ask why he was still here. There was simply no time for that.

"That is not surprising, Colette, it is one of the best kept secrets of the noble families. It is not really a curse, but a chemical reaction of the body. When you drink tainted blood and then drink good blood, or bloodberries then it provides a reaction that makes some kind of zombie. It is forbidden and kept secret by the noble families." Leo sighed, they didn't have time here for a history lesson. They had to go to Kailey, who was getting closer to the same fate as Alexandra every minute. He shivered for a moment and shook off these thoughts. He hoped there was still time to safe her, no there had to be time to safe her. She was so stubborn that she could fight the reaction. But for how long?

"How do we protect ourselves against that." The Headmaster chuckled, as if Leo had said something funny.

"With garlic and silver." Leo looked at the Headmaster in surprise, he could not mean this. With stuff used in bad vampire movies, the Headmaster shrugged. "My old uncle Vladimir Dracul wanted these attributes in the movies and because he was already a star at the time, the filmmakers agreed. Somehow smart, but also so annoying." Leo could understand. He praised himself lucky that his family didn't had somebody like that. Collete ran to the kitchen and came back with a basket filled with garlic.

"Now I understand why Nirrox insisted that we always stock up on garlic, darling where is the silver you have been so anxiously hiding from me?" Nirrox was already ahead of the question and slapped a chest with chains on the table. Silver crosses hung from the chains.

"You can not be serious." Leo said still in disbelief, pulling a chain from the box.

"I've never been more serious in my life, Lion cub. Put it on and everyone brings an extra chain for Kailey."

LEO WAS SURPRISED TO be allowed to go with the *adult* vampires, when they were sitting in the car the Headmaster called Kailey's father to tell him what was going on.

"The hunters are also coming, let's hope that van Helsing's name means something, or otherwise Mikan has what he wanted." Leo's throat grew swollen, a Second war. His neck hairs lifted from something.

"Leo." There was Alexandra.

"By my soul, Alex can you stop that!" Alexandra sat between him and the Headmaster, but she floated between them.

"Since when have you been so scary cat?" She asked, there was a hint of teasing in her voice.

"Since my sister has become a ghost!" He snapped at her. She seemed to consider his answer, then nodded, as if it sounded very logic.

"You have to hurry up Leo, her transformation is almost complete and Mikan is ready with the tainted blood. She's doing her best to keep him and Alexia talking."

"What wait a second, Alexia Crystal is there too?" Alexandra nodded and Leo swore. In the front of the car, Nirrox did the same.

"I knew there was something wrong with that girl. Alex is she the one who gave you the tainted blood?"

"Yes, she was dressed as a girl scout. She said that they gave away a new type of candy." Leo looked at Nirrox.

"She is saying yes." Again, Nirrox cursed, stepping harder on the gas.

"Alexandra, do you know why she is doing this?" Alexandra nodded before she gave Leo her answer.

"Kailey's parents killed Alexia's parent on, I suspect they broke the law. Especially if one of Helsing's killed them." Leo told the other in the car and the Headmaster nodded in agreement.

"I agree with your sister. Unfortunately I don't know what their crime were. Normally if the hunters suspect that a vampire committed a crime they take a representative of the noble families along. To spread the message a bit faster, also that representative keeps the hunters in check." Nirrox grumbled something unintelligible, but Leo could hear something about the Lazar family, then Nirrox hit the brakes. Leo praised himself lucky that he put his seat-belt on, otherwise he had flown through the front window.

"We are here." Said Nirrox a bit sinacter.

EVERYONE GOT OUT OF the car, Axel-Lucas and Velika got out of another one.

"Nirrox are you sure that we need to take the lion cub with us? It seems a little irresponsible to me." Leo gave Colette a dirty look. In that moment he agreed with Alexandra, Nadia was more suited to be Nirrox's wife. But then again Nirrox has to live with her.

"Angel of the night, if we don't take him with us, he will follow us. In other words we are stuck with him." There was some truth in that. But they were wasting time discussing this. Leo cursed and tried to run in, but he was stopped by the Headmaster.

"Wait a minute, the hunters are not there yet. It is not safe to go in there without back-up." Leo gave him the same dirty look.

"We don't have time, Kailey is about to turn into a zombie and I'm not going to stand here and wait for some guys in black to show up." He shook off the headmaster's hand and stormed into the abandoned house. He didn't have to bother to find them, Alexia's sickening sweet voice led him to the basement. He kicks the door open with a number of stairs and storms down the stairs.

"Leo behind you!" Kailey screamed and he turned as fast as he could, just not fast enough.

16

"Leo?" Why did Kailey sound so desperate. "Leo, please wake up!" Leo's eyes shot open quickly. He lay on the floor of the filthy basement, scrambling to his feet, but was pushed back down by somebody. It had to Mikan because the person holding him down was very strong.

"Not so fast, lion cub." Wait it was Alexia holding him, how could this be. He had heard that vampires who drink human blood are stronger then the once that drink Bloodberries. He shivered, that meant that Alexia had committed a crime. "I smell that you have eaten some garlic, which means that you have found out our little secret. My only question is did you find out yourself or did you have help. Unfortunately I cannot ask your death sister because her ghost is missing." Leo tried to fight Alexia's grib on him, but she was simple to strong for him. Luckily he could move his head slightly, looking straight into Kailey's tear-covered face. Her lips had turned in a brownish red, they had given her the tainted blood, and he could tell she was fighting it. Her skin was gray, but not yet gray, and her irises had a small red border.

"I'm sorry Kailey, I wasn't fast enough." She shook her head slowly. He could she that she wanted to say something but the words couldn't leave her lips.

"Alexia puts a sock in his mouth, he's diverting our weapon." A male voice filled the room and something was indeed put into Leo's mouth.

"I love you." He tried to say through the sock, but the words where nothing more than murmurs. He hoped with all his heart that she understood him anyway. Leo tried to push the sock out of his mouth with his tongue, trying not to wonder if anyone had washed this thing. But there was no use, the thing was to big.

"Master, I doubt that this lost cub is trully lost. Shall I go and have a look if there are others outside?" Leo didn't hear an answer, yet he felt Alexia's foot go away from him, he heard her footsteps run away. He was lashed to his feet, looking straight into Mikan Stryder's red eyes. He had always heard that he looked like an adult version of Realm, well then a lot had changed.

"I'm so glad I did listen to that girl and let her put a collar around your sisters neck, it was very effective. Of course you wouldn't agree with me, Lion cub." Mikan Stryder pushed him roughly toward the wall out of Kailey's view and forced Leo to sit. Still, he let out several mumbles.

"Kailey don't give in, I'm just here. Your father is coming." Not to tell her all this, but just to let her know that he was still there and that he was fighting for her. She couldn't give up because he certainly wouldn't. Leo heard a metal cuff wrapped around his wrist above his head.

"Master! Master flee. The Suits, the Suits are here!" Mikan shot up and started to run. Leo shook his head gently and kicked one of Mikan's legs out from under the man. He pulled the sock out of his mouth with his free hand.

"Do you actually think you can escape for a third time? I do not think so." Leo got up as far as he could and put his foot on the man. So that he had to fight to get up, there was a thumping on the stairs. It sounded like multiple footsteps in heavy shoes, so it wasn't Alexia.

"By my soul, Kailey!" A man's voice echoed across the room.

"Mr. van Helsing," at least Leo hoped it was Kailey's father. "Somebody, I have a hard time holding Mikan Stryder down. Can some get him of my hands?" Immediately someone came into his sight, it was a woman who looked like an adult version of Kailey. "Mrs. van Helsing, I assume." The woman nodded and bent down to pick up Mikan. Leo only took his foot off his back when he saw that Kailey's mother was holding him tight.

"Thanks for your help." She said with a forced smile that Leo knew from her daughter. Nirrox ran past the woman and snatched a bunch of keys from Mikan's belt. Leo looked at it in surprise, he had not seen those. But then again he was to busy with other things. Nirrox untied him and Leo painfully rubbed where the handcuff had been.

"If you had waited." Nirrox snapped at him, but Leo shook his head.

"If I had, Mikan would have been gone again and we would have bigger problems." Leo said irritated. "Kailey!" He pushed Nirrox aside and ran to the chair where Kailey was sitting. Her father was loosening ropes, Kailey's head hung on her chest. Leo's heart stopped, her skin ashen and gray. Did this mean he was late? Tears sprang to his eyes and a hand appeared on his shoulder.

"Don't worry, she fought so hard against the tainted blood that it knocked her out and I think we owe that to you." Said the voice of an unknown man, his hand slightly squeezed his shoulder and the man walked over to the unconscious Kailey. "Abraham. Let me." The man pulled the ropes and picked up Kailey. "Nirrox, what are you standing there boy."

"Colette, is already going to your place, father. I will do a check-up by the lion cub if he let me. So take it easy on my soul, father." The man shrugged and walked away with Kailey. Nirrox put his hand on Leo.

"You stay with me and let me examine you." Leo was carefully checked by Nirrox.

"Where is that man going with Kailey?" Nirrox just shone with a bright light in Leo's right eye. Leo wanted to shot his eye, but he knew from Cousin Rhain that he need to keep them open.

"That man is my father and he takes her to his house. That us where he treats vampires." Leo felt a relief that made his legs wobble. Or was it because of that blow earlier, he didn't know or care. Kailey was in the hands of Jorin Barnier, the best doctor in Traimora. "Looks like I'm going to take you there too. You've got a big wound and I suspect that this dirty thing." He held up the filthy sock that had been in Leo's mouth. "Has some tainted blood on it." He put a hand on Leo's shoulder and pulled first, then pushed Leo toward the stairs.

"I have eaten the garlic and I have the silver cross around my neck. Then why do I have to go to your father's house?"

"Out of precaution." Nirrox said briefly when they got to the top of the stairs. Leo wanted to argue again, but as they walked around the house, he saw the headless bodies of Mikan and Alexia lying in one of the rooms. His stomach started to turn, why had Alexia been killed too? He wanted to ask Nirrox, but he pulled him with him. In the car, Leo felt he could breathe again.

"Alexia, she was only seventeen!" Leo burst into rage.

"Which makes her old enough Leo, she confessed that she volunteered to help Mikan. That was all the information the hunters needed to kill her. And before you are going to say something about the noble representative, nobody and I repeat nobody of the nobles is waiting on a Second war."

"She was..." What was she to him? A friend she, he shook his head. She was not a friend of his, but she was going to the Red Tempest Academy. She'd lost her parents, and she'd blamed Kailey and her parents for that. What would he have done if Mikan had approached him after what happened to Alexandra, would he have helped him? He didn't knew the answer to that question, and if he was to be honest, he didn't want to know the answer.

17

Leo sat next to Kailey's bed, his head lay on the edge, his eyes closed and his breath slowly rising and falling. Still, he didn't sleep, he only pretended that he was. So could he be with Kailey without somebody sending him away. Kailey however was asleep and she had been doing that for a few days. According to Jorin Barnier, that was a good thing, the poison from the tainted blood could leave her body in peace without Kailey being bothered by it. Leo wished he had been asleep too when the tainted blood left his body. But they feared that he had got a concussion so they kept him awake, he didn't know what he hated the most during that period. The lack of sleep or the pain of his muscles cramped from the lack of Bloodberries or anything else to eat or drink. Jorin thought even simple tap water was too risky. The room door opened and Leo heard two sets of footsteps enter.

"He still hasn't left her side?" Leo recognized the voice of Kailey's father, who came by every day.

"If you don't count him going up and down to the toilet. Then no, he sleeps here and eats here." Nirrox couldn't leave out the sarcasm. "He and your daughter have spent time in my household and I have seen them grow closer to each other. He truly cares about her and if she were my daughter it would fill me with satisfaction."

"Don't tell me what to feel, Barnier. But you're right it fills me with satisfaction and even though Sarah doesn't say it, she agrees with me in silents. Although are daughter is a vimpre we will never treat her in the same way as the Lazar family treated Velika." Leo had to hold back from coming up, but he knew that her father meant every word.

"Let's continue this conversation outside the room, we don't want to wake up the lion cub or your daughter for that matter."

"Why does everyone call him that, I know his name is Leo which means lion?" Nirrox shrugged and chuckled.

"I really have no idea, his sister always called him that and we took it over from her. But I think that we now call him that because Alexandra can't do it anymore." Leo's heart stopped beating, he never thought that the tried to fill up the teasing part that Alexandra left behind. In silence he thanked everybody for doing that.

LEO RESTED HIS ELBOWS on the sheets and sighed, the sunlight was kept from the room by sunlight blocking curtains, but the simple clock on the wall told him that is was evening. Which means a week had passed since their basement adventure. He took Kailey's hand, his parents told him that he had being away from school to long and that they wanted him to go back there. He fought them as his name sack. Telling them that Kailey needed him here. But it hadn't helped, they were as stubborn as he was and their decision was final.

"Kailey, I'm sorry, but I have to go get my things." He squeezed her hand gently and, to his surprise, she squeezed back slightly. He sprang to his feet and saw that her gray eyes were open with a green glow. A warm but thin smile was on her mouth.

"Do not worry about me, I'll be there soon enough." Her voice creaked a little, yet it was clear. He brought his lips to hers and kissed them gently.

"Kailey, I'll always worry about you. If you like it or not, you are stuck with me." She nodded and sighed.

"Well then I need to find a way to life with that." She took a deep breath before she continued."Leo, can you see if my dad is here?" Leo nodded and walked away from her, pausing before releasing her hand. A strange and dismal feeling crept over him.

"Leo do not release her hand, if you let her go you won't see her again, in this life time." Alexandra appeared on the other side of the bed. Kailey looked at her too.

"Alexandra?"

"Call for the doctor Leo and tell him that Kailey is suffering from food poisoning." Leo's eyes widened.

"Doctor Barnier!" It didn't take long for Jorin to burst into the room. He was genuinely worried about Kailey and Leo.

"What is it Leo?" Leo explained to him in a shaky voice what he had heard from Alexandra, Jorin looked incredulous for a moment, but quickly checked Kailey.

"By my soul, you're right. Leo won't let go of Kailey's hand, I believe she's still with us thanks to you." Jorin called Colette into the room, and the two went straight to work.

"Barnier, what's souls name going on here?" Abraham van Helsing 8th entered the room.

"Food poisoning. Late stage, I can't talk right now. I'm sorry Abraham." Leo looked at Kailey's father standing in the doorway as pale ashen.

"You said she was fine!" Kailey's father snapped at Jorin. The dismay and anger were clearly audible.

"I know what I said." Jorin said, slightly annoyed. "And it seemed to be going well for her too, only now I know why." Jorin nodded to Leo. "Somehow she fed on his energy, something only strong vampires can do that. It is good that he is still with use, because if we would have found out when he was gone." Jorin did not have to finish his sentence, everyone in the room understood what he wanted to say.

PEACE HAD RETURNED to the room, and Kailey was to Leo's relief out of danger. This time he sat next to her on the bed with her in his arms. Her head rested on his chest, her eyes closed. She fell asleep right after he sat down next to her. He rubbed her shoulder with his thumb. Jorin Barnier had called his parents and explained the situation to them. Leo wouldn't return to the Red Tempest Academy until Kailey was going to. Alexandra appeared next to the bed, this time he wasn't shocked.

"Leo, I am so happy for you and I am proud."

"Thanks Alex." He looked at her a little more closely, she was a bit more vague than usual. She saw him looking and nodded slowly.

"Yes, lion cub. My time in this world is up, I have to move on." A lump appeared in his throat, tears formed in his eyes. "Don't cry or I'll start." She was already blinking a little out of the corner of her eye.

"Alex..." He started and she nodded.

"I will miss you to, lion cub. Be your warm self, shower Kailey with all your love. Be a good father to your children and an even better grandfather to your grandchildren. We will see each other again, I firmly believe in that." He nodded and a tear ran down his cheek. Alexandra caught the tear just in time before it hit Kailey's face. "Goodbye, little brother and good friend." And Alexandra disappeared. Kailey woke up and looked over to where Alexandra had just stood.

"Has she moved on?" Leo nodded and Kailey put an arm tight around him. "I'm so sorry Leo. Now you lost her for a second time." He smiled softly to her.

"It wasn't your fault, it was Mikans. But she's in peace or she otherwise wouldn't have gone." Kailey let go of him and crawled up.

"That's a soothing thought. Thank you for saying that." He could look her in the eye, she looked better than before.

"Leo." She started.

"Yes?"

"I love you too." He looked at her in surprise, where did that suddenly come from? She had seen the surprise on his face. "In the basement, you said through your that sock that you loved me." He nodded. That was true. "Well I love you too." He pressed his lips against hers and kissed her fervently. He broke away from her and immediately regretted it.

"I love you Kailey van Helsing and I will prove that to you every day of my life. If your father were here I would ask for your hand."

"It's her choice!" Her father's voice came through the door, Kailey and Leo looked at each other for a moment before laughing. Her father's head came through the door for a moment. "Just to be clear, I wasn't eavesdropping. I just happened to walk by." Kailey nodded and her father's head disappeared.

"He's a liar, he's been sleeping next door for a few days." Leo said with a smile on his face. Kailey's eyes sparkled with pleasure.

"Well, I'm glad he didn't cast me out like the Lazar family did with Velika." Leo looked at the door, where her father was most likely sitting next to the door, listening.

"The Lazar family has lost sight of where they came from, the van Helsing family hasn't. But where are those sweet lips of yours?" He pressed his lips to hers. Knowing that he couldn't go any further with her father at the door, yet he felt that this was the beginning of his life with Kailey van Helsing.

Dedication

This is for the ones who helped me with putting toghter this collection of books.

———— ⟡ ————

EDITS
Diane (SableAradia)

———— ⟡ ————

COVER
Nathalia Books

———— ⟡ ————

MENTAL SUPPORT
Darth Nickolas
Realm of music
LordGalakrond
Dazzlinkat
Siobhan
Authorgoddess
Diane
Dennis
My Dad

Don't miss out!

Visit the website below and you can sign up to receive emails whenever Nathalia Books publishes a new book. There's no charge and no obligation.

https://books2read.com/r/B-A-MVSL-MZQSB

BOOKS 2 READ

Connecting independent readers to independent writers.

Did you love *Red Tempest Academy Omnibus*? Then you should read *Dance of the Crane* by Nathalia Books!

The magic dance begins. Diàsha Sumero waves her fans. The sun perks over the horizon. Purple blossoms unfold. It is a new day. A new beginning.

   ... The end of a normal life...

   Read more at https://nathalia-books-1993.webnode.nl/.

Also by Nathalia Books

A Thicket of Thorns story
Book of Secrets

Nova Babylon
Nova Babylon
Flaming Arrow

Realms of Carminba
Black Swan
Brothers in Crime

Red Tempest Academy
Unexpected
The Rose and Serpent
A Stryder
Curse of the Ancestors
Red Tempest Academy Omnibus

Standalone
The Steria

Watch for more at https://nathalia-books-1993.webnode.nl/.

About the Author

Nathalia Books is a real dreamer and turns these dreams into stories. Each with their own world and charm, she prefers to write all day long, and she loves to forget the world around her. Her worlds take you to deserted places and new unknown cities. She introduces you to new unknown races and beliefs.

Read more at https://nathalia-books-1993.webnode.nl/.

About the Publisher

Purpleheart publishing is the name Nathalia Books and Mariposa Floresce are using to publishing their work. With a good cup of coffee, the books are coming together.

CPSIA information can be obtained
at www.ICGtesting.com
Printed in the USA
BVHW072039261222
654951BV00005B/41